I0732599

The Memory of Flight

a novel

by

Debra Bowling

THE MEMORY OF FIGHT
a novel

Copyright © 2014, 2021 by Debra Bowling.
All rights reserved.

Originally published by Little Feather Books, 2014.

This novel is a work of fiction. Characters, names, places, and events are either the product of the author's imagination or are used fictitiously, and any resemblance to actual persons, living or dead, or to actual locales is entirely coincidental.

No part of this book may be reproduced or transmitted in any form or by any means, graphic, electronic, or mechanical, including photocopying, recording, taping, or by any information storage or retrieval system, without the permission in writing from the publisher. For permission requests and other information, please contact the author at www.debrabowling.com.

Published by 2nd ER

Print ISBN: 9781736369715
Ebook ISBN: 9781736369708

Dedication

To those struggling to find a way forward.

The Memory of Flight

a novel

Debra Bowling

CHAPTER 1

THE BRIDGE

MARILYN, 1960

She crouched forward on the car seat and leaned sideways against the door as they turned a curve in the road. The metal of the door handle was cool to her touch, and she looked down at her pale, thin fingers with long, red nails. She carefully filed and polished them in the early morning hours while CB and the girls banged on the bathroom door begging for her to come out. CB threatened to take down the "god-damned door," but she waited until each nail was perfect before pushing back the latch.

They were all asleep when she slipped from bed and quietly locked herself in the bathroom. She counted thirty-four aspirin in the bottle and ran her finger against the blade in CB's razor, gummed with old soap and tiny hairs. That's when she noticed the chipped polish. Now, in the car, their shiny redness seemed to stand out more against her pale white skin. The white fingers looked bloodless; maybe they were already dead.

She quickly let go of the door handle and smoothed back the soft waves of her hair, trying unsuccessfully to twist the ends into a knot. Moments later, she gave up and flipped the strands back. One foot tapped nervously as she remembered the plan she made this morning to get CB to take her to the lake when he got home from work—and cross the bridge that recently opened after major renovations. The bridge had always loomed in the distance when she came with family to the lake as a young woman, but she never crossed it before, never saw the other side.

"The other side is miles and miles of trees on a bunch of little moun-tain tops. If you keep going, you get to Scant City, then Arab if you go south. Ain't really nothing to see, especially by the time we get there. It will already be dark."

He was sniffling now, and Marilyn shifted her eyes to look at CB next to her, his left hand on the steering wheel. He was a tall man, still lanky at thirty-six with huge hands and feet. His eyes glanced at her and she weaved her fingers together and dropped them into her lap.

Resisting the urge to bite her lip, she studied her hands. Red nails and white skin. Red and white. Red like blood. She closed her eyes tightly, comforted for a moment by the darkness. Then all she saw was red—liquid red. She wanted to open her eyes, instead she watched red blood trickling down her long, white fingers, dripping off the tips of her nails and falling in fat splotches that covered her dress and began to fill the car. She cupped her shaking hands trying to catch her blood into her hands then pressed them together, then tighter together.

Stop!

Did she say it out loud? Her eyes opened to see CB light a cigarette and she shifted slightly to keep him visible from the corner of her eye. His head turned toward her as she moved, and she stiffened. The blare of a horn made him lean forward suddenly and swerve closer to the curb. Several thick black curls fell on his forehead, and it reminded her of how good he looked. Even now. Even half drunk.

He slumped his six-foot-four frame back down to fit into the seat. Still, she knew his head was touching the headliner where a dark wet spot continued to grow from the daily squirt of Vitalis he religiously combed through his hair. One hand touched her stomach, almost flat. She wondered if this baby would be a boy and would he look like him.

"Still upset?" CB's voice was deep and loud in the car, and she turned her head slightly toward him but did not answer. She flinched and squinted to see him in the darkness when he moved forward suddenly, his hand searching under the seat. He pulled out a brown paper bag. "Why don't you take a sip with me?"

Again she did not answer, but turned toward the window, annoyed by the sound of whiskey sloshing in the bottle when he raised it several times. The highway was lined heavily with trees, dense and overgrown, blocking out much of the fading light from the sky.

As they turned the curve, two eyes glowed in the distance returning the headlight's glare. The eyes held hers, and she wondered what animal had stopped, blinded by CB's lights, its motionless body waiting, frightened by the sound of the motor racing toward it. Maybe it was waiting for fate to decide if the car would smash it to death or pass on by. Was it too scared to run?

The road twisted to the right, and the eyes disappeared. Marilyn felt vaguely disappointed as if the car failed its mission. She must have let out a sound because CB's fingers suddenly touched her shoulder, stroking the only part of her he could reach. She imagined their imprint on her skin like the dark purple spots his hands left around her neck and shoulder last night. She pulled her body closer to the door, and his hand slid to the seat. After a few seconds, he sighed loudly and returned his hand to the steering wheel.

Marilyn rolled down the window halfway as they turned another curve, and then sped down the mountain. The wind blew back her hair and filled the car with the sharp scent of pine trees. A string of lights revealed a clearing with two block buildings with peeling paint and a large metal white sign with black letters, LITTLE TEXAS. A smaller, hand-lettered sign was near the door with GO TO THE BACK FOR BAIT. She wondered again why this dump on the side of the road in Guntersville, Alabama would name their place after Texas, but it was one of the few places in the surrounding dry counties where CB could go to the back and buy liquor. This liquor was packaged, safer than the moonshine that almost killed CB when he was a teenager, but nearly twice as expensive. Although he was a frequent visitor, CB rarely stopped when she was with him, telling her it was too rough a place for women.

"If you weren't going to talk to me Marilyn, why did you want to take a drive together to see the bridge?" CB's voice whined like a child and as if she had no right to be upset with him. Pressing her lips together, she turned to face the window and wondered if her lipstick had worn off. She forgot to check before leaving the house even though she stared at a mirror while waiting for CB to get a neighbor to watch the girls.

CB turned the radio on and then quickly snapped it off, slowing down as they circled the last curve to Guntersville Bridge. From the side, the lights created long shadows from the tall, metal beams that soared high above the bridge and then dropped to disappear into the dark waters below. Even the road disappeared into the wilderness on the other side, or maybe it was just too dark to see it ahead.

Her heart fluttered, and she turned in the seat and looked back from the direction they came and saw the darkness closing in behind them; not even the lights of Little Texas shined through the trees.

"I told you it would be too dark to see anything by the time we got here."

There were no other cars in either direction on the bridge. Satisfied, she sat back, listening for the sound of water while trying to smell it in the breeze that lifted her hair. Shutting both eyes, she imagined the cool water washing over her and closing everything out. Her heart began pounding in her ears; irritated, she leaned closer to the window and struggled to hear the water. She thought she heard a voice then, "Maybe the baby's heart is beating hard, too." One hand pressed on her belly to comfort him, and she opened her eyes to the bridge looming before them. They drove up and inside the huge, metal cage that wrapped around the concrete with big, strong metal arms.

She wondered if the arms made the bridge safer or if it was only to make people think it was. The holes in the cage were still big enough to fall through. Or jump through. A shiver began but stopped as she looked at her husband, quietly sneaking sips of whiskey, the bottle still covered with a brown paper bag. He turned to her then, his eyes pleading for her, full of sadness and regret. His sadness always filled her, and she trusted it, took it in even with the drunken outbursts. This used to be all it took to get her back. She used to think she could make the sadness go away.

Her head quickly turned back to the window, and she heard him screw the cap on the bottle as she craned her neck out the window to see the water below. The side of the bridge was too high. The smell of damp earth and fishy water filled the car.

She turned back to CB. "I need to see it. I need to see the water."

CB's face grew soft, then relieved. He quickly slowed the car and pulled in closer to the edge. "Can you see it now, baby?" Her back stiffened at his voice. She would only be able to see it when she got out. They were near the center of the bridge. It had to be now.

He continued, his voice kind, almost a whisper, "If I had known you wanted to see the water, we would have gone to the swimming area on the other side of the lake."

Her hand grasped the handle, and she drew in a slow, shaky breath. She jerked the handle up and pushed against the door and used one foot to help shove it open.

Feet first. This was as far as she planned. The pavement scraped her foot, and the wind pushed the door against her. She held to the door to move her body out, but the car lunged forward, going faster. For a moment, she was afraid the car would pin her against the railing, but it swerved away, then back again, the headlight scrapping against the railing when it stopped and her body jerked forward. The door stayed open, and she was almost out when a big hand grabbed at the back of her head, taking strands of hair when it dug deep into her bruised neck and shoulder, tearing her blouse and she felt herself falling back.

Screams tore from her throat when she realized that his hands held her tightly inside the car. "I'm gonna jump. I'm gonna jump." She couldn't stop saying the words while trying to tear herself away from him.

"You goddamned crazy woman!" He released his hold on one shoulder for a second and leaned forward, quickly grabbing under her arm and pulling her back in toward him.

"Her arms and legs continued to lock on the door frame until he stopped pulling and slapped her over and over, then pulled her fully inside. He reached over her, locking the door even through it wasn't shut tight.

A car from behind slowed down, then went around them. CB's hand held to her hair, pulling her head back. He glanced back to look at another car stopping behind them, then turned back to her, his eyes red from the liquor and rage. She flattened her body against the seat.

"You were going to jump the damn bridge!" He accused her, his breath hard and labored. She remained quiet and limp, matching his breath. "You're trying to get me in trouble, trying to make people think I threw you!"

Her head moved slightly to try to ease the strain from her scalp. His eyes narrowed at her move. He raised his other hand as if to slap her.

It was only a warning. A rush of anger stiffened her body. His face was so close to hers that she wildly thought about plucking out his blue eyes and flinging them into the water.

"Let go." Her loud voice seemed to startle him. Her fingers were only tiny claws pulling at his huge hands, but his hold weakened when they both heard slamming car doors and strangers from cars talking to one another.

"Keep your mouth shut, Marilyn, or I swear I'll kill you and you won't have to jump off no damn bridge." She thought he smiled at her then, a twisted curl of his lips before he turned in his seat and opened the door.

"My wife and I are fine. Lost control of the car, but we were going so slow that everything seems okay." He got out and unsteadily walked in front of the car, stopping to examine the fender and headlight while talking to the two men. He moved over to lean against the railing, continuing to talk while watching her.

It was a mistake. Why did she choose this? Her face was burning and she could feel sweat trickling down the sides of her face. Blood circled around her red fingernails, and she wondered if it was hers or CB's. She pulled back her hair with one hand while pulling the rear view mirror down. She flinched at her swollen face and left eye and slowly pushed the mirror back in place.

She should run now. Her eyes focused across the bridge where the forest continued for miles without houses or people. It would be daylight before he could see to search for her.

She took a cigarette from his pack and lit it with shaking hands while imagining herself lighting a campfire. Breathing in the smoke made her calmer. As a child, she played in the woods, ran barefoot through the creek behind the family farm and sunned herself on large rocks. Could she get through the night here? She looked down at her skirt and bare ankles, the patches of scraped bleeding skin and one foot swollen over the edge of her shoe. Where would she go at daybreak?

CB moved from the railing and back around the car, still talking to the men. With the cigarette pointed up, she watched the tip burn down, breathing in the smoke through her nose. The door opened and CB slid in, moving the rear view mirror to watch the last man get into his car behind them. He waved as the car passed and sat silent until the glow of taillights disappeared before turning suddenly and grabbing her arm, taking away the cigarette and throwing it out the window.

"I know what you're doing. What kind of wife and mother are you anyway? Don't you even think about the girls or the baby?" He stared into her eyes briefly, his eyes no longer sad, but cold and unrecognizable. Fear gripped her stomach. It was this stranger she feared the most. His nostrils flared, and he jerked her arm as he released his hold and found the keys in his pocket.

The car started quickly, and CB slowly continued across the bridge, then pulled the car onto the left side of the graveled shoulder of the road and reached for a cigarette. A metal railing continued from the bridge into the edge of the forest, holding back the baby pine trees and thick vines with tentacles that held to the metal and reached out for something more. A breeze made them sway like waving arms. Marilyn watched, shaking her head slightly, wondering again if she could have made it in the forest. Her arm slowly slipped out the window, her hand wide open and palm up. It began to shake, and she quickly turned the palm down, glancing at CB as he backed up the car, smoke streaming from his mouth. It was too late. She waved slightly to the vines before bringing her arm back inside the window.

The car sped back over the bridge, and she fanned away the fishy, damp air that filled the car along with CB's cigarette smoke. The car zipped back into the winding road and the waiting darkness where there was nothing more to see.

They were both silent as CB drove up the mountain, slowly turning sharp curves. There was no moonlight, and the headlights lit only a few feet of the pavement before the next curve. She rubbed her arms and neck where they had begun to ache and patted her swollen face. Her throat was sore and dry when she tried to swallow.

As the twists and turns of the road straightened out and they came into the edge of town, CB slowed down and turned the car into the driveway of a service station. "Can I trust you to stay put while I get us a Coke?"

Turning away, she stared at the screen door with a picture of a rosy cheeked little girl eating bread, and then changed her view to study fading letters on a wooden bench in order to keep from watching CB walk inside the store. A breeze cooled her face, and she heard the distant sound of thunder.

Children ran out of the store, slamming the screen door and laughing as they all crawled into the back of a truck parked near her. A tall older man came out next, nodding in her direction. "Evening."

She didn't answer. She knew CB would be watching her while in the store. He walked out then, holding two Cokes. He swallowed from the first can and held the other one out to her.

The older man started his car and waved, then pulled out of the driveway.

"Who is he?" CB turned and watched the car drive away.

There would be no right answer, so she gave none.

"Will you take the damned Coke?" He set his on the top of the car, then reached inside the window and pulled her limp arm from her lap. There were bloody scratches on his hand, and she wondered if he noticed. He put the can in her hand, grabbed his own, and then walked back to the other side of the car.

Her throat ached, and she slowly brought the can up to her lips. A small sip of Coke fizzed against her raw throat moments before CB screeched the car out of the drive and onto the road. His hands tightly gripped the steering wheel, and she wondered why he stopped her from jumping? Was it only because he feared that everyone would think he did it? Sinking back, she closed her eyes, too weary to think anymore.

Maybe she was too tired. Maybe he put something in her Coke. She sat up and carefully brought the can up to her face and pretended to take a sip while rubbing a finger across the top, then smelling it. Only one side had a triangle cut into it; as usual, he didn't bother to make the second hole.

Glancing at CB, she wondered how long he would punish her when they got home. She just wanted it all to end. She leaned her head back and closed her eyes. If only she could just go to sleep and not wake up. She felt comforted at the thought and rose up to take large sips of the sweet Coke.

CHAPTER 2

BABY CHICKS

GINNY, 1960

Tearing off a wad of toilet paper, Ginny stretched to reach over the sink, but had to climb back on the stool to reach the streaks on the mirror. She stopped to shake her head and watch the long brown pony-tail swing back and forth. The hair on top was still pulled back too tight. Sheila combed it back that way, then laughed and said Ginny's face looked fat. Mother laughed too. When Ginny tried to pull the rubber band out, her mother told her to leave it like her sister fixed it and for both of them to go clean up their room. That's what she always says, especially if she and Daddy are fighting.

"Go clean your room." Ginny said it to herself rubbing the mirror. But they never did. She would just go back to the room with Sheila and find something to play until they could sneak back out.

A noise in the hallway made her jump and she wondered if God had watched her mark the mirror with her mother's lipstick and decided that He had, since He saw everything. She hesitated then decided she would have to fix it and took toilet paper and wiped the top of the lipstick, trying to make it smooth again. Little pieces of tissue dissolved into the waxy red stick, and her fingertips left marks where she tried to pick them off.

The medicine cabinet opened quietly, and she carefully put the case back between the toothpaste and the little red plastic box that held a tiny brush and black paint that mother used on her eyes. She reached to take the red box then remembered she needed to hurry, so she grabbed the bottle of black shoe polish and tucked it inside her shorts where the elastic waistband would hold it in place.

She crept down the hallway. The television was on in the playroom, so she stopped and sneaked a quick look. Her mother's back was to her, one hand holding the iron while she watched the TV. Ginny tiptoed past the door. Once outside, she made her way past rows and rows of red brick apartments that looked just like hers. Every other row had long clotheslines held up by poles that made capital Ts. When she walked past them, she was surprised at the way the Ts lined up; they looked like steps stacked slightly out from each other. When she got exactly in front of the first pole, she could not see the others; they were straight behind one another. It reminded her of lining up dominos with Grandmother.

At the end of the block, the gate to the playground was open, and she stepped inside thinking about the tall slide that she wasn't allowed to climb. Now, there was a woman wearing a pink poodle skirt and big, black sunglasses who stood at the end of the slide grabbing a boy as he zipped out the end. The woman laughed and whirled around, her skirt flaring up in back.

Ginny walked toward them, then whirled around too and held out her arms on either side as if her own skirt would flair out. The pretty woman twirled around again while holding the boy tight. Her skirt twirled around higher this time in a circle, and Ginny laughed out loud, then covered her mouth with both hands when she saw a flash of the woman's white panties underneath. The boy slid from the woman's arms and ran to the back of the slide and up the ladder again. Once again she scooped him up, twirling around and around, then carried him away from the slide. Throwing out her arms again, Ginny imagined the pink poodle skirt circling around her legs as she twirled around then stopped suddenly to see where the woman was going next. Her eyes searched in the crowd but did not see her. Disappointed, she turned to go out and stopped to pick up the bottle of shoe polish where it fell on the ground and ran out the gate and through a grassy field where some boys played ball. Soon, she saw the tall trees near a short muddy road with piles of garbage on either side. At the back of the garbage dump were several huge rocks, the tallest one was higher than a house, and she climbed up one just as she did when she came with Sheila. Finally, she carefully stepped down into a small flat area in the rock quarry that Sheila had found. It was their playhouse.

It was bigger than the living room at home, only it didn't have a top. Two cracked plates and a big yellow plastic bowl with a melted hole set on top of shelves that Sheila made by layering old cans and pieces of wood from the dump. Two smelly glass jars with small rocks in them were on the bottom shelf, and Sheila told her they were pretend ice cubes for when they had a drink. They had one of Daddy's flat bottles with a little of the brown liquid left in it and a pack of cigarettes, but these were hidden behind the shelves in case someone found their place.

Ginny suddenly missed Sheila and wished she had come with her instead of going over to Betty's house. Her fingers pulled out the bottle of shoe polish and twisted the cap. Sheila would be so surprised to see that she had painted the little rock they used as a chair. It would be a beautiful shiny, black chair. Maybe Sheila wouldn't want to go play with Betty anymore.

Ginny pressed the sponge against the rock like she saw her mother do when she polished shoes. The polish came out slowly as her hand moved back and forth. The black streaks covered only a little bit before sand stuck to the sponge. She tried to brush it off with her hand, then impatiently, she rubbed the sponge on the back of her hand to get the polish started again. It began to glide smoothly and she continued until she totally covered her hand. It looked like black velvet, like the dress that Sheila wore to her first big girl party. Mother made it from one of her old dresses. The polish glided smoothly on the top of Ginny's other hand. She hoped her mother would make her a black velvet dress too. When she asked her, Mother just said, "maybe one day."

The distant noise of a plane made her look up. It was straight overhead. She liked the long streak that planes left in the sky; you could see where they came from. Sheila told her it was just smoke, but Ginny wasn't sure if she believed her. It looked more like the clouds were parting for the plane, like the sea did for the man in the Bible. Grandmother told her about him and showed her the pictures.

She pressed the sponge firm against the rock again, zigzagging until bits of the sponge stuck and tore. Gritting her teeth, she threw the bottle on the ground. Grabbing it again, she threw it again—harder—and it bounced against the shelves. Sheila could have done it better.

Sitting on the streaked rock, she wondered what Sheila would be doing at Betty's house. Betty never asked Ginny to come over; just Sheila. Even though Betty was only a year older than Ginny, she always tried to pretend she was a lot older and called Ginny the "kid."

Betty no longer was allowed to come to their house. Once while there, Betty saw daddy's flat bottles in the garbage and told Ginny that she was going to tell her uncle. He was a policeman, and she said he would lock him up in jail. After Ginny told Daddy, he told them to never bring Betty back in his home again; he "didn't need nobody going through his damn garbage." They didn't have to tell Betty because she never asked to come over anymore, only for Sheila to visit.

A loud crashing noise made Ginny jump. She sat very still and waited to see if someone was coming, but didn't hear anything else. She climbed up a few steps and peeped around the side. "Johnny, I don't see anyone." She looked back at her pretend friend standing back near the streaked chair. Even though he was taller than her, he looked small against the big rocks all around them.

"It's too spooky here. Maybe if we just go to Betty's house, they will let me play with them." While continuing up two more steps out of the play-house, she remembered the last time she was with them and they made her eat squashed tomatoes out of an old mayonnaise jar first. Her nose wrinkled up remembering the smell. She looked around carefully then started down, finally turning backwards so she could hold on while stepping to the ground. She smiled at Johnny right behind her, "Be careful to go around the garbage."

The playground had lots of kids in it now, and she hesitated at the gate then walked quickly for several blocks to get to Betty's house. The two girls were sitting on a blanket in the front yard, their heads bent over their laps painting their fingernails. A radio blared from the open window of the house. Neither girl spoke or looked up as she edged near them. She shifted her weight on one foot and placed one hand on her hip.

"Hey!" Neither girl looked up. Ginny sat on the grass, careful not to touch the edge of the blanket.

"Can I polish my nails too?" Ginny looked first at Sheila, then to Betty.

"Ginny, our song is on. Shut up will you?" Betty frowned but did not look up.

Ginny sat still watching until "Wake Up Little Susie" came on. It was her favorite song. Daddy always turned the radio up loud for her when it came on while they were in the car. Ginny sung along, sure that Sheila would be impressed that she now knew all the words.

Sheila looked up from her hand at Ginny. "I thought you were going to stay home. What have you got all over your hands?"

Ginny raised her chin and then held out a hand for her to see. "I polished them."

"Mother's going to whip you! What is it, shoe polish?"

"No, she won't. I'll wash it off before I go home." Ginny nodded yes and rubbed the back of her velvet hand.

"It won't wash off, silly." Betty stared at Ginny's hands. Sheila put the brush back into the bottle of polish she was using then blew on her nails. "Betty, can I use some of the nail polish remover to see if it will take the shoe polish off?"

"No." Betty grabbed the bottle from the blanket and put it in her bag. "The bratty kid can just get into trouble. I didn't invite her here anyway."

Ginny stood quickly and tried to decide whether to smack Betty's head before leaving. "I don't want your ole polish mover anyway." Neither girl spoke so she kicked at the blanket and ran back behind Betty's house.

"Ginny."

Ginny heard Sheila calling after her, but kept going. She cut through the yard and through another yard and came out on a different street. She kept running, half expecting Sheila to come after her and ask her to come back. If they had been at home, Daddy would have made them let her play with them.

At the corner she hesitated, looking back and seeing the side of Betty's house and the backyard of the old mean man next door. She didn't want to go back. This really wasn't very far from Betty's house.

This was as far as she ever walked alone. She and Sheila went to look at the chicken hatchery a couple of times. They watched from the side as boxes and boxes with little round holes holding baby chicks were being put in a truck. Two men sitting at the side door smoking stared when she asked what happened to the mothers of the chicks. One said he guessed they were all dead, and they both laughed. Sheila pulled her away then, and they ran back across the street.

Now, it looked like no one was there. Daddy said the workers only came there at times to process the chicks. She wondered if there were chicks inside by themselves now.

"Johnny, you'll come with me won't you?" She whispered the question then turned her head to see him nod yes, and they continued. Walking slowly in the drive and near the building, she listened carefully but couldn't hear any chicks crying. She wished Daddy hadn't told her about the hatchery where baby chicks stay without their mothers. He said they gave them medicine. But mother said that the medicine killed them.

"Maybe they're all dead Johnny." She looked at him, and Johnny shrugged his shoulders.

Ginny and Sheila once found a bunch of little bottles in boxes stacked next to the outside gate of the hatchery and took them home. The bottles looked like tiny glass milk jugs like the kind the milkman brought. But mother said that they once had poison in them, and they used it for the baby chicks that had something wrong with them. She made Ginny throw all the bottles away. Ginny wanted to ask more questions, but she was afraid. Mother got mad when she asked too many questions.

Johnny walked around the doors of the hatchery, and she followed him. They found cartons and cartons of the empty bottles lined up near a ramp. "See them Johnny?" She pointed, and then stared up close so she could see any poison left in them. "Why doesn't someone stop them from hurting the chicks?"

Johnny didn't answer and just stared back at her. For a moment he faded a little and she got scared. Maybe the hatchery people would give the medicine to her if they caught her here, and she wouldn't ever see Daddy or Sheila or Mother anymore. She turned quickly and walked back around the side of the hatchery, then stopped when she thought she heard something. Three baby chicks dashed out from the crates, making loud cheeps.

"Come to me." She yelled to the chicks while running toward them. She held out her hands. The chicks separated and raced away from her and Johnny. One was blocked near a door, and Ginny put a box over it. The other two kept running until they hid in the stacks of crates and cartons at the end of the building. She tried to climb over to get closer to them but slipped down each time.

"Johnny, can't you help?" But she knew he couldn't. "You're not even real!" Johnny faded totally away, and she was sorry she yelled at him. Her heart was beating hard and she was afraid to stay any longer but afraid to leave the other chicks. She carefully collected the trapped chick by sliding a lid on top when she turned the box over.

"Johnny, can you help the other chicks? Johnny?" Johnny didn't appear. She walked quickly to the end of the block and across the street, stopping once to briefly look down the road behind her. Only when she got near Betty's house did she stop. Gasping for air, she began to cough and sat down on the curb.

The chick was making lots of noise, so Ginny peeped in the round hole of the box and talked softly to it. The chick didn't look like anything was wrong with it, and she wondered if maybe something was wrong with its nerves or mind. Aunt Adele once said that her mother's nerves were breaking; that's why Mother said things that didn't make sense. She wondered if her mother would be given medicine after the nerves completely broke. The little bottles of poison came to her mind, and she shivered. A wheezing noise escaped each time she breathed through her mouth, and she stood slowly and continued home.

The house was quiet as Ginny came into the front door and stood still. The chick was making a lot of noise, so she quickly ran down the hallway to her bedroom and put the chick in the closet. She thought about something to feed it and went to the kitchen.

"Mother?" Ginny listened for a few seconds, but the apartment was quiet. Maybe mother went looking for her. Her stomach fluttered. She wondered if chicks would eat bread crumbs and opened the bread bag and took out a slice. The back door popped opened, and she jumped.

"Where have you been?" Her mother was carrying a load of clothes from the clothesline.

Ginny didn't want her to know the bread was for the chick, so she stuffed a small piece of the bread in her mouth. Her mother piled the clothes on the kitchen table and turned to look at her. They both looked at the white bread in her black polished hand.

"What is that all over your hands?"

Ginny couldn't swallow the bread, and her face began to itch. She rubbed her face and tried to swallow again, but only part of the bread went down.

"It's shoe polish." Her voice came out a whisper, and her breath was short.

"Where did you get it?"

Ginny shifted to one leg and tried to think of an answer. She kept her mouth open to breathe, and the wheezing was louder. Sheila once said that it sounded like a bunch of men singing far away.

"I asked you a question." Her mother turned from the table and grabbed Ginny's arm and pulled her forward then stopped suddenly. "You're wheezing. That stuff is probably making you sick. Go wash your hands and face."

Ginny didn't answer, but ran to her bedroom and crumbled bread into the holes of the box, then went to the bathroom and rinsed her hands and patted her face. The polish didn't come off, and she was glad. She dried her hands.

"Ginny." Silverware clinked in the kitchen. Ginny checked on the baby chick again.

"Ginny!" Ginny's stomach fluttered as she ran back to the kitchen. Her mother stirred something in a pot. "Where did you get that shoe polish?"

Ginny held to a kitchen chair to catch her breath. "At the dump in the quarry." Ginny lied, sure that God would understand.

"You know better than to be messing around there. I ought to blister you." Her mother's voice was high. It scared her more than when she just yelled. Avoiding her mother's eyes, she stared instead at the rows and rows of round flat curls held down by hairpins. The curls circled all around the edge of her head. It made her look like she had on a cap.

A pot began to boil over and her mother turned back to the stove. Ginny inched toward the door.

"Where's Sheila?"

"Betty's house."

"I've told both of you that you are never to come home by yourself."

They both turned as the front door opened. Ginny escaped the kitchen and ran to her father and jumped as he caught her and lifted her up high for a kiss. He usually threw her in the air, so she tried to catch her breath for the ride. Instead he kissed her then gently pulled her to his face.

The short dash to her father made the singing men louder and Ginny held tightly to his neck.

"You're wheezing." He carried Ginny to the kitchen. "Marilyn, have you given her a pill?"

"No." Marilyn stared at Ginny as CB set her on a chair.

"It's too late. We're going to have to take her for a shot. He leaned down to look closely at Ginny's hands. "I don't know what we'll use to pay for it."

"No, Daddy." The tears came up as she thought about the needle and gasped for air.

"I guess you won't be able to buy liquor."

CB ignored Marilyn and looked back at Ginny. "Where's Sheila?"

"At Betty's," Marilyn answered before Ginny. "Try giving her a pill first. It still might work."

"It's too late. You should have given her one earlier… can't you see how sick she is?" CB picked Ginny back up and walked down the hall toward the bedroom. "I'll wash her face and hands. We'll have to go find Sheila."

He set Ginny on the toilet and began filling the sink with water. "What have you gotten all over you?"

"Daddy, I…"

He held up his hand to hush her as he turned his head sideways straining to hear. "What's that noise?"

Ginny sat still as he went into the bedroom. She heard the closet door open and the chick cheeping louder.

"Damn it, Ginny! This chicken is making you sick. Do you not understand that?" He came into the bathroom holding the box sideways with one hand. She looked from the deep frown on his face to the box as he waved it back and forth.

"Where did you get it?" For a moment all they could hear was the scraping sounds coming from the box when CB turned it back and forth.

"You're hurting it, Daddy." Ginny began to cry again. Struggling for breath and grabbing onto the sink.

"I'm not hurting it." Setting the box on the floor, he picked her up, "Calm down."

"I went outside and called for Sheila but didn't get an answer… what is that noise?" Marilyn was at the door and looked down at the box in the floor. Two curls escaped the hairpins and fell in her face.

"Where did that thing come from?" Marilyn impatiently pushed the curls back and looked from the box back to Ginny. Her voice was high again, and Ginny buried her face into CB's neck.

"Let's go. We'll go by Betty's house." CB carried Ginny out, and Marilyn picked up the box and grabbed a hair brush.

Sheila came in the back door as Marilyn walked to the front. CB yelled to her as he carried Ginny out. "Sheila, lock that door and come on. We're going to the clinic."

After turning the lock, Sheila ran up beside Marilyn and tried to look in the holes of the box. "What is that?" Marilyn's tapped Sheila's chest with the hairbrush until Sheila moved back.

CB put Ginny in the front seat through the passenger side then stepped back. Marilyn came up behind him.

"What the hell are you doing with the damned chicken?"

Marilyn held the box out from his reach. "I'm not going to leave it in the house, CB. We'll throw it out at the hatchery when we go by."

"No, they'll kill it." Ginny pictured the medicine bottles and protested louder, "Daddy, no, they will kill it."

"Good God. Ginny stop it."

"Daddy…"

"I said stop." He yelled at her and continued to frown as he moved back from the car.

"We are not leaving the chicken in the house." Marilyn leaned over and gave Ginny an icy stare. More curls were sticking out around her face.

"Marilyn…" CB lowered his voice and walked around the car. "Put the chicken in the back seat. We'll take the damned thing to your mother's after we get Ginny's shot.

Ginny propped herself forward on her arms to help catch her breath. She imagined the chick at her grandmother's farm, running around eating corn with all the other chickens.

Marilyn put the box in the backseat and then sat in the front seat next to Ginny, pulling out the rest of the hairpins and letting them drop into her lap. When the car pulled quickly away from the curb, the hairpins slid in the folds of mother's skirt beneath her big belly. The hairpins began sliding to the floorboard, and she wondered why her mother didn't want to take care of the chick and why she got so mad. She raised her hand to pat her mother's leg, but Johnny appeared at her side in the skinny space between them. Smiling at him, she silently formed the words that only he could hear. "It's okay, Johnny. Daddy will take care of the chick."

Chapter 3

SLEEP

Marilyn, 1961

Marilyn awakened with the warmth of the morning sun on the side of her face. Fingers from one hand held to the edge of the bed and her pillow was on the floor. Softly, she turned her head to see if CB was still beside her. He was gone. The baby was quiet in the crib so she dropped her head back down then rolled over.

She closed her eyes. The tiredness always seemed to stay with her. One hand smoothed over her stomach. Maybe it was childbirth. Even though her mother stayed with her for the first two weeks after the baby was born, this last week without her was exhausting.

The faint sound of laughter startled her. She heard CB's voice somewhere in the house. He was whispering. She wondered if he talked about her to the girls when she wasn't around. They always listen to CB more than they do her. He practically controlled them. She sat up quickly and threw aside the white sheet and chenille spread. God, was that his plan?

The linoleum floor was cool to her bare feet as she stood up and stopped briefly to stare at the small, bloody spots she left on the bed. Leave it. Just check on the girls. She moved toward the door.

"Hurry. Hurry." Whispering the words out loud made her walk more quickly down the hall and into the kitchen.

"What are you doing?" Her voice was angry and loud, even to herself. The girls stopped talking and stood, watching her as if they were caught. Their eyes searched back and forth among daughters and mother, then finally between sisters. They didn't look back up at her but at least they didn't look to CB. She could tell they were frightened, and their fear made her angry. She knew they thought she was crazy.

CB continued to turn bacon strips over and then reached for the rest of the package from Ginny. Sheila took another egg from the carton and broke it into the bowl, letting pieces of the shell fall as well.

"We decided to cook breakfast." CB's calm voice sounded like he was talking to a child. He didn't look up from the pan as he spoke.

"I can fix breakfast." Marilyn moved quickly to Sheila and took the bowl of eggs. "Go clean up your room."

They rushed out, Sheila pushing against Ginny to get out quicker. CB slowly took the last piece of bacon from the skillet, holding it up and allowing the hot grease to drip. "They were just trying to help."

He poured more coffee in his cup and pulled out a kitchen chair to sit down. "You know you could have taken time to change. Or get dressed." He raised his cup to his lips. "There's blood on the back of your gown."

The egg yolks broke quickly as she beat them with a fork. They both looked up as Lenny began to cry. CB smiled as he stood up from the chair. "Since you're getting breakfast, I'll get Lenny."

She listened to CB talk to their son while she added cheese. Before she finished buttering bread for toast, the girls joined him in the room. Their laughter was loud. CB always kept everyone laughing, and for a long time, she laughed too. Then it got where she only smiled at his jokes. Now she didn't do either.

The stack of Blue Willow plates rattled as Marilyn pulled them from the shelf and set them on the table. His sister once told her that CB had pinned her picture up next to Rita Hayworth's, showing his friends how much she looked like her and that he planned to marry her one day. Other boys told her she was beautiful before CB, but most of them didn't last; they said she was too quiet or they were tired of trying to find ways to get around her father in order to see her. CB told her he liked a challenge, that he liked it that she hadn't dated much. But even now, it was always her beauty that he whispered about when they were close.

The last plate and all the silverware were in place, exactly one inch from the edge of the table. Maybe he is happier that he has a son and will act better. At the hospital, he kept saying how happy he was, that he so wanted a son.

The smell of heated butter reminded Marilyn of the toast, and she took the hot pan from the oven. Eight slices of perfectly browned toast stacked nicely on the Blue Willow platter and looked like a picture book set beside the dark blue serving dishes holding the bacon and eggs.

Twice she tried going back home. The first time, her father told her when she arrived that he thought it best that she go back to live with him and work it out. The second time, a neighbor insisted on driving her home after CB left for work. Her father sent her mother back to live with them for a few days, thinking she could show Marilyn how to work things out. CB was the perfect apologetic husband that day. After he went to work, Marilyn tried to explain CB to her mother. She patted Marilyn on the shoulder and told her to find some sewing to take in, something to occupy her mind. Marilyn wanted to ask her mother if that's what she did when Daddy threatened her. But she didn't. She knew the answer.

Marilyn stood still, staring at the beautiful table. Both hands held to the back of a chair, the fingers pressing tightly against the padded vinyl. She was tired of trying to figure it all out. Softly, she went to the china cabinet and set out the good blue glasses for milk. There was no reason to save them anymore.

* * *

It was after midnight. Trouble was coming; this she knew. CB didn't go to work and insisted it was Saturday so he shouldn't have to go in. He refused to go pay the rent and after arguing with her he left. Hours later he showed up with his buddy Mack and a collection of beer and liquor, all from Little Texas.

An aching back made her feel worse than tired. She wished she slept longer this morning when she had the chance. Her bare feet padded to the living room. Both CB and Mack were still sitting at the small card table and both managed to lay down a card when it was their time, although both insisted that the other was cheating at every turn.

Continuing past the men and down the hall, she stuck her head in the girls' room and saw their eyes were closed. She knew they would probably sneak back up, so she left the door cracked open and went back to the kitchen. An RC Cola was left in the refrigerator, so she took it and pressed the cold can against the side of her face before digging out the can opener from a drawer.

She was afraid to go to bed. If they argued too loud, neighbors would call the police, and they would pick him up again. Pushing empty beer cans aside on the counter, she found a pack of CB's cigarettes and took one and lit it. She set it in the ashtray, content to breathe in the smoke streaming in the air. The men were no longer talking, so she took the cigarette and sucked on the tip, swallowing the smoke and holding it in her lungs before a fit of coughing let it go. She walked back into the living room. Mack's head was face down on the table. Passed out, she supposed. CB was staring into space muttering.

She touched his arm, "CB, let me help you to bed."

He flinched as if her touch burned him, then frowned, "I told you no, Marilyn." He looked up at her, winced, then slumped back into his chair, still muttering words too low to understand.

There was nothing to do now but wait. CB continued to mutter and look up at her as she left them. The bedroom was cooler, and she sat down and lay back. Closing her eyes, she tried to relax. Just a short nap and she would check on them again.

*   *   *

"Get up! You bitch, you little whore… you think I don't know what you were doing?" Hands pulled her shoulder then lifted her from the bed. She made an attempt to fight, but her mind was too groggy. For a second her body was airborne, then it slapped against a door. Before she could get up, CB pulled her into the bathroom and pushed her head down to the toilet.

"I should kill you. You and all those children."

He pulled her face up to his. "Whose baby did you have? Whose?" He suddenly released her, and she fell to the floor. He swerved around and stormed from the room.

She tried to think of what to do or where to go. No money for a cab. She impatiently wiped at tears and realized blood was streaming from her nose. If she got the baby, maybe she could make it to the store and use the phone before he caught her. The window was dark behind the curtain. It would be too early for the store to be open, and she couldn't risk having the baby if he caught her.

Crawling forward, she began to pull herself up by holding on to the toilet. CB's footsteps were loud as he stumbled back to her. Dropping back to the floor, she hugged the base of the toilet.

"Now, I'm going to get the truth." He was in the doorway holding his rifle. The bowl of the toilet couldn't shield her, but she tried to wedge her face between it and the wall. She didn't want to see him pull the trigger.

CB pulled on her leg with one hand, then her arm. Swearing, he stood and kicked her backside. "Get up. I want to see your face when I get the truth out of you." He kicked again and again. The pain forced her to loosen her hold. She allowed him to unwrap her from cold white seat and pull her up. As he barked orders, she obeyed, going back to the bedroom.

As they went down the hall, she saw the girls' bedroom door wide open. One of them must have gotten up. Searching the length of the hall, she saw nothing. Maybe they sneaked out to get help. A spark of hope straightened her body, and she prepared herself to run.

Mack startled her. He was sitting on the edge of the bed, his hands shielding his eyes from the overhead light as he tried to look up when they entered the room.

"What the hell is going on CB?"

"You tell me Mack." CB stood in front of Mack. Marilyn looked from man to man. Mack was drunk and out of it, and CB seemed the most sober she had ever seen him while in a rage. It gave her no comfort.

He shoved her toward the bed beside Mack and raised the rifle threateningly. "I want you both to tell me how you got together behind my back. You thought I didn't know why you keep coming over… Mack the man."

"CB, you crazy son of a bitch." Mack waved his hand impatiently.

"Don't call me crazy, Mack, I'll kill you right now. I'll kill you just like I'm going to kill her and your baby." He turns to Marilyn, a sneer on his face. "You thought I didn't know. I know. I know all about you. That baby's not mine. Couldn't be…"

"CB, stop the crap." Mack jumped from the bed, his arms held out slightly from his short stocky body.

The rifle swung suddenly, brushing past Marilyn's hair and stopping in Mack's gut.

Mack curled his arms and legs around the barrel and fell to the floor.

"CB, stop." CB ignored Marilyn as Mack groaned and slowly pulled himself up to his knees.

"Try again, Mack." CB's voice was a whisper. "Tell me how you slept with my wife and left her pregnant." He held the butt of the rifle over Mack's head.

"CB, Lenny is your baby. There was no one else." Marilyn pictured CB shooting them all. "Stop before you hurt him." She wasn't sure whether she meant Lenny or Mack.

Mack pulled himself up and sat on the edge of the bed.

"That's right, get back on the bed with your girlfriend. I've got it all planned." CB's voice got louder. "The two of you are going to take off your clothes, and I'll shoot both of you in bed together. No one will blame me."

"Stop it. Just stop it." Marilyn screamed the words, but CB continued to look at Mack.

Lenny's cry from the other room silenced both of them. CB frowned then glared toward the closed nursery door. "Shut up, or I'll kill you too. I'll just kill every damn body."

As he swung around, CB shifted unsteadily, and Mack grabbed at his legs and knocked him down. The rifle fell from CB's hands, and the two men scrambled on the floor. Marilyn climbed further back on the bed, surprised that Mack continued to hold on to CB. She stood up on the side of the bed next to the wall, hesitating before reaching down and pulling the rifle toward her. One of the men screamed her name as she took it and ran out of the room.

The rifle easily slipped beneath the old couch in the playroom and she slid down on the floor behind the toy chest until she heard someone race past the room. She listened for a second set of footsteps and thought she heard a door shut.

Finally the second steps came with someone dragging their hand along the wall. "Think you can get away bitch, you think again. I'll kill you with my bare hands. I don't need no rifle." It was CB. Mack must have been first and ran out. The sound of empty beer cans crashing on the floor made her jump. He was in the kitchen.

"God damn you, Marilyn. Where's my rifle?"

A door slammed. Did CB leave? She knew Mack wouldn't come back and he wouldn't call the police either. She stood and crept silently to the door. Better to keep him at the front of the apartment and away from the kids.

"Marilyn!" CB screamed her name outside while holding to the back door. He came back inside and slammed the door shut when he saw her come in the kitchen. They quickly circled the table. She had to keep it between them. He stopped. She stopped. "Where's Mack, Marilyn? What happened to your boyfriend?" He picked up a glass from the table and drank the brown liquid in it.

Lenny began crying again, and CB looked at her and smiled. He dropped the glass and turned. Even with his unsteady gait, she could not circle the table and catch up to him as he raced down the hall and inside the nursery. He slammed the door shut, and she heard the lock click as she reached for the knob.

Lenny was quiet as Marilyn pounded on the door. "CB, open the door. Don't you dare touch him. CB!"

The second door to the nursery was through the bedroom, and she ran around to it. The door crashed against the wall from her shove. CB was sitting in the rocking chair, and the baby's bed was empty. Her eyes searched the room for Lenny then stopped back at CB, slowly rocking and watching her.

"What did you do with him?" Her mind started racing, and she could picture the rifle under the couch. She imagined herself using it to shoot CB's cruel face over and over.

"I've not touched him." CB waved his hand back and frowned, his face suddenly sullen.

"Where is Lenny?" Her body bent over as she screamed each word slowly, her throat raw from the effort. She wondered if she could aim the rifle before CB took it away.

CB frowned, and the thick ridge of his brows made it hard to see his eyes. He sat forward in the rocking chair, squirming as she continued to stare. "I don't have him."

"Lenny! Lenny!" She stood uncertain in the center of the room watching CB lean back again, staring past her into their bedroom.

Marilyn turned to follow his gaze. A slight noise from the closet filled her with relief as she jerked the door open and found herself staring into Ginny's eyes. Lenny was propped against her leg with an old bottle in his mouth.

"What are you doing?" She didn't wait for an answer. "Give him to me."

Ginny continued to hold one hand on Lenny, while raising the other holding a clothes hanger. Marilyn stooped to take the baby, and Ginny raised the hanger higher.

Marilyn pulled back, anger burning through her body. "What are you doing? You'd better put that thing down and get back to your bed. Right now! Go! You nearly scared me half to death." They stared at each other until Ginny dropped the hanger.

"Leave her! I said to leave her alone." CB stopped rocking to yell from the nursery. "Come here, baby. Come on and stay with me."

Ginny avoided the nursery and slid sideways along the wall watching them until she was out of sight.

"To hell with you then. To hell with all of you." CB stood up and started toward her. "You hear me, Marilyn?"

Marilyn frowned at him, pitching the old bottle down while holding Lenny tight against her chest. She watched CB as he began to cry, then fell across their bed.

"Sheila? Sheila, come here, baby." CB was crying hard now. "Sheila, your daddy needs you, honey. Come to me."

Sheila softly walked up the hall and through the nursery with big, fearful eyes. She was fully dressed, and Marilyn wondered if she was ready to leave.

"Come here, baby. CB patted the space beside him. Sheila obediently went to her father and sat on the bed near him, patting his hand.

"It's ok, Daddy."

Ignoring them both, Marilyn took Lenny to the nursery. She put him down and heard the snores from CB. Nausea rose in her stomach when she saw the streaks of blood left on the blanket and now on Lenny's tiny hand. Her own blood.

He would be out for the rest of the night, but it gave her little comfort. Tomorrow, he would act like he didn't remember anything.

Sheila was lying on her side, one hand continuing to pat CB's arm. Her long dark hair was spread out around her head, and she stared at Marilyn, eyes still fearful. Who was she most afraid of, Marilyn or CB? She wanted to shake her, to slap her hand away from CB's arm; instead, she turned and followed the slightly worn path on the linoleum to the girl's room. Ginny actually hid Lenny from both of them; she no longer trusted them. CB had already taken Sheila. It was only a matter of time before he took Lenny, too.

Ginny's breathing was unsteady; she was still awake. Marilyn paused briefly and then left the door open to go the bathroom, the only room she could usually get some peace. She left this door open too, not because she needed to listen out for CB, but because she no longer felt connected to any of them, or even to her own body. Both her hands were bruised and bloody, but nothing ached. A loud silence rushed in her ears, filling her head with tiny waves that seemed to take her further out, she was bobbing away from herself.

She held tightly to the edge of the sink and looked into the mirror.

For a few seconds it held a stranger with a swollen nose and blackened cheek. Touching first the mirror then her cheek, she felt it, warm and soft, but her cheek did not feel the finger.

She propped one foot on the edge of the tub and rubbed the swollen snakelike shape that started below her knee and looped almost to the ankle. Was it the blood vein that had swollen and popped up? Shouldn't it hurt when it was swollen this much?

Putting her foot back on the floor, she reached up and pinched her cheek. Nothing.

She wondered if it meant something was broken when you couldn't feel anymore.

"Does it?" The woman in the mirror didn't answer.

CHAPTER 4

DOUBLE BRIDGES

GINNY, 1961

Grandfather's baldhead was shiny and smooth. A little fringe of hair rounded the back of his head like a hula girl's skirt. Ginny wanted to touch it, but did not. He was crowded into the front seat of the car with Grandmother and Uncle Jack, while Ginny, Sheila, and their cousin, Marti, sat in the back seat on their way to Uncle Jack's house.

The car moved slowly. Grandfather didn't like to drive fast. Not like Daddy. Thinking of him made her eyes water, and she wondered where he was. Uncle Jack brought Sheila and Ginny to stay with Grandmother several days ago, but he and Aunt Katie kept Lenny. When Grandfather left early this morning and brought back Uncle Jack and their cousin, Marti, Ginny had only been able to ask if they had Lenny before dissolving into tears and running back to the guest bedroom.

She rested her head in the crook of her elbow, comforted by the sound of Grandmother's voice, excited and laughing while telling a story to Uncle Jack. It was Grandmother who came to the bedroom and told her to stop crying. "Your momma left the hospital this morning, and she is with Aunt Katie. We'll take you to see her later today."

Sheila's finger poked into Ginny's side. "Sit back and scoot over."

Ginny glared at her and stubbornly stiffened her back and pressed forward a little more.

"Ginny, sit back and move over to the center."

"Well, I don't want her over here either!" Marti took a deep breath and expanded her chest and arms to take up more space. Ginny looked at Marti from her narrowed eyes and then slid them to the other corner to look at Sheila on the other side.

"Girls." Grandmother stopped talking to Uncle Jack and shifted her body to turn her head back and glance at them in the back seat. "Now let's all be pretty and act like ladies."

"I don't want to sit in the middle." Ginny frowned at the back of her Grandmother's head then focused on the brown and green threads that looped around each other to make the fabric of the car seat. She thought of the potholders she and Sheila made out of loops in a kit they got for Christmas.

"Well, the prettiest girl always got to sit in the middle when I was growing up." Grandmother turned and winked at her.

"If you girls don't behave, we'll just not tell you about the surprise." Uncle Jack's forehead rose up along with his bushy eyebrows as he turned and stared for a few seconds at each one of them.

Marti leaned forward quickly, her elbow nudging Ginny over. "What surprise, Daddy?"

"You just wait until we get home. They will want to visit with their mother awhile, first." He looked at Ginny and smiled, "And with Lenny, too."

Ginny looked away from Uncle Jack to Sheila while scooting all the way back; both feet on the hump in the floorboard. It was hot in the middle, and her stomach hurt. She stared at her big toe that had a scab on the end where she stubbed it yesterday. Glancing at Sheila, she started to tell her she felt sick, but decided that everyone would hear her and stare. Swallowing several times, she tried to think of something else, but instead, remembered the trip Daddy took them on last year when she puked on herself and Sheila.

She wondered where Daddy went. No one talked about him. When she asked, no one seemed to know. He might have gone back home and found no one there and not known where they were. He would be all alone, or maybe he would just leave and never come back. He said before that she would have to choose between them and if she chose her mother she would never see him again. Tears came to her eyes and she quickly wiped them away when Marti sat back with sudden impatience.

"I bet I can guess what it is." No one answered and Ginny watched Marti's foot pressing in the back of Grandfather's seat. Marti's socks and T-strap shoes were very white and new. The socks had yellow lace and tiny, yellow flowers.

Ginny looked past Sheila outside the window, noting each house until they passed a big, white house with a porch. It would do. Quickly she warmed to her favorite game. Softly laying her head back, she closed her eyes and imagined herself sitting at the house in a porch swing, wearing a black, velvet dress and pretty socks and shoes like Marti's, except her socks had tiny, pink roses and her shoes were black. Lenny and Sheila would be there too, all dressed up, and they would all go out together with daddy in his convertible for chocolate ice cream.

"It's a horse, Grandfather! Can we stop and ask if we can ride him?" Marti's voice compelled Ginny to open her eyes and see the fenced horse on the side of the road.

"I don't think we can do that." Grandfather laughed at Marti's suggestion. Ginny watched the horse and imagined it fenced in the back of her house. "Daddy will get us a horse, and we will ride it every day."

"Daddy ain't gonna get you no horse." Sheila voice was angry, and her eyelids were bunched tight when Ginny turned to look at her. "We don't even know where he is."

Everyone else stopped talking. Ginny thought Sheila was mad about Daddy, and she wanted to tell her how to pretend so she wouldn't feel so bad. But Sheila thought pretending was silly. When Ginny told her about her friend, Johnny, Sheila said he wasn't real and people were going to think she was crazy like mother if she kept talking about him. Ginny swore she wouldn't ever talk about him again and after that, whenever Ginny tried to call him, Johnny didn't come back, not even when she cried for him at night.

"Well, you never know what will happen in the future. Maybe Ginny will get to go horseback riding someday." Uncle Jack's voice was soft. "It doesn't hurt to wish for it."

That's our surprise isn't it? You're taking us horseback riding!" Marti bobbed her body up and down, first pulling her legs and feet up under her on the seat then back down, the buckle on her shoe catching and pulling a thread from the seat.

No Marti, that's not it." Uncle Jack's voice was loud and irritated, and Ginny avoided looking at him. "Sit straight with your feet on the floor."

"My feet don't reach the floor. See, they don't reach." Marti frowned at Uncle Jack, her voice loud. "I don't like Grandfather's old car anyway."

"Guess Ginny and Sheila will be the only ones getting a surprise."

"No, Daddy! I'll be good." Marti sat quietly and twisted a long blond lock of hair then dropped it to chew her fingernail.

The drive through small streets with crowded houses was familiar to Ginny as Grandfather drove them to Uncle Jack's house. They were almost there. Her stomach began to hurt again, and when she tried to swallow, her insides seem to get bigger and bigger. Maybe she was dying.

Clamping her eyes tight, she leaned back and waited. At least if she died, she wouldn't have to go inside.

"You're not asleep Ginny." Sheila nudged her. "We're here, get up."

"I am too." Ginny kept her eyes closed.

"Then you wouldn't be talking."

She opened her eyes and frowned. "I was too asleep until you woke me."

Marti got out of the car quickly, running toward the door and yelling for her mother.

Uncle Jack leaned inside the car from the open car door Marti left. "Well, sleepy head, come on and get out.

"She just always pretends to be asleep so Daddy will pick her up when he gets home." Sheila grimaced at Uncle Jack then turned to follow the others inside the house.

"Missing your dad a lot, aren't you, girl?"

She nodded.

"Are you scared?" She didn't want to talk to Uncle Jack.

"You know you have to be brave." His hand patted hers and then squeezed it tight. "You know, kid, God is watching. He hears our prayers, and he takes care of us."

Maybe Uncle Jack could get God to help take care of Mother; he didn't do it when Grandmother asked. She already prayed every night for God to make Mother well. Maybe God would listen to Uncle Jack since he was a minister, part time. The need to puke stopped but she noticed his hands were sweaty and shaking, and she pulled her own away.

"I want out now." Uncle Jack didn't move, and Ginny started to repeat herself when Aunt Katie stepped out from the door to look at them. Uncle Jack got out quickly, and Aunt Katie paused until Ginny stepped up to the porch and then softly resting a hand on her head. "Girl, haven't you got some shorts instead of that dress? It's going to be hot today."

Ginny shrugged. Shorts were not what she wanted to wear. She hoped Daddy might come by to visit this morning and if she looked real pretty in her dress, he might want to stay with them.

From the kitchen, Ginny entered the living room and, for a moment, it was too dark to see. As her eyes adjusted, she saw her mother sitting on a cot with a sheet draped around her body and her back against the wall underneath two large windows. The blinds and curtains were closed, yet the bright sunlight managed to leak through them both, highlighting the red flowers of the curtains.

So absorbed was she in the light, Ginny did not immediately see her mother's bandaged arm urging her forward, while allowing Sheila to briefly hug her neck. Both arms were heavily bandaged from the fingers to the elbow.

Aunt Katie nudged Ginny firmly in the back. "Go on honey. I know you want to give your mother a big hug."

Each foot moved in front of the other until Ginny found herself near the cot, and she looked up. Big dark red flowers spread into paler ones, over and over on the curtains. Some of the petals were so red they had become partially black. She tried to find where the dark red spots came from, but the spots all bled into other spots. Trembling started in her legs, moving slowly up to her back, into her arms, then into her hands that held tightly to the gathers in her dress. Where did the spots start? It was important to find where the flowers started, but she didn't know why. She remembered a hole torn open in her mother's arms and blood gushing out. A small scream started in her throat. Quickly Ginny felt herself float away, and she could see herself standing in front of her mother. She watched over her; there was something terrible happening. Marilyn raised her bandaged arms, urging her to come closer so she could reach her.

"Run. Run." Ginny whispered it to the little girl, to herself. The feet raced the little girl from the cot, from the bleeding red flowers, from the calls of her name, and from the house. The sun was bright outside as her feet fought to climb through the thick gravel in the driveway. Then she was the little girl again, back inside her body. Ginny stood still, uncertain if she was herself. She picked up a rock and held it tight and felt her own hand holding it.

Cousin Marti's bright red swing set in the back yard caught her eye, and she went to it, carefully tucking her dress around her legs as she sat down. The black shoes were soon covered with a film of dust as she pushed herself over and over but always swinging low.

It must have been her spirit leaving her body then coming back in. That might mean that she was dead but didn't know it yet. The black shoes scraped as she tried to stand up suddenly. She didn't feel dead. Maybe spirits leave the body for short periods of time.

The back door slammed, and Ginny looked up to see Uncle Jack. She sat back into the swing and pushed herself again. She wondered why her mother slept on Uncle Jack's cot instead of coming to Grandmother's. What happened to her arms?

Uncle Jack began walking towards her. Her hands held tight to the chains of the swing, and she put both feet on the ground and stood, still inside the swing, waiting.

"Your Grandfather is about ready to go, hon. You and Sheila are going to stay with them this week."

Ginny said nothing, but wanted to ask if Lenny could go, too. She didn't like leaving him here.

"Don't you want to tell your mother good-bye?"

"No." The chain twisted as she turned herself around and around.

"Ginny, sometimes people get very sad. They do things that they wouldn't ordinarily do." He stared at her.

"What's wrong with her arms?" She blurted it out, afraid to say the wrong thing.

"Don't you remember?" His voice was almost a whisper.

She shook her head.

"She… tried to commit suicide."

She looked at the ground. He squatted down in front of her.

"It means she tried to kill herself, Ginny. She cut the veins in her arms." His pale finger tapped his wrist, and she saw it then, bleeding from her mother's arm making red flowers on the sheets and on her. She slapped her hand over her mouth when her stomach lurched.

Uncle Jack stood up. "Are you okay? Are you getting sick?"

She knew he was staring and wished he would go away.

"Maybe we should go back in and get something for you to take if you're feeling sick."

The trembling was starting again. She allowed the swing to twist back around twice to unwind and she stood, uncertain what to do. "I'm not sick."

"Ok, if you're sure." He stood closer to her. "You're very pretty, Ginny. All of us love you."

The swing seat was touching the back of her legs, and she sat back down, wanting him to move.

"You left before I told you what the surprise is." He waited. She didn't answer.

"Don't you want to know?" His eyes were open very wide. She knew he wanted her to say yes.

She nodded while holding tightly to the chain and looking at the bluish line in her arm. Mother wanted to die. She wanted to leave her and Lenny and Sheila. Her hands held tighter while she pushed backwards as far as she could and planted her feet in the soft dirt.

Uncle Jack moved over to the side, his smile leaving. "Marti and I are coming to Grandfather's to be with you and Sheila tomorrow. We'll have a picnic at Double Bridges. That's where we went last year, or didn't you get to come to that?"

Ginny shrugged. She wanted to ask to see Lenny, but didn't want to go back inside the house.

"Anyway, it's a long road that crosses two big creeks that join near there to make a huge waterfall. They had to build two bridges close together so they call it Double Bridges."

One hand released the chain and rubbed her arm. Her head bobbed when he stopped talking, but she didn't look at him.

"You kids can go wading under the bridges--but you have to be careful so you don't get pulled in and go off the waterfall."

She wondered if all the blood came out of her mother's arms and if it hurt. Once she cut her finger, and it hurt real bad.

Grandmother came out the door. "Come on, Ginny, come say good-bye to your mother.

Relieved, she walked forward with the swing coming behind her.

"Give me a kiss goodbye, and we will see you tomorrow." Uncle Jack's hand lifted her face as he bent down and covered her mouth and her nose with his own mouth. His kiss made her face all wet and mushy, and she struggled to pull away to catch her breath. He stood up finally, his hand patting her behind, "Now you be good and mind your Grandparents."

While racing to the car, she pulled up the bottom of her dress and wiped his kiss on the hem. Hot air escaped from the car as she opened the door and sat in the back seat. She pushed the lock down and slightly rolled the widow open, impatient for Sheila to come out.

*   *   *

The lawn chair began to feel hard against Ginny's bottom, but she knew if she got up, Marti would take it. There were only two lawn chairs in the side yard, and Sheila was in the other chair.

"Okay, kids, it's time to go." Uncle Jack came out of the house followed by Grandmother. Ginny ran ahead of Sheila, who got up and walked slowly with Uncle Jack.

"Jack, are you sure you know what you're doing?" Grandmother stood shaking her head at the sight of the three of them crawling in the back of his station wagon. "Now, you girls all behave, and you mind your uncle."

"Don't you worry, Grandmother, we'll all have a good time, and you can get some rest." Uncle Jack stood at the back, his hand on top of the hatch. "Ginny, honey, why don't you come up front with me? There is really only room for two big kids back there."

"Why is she riding up front?" Marti frowned at her father.

"Because Ginny is special right now." Uncle Jack smiled at her and then glanced at Marti while picking up a marble from the carpet. "Remember what I told you?"

The front seat looked far away. Ginny watched Uncle Jack's fingers roll the marble around and around and knew he was looking at her. "Marti can sit up front, I'll sit in the back with Sheila."

"I don't want to sit up there. I want to be with Sheila." Marti turned back to flipping through a magazine.

Ginny climbed out of the back of the station wagon while Marti asked Sheila if she could fix her hair so it would flip up like hers. She got in the front seat and rolled the window down, jumping when Uncle Jack unexpectedly dropped the marble down the front of her shirt before he began to back out the driveway. She felt her face get red with embarrassment, unsure where the marble went. She gently pulled her shirt out but did not see it fall out.

They turned to go in the opposite direction of the church, back through miles of dirt roads with little farmhouses she saw many times while on the school bus. Once they got to the highway, Ginny started looking for a magic house she could dream about, one with porches and an upstairs. It would be fun to live in a house with an upstairs.

His hand on her leg started her, but Ginny did not turn away from the window.

"You seem very far away. What you thinking about?"

The yellow and blue spots on her dress hid his hand, which began to softly nip at her thigh. It didn't hurt, but she was embarrassed and pushed his hand away gently, glancing at his face to see if he was going to get upset.

He put his hand on top of her skirt and patted her leg again. "You're very pretty, I bet you have a boyfriend."

She shook her head no, remembering the boy in class that sent her a note telling her he liked her. He had brown eyes and she liked him too, but had been too embarrassed to answer his note. That was before summer break.

"Well, I'll be your boyfriend then." He smiled and continued. "I love you." He looked up in the rear view mirror, "In fact, I love you all. You're all my girlfriends." Marti and Sheila giggled from the back.

The road came up a hill then ended on a paved highway. They turned and continued past a church made of large flat rocks with a huge graveyard. Soon, they crossed over a long bridge.

"That's the first bridge. We'll stop at the second one. The creek used to be easier to get to on this side." For the first time, Ginny felt an interest in seeing the creek and waterfall.

A tiny dirt road took them from the road and looped down the hill. Uncle Jack stopped the car. Dust continued to rise from the road behind them, and Ginny fanned the dust from her face as she got out of the car quickly. Marti yelled for her father to hurry and open the back hatch so she and Sheila could get out.

Ginny did not wait. She ran down the hill to the creek under the bridge with Uncle Jack cautioning her to wait for them. The creek was so small; it hardly seemed worth a bridge being built over it. She craned her neck to see the bridge high above their heads, listening to the occasional car cross. It felt like a secret. The people in the cars didn't even know they were here.

"Okay kids, we've got a ways to go yet." Uncle Jack set a small water jug on the ground and pointed towards big rocks in the distance. "Out past those rocks, the creek gets bigger and the rocks make a flat floor. Kind of like an uneven swimming pool. That's where you all can wade in the water. But you have to mind me. Out from the pool area is a waterfall. It's dangerous to get too close." He looked sternly at each of them. "Everybody understand?"

All the heads bobbed in unison. "Good. If you all do like I say, then on the way home, I'll stop at the store and get us all a Coke."

"Daddy, can we get a candy bar too?" Marti began to chew on her fingernail.

"You certainly will not get anything if you keep biting your nails. Ginny and Sheila don't bite their nails." Uncle Jack picked up the water jug and pointed them in the direction of the rock.

They started on a trail that sometimes disappeared in the sandy ground near the edge of the creek. Sheila led them since she was the oldest. As they continued, the creek got bigger. They passed a makeshift diving board and several old tennis shoes that didn't match. Sheila tried one over her shoe and marched a few steps singing a phrase over and over, "I'm stamping out the vintage where the grapes of wrath are stored."

Marti and Ginny laughed at her and tried to take a turn with the shoe before Uncle Jack directed them to hurry so they would have time to play before having to return.

"Daddy, I'm tired. How much further?"

"It's still a little ways, Marti. I thought you liked to hike."

"I do, but I'm tired."

Uncle Jack stopped and handed the water jug to Sheila. "Okay, step up on this rock." His head nodded to the rock near him. "I'll be a horse for a while."

Marti jumped on to the rock and tightly held him around the neck while he looped an arm around each leg. "Okay, ready?"

"Faster horse." Marti slapped his head slightly.

Ginny wished Daddy were here. She didn't care about the falls anymore; she just wanted to go home. Sheila was quiet, too, and they both hurried along the trail.

The creek became wider and then opened up like a lake. The water was so clear she could easily see to walk. But it was cold, barely covering her feet when she dashed through it. They walked in further and the water came up to Ginny's knees. They stayed in this spot, pausing to listen to the sound of the falls further down before picking up smaller rocks and throwing them, trying to guess if the other side was deeper.

Uncle Jack said another creek fed the lake from the other side; it was deeper and the current was stronger. "Don't go out very far, you could get pulled into the current and carried to the falls. He yelled a few times, reminding them to come back nearer to the edge where he sat bathing his own feet while sitting on a rock.

"Goodness, your feet look like raisins." Uncle Jack had each of them to sit on a rock, letting their feet dangle to get them dry before putting their shoes back on. He passed the water jug to each of them.

The tennis shoes were hard to get back on with wet feet. Soon they were walking back to the car, but now it seemed much hotter.

"Daddy, do we get candy and a coke?" Marti stopped to talk to her father.

"I guess so. You've all been pretty good." Uncle Jack smiled and placed a hand on Marti's head.

"Will you carry me again?"

"Not this time. In fact, it's Ginny's turn to ride the horse."

"But I want to ride. You're my daddy."

"Marti, you're not being very good right now." Uncle Jack stood near a rock. "Come on, Ginny."

"I don't want to. Marti can ride." Ginny stood a little closer to Sheila.

"No. Now, it's your turn."

Ginny hesitated, then slowly walked to the rock and held her arms around Uncle Jack's neck. Her legs circled his waist and he held on to each one. "Okay. Let's go."

They walked behind Sheila and Marti. She felt herself slide down, and Uncle Jack shifted to help push her back up. "Hold a little tighter, to my neck."

She propped her arms higher and held tighter. He grasped his hands beneath her bottom. She struggled to straighten her dress and pull it back down.

"You're such a little wiggle-wart." Uncle Jack patted her bottom then pinched slightly, the fingers of one hand sliding underneath the elastic of her panties and staying there. She could feel her face flush; she was embarrassed and tried to raise herself away from him.

"Ginny, be still. It's hard to carry you when you wiggle around so much." He walked slower, but kept Marti and Sheila in view. Two fingers kept fluttering until they rubbed inside her and made her want to pee.

"Doesn't that feel good?"

Tears came to her eyes, and she began to struggle to get down, pushing away from his back. "I want to be with Sheila."

"Hold on, honey. There's no need to get upset. Sheila is right up in front of us." He stopped and allowed her to slide down. His hands shook slightly as he smoothed down her dress and her eyes searched for Sheila, suddenly out of sight.

"I love you, Ginny. Now you know that. I just want to make you feel good. Okay?" His face was close to her, and he kissed her on the check, one hand rubbing her back.

They both turned at the sound of Sheila and Marti running back towards them. "We lost you, Daddy. Come on."

"Okay. Ginny wanted down so she could walk with you guys."

Ginny ran to walk in front of Sheila and tried to stay far away from Uncle Jack.

*　*　*

The car was hot as Ginny crawled in next to Sheila, refusing to get out when Marti demanded her to move. Uncle Jack let them all sit crowded in the back and then stopped at the store to get them a candy bar and Coke before going back.

Grandmother was outside watering flowers when they pulled into the driveway. She set her bucket down while they got out of the car. "Was everyone good, Uncle Jack?"

Ginny held her breath, afraid he might say she wasn't good. She glanced at him, and he smiled at her. "Everyone was real good. I'm real proud of all three of my girlfriends."

Everyone laughed but Ginny looked closely at a cactus.

"Ginny, don't touch that. You'll get stickers, and they will hurt."

Ginny nodded. Grandmother told her that many times already.

"Marti, get your things ready and tell Grandmother and the girls good-bye. We've got to get back home." Uncle Jack and Grandmother walked around the house and inside the kitchen. Sheila and Marti went to gather Marti's things while Ginny walked around the house, staring at each flower. She glanced up when everyone walked to the car but pretended not to see Uncle Jack wave at her.

CHAPTER 5

THE SAND MOUNDS

MARILYN, 1961

Years of walking on the dirt ground inside the old building resulted in a hard packed, hilly floor. Marilyn and her father unrolled a large piece of linoleum over it, trying to keep loose dirt off the top.

They closed off the part of the building that was once a garage and made two rooms out of a large one that had been used for storage, including the winter supply of home canned fruits and vegetables, salted pork, sacks of peanuts, and all kinds of worthless junk her mother kept because she remembered the depression. Most of it looked like labels and old bottles.

"Grit is going to scrub off the design in no time." Her mother shook her head. "You'll have to be careful when you mop."

Marilyn looked up from the linoleum to her mother's blue-gray, curly hair and used her hand to fan away the scent of dime store cold cream and Juicy Fruit gum.

With the linoleum flattened out, she saw that a good four inches of the ground at the back of the room would not be covered. Her father yelled for her two brothers to start bringing in the furniture, and Marilyn walked across the shiny floor and outside to the makeshift porch.

The cigarettes were inside a cinder block. She pulled out the pack while silently counting the blocks that lined up to make the porch. There were eight of them on top, sixteen in all. As she tore a match out of the cover, her youngest brother came to her with his hand stretched out.

"You're going to have to start buying your own, Bobby." She could feel her forehead knot with irritation as she threw a cigarette toward him which he easily caught with one hand. "I don't have any money from CB yet."

"I know, I know." he nodded and hurried past her to help inside.

The step was cool next to her bare legs as she sat down. Gnats immediately swarmed around her ankles, and she waved them away with her lit cigarette.

The old cottonwood tree provided a welcome shade for her new home even though she hated the pods that grew on it. Her eyes followed the branches and limbs, and she remembered how much smaller it was when she was in her teens, watching her sisters and brothers play card games underneath it. Occasionally they would play baseball down near the barn if her father left to go into town. She rarely joined them, but was often the lookout, warning them if she saw his truck coming down the road. But fear of her father kept them from playing very long.

Breaking glass made her jump and after a long drag on her cigarette she whispered, "Whatever is broken, can't be fixed." At first, she was relieved when her mother told her they planned to make a home for her in the old garage until she could work things out with CB. Up until then, she refused to talk about CB or what to do.

Flicking her cigarette, she watched the ashes scatter across the ground. Nothing but sand. The entire front yard of the garage was like a giant sandbox just like everywhere else on "Sand Mountain." People used to come from all around the state to get sand for graves, stopping alongside the road, standing in ditches holding shovels that piled sand in the back of their trucks, sometimes in the trunks of their cars.

The back screen door of her father's house flew open with Ginny racing out and Sheila chasing close behind her. Marilyn watched them, then leaned sideways as her father hurried past her, gesturing with his bad hand with the missing fingers and yelling something about how they were going to act at his house. Crushing the lit cigarette butt in the sand near the porch, her yellow-stained fingers scooped up more sand and made a mound to cover it. It looked like a tiny grave so she peeled a red stamp from the cigarette pack to make a marker, but lost it in all the other little mounds in the sand.

"A hundred little deaths," she whispered. The words popped out, and she poked a finger in several mounds, stopping to watch her father's boots as he stepped past her on the cinderblocks. She didn't look up; continuing to push her finger in the sand until she found the one with the cigarette butt and put the marker in place.

How was she was suppose to live here? To do this? CB promised her mother he would send money every month, but she knew it wouldn't happen. It was hard enough to get money from him when she lived with him.

Last week, she stood for several hours to get an interview at the chicken plant after a neighbor, Mr. Canton, told her they would be hiring. After all that waiting the man told her they required a high school diploma.

"You need an education to pull out chicken guts?" She meant to say the words to herself and the man slightly smiled while smoothing back thinning hair with one hand.

"Actually it's a new requirement. If you had of come in last week you wouldn't need a diploma. But now all new folks need to have finished their schooling."

Relief had flooded her, and she quickly reached for her purse on the floor. It was okay to go now; she wouldn't have to stand all day in this freezing plant and dress chickens. The neighbors talked about how hard the work was, and their expressions told her they didn't think she could do it.

"You know, I really wish I could help you out." His tiny eyes stared her in the face then traveled down her arm and stopped on her wrist. "Mr. Canton says you really need the job… to keep yourself busy and all."

A faint, red ridge circled his forehead, and she followed it, guessing it was from a tight fitting hat. He did not look up even as she spoke. "I have three children to keep me busy. I need a job to take care of them." Standing up quickly, she bumped the edge of the lampshade. He stood as well, one hand quickly steadying the lamp. Glancing behind her at the door, he moved in closer, cupping his hand on one side of his mouth, his words soft. "We had to do this to keep the coloreds out."

She stared into his eyes, even with her own then leaned closer, whispering. "There ain't but a handful of colored families who even live near here."

His head moved back a little, his eyes squinting and his voice impatient, a little louder. "Not those families." One arm waved outward while his head jerked back in the opposite direction before leaning in toward her. "We think they might try to move here and take our jobs."

The flicker of fear in his widened eyes startled her. She tried to control her face, but a ripple of laughter came rumbling up from her belly. Even though she tried to whisper, her words were still loud. "You think they want to move here just to work at your plant?"

He blinked, then leaned back and sat down, his head settling into his white shirt collar. His tongue pressed out slowly between pale, pink lips, reminding her of clothes coming out between the rollers on their wringer washing machine. She wanted to tell him about the real things she had to be worried about, but she thought of Mr. Canton waiting outside, taking time to try to help her. In a quiet nice voice she tried to smooth things over, "I don't have a job, but I need one to take care of my children."

"The rest of us here do have jobs, and we are going to keep 'em." His voice was flat, businesslike as he quickly stood and walked around the desk. She turned as he came near, offering her hand to him. He stared down at her open hand with the two puckered lines wavy on her wrist. She left it there in the air, holding it out until it filled him and he looked away. Small bubbles of laughter escaped her, and she dropped her arm and walked out the door. The giggles came back to her now just remembering him.

Her father stepped up to her and stood, blocking the late day sun. "What's so funny?"

The laugh stopped, and she looked up, unable to see his face with the late day glare of the sun behind him.

"Marilyn…" he pointed to the cigarette pack and back to the boys struggling to set up a potbellied heater in the center of the room. "You be careful with those cigarettes and this here house. A cigarette could start a fire real easy." Three middle fingers of his good hand began directing his words. His loud voice grew louder, and she felt her back stiffen. "If that heater got too hot, this place could burn up in a minute." His chin jutted upward as he paused.

What did he want? For her to tell him she knew a fire would burn up the house? She continued to look at the face she couldn't see, and as he shifted his weight to the other hip, she ran her eyes down the faded overalls. Maybe he wanted her to tell him how grateful she was that he let her stay. Her stomach quivered.

"The boys here, they'll bring in the rest of your things. But now you have to take the key and lock the door. You want to keep CB out, lock the door. That's what your lock is for."

Maybe it was the nature of men to always take over, to try and tell you everything, even simple things you've known all your life.

His feet were laced up in Red Wing boots, and her eyes studied them while her face automatically nodded. Nodding meant you understood. Or did it mean you agreed? It was what she did with CB. She nodded when she knew he was lying. Even after he tried to kill her, then said he didn't. Her index finger touched the inside of her wrist.

They said she took a new razor blade from CB's box and tried to kill herself that last night. That she lay next to Ginny in the bed, and when Ginny woke up and saw the blood on the sheets, she screamed so much the neighbors called the police. They say CB was still out when the police got there. Shutting her eyes, she tried to force a picture out. No memories came to defend her; she couldn't remember anything.

It was quiet. Her father stopped talking. Maybe he asked her a question. A slight chill started from sitting in her father's shadow and she began rubbing her hands. Opening her mouth to speak, she stopped when he stepped back, his heel nudging the marker down at the mound she made earlier. Raising one leg then another, she sat on her hands to stop their shaking.

Her father walked away abruptly, and the sun glared fully in her eyes as she followed his tall, slightly stooped body as it disappeared into his house. Both hands slipped from underneath her legs and clasped her body tight. There was a sickening, cold mass gathering inside her stomach. The cigarette pack was almost empty. There was nothing near her; no rock or stick, only damned sand. She dug her thumbnail into the fleshy palm of her hand until small drops of blood rose up and slid off. Her breath came more easily, and she continued to stare at the ground and the sand-covered dots at her feet.

They managed to get a dresser, chest, and full-size bed into the tiny room for the girls, made smaller by the big built-in cupboard that held the canned jars of food that would carry them through winter. The original wide back door was left, and it opened to a tiny piece of the tin covered porch; the rest was enclosed by tin years ago to make a shop for her father.

They had two rooms for four of them to share. In the main room, they placed a full bed for Marilyn, a twin bed for when Lenny got older, a couch, a dresser, a chair, a rocker, and her old, metal kitchen table with four chairs. Everything was arranged around the coal heater in the center and the sink under the window. The walls were unpainted sheet rock. The new linoleum covered the center of the floor, and both beds covered most of the border of dirt. This was the worst home Marilyn ever lived in. As the boys stepped out to go to their homes and wives, Marilyn stood in the center and swallowed several times. The girls would have to get used to an outhouse and going to their Grandfather's house for meals and baths.

* * *

It was close to suppertime, and all the boiling pots were in the way, taking up all the stove burners. Lenny's wailing made her grit her teeth, and she poured out the milk from the bottle her mother made. A waste of milk and syrup. "You know that I don't let anyone feed Lenny but me. Nobody's gonna poison my baby."

"Marilyn, you know I wouldn't do such a thing." One arm stopped midair, a slotted spoon in her hand above a pot on the stove, the other holding a wailing Lenny near her shoulder. Her round eyes stared from behind glasses spattered with specks of food

Cutting her eyes to her mother's face and back, she poured milk in a clean bottle and set it in the pot of hot water. Mother looked slightly scared. The way people look when they are trying to look like nothing is wrong, trying to sneak looks to see if you are doing something else they think is crazy. Taking the bottle out of the water, she shook it, and then tested the temperature on her arm.

"Marilyn, it's not been in there long enough. It's not warm yet."

Marilyn pulled Lenny from her mother's arm and took the bottle, slamming the door behind her. "You're my baby, and no one's going to hurt you."

CHAPTER 6

WINGS

GINNY, 1962

Ginny slipped inside the narrow opening of the old gate and then turned, poking her fingers through rusted wire squares and pulling it forward. The old unpainted gate was covered with vines full of green grapes and very heavy, making the wire pull away from the top of the frame. Still, she managed to shut it and hook the latch. Choosing a large bunch of grapes, she tore them off the vine and bit into one and immediately spit it out when the bitter taste filled her mouth. She wondered how long it would be before the grapes tasted right.

Freshly plowed rows of dirt curved to the end of the huge garden, and Ginny's eyes followed them down the rows until she caught a glimpse of her grandmother's pink bonnet and blue flowered dress far at the end inside the small chicken pen. She dropped the rest of the grapes and quickly ran inside the row until she got to the end at the smaller gate, slightly out of breath and sweat running down her face.

It was her job to help Grandmother with the chickens. No one asked her, but she knew it ever since she saw the baby chicks in a big cardboard box with no mother and only a light bulb to keep them warm. Every day after school, she talked to them and when no one was looking, she would softly stroke their heads and backs as long as she could hold her breath so she wouldn't breathe in the chicken dust that would make her wheeze. When they got bigger they didn't need the light bulb, and Grandmother let them run around a fenced pen with a chicken coop inside that sat on long wooden legs with tiny ladders at the door so they could climb up.

Ginny's bare feet tiptoed carefully around the dark spots of chicken poop and tiny feathers and caught up to Grandmother carrying a metal bucket.

"Did you lock the gate behind you?"

Ginny nodded and began counting chickens, knowing there should be thirty.

Grandmother stopped and turned to her, pushing her bonnet up with two fingers. "Well?"

"Yes, Grandmother. I nodded yes." Ginny lost count as chickens crowded around their feet.

"Always answer when an elder talks to you." She threw out a handful of corn. One chicken turned its head sideways to look at the kernel before turning back and snatching it up.

"Why?" Ginny thought about her mother, saying things and talking to nobody she could see. Sometimes she got mad when Ginny answered her when she was talking to her pretend friends.

"Because it shows respect." Grandmother paused and held the bucket of corn out to her. Taking a double handful of corn, Ginny stood on one foot hoping none of the chicks would think her toes were corn.

"What if you don't respect them?" Much of the corn fell from her hands, but Ginny threw the rest to the chickens in the back and continued to balance by resting one foot on top of the other one.

"If they're older, you should always show respect." Grandmother set the bucket on the ground and caught one of the young chickens that flew up and landed in the corn. Taking a pair of scissors from her dirty apron, she cut off the ends of the feathers on one wing. The chicken thrashed about, fluttering her other wing and making a dreadful squawking noise.

"Grandmother, you're hurting her!"

The scissors continued. "It doesn't hurt her." She looked up as she let the chicken go. "It's like cutting your hair or your toenails."

The chicken flapped her wings, then dug her beak into her own flesh and loosened all her feathers. As Grandmother threw out another handful of corn, the chicken ran to join the others, and after a few seconds, Ginny couldn't tell her from the rest.

"Why are you cutting her feathers?"

"So she can't fly."

Ginny couldn't remember ever seeing chickens flying like birds. Pieces of feathers blew along the ground and she wanted to catch them but stood still instead. "Why do you not want them to fly?"

"Because they'll get out of the pen. Some breeds of chickens can fly up as high as that tree. Others fly up in steps. They would fly up the ladder, then to the top of the coop, then over the fence. If they get out they'll nest all over the place, and we won't be able to find their eggs."

Ginny reached for more corn. "Why do they try to get out? Don't they like it here?"

Grandmother sighed and let go of another chicken that had been clipped. Ginny knew she was getting tired of the questions.

"Chickens don't think. They don't know it's dangerous outside the fence. So we have to take care of them and teach them to nest in the coop so we can find the eggs."

"Are the wings too short for them to fly when you cut them?"

"No, child. You only cut the feathers off one wing. It makes their wings uneven."

She spread out the wings of a chicken she was holding for Ginny to inspect.

The wings looked okay, but when Ginny tried to look in the chicken's dark eye, the head stretched forward and pecked at a blue button on her blouse.

"Ouch!" Ginny fell back and began rubbing the skin under the button.

"Don't get too close." Grandmother's voice was sharp, "Remember your asthma."

"Grandmother, do the chickens know I'm not clipping their wings?"

"Oh, Ginny." The older woman stopped and pushed the bonnet up so she could look at her. "These aren't pets, honey. On a farm, we raise animals for food. Don't you like eggs and fried chicken?"

Ginny thought of the chicken leg she ate on Sunday and immediately pushed the memory away before the chickens could see it.

Grandmother stood and dropped the scissors in her apron pocket. "The chickens don't remember that their wings were clipped." Her voice lowered, "They just can't fly anymore, and they don't remember why or even that they once could."

Ginny stood still with corn in both hands. If she ever flew, she was sure she would always remember it. How could they forget?

Her Grandmother walked away, stopping to scrape the bottom of her canvas shoes in the grassy area. Ginny stared at her back, one leg twitching. She threw the last corn from both hands as hard as she could, hitting the tin roof of the coop.

"Don't throw the corn so high. They can't get to it up there." Grandmother frowned at her as she set a bucket of water next to a row of canning jars that were turned upside down in saucers to let water out a little at a time for the chickens. She turned back to Ginny.

"I was thinking that maybe I should make you a bonnet. I have a pretty piece of material with blue flowers that would be real pretty."

Ginny pulled back a strand of hair and twisted it while staring at Grandmother's bonnet with the gathers in back and bow tie in front. She didn't like Grandmother's bonnets. Grandmother couldn't see to the side because it stuck out too far, and her hair was sweaty and flat when she took it off.

Grandmother reached down and poured out the dirty water in several jars. She stood for a moment, then continued talking. "You know, once when I was a young girl, there was this newly wedded couple from Hariken's Hollow that moved next to us. They bought a mess of chickens one day, and the boy came over and asked Papa about how to keep them. Papa told them about clipping the wings and so the boy went home and he and his wife trimmed the feathers a little on both sides." Standing with her hand on the edge of the fence, Grandmother stared off into space then laughed.

There wasn't anything funny. Ginny quickly looked away, wondering if she was going to laugh a long time like mother did.

Grandmother continued, "That night most of the chickens got over the fence."

Ginny tried to imagine a pen full of chickens with short wings flying together in the sky. "Did they ever catch them?"

"A few. But the boy got real mad. The family started a rippet with ours because they thought Papa had told them wrong." Reaching for the bucket again, she shook her head and looked at Ginny. "One day you'll know all about these things when you get married and have a family and a farm of your own."

"I don't want no farm." Now she was sure. "I'm going to be a missionary and go far away to Africa." Until now, she hadn't told anyone her plans to become a missionary and go to Africa, just like the story she read at school.

"Good Lord, child!" A snorting sound came from her nose, "You don't even know how far away that is, with jungles full of wild animals."

"I don't care. I'll be a missionary and help all the little children and the animals." Ginny swallowed and thought about the wild animals she saw on television.

"Missionaries have to get the calling." Grandmother squatted down and emptied the rest of the watering jars and left them right side up.

"Maybe I'm getting the calling now." Turning her eyes toward the blue sky, Ginny watched a swirl of fuzzy clouds as she listened to the sound of water filling glass jars.

"Do you know what a calling is?"

She answered quickly, remembering the story at school, "A call from God." The words reminded her of Uncle Jack telling her about his call from God. She dug her toes in the dirt and quickly tried to see Grandmother's face. She wanted to tell her about Uncle Jack, but she found it hard to breath and her throat felt fuzzy, like she tried to swallow the cloud.

"Well, you'll never get any man to go off to Africa with you, and women don't go off to those places by themselves." Slowly Grandmother stood up and picked up the empty buckets. "You'll forget about all that when you get married and have a family to take care of."

"But if God called me, I'd have to go. Even if my husband didn't want me to, I'd have to go." In the storybook, the missionary woman told her husband she had to obey God first. As she ran toward a cluster of chickens and watched them scatter, Ginny tried to imagine what it was like to be married.

She turned back to her grandmother suddenly, "Because God is more important, right?"

Grandmother was already outside the first fence walking up a row. "God wouldn't ask you to do anything your husband didn't want you to do."

"He might." Ginny ran to the first gate and tried to imagine God asking her grandfather to let Grandmother go away. Maybe he didn't call Grandmother because he was afraid of Grandfather; everyone else was. She stood pressing her face against the cool wire in the gate. "Anyway, I might not get married."

"Of course you'll get married." Grandmother turned toward her and shook her head, "You'll not want to be an old maid with no one to take care of you." Nodding her head, she turned back around. "Pick up that other bucket and bring it back to the house with you."

Ginny thought of the goofy-looking woman on her old maid cards as she grabbed the wire handle of the bucket and ran through the group of chickens clustered together. They flapped their wings, and two of them lifted up a short distance. Imitating their squawking sound, she latched the gate behind her and ran to catch up, carefully stretching to match her feet in her grandmother's footprints. When she caught up to her, she grew impatient and ran around to be in front, walking backwards so she could see Grandmother's face.

"Grandmother, what happened to the chickens?"

"Watch where you're going. You're stepping on plants. What chickens?"

Ginny carefully stepped in the row with no plants. "The married couple's chickens that flew away. Did they find out where they went?"

"I don't remember. They were probably caught and ate up by some stray dogs or wild animals."

A shiver ran up her back as Ginny imagined the wild animals corner-ing the chicks. Grandmother lifted the latch and pushed against the big heavy gate, then stopped to stare at Ginny.

"What have I told you about picking green grapes?" Ginny didn't answer but looked at the bunch she threw down earlier.

"I don't want to have to tell you again. Come on out and latch the gate behind you."

Walking through the gate, she heard her Grandmother hum a song repeating "old rugged cross" several times. The fried chicken leg came back to her mind, and she turned back toward the chicken pen wonder-ing if it was one of them she ate. She shoved the heavy gate shut and latched it quickly, resisting the urge to pick more green grapes.

*   *   *

Her mother left out the front door with Lenny to go eat supper at Grand-mother's while Ginny waited quietly on the little back porch, slipping in the back door to her room as soon as she knew they were gone. The biscuit and fried pork was still warm in her hand, sneaked off the supper table when Grandmother turned her back to pour milk into glasses at the counter. She took a bite now while standing in her room, thinking about daddy's old, brown camera. Tiger rubbed against her leg, then raced in front of her when she stepped down into the larger room. She took one more bite of the biscuit then dropped it on the floor at the edge of the table. Tiger snatched the pork and disappeared under her mother's bed making slight growling noises. Ginny laughed and pulled up the sheet to try and see him.

A noise outside made her stomach flutter and she dropped the sheet and went to the window and peeped out to make sure it wasn't her mother coming back already. There was no one, so she quickly went to her mother's dresser and opened the bottom drawer. Carefully she took out a long box that held two cameras. Her mother always used the black one, looking down into the tiny window when she took their picture. Daddy's camera was an "old Brownie," as he called it, held up to his eye while he looking at them through the square. She carefully took the Brownie out and set it on the table, and then closed the box and put it back in the drawer.

Tiger darted out from under the bed, briefly smelled the biscuit, and then turned to rub against Ginny's leg. She pushed him away. "Hurry and eat before Buster comes back." Lenny's dog, Buster, didn't like Tiger.

Instead Tiger jumped on the dresser, then back down to follow her to her room.

The little window on the camera was dusty when she held it up to her eye and searched the room for enough light to see. She framed a doll on the shelf and clicked the button, while imagining a chicken flying up from the coop and out of the pen. Her body shook slightly. She pretended to wind the film and turned the knob just like daddy showed her once when he let her take a picture. Now, she could take pictures of the chickens when they fly so they would remember they could.

Ginny told Grandmother yesterday that Daddy said she could use his camera the last time he was here. She lowered her eyes, keeping her gaze on the pods of okra on the table, trying to act like it was the truth and no big deal.

Grandmother stopped cutting okra and Ginny knew she was looking at her. "Marilyn won't like it." Ginny shrugged her shoulders and tried not to get scared. After Grandmother dusted cornmeal on the okra, she washed her hands and left the kitchen. Later Grandmother came back with a mailer envelope and explained how much it would cost to develop film. She agreed to show Ginny how to load the film in the camera when she got her mother to buy her a roll.

The screen door slammed at Grandmother's house, and Ginny hurried to push the camera under her bed, then took it back and put it in her drawer in the dresser and covered it with papers. The front door opened, and then shut, Lenny was jabbering but her mother was quiet.

Ginny moved over to the bench in front of the dresser and grabbed a hairbrush and began to pull it through her long curly hair. Her mother appeared in the doorway, holding Lenny, who smiled while holding out one arm, his hand making a tiny fist.

"If you're going to eat supper you'd better get over there." Her eyes narrowed while she watched Ginny brush her hair. "What are you doing out here by yourself anyway?"

"Nothing. Just combing my hair."

Her mother continued to stare until Lenny began to struggle to get down then she turned from the door. Ginny set the brush down and left out the back, running across the sandy yard and jumping over the little rock wall that held in the grass in Grandmother's back yard. Just as she reached Grandmother's kitchen door, she heard her mother scream her name. She stopped walking and stood very still. Her mother opened the front door, and Ginny turned her head to see Tiger pitched out. He hit the ground then quickly ran around the house.

"What have I told you about feeding the damn cat in here?" Her mother disappeared for a moment, then threw out the biscuit and slammed the door shut.

Ginny continued to stand very still until Grandmother came out and reminded her that it was time to help Sheila do the dishes.

*　*　*

The sun was hot, and her slip clung to her legs. Beads of sweat rolled down her head and made her hair damp. Standing next to third base, Ginny watched as Lucille Swears walked up to home plate and stood ready to kick the ball. The girls in the field backed up and fanned out in anticipation of the force of Lucille's kick. There was the thud of the ball and Ginny watched Lucille run past first base, then stop at second.

Lizzy, the most popular girl in class, stood and then paused, tossing back long blond hair before slowly walking up to kick next. Lucille danced off second base with the pitcher threatening to throw the ball to someone to tag her out. As the pitcher prepared to throw the ball, girls started yelling and Lucille was suddenly standing next to Ginny, her hair wet with sweat and curly like she just had a perm. The pitcher protested to the teacher that Lucille was cheating.

Lucille smiled at Ginny before leaning down to pull up her socks that were being eaten by her shoes. "Do you have all the math problems done yet?"

Ginny nodded, noticing the dark hair covering Lucille's long thin legs below her short pleated skirt.

Lucille pushed up the sleeves of her sweater, before edging away from base, her eyes focused on the ball. "Can you help me before class?"

Ginny nodded just as Lizzy kicked the ball, and Lucille took off for home plate.

"Ginny get it!" The ball bounced between her and second base and then continued past the outfielder. Ginny watched other girls run after it while keeping her foot on third base. Moments later, Lizzy ran over third base without looking at Ginny even though they both stood at the blackboard in front of math class yesterday and often competed for the highest grade in English.

Lucille climbed up the wooden bleachers to sit alone at the top. She became her friend, but Grandmother wouldn't like it. She didn't like the Swears because they rented her mother's old house and left old cars and garbage all over the yard. Whenever Ginny left her play house things in the yard, Grandmother always yelled, "You want people to think that the Swears live here?"

The bell rang, and the girls moved toward the building. Ginny glanced at the bleachers and saw Lucille nodding at a teacher, who was talking to her, one hand on her shoulder. They might not have time for Lucille to copy her math problems before class. Maybe she would just copy them for her instead. She walked faster to the classroom.

*　　*　　*

When they got off the school bus, Ginny ran straight to Grandmother's kitchen and Sheila went to their house. A big covered pot was boiling on the stove, and Grandmother was searching through bags of frozen food in the freezer chest.

"Your pictures came in the mail today. They're on top of the TV in the living room."

Ginny hurriedly opened the envelope, slipping out her Grandmother's front door and to the side of the house where she could be alone. There were several pictures of the chickens, two of Lenny, and some that were so dark she couldn't tell what were in them. But her fingers held tightly to one of Lucille and her mother. It was from the day Mrs. Swears and Lucille walked past the house on their way home.

It rained hard all day, and the sky stayed cloudy and dark. Ginny was at home sick and saw two figures walking on the road and watched them until they were close enough for her to realize it was Mrs. Swears in a big dark raincoat and hat, huddled close to Lucille, their arms looped together. For a while she couldn't turn from the window, the longing to follow deepening as they passed the house. It occurred to her to take a picture, and she raced to get the camera and stood on her Grandmother's front porch, taking pictures of them even though they passed the house and were far down the muddy dirt road. Only one picture turned out, with the figures so shadowy they looked like they might not really be there after all, like the rain was playing tricks.

Ginny put all the pictures back in the envelope and ran across the yard and into her room through the back door, ignoring Sheila who was sitting at the dresser writing in a notebook while playing the radio loud. With her back to Sheila, she pulled open the dresser drawer with one hand and quickly slipped the envelope of pictures inside, glancing back to see if Sheila noticed what she had done.

The bed creaked as she sat down and untied her shoes, thinking about developing the roll of film she took out of the camera yesterday. It was difficult to get the film in the camera, and she hoped that the pictures would come out okay. Maybe she could also get an enlargement of Lucille and her mother. She closed her eyes to count up the lunch money she would save by next week if she secretly carried her lunch to school. She sighed. If she took something for lunch every single day, she still wouldn't have enough money by the end of the week. She sighed again.

"What's wrong with you?" Sheila was looking at her through heavily painted eyelashes.

"Nothing." Ginny shook her head several times, looking down at her feet when Sheila didn't look away. Finally, Sheila looked relieved and went back to her writing. The cool floor felt good against Ginny's feet as she stood and quietly left to go back to Grandmother's kitchen.

CHAPTER 7

LEAVING SCARS

MARILYN, 1963

Marilyn pulled the heavy pick-sack up against her leg and put a handful of hard dried cotton bolls inside, feeling the sharp stab from the pointed ends. This was the last field with enough cotton to pick. The bolls were closed tight with the last of the season's cotton and the last chance to make a little money. She pushed the sack backwards and folded it over to make a seat, sitting carefully while pulling off a glove. She inspected the cracked open skin on her thumb and two fingers, gingerly smoothing the bandages before taking out the pack of cigarettes tucked into her shirt pocket. She eagerly lit one, glancing up at the sounds of chirping birds, growing louder. She exhaled the smoke, startled at the huge mass of birds overhead. There was no part of the sky as far as she could see that was not tied together with the little black bows.

The birds reminded her of the coming cold, of Thanksgiving, then Christmas. CB wasn't sending money, and she doubted he would for the holidays either. Her gloved hand crunched dried leaves on the cotton stalks, and she watched the crumbs fall freely on her dirty tennis shoes. She wondered if Lenny was okay; she was so far away from the old truck parked in the middle of the field. There wasn't much to get into here, but she worried about him climbing up the back of the truck railings and falling. The cotton filled it to the top. She willed the worry from her mind. It was only a short time before they had to stop work anyway.

Finishing the cigarette, she found a second one and watched birds roost nearby in the cornfield and thin strip of trees separating the field from the road. Their chirping was like a jabbering crowd of people, watching while standing around and talking about her.

"Shoo!" She yelled, dropping the pack of cigarettes when she stood up. A few birds flew away. She pulled off the one glove, dropping it while she clapped, wincing at the pain in her thumb and fingers but yelling louder, "Shoo! Go on!" A flutter of wings took them to the sky where they circled overhead.

Sitting back down, she covered her head with her arms. The noise was louder and the birds settled down again, many filling the power lines that ran over the field from the woods and connecting to a massive tower in a neighbor's field in the other direction.

She studied the tower, wider at the bottom and thinner at the top, a huge metal frame that looked like a giant dress with no head or arms, just wires. The chirping birds sat on power lines crackling with commands being threaded into the headless giant. Who gave the commands to the tower?

It shook slightly, and Marilyn blinked, then stared, unbelieving. Maybe it was some kind of earthquake. It shook again, and she looked behind her, back in the rows of cotton to see if anyone else was near. There was no one. She turned back just in time to see the giant frame shift and lean forward toward her.

With trembling hands she put the gloves back on, avoiding looking at the tower but searching the wires back towards the woods. There was nothing but the birds. Maybe she should try to lift the pick-sack over her shoulder and just go to the truck. Everyone would think she was quitting early. She slipped the shoulder strap back over her head, estimating the sack to be over fifty pounds and wondering if she could lift it high enough to go over her back.

"Marilyn." She glanced at the tower, then quickly away, not moving, but breathing hard. She took the pick-sack strap off getting ready to run.

"Marilyn."

The voice was her father's. She turned to see him walking toward her.

"Marilyn, we're quitting now. I came to carry the sack back to the truck for you."

She nodded and she looked back at the metal dress, still and quiet. Relief flooded her body.

By the time they finished weighing and emptying the sacks, the sun completely disappeared. Cutting through the cornfield shortened the walk home, and she moved quickly. The kids rode back in the truck on top of the cotton bolls, now above the railing. She almost insisted they walk with her but let them stay, watching as the truck slowly cut through the field and back to the road. Just as she made her way into the yard, the truck pulled up in the driveway.

It was cold inside the house. The wind picked up and blew through cracks around the windows. She dashed outside and filled one bucket with coal and another with kindling. Once back inside, she threw a kerosene soaked rag into the potbellied stove, arranged the kindling on top, and then lit it. While standing near the stove, she carefully removed the bandages from her fingers and threw them in the fire as well. She washed her hands with soap and cold water, examining the cuts on her fingers and the unpolished nails, then took strips of an old sheet to wrap each finger.

A car pulled up the driveway, and she hurried to wrap the last finger so she could sneak a look. Before she got to the window, someone knocked. CB's smile greeted her when she pulled the door open. His mouth opened to say something, but she didn't hear the words because Lenny began screaming with excitement as he ran up the porch steps. She stepped back to let them both enter.

"Hey." He hugged his son in the opened door, then set him down and picked up a grocery bag and small suitcase and brought them inside. "It's just me."

Marilyn tried to smile, moving quickly to close the door behind him. Her father was standing on his porch watching them, watching her.

"Get away." She muttered the words under her breath and pushed the door shut and the curtains together. Turning towards her estranged husband, she searched for a sign of whether he had been drinking. He hugged her and briefly she found herself returning the embrace, grateful for his warm body and strong arms holding tightly to her.

"How are you Marilyn?" His muffled voice was in her ear. Lenny began to tell his father about Buster, and she pulled back and turned to the table, taking a deep drag on her cigarette. She steadied herself and watched the cloud of smoke she exhaled.

"Lenny, let me look at you." She turned back as CB pulled Lenny toward him, pulling on his jeans that were low on his hips. The shirt was too short on Lenny's tall, thin frame, but she hadn't noticed that until now.

"You've been a good boy haven't you?" Lenny nodded and CB grabbed him and threw him in the air, then set him on the floor. "Well then, here's the key to the car. If you look in the back seat there's something for you."

Lenny grabbed the keys and ran outside, knocking the screen door back against the house. The curtains fluttered with the breeze from the open door, and Marilyn watched them, not sure she wanted to look at CB when he stood and closed the door.

"He needs some clothes, Marilyn. That shirt is way too little."

Her fingers tapped the table as she resisted the urge to ask why he didn't send money for clothes. "I just bought him clothes. All I could afford." The words were cold, and she turned to watch his face.

He shrugged as he sat on the sofa. "Well, he must be growing real fast, they're too small already." He leaned his head toward the bedroom. "Where are the girls?"

"They are out at their grandmother's. They live out there most of the time." She waved her hand outward, and a steady stream of smoke followed.

"That must make you real lonely." He stared, and she looked away, picking up the metal rod and opening the potbellied stove. The black lumps of coal from the bucket were still damp and made a short sizzling sound when she threw them into the fire. Bright sparks flew up just as tiny flames danced across the dark pieces; crackling while taking over.

CB stood up and took her hand, fingering the bandages she had put on earlier. "I asked earlier how you were."

Pulling her hand away and stepping back, she threw out her words quickly. "It ain't easy, CB. It's like it was before I left here with you, only now it's worse because I came back, and nothing good is ever going to happen…" Her voice choked with anger. She stopped, but then needed to continue, louder so he could hear. "Picking cotton, pulling corn, the gardens, the canning, and this." Her hand waved in the air. "This shack, the…"

His hand touched her face, and she stopped. A knot of fear rose in her throat, and she took a step back. "This shack, the welfare workers coming by, the kids, and Daddy always watching my every move. All this and seventy dollars a month welfare."

He leaned forward, his eyes soft and concerned. "Maybe I'll stay awhile and help." His large fist pulled a wad of money from his pocket, and he dropped it on the table.

Protests sprang to her lips, but she heard Lenny bounding up the steps. He opened the door, a BB rifle slung on his back.

"It's real, ain't it Dad?"

CB laughed as he took out a small sack from his pocket and threw it at his son. "I don't know if it's real or not, but here's some BBs. Try it out." His laugh filled the room again, and they all turned as the door opened again and Ginny came inside.

"Ginny, you are getting tall." He turned to Marilyn, "She's looking more like you, Marilyn. Only I think she'll be taller."

Marilyn looked quickly at Ginny, and saw her slightly shake her head. "She looks like she always has CB. She'd look a lot better if she'd do something with that hair."

"Where's Sheila?" CB looked back at the door while hugging Ginny. She sat down with him on the couch, and his hand stroked her hair. Lenny sat at his feet loading BBs in his rifle. Ginny didn't answer, and CB searched his pocket. "I got something for you too." CB pulled out some change before digging in his pocket again and finding a Virgin Mary pendant, still attached to a broken chain. He held it out to her. "I'll see if I can fix the chain for you tomorrow."

Ginny stared at the image of the Virgin Mary on the pendant, while CB playfully pushed the rifle down, causing BBs to spill out of Lenny's small hand and roll all over the uneven floor.

"Dad!" Lenny crawled on the floor, his fingers picking up BBs one at a time and putting them into the rifle.

Ginny looked up from the pendant. "What does it mean, Daddy?"

CB glanced at Ginny then back to Lenny, who held the rifle up to a squinted eye, moving slowly around the room to find a target. "Don't you know about Mary, the mother of baby Jesus?"

"Yes. But in this picture she has a halo and there is a prayer to her written around the edge."

"I don't know, Ginny. Probably something to do with the Catholics." CB sought Marilyn's eyes then laughed. "Hell, they pray to everybody." He looked back at Ginny, whose somber eyes were still staring.

"If you don't like it, put it on the table and I'll give it to someone else."

Ginny stiffened. "I like it, Daddy."

Marilyn wanted to smile. CB was not used to this Ginny, always questioning everything she was told.

Ginny stood, quietly taking the pendant to her room.

"Ginny." CB and Lenny looked as she spoke. "Go eat your supper at your grandmother's and bring us back some coffee when you're done. Lenny, you go too."

"I don't want to go." Lenny frowned as he lowered the rifle and stared at her.

"Go on, both of you." CB nudged Lenny forward.

As the door closed behind them, CB opened the grocery bag and took out a bottle of whiskey. His face became sullen when he glanced at her and then cracked the cap open.

"Hell yes, Marilyn, I still drink." He stood near her while putting his lips on the bottle and turning it up. He screwed the cap back on. "I'll probably drink until the day I die, which won't be long now."

Taking the last puff of her cigarette, she moved away and sat down, crushing the butt in the full ashtray, then took out another and immediately lit it without looking back at him.

*   *   *

Listening to Lenny's even breathing allowed her to relax a little. She looked over to his bed and felt CB's impatience as he turned her head back around to him and kissed her.

"The kids are asleep, Marilyn. In fact, it's almost time for them to get up." His hand moved from her face to her throat, and she looked at the clock barely visible on the wall. He tried to draw her closer to him, but she resisted.

"I'm your husband, Marilyn." The words he spoke repeated themselves in her mind over and over like echoes until the last one, a deep voice that mimicked CB with a whine. "I'm your husband, I'm your husband, I'm… your husband."

She turned away, but he pressed his body closer against her. She closed her eyes. Once the kids came back from her mother's, she thought he would leave. Not even the whiskey could keep CB from feeling Sheila's icy stare when she came home, or her reluctance to hug him. He lost both girls, but didn't seem to care. Instead of leaving, he continued to drink and talk, finally stopping and telling her he knew she was really tired from working all day and they should lie down.

Maybe she would sleep better with him holding her. He was still her husband. A sigh escaped from her lips, and she tried to relax. He raised up quickly, lowering the sheet while pulling off his t-shirt. One arm braced on the bed near her shoulder when his body covered her. Her mind unraveled back to the last time they were together and her hand wadded up the edge of the sheet in her hand and pulled it up as she shivered. She burned the sheets from that last time while trying to think of a way to burn him.

He pulled the sheet from her hand. "I know you're cold, hold on."

Both her arms crossed her chest as CB fell against her. He began slowly to kiss her bandaged hand, then moved up her arm to her face. She tried to think back to when they first married and when she felt safe with him. Momma said it was the alcohol that made him hurt her. He said it was her. He screamed that it was her, that she made him drink.

"Marilyn, I've missed you." He whispered the words close to her ear. The voices began to repeat the words, only they sounded angry, like jealous men, jealous lovers. She tried to reassure them, sending them thoughts. CB's words are useless. They mean nothing. Now, they mimicked her, saying she was useless, she was nothing.

She put both arms around his neck, trying to get closer, wanting him tight against her, no longer here, no longer in this place. While squeezing her eyes shut, she imagined squeezing her head until voices could no longer get in to talk to her.

CB jerked back angrily and she dropped her arms from his neck as he rose to his knees. She couldn't make out his face in the darkness. There was silence in her head.

"You would probably enjoy this more if you'd have a drink with me." He reached for the whiskey bottle. Sliding up from underneath him, she sat with her back against the headboard and reached for cigarettes on the table. She lit one and stared at his fist tight around the neck of the bottle.

"Nothing's changed has it, Marilyn?" He took the cigarette from her hand and began smoking it. "Always trying to get away. Do you know what the hell it is you're trying to get away from?"

He was almost drunk. Her hand tugged at the bottle, and he let her take it, continuing to hold the cigarette while leaning further back.

"It's been a long time, Marilyn. Aren't you lonely here?" His hand passed the cigarette butt to her, then dropped down to brush across her breast. Before she could drop the cigarette in the ashtray, his hands were on the outside of her legs, pulling her back until she was flat on the bed again. The smell of whiskey repulsed her, and she turned her head. He didn't try to kiss her anymore. She didn't put her arms around him or try to hold tight; he liked it better this way. His body was warm. The room had gotten very cold. She closed her eyes following the warm touch of his hand and his body. As CB arched his back and pressed inward against her, she heard the voices. They disapproved. They watched and narrated CB's moves.

"Go to hell." Her voice was low but forceful. She imagined the shock of the faceless voices, and spasms of laughter made her belly quiver. She tried to think of something else, to stifle the laughter, but it kept coming back.

CB rolled away from her. Did he hear her? Crazy talk. That's what he would say.

A noise at the door to the girls' room made her turn her head. Was Ginny or Sheila up already? She raised her head up and listened. The back door softly opened and shut. It would be Ginny; she left to go to her grandmother's.

"It's all right, CB. It's good that she knows what it's all about."

Getting no answer from him, she leaned in closer and heard his steady breathing. Finding her gown, she pulled it over her head before getting up and checking the fire. A faint, red glow was all that was left. Shivering, she threw in several pieces of coal and watched the glow disappear and thick, black smoke circle inside the heater. She hoped it didn't put out the fire. There were several loud bongs outside, and she knew her mother was walking past with the milk buckets on her way to the barn. While lighting the cigarette, she looked at the clock. Almost five-thirty.

She quietly looked for clothes, setting the cigarette on the edge of the chest while slipping into a flannel shirt and buttoning it to the collar. The cold water felt like ice when she splashed her face and eyes, getting the cuffs of her shirt wet. She thought of nothing but the hot coffee that would be next door.

The gloves were on the back of a chair, and she grabbed them while walking to the door. She stopped, remembering her cigarette on the chest and reached for it but saw nothing but a stick of white ash burned into the wood. Her hand brushed the ashes off into the floor, and the scar was lost in the maze of groves left from earlier burns.

Glancing at Lenny, she walked quietly out the door. She would send Ginny back with some coffee for CB and tell her to get Lenny dressed. By the time they left on the truck, she would have walked back up to the field alone. CB would leave long before they broke for lunch, and there would be no money left on the table.

CHAPTER 8

THE PICTURE

GINNY, 1965

Ginny held tightly to the straps of her oversize purse and tried not to shake the camera inside while running to catch up to Lucille, who was disappearing behind a dark, green cedar tree. When she reached the opening in the line of trees separating the school parking lot from the church yard, Ginny paused, slightly out of breath. She looked briefly over her shoulder to see if any teachers were at the classroom windows watching them cross the parking lot.

Her fingers slid to the inside pocket of her purse and followed the straight thin line of the envelope holding the picture. Once she was sure it was there, she quickly removed her hand and ran past the trees and down the church walkway.

Lucille was standing still, clutching a brown paper bag at the foot of the steps to the church. Ginny continued past her and up the stairs, stopping at the one window while shaping her hand into a funnel to see inside the church.

Rows of wooden pews lined up on either side of the aisle stopping just before a short fence and wooden gate enclosed the stage. She remembered coming to a funeral here once with her mother. Sheila was in school, and Daddy was at work. Grandfather and Grandmother picked them up, and they sat on one of the pews for a long time listening to a man shouting while pacing about the stage until sweat rolled down his face. A few women cried really loudly. After a while, they all stood and then circled around the front where her mother looked down at the dead man. Ginny stretched on her tiptoes and then tried to hold on to the edge of the casket so she could see him. Mother quickly grabbed her by the arm and yanked her forward, partially dragging her when she fell down on one knee. She cried walking back to their pew, but she was careful to make no noise. No tears were ever on her mother's face that day, and she frowned when she looked at Ginny or her scraped knee.

Now there were throne chairs with red, velvet seats onstage, and she longed to go sit in one of them. On the wall above them was a big picture of Jesus, lit with a light and surrounded by a heavy red drape. The latch clicked when Ginny reached over and turned the doorknob. Hesitating, she glanced at Lucille, trying to hold her full skirt down from the wind while she slowly climbed the steps.

"Do you want to go inside?"

Lucille shook her head.

Ginny watched until she stood even with her. "There are throne chairs. Two of them. Let's go sit in them."

Lucille licked her lips. "I can't go in there; I don't believe in God."

Ginny stared at her, then quickly looked back through the window at the picture of Jesus with his long hair and white robes and wondered what he might do. Nothing happened. After a few more seconds, she turned her head from the window disappointed and watched Lucille, whose hands were tightly rolling and unrolling the top of the paper bag.

"Why don't you believe in God?"

"When your mother dies, Ginny, you'll understand."

Ginny's eyes shut as she tried to picture her mother dead and lying in a casket. Instead, she saw her sit up and stare, cigarette smoke streaming from her flared nostrils and open mouth. Then she started laughing like she wasn't going to stop. Ginny opened her eyes wide and tried to shut the image from her mind. "Maybe sometimes it's better to be dead."

Lucille flinched, her eyes tearing up just before she stormed past Ginny and ran across the church landing and down several steps on the cemetery side. Ginny followed slowly, trying to find the right words to say, to tell Lucille that she didn't mean her mother.

The wind parted Lucille's hair at the back of her head, and her back was very straight and stiff. Ginny stood behind her, looking ahead at a small grave with a picture of the baby on the front of the tombstone and a lamb lying on top. There was a bench at the foot of the grave and a small tree that made a shade. The last time they sneaked here during lunch, they sat on the bench and wondered why God would let a baby die. Now she wondered why God let her be born or why he didn't just let her die when she was a baby. She pictured herself still and quiet in a little casket, her picture on the front of the tombstone with a lamb asleep on top. She wondered if her mother would cry to see her gone.

Lucille did not look up, so Ginny sat down beside her, patting her arm, ready to try to explain. But Lucille held a finger to her lips and pointed to the trees behind the church, and Ginny could see the feet of a group of girls standing on the other side in the school parking lot. They quietly stood and ran down steps and through rows of graves and down a grassy hill.

Ginny stopped first, grabbing on to one of the bars of a spiked iron gate that closed off the front of a tiny building with cinder block walls. Behind the locked gate a smiling young woman with teased hair looked up at them from a big picture hanging on a three-legged easel. Next to the picture was a huge wreath of plastic flowers.

Ginny set her purse in the grass, and Lucille rested her forehead against the bars and stared at the girl in the picture. "She was only sixteen."

"I wonder how she died?" Ginny stretched her arm between the bars to pop a plastic flower from the wreath, its pale yellow color almost gone.

Lucille closed her eyes. "She will never change. She will forever be just like she was when she died."

Ginny tore the leaves away from the flower and let them drop to her feet. "Her body is probably dust by now. Bodies don't stay the same. Grandmother says that only the spirit remains and it goes to heaven or hell."

Lucille's head jerked back, "She's wrong! They're still in their bodies when they come back. I know! My mother comes back and talks to me sometimes."

Ginny looked down at the flower in her hand, tearing away each petal until they were all off the stem and wondered for a moment if real flowers felt anything when you tear them apart. She looked up, returning Lucille's stare until they both looked away.

Maybe Lucille's mother kept her body because she wanted it in order to come back to be with Lucille. The petals from the plastic flower jabbed her palm when she closed her hand so she closed it tighter and made a fist. With a jerk of her arm, the faded petals hit the back of the cinder block wall behind the smiling girl's picture. What it was it about Lucille that made her mother want to stay with her?

"Are you mad at me, Ginny?

She started to ask Lucille what her mother told her when she came back, but she stopped herself. Once when Ginny's mother kept laughing, she asked her what her voices were saying. Her mother turned her head, covering her mouth with her hand and laughing even harder while making quick little glances back at Ginny. It made her think the voices were whispering jokes about her.

Staring into the eyes of the smiling girl's picture, Ginny whispered, "You're dead." For a moment she wished she were the girl with the teased hair, safe behind the bars, no longer here. Suddenly, her body was weak - like she might fall and Ginny grabbed the bars, afraid.

"Let me show you my mother's scarf. I want to wear it when we take the picture." Lucille moved closer to Ginny, nudging her elbow.

Ginny reluctantly turned from the girl's eyes to see Lucille wrap a wad of fuzzy red material around her neck. She held the end up to her face and took a deep breath. "It smells like her." Lucille's voice was a strange high pitch. "She wore it a lot. Here. Touch it."

Lucille's flushed face was smiling, and Ginny let go of the bar to take the edge of the scarf. The fabric was so soft.

"Mother said it has rabbit in it. That's what makes it soft."

Ginny pulled the end of the scarf with both hands, leaning in close to Lucille and picturing her mother hugging them both. She whirled a half turn and pulled the scarf tighter around them, burying her face into the side of Lucille's hair.

"I miss her!" The screeching words frightened Ginny, and she unwound the scarf, her heart pounding. Tears ran down Lucille's face, and she sucked in her breath making choking sounds.

"I miss her too." Ginny blinked tears and patted Lucille's face with the edge of the scarf. For the first time, she smelled the faint scent of Vicks VapoRub and sweet flowers.

Lucille raised her face with tightly closed eyes, and Ginny patted her eyes again and then pulled the scarf up and smelled it, noticing the tiny white hairs sticking out from the red fabric and knew it must be the dead rabbit's hair. Her fingers quickly let go of the scarf, and she bent down to pick up her purse. "Come on, Lucille, we've got to hurry if we are going to take the picture."

Lucille followed her further down the hill, sniffling before talking in a shaky voice. "I don't know what's going to happen to me. To us."

She had been talking this way for days. The aunt and grandmother fought over who should take care of Lucille and her brothers since their mother died. Her stomach fluttered, and Ginny's fingers gripped tightly to her big purse. "What do you think will happen?"

"I'll probably go live with my grandmother." Ginny waited, and Luci-lle walked past her. "She's mean, but my aunt doesn't want all of us. Some of my brothers would have to live with grandmother anyway." She stopped at the edge of her mother's grave. "So we may as well just all go there."

The aunt was living with Lucille's family now. Ginny knew because Grandmother discussed it with Aunt Justine last weekend. They wanted the Swears to move out because now the yard and house looked worse than it did when Mrs. Swears was alive. Ginny wanted to tell them that day that Lucille was her best friend. But she couldn't. Whenever Grandmother asked her about the little Swears girl, she just shook her head like she didn't know.

Ginny linked her arm through Lucille's and pulled her forward. There was nothing she could think of to say except she wished she were going away to live with someone else, but she knew Lucille wouldn't understand.

They reached the grave and stood looking at the new headstone, just put in place. Ginny watched her friend softly touch her mother's engraved name. After this week, Lucille will be gone, and she will probably never see her again. Ginny swallowed several times before her fingers pulled her father's camera from the big purse and looped the strap around her neck. She began to think of the camera as hers; neither Mother nor Daddy seemed to remember it.

Lucille moved in closer to Ginny, staring with feverish eyes. "Be glad you still have her… your mother."

Quickly raising the camera between them, Ginny stepped back and pointed the lens at the tombstone then up to Lucille's face.

"Wait." Lucille took off her sweater and dropped it to the ground, draping the scarf around her bare arms and a faded blouse. She rolled the top of her skirt to show more of her thin legs, and then shifted her weight onto her left hip where her hand was clutching her waist. Her right elbow rested on the top of the tombstone with her fingers dangling off the edge.

"Make sure you can see my mother's name."

Ginny stared at Lucille in the square, and then nervously peered around the edge of the camera at the real one. Lucille in the square looked different, suddenly older. Her face was frozen, her eyes half-closed and a slight smile on her lips. The engraved name was just below her fingertips. The wind lifted the scarf as Ginny snapped the picture.

Lucille continued to stay in pose while Ginny wound the film carefully.

"Take the picture again." Lucille's lips moved but the slight smile stayed on her lips. "Will you take it again? I need to make sure. I don't have any pictures of her."

Ginny let go of the camera, letting it swing freely from her neck, her eyes staring at her purse at her feet. "You told me that already." She was breathless like she had been running.

"Ginny, what's wrong? Why won't you take another picture?"

She made her voice calm and tried to breathe normally. "Nothing's wrong. You already told me you don't have a picture of your mother."

Lucille dropped to the grass, pulling her skirt down and covering her bare knees. "Will you mail the negative with the picture when you send it to me?" She put her head down onto her arms propped against her knees.

"Where am I going to mail them?" Ginny gritted her teeth, wanting to leave.

"I don't know." Lucille's voice was low and muffled, her arm muscle tightening as she pulled her legs in closer, making her look even smaller.

Quickly, Ginny bent down and slid her hand into her purse and pulled out the envelope. She took out the small snapshot and allowed herself to study the two grey figures huddled together walking down the dirt road in heavy rain. For one last time, Ginny imagined walking with Lucille's mother, pressed together against the rain and so close she would be able to smell Vicks VapoRub and flowers. Her fingers held tightly to the picture—her picture. The picture she took with her camera. She trembled.

This mother was Lucille's; she had to give the picture to her. Quickly she held it out to Lucille, brushing it the edge against her hair.

"What?" Lucille's voice sounded hurt. She raised her head slightly but not enough to see.

"Take the picture."

Lucille's fingers took the white edged corner of the photograph. Ginny took the strap from around her neck and returned the camera and the empty envelope to her purse. "It's a picture of you and your mother walking home in the rain. It was raining so hard you can barely see the two of you in the corner."

"It is her... and me." Lucille looked up to Ginny. "Where did you get this?"

Ginny closed her purse and held the top together tightly with fingers from both hands. "I took it. It's mine."

"When?"

"A long time ago. Back when we first became friends. I was out sick that day and your mother walked you home from school."

"I remember. The car wasn't running, and she walked to school in the rain just to walk me home." Lucille's voice became whispery. "We're like shadows. Like she is when she comes to see me now."

Little burning flickers started in Ginny's stomach. Lucille looked up. "You had this picture all this time?"

The school bell began to ring in the distance. Ginny flinched.

Lucille's eyes narrowed. "Why didn't you ever show it to me?"

"You can't even see your faces… I didn't think about it."

Lucille looked back at the picture but not before Ginny saw the flash of anger in her eyes. One cheek quivered slightly, and Ginny felt a jab of fear. "I just liked the picture, Lucille. I didn't know you didn't have any pictures of her." Ginny's hands were shaking but she picked up the paper bag and the sweater and handed them to Lucille. "We've got to go."

Lucille took the sweater, then dropped it back on the ground; reaching out her other hand for Ginny to help her up while continuing to stare at the photograph.

Ginny pulled her up with both hands. "Let me look at it one last time."

Lucille flashed the picture before her face and then quickly took it back and tucked it inside her shirt, holding it in place with her hand like she was pledging alliance to the flag.

"Let me hold it one last time."

Lucille grabbed the sweater from the ground and began running up the hill.

"Lucille, wait!" Ginny picked up her purse and followed, still holding the paper bag and trying not to shake the camera.

Without stopping, they ran up the hill, passing the graves and the picture of the smiling girl. Lucille ran across the parking lot and then up the steps. Then she stopped. Slowly she put on her sweater while staring at Ginny.

There were no teachers looking out the classroom windows, and Ginny crossed the parking lot and ran up the stairs. Lucille pulled open the heavy side door and waited for her to go through the door first. They silently joined other kids in the hallway.

The noise from the classroom was extra loud, and Miss Lauren wasn't at her desk. Ginny handed Lucille the paper bag, searching for something to say to make things better.

"Have y'all heard about Cindy Davis?" Jackie, the girl who sat in front of Ginny, walked up to them. Ginny shook her head and turned back to Lucille. Jackie was mean, and she wanted no part of talking to her.

"She is moving away 'cause the police locked her daddy up."

"Who told you?" Lucille asked, and Ginny tried to catch her eye and slightly shook her head.

"My momma heard it from a neighbor that lives next door to them."

Shuddering, Ginny shook her head again at Lucille, memories coming back of when Jackie told everyone that Ginny moved here because her mother was crazy and they kept her locked up.

"Don't shake your head no at me, Ginny. Go ask Lizzy if you don't believe me—since Lizzy is Cindy's best friend." Jackie's voice was loud now, and other kids began to circle around them.

"It's probably a lie." Ginny blurted it out, hoping Jackie would go away and the other kids would go away.

"It is not a lie. My momma said that Mr. Davis made Cindy's older sister pregnant." Jackie tilted her head upward and stood still with one of her hands holding on to the other one as if posing for a picture. Ginny disliked the urge she had to take her picture; she pushed the thought back. Cindy's father made her sister pregnant? Grandmother said that you couldn't get pregnant unless you were married.

Lucille glanced at Ginny. "Jackie, you shouldn't say things like that."

"My mother said he had sex with his own daughter after his wife left him."

One of the girls behind Jackie put her hand over her mouth, while others began whispering to each other. Ginny became light-headed, an image of Uncle Jack pulling her panties down. Nausea began rising as another image came to her. Jackie was still talking. Ginny stepped back from the group. "Stop spreading stories, Jackie. You're so hateful!"

Everyone got quiet and watched Jackie when she stepped up closer to Ginny. "You just shut up, Ginny. I'm not lying."

Ginny turned away, certain she was going to be sick. Her fingers were tightly holding her purse straps, and she thought of quickly running to the bathroom. Jackie was just getting started.

"You're one to talk Ginny. You're the one that's hateful." Jackie paused, "Like the time you said that Lucille's family was so trashy that your grandmother wouldn't let you go to her house or even be friends with her."

For a moment, everything seemed to get smaller and far away. Ginny closed her eyes and tried to swallow and then opened her mouth to speak but nothing came out. Helpless, she continued to look at Jackie, waiting and smiling like she hadn't heard what she said. Slowly her eyes shifted down to her feet, and she studied the red mud on her shoes from the graveyard.

Miss Lauren came in, clapping her hands and telling everyone to take their seat.

Lucille's hand touched Ginny's arm as she turned and whispered, "It's okay."

Nodding, Ginny kept her eyes down and walked to her seat. She studied the scratched initials, flinching when the teacher clapped her hands again and sharply warned them to be quiet.

Jackie sat in her seat in front of Ginny but did not turn around. Ginny had forgotten that she once said such an awful thing about Lucille's family. Her body felt too hot, and her hand pressed against her mouth. Was she sick? She just wanted to go home.

When the school bell rang an hour later, Ginny ran from the room and hid in a bathroom stall for a while before getting on the school bus. She didn't sit close to the window in case Lucille was looking for her.

* * *

It was quiet and cool when Sheila and Ginny walked into the school building. It was still too early for other students to be there. Grandfather brought them to school instead of their taking the bus because Ginny had been sick for three days, a punishment from God for saying such awful things about Lucille. She deserved to wheeze and cough, so she didn't take the little bitter asthmas pills so she would suffer longer.

Sheila quickly disappeared down the hall to the opposite end of the school to her own classroom. Ginny stood and watched her go, afraid to be alone. Whenever she thought about seeing Lucille, it got harder to breathe. She slowly walked to her room.

"Hello, Ginny. Are you feeling better?" Miss Lauren was at the back of the room, standing near the large wastebasket.

Ginny nodded and went to her desk and sat down, her breathing labored. She took out the letter she had written for Lucille before putting her purse under the desk.

"Ginny, since you and Lucille were such good friends, I think she would want you to have her things." Miss Lauren walked up, setting a notebook and a pencil box in front of her. Ginny studied the box before looking up. Why was she giving away Lucille's things?

"You did know she moved away, didn't you?"

Ginny shook her head, feeling sick and relieved at the same time. She didn't have to give her the letter and apologize. But she probably would never see her again or be able to give her the picture at her mother's tombstone.

"Oh, that's too bad." She set the notebook and pencil box on the edge of Ginny's desk.

"I know you've been out sick, but I thought you girls probably talked on the telephone."

"I… we don't have a phone."

"Oh." Miss Lauren nodded. "She went to live with her grandmother."

Ginny lowered her eyes, opening Lucille's pencil box and staring at the two short pencils and four new ones. They both looked up when several boys came in, laughing and loud. Miss Lauren patted Ginny's hand. "I didn't get to say goodbye either. Her aunt called to tell us her grandmother took her and her brothers earlier than expected."

Ginny closed the pencil box and unfolded the letter she wrote to Lucille and then tore it in half. She continued to tear the halves into smaller pieces before grabbing them and taking them back to the wastebasket where she sprinkled them inside to keep someone like Jackie from putting it back together. But then she saw Lucille's name printed in large neat letters on her old spelling book. Homework papers and her math workbook were underneath. Ginny took them all, sucking in a deep breath when she saw a piece of the fuzzy, red scarf. Part of it was still in the brown paper bag.

For a moment, she was like stone remembering how the scarf had held them tight together. She pulled out the scarf and bag, glaring up at Miss Lauren, now in front of the room talking and laughing with a silly group of girls. How could she throw out Lucille's scarf? Ginny quickly stuffed the scarf back in the sack and rolled the top down tight. Back at her desk, she wondered how Lucille could have forgotten and left it. How sad she must have been when she realized she didn't have it anymore. But Ginny knew. She must have been very upset and left quickly, either to get away or to catch up with Ginny. Her body crumpled forward, and she laid her head against her arms on the desk. Don't cry, don't cry.

Then she heard Jackie's voice, loudly asking Miss Lauren if she could move to Lucille's old seat near the windows. Miss Lauren said yes, telling Jackie to move quickly; class would start soon. Hateful, old Jackie. Quickly Ginny sat up and watched her squat down beside the desk in front of her. Jackie pulled out her books, glancing at Ginny when she stood up. But her eyes quickly looked again, and for a moment, Ginny saw the fear before she turned and walked to her new desk.

Opening Lucille's pencil box, Ginny took out the four new pencils. The pencil sharpener was at the back of the room, and she took them back, turning the crank until each one had a fine point. Her fists held the pencils tight, a couple in each hand, the sharp tips down. There was now an empty desk in front of her and behind her. Slowly she walked back and sat still, continuing to hold the pencils.

The late bell rang. Two boys, Gary and Ferris, rushed through the door with Lizzy, their arms full of books. Lizzy stopped in front of the room, her eyes narrowing when she saw Jackie sitting behind her desk. Miss Lauren thanked the boys for helping Lizzy bring back Cindy's books. Lizzy turned and leaned in to talk quietly to Miss Lauren, whose forehead wrinkled for a moment, then nodded.

Spelling was first, and Miss Lauren asked the class to take out their spelling books. Ginny thought of pulling Lucille's book from the trash to use, turning to look back at the wastebasket. Instead, she slowly put all the pencils back in the box but one.

Miss Lauren began reading out the new spelling words and using each one in a sentence. Ginny looked for her own book underneath her desk.

Lizzy got her books and was now at Jackie's old desk in front of her. She leaned in toward Ginny, whispering, "I heard what that Jackie girl said about Cindy. I don't want to sit near her."

Ginny nodded, and they both looked over to Jackie, who was frowning. Lizzy sat down, and Ginny quickly began writing the sentence Miss Lauren wrote on the board. She stopped at the end of the sentence and took out another pencil from the box and held it out to Lizzy. After she took it, Ginny snapped the plastic lid shut and began writing the next sentence.

CHAPTER 9

MISS SLICK CHICK

MARILYN, 1967

Her fingers felt a small bump below her chin, and she continued to rub it while getting up from the couch to look in the magnifying mirror. She picked up her tweezers then moved the mirror closer to the light from the window and propped it against a pink towel on the sink.

Father's truck pulled up outside, close to her porch and door. Clenching her jaw, she used the tweezers to scratch at the bump while the engine raced outside. He had been in the shop for the last hour, hammering—hammering so much she thought she should be bloody by now. The smell of gasoline became strong, and she moved quickly to the door, raising the curtain to send a warning to him. The back of his blue, pressed shirt and overalls were all she could see of her father, who leaned halfway inside the hood. He pulled the water hose from the lips of the radiator and pitched it behind him, jerking his head back to look again after he saw her in the window.

"No sense you getting so close to the house, trying to make me smell like you." She yelled the words while throwing the tweezers back at the sink even though she knew he couldn't hear her through the closed door and running engine.

He continued to look while replacing the cap on the radiator. Music blared suddenly, and she turned from the door, letting the curtain flutter back in place while standing still to let her eyes adjust to the dark.

"Sheila! Turn down that music."

There was no answer, and the music stayed the same. Marilyn walked over and poked her head through the doorway of the girl's room. Sheila was sitting at the dresser, her face close to the mirror as she marked a black line on her right eyelid.

"I said to turn down the music."

Sheila dropped the pencil into her makeup bag and pulled out two remaining curlers from her hair. "I can't hear it with you yelling."

Marilyn was sure it was a drop of blood rolling down her neck as she stepped further into the room. "I'll yell whenever I want." The blood felt like a bug crawling, and she swatted at it just in case.

Sheila sighed while reaching over to turn down the radio.

"Why you putting all that on for?"

Sheila picked up a comb with short, small teeth and began to tease a thick wad of hair.

"I asked you a question." Marilyn's fingers found the bump just below her jaw line and pressed her thumb against it.

"Because we're going to the parade."

"What parade?"

"Miss… Slick… Chick." Sheila's words were slow and deliberate.

Sheila's words repeated what her mother told her at breakfast. Marilyn had forgotten. They were going in the old truck because the car still wasn't fixed. The kids would ride in the back, and the three adults would squeeze together in the cab. "Why you going to that for. You think you going to be her?"

Frowning, Sheila looked up from the mirror, her eyes lingering at her mother's hand wrapped around her own throat. She dropped the comb and smoothed the bird nest hair with both hands. The pounding of Marilyn's heart bumped against her thumb. She released the bump, holding her eyes steady on Sheila's hair.

Sheila looked again at her mother with lipstick in hand, one orange, chalky stroke already across her bottom lip. Her eyes looked at Marilyn's neck, and she leaned back, her nose wrinkled with disgust.

"You want to see it better?" Marilyn jerked the neck of her white shirt open then turned back from the room. "You ain't Miss Slick Chick… just as well take that stuff off your face."

Her legs felt stiff, and Marilyn fell back into the couch, her cigarettes bouncing off the vinyl covered cushions onto the floor. She thought about going to town, then about being stuck in the cab with her mother and father. Maybe she would just stay at home. Stretching her leg, she nudged the cigarette pack closer with her foot and then reached down to pick it up. It was almost empty, and the small lighter wasn't inside. Squinting, she searched the floor for the lighter.

"Damn it, where's the lighter?"

The music from the radio was loud again, and Marilyn's head turned to stare at the doorway. After a few seconds, she stiffly lifted her body from the couch to search the junk drawer for matches or an old lighter that still worked.

The front door swung open, banging against the small table behind it. "Momma?" Lenny's thin body was surrounded by the glare of the sun spilling into the dark room. "It's time to go."

"Go where?" She knew the answer but wanted him to explain anyway.

"To town… to the parade. You promised to buy me more BBs when we went back to town."

Her hand pushed the drawer shut as she turned to him, seeing the short dirty shirt and mustache of chocolate milk on his upper lip. "Close the door." She leaned over the mirror to look at her neck.

He slammed the door shut, and she grabbed a washcloth and ran cold water over it. Pulling the string from the dangling light bulb above her, Marilyn pointed a finger at the front of his shirt. "You'll need to change." She gripped the back of his head and blotted the cloth against his eyes and wiped off the mustache.

His body struggled and he sucked in his breath. "It's too cold."

Giving his face one more swipe, she looked into his bright eyes dancing with light reflected from the bulb swinging from above them. He squirmed to be free of her hand, his face flushed, his mouth pressed together in case the wet cloth rubbed against them again. His hair was too long. When had his blond hair turned brown? She ran her fingers through it now, looking closely at the roots. A dull ache started in her chest.

"Go find a clean shirt."

*　*　*

The girls were going to sit in the back on a wooden bench her father made just for the occasion by anchoring a plank with nailed wooden stubs that was then hammered into the holes in the front corners of the bed of the old truck.

Ginny sat perched on one side, tightly holding a big straw purse and eating an apple.

"Throw that thing away. You want people to stare at you eating?"

Ginny stopped and dropped her arm to her side.

"Marilyn, I gave the kids apples to eat. It will be late by the time we get back here to eat." Her mother stood behind her. Marilyn could smell the cold cream again.

"I don't want them eating in public with people staring at them." She did not turn around and clenched her teeth together.

"Oh, they will be finished with them by the time we get anywhere close to town."

"I don't want them eating on the back of the truck where people will see them." Her face flushed. Why was everyone ignoring what she said?

"I'll put it in my purse for later." Ginny quickly opened the boxy, straw lid and tried to shove the apple inside. The lid popped back up when she tried to close it.

"Why are you carrying that big thing for? What's in it, anyway?" Marilyn stepped up on the running board of the truck to get a closer look.

"My stuff."

"What stuff? Let me see." Marilyn did not wait, but leaned in and pushed aside Ginny's hand, knocking the apple into the bed of the truck. Ginny leaned back but held the tight to the strap.

"What is that?" Marilyn's nails tapped on brown plastic. Ginny looked behind her to her grandmother, her eyes darting back and forth.

"What is it?" Marilyn was irritated that Ginny kept looking at her grandmother instead of answering, and her fingers gripped the edge of the plastic box to pull it out.

"My camera." Ginny said it quietly while pulling the purse out of reach and looking back to her grandmother again.

"Your camera?" Ginny was always trading her good things with other kids at school for junk. "What did you trade for a camera? It probably doesn't even work, and I'm not going to pay for film. Whatever you traded for it, get it back."

"Marilyn, did you know there's blood on the front of your blouse?" Her mother's voice was close to her ear. "We can wait until you change… ..if you want."

"Mother, please move. I need to get up there." Sheila's irritated voice was behind her.

Marilyn stepped down off the running board; watching Sheila step up, then lift a leg over the side of the truck bed, holding down her straight, tight skirt. She was surprised that Sheila had on hose and small-heeled, dressy shoes.

The smell of hairspray was strong, and Marilyn waved her hand near her nose, waiting for her mother to get inside the cab. Voices whispered for her to get in ahead of her inside, and she frowned. No. No, she would not sit in the middle and be by him. Her eyes cut over to her father, silently sitting behind the steering wheel holding a hand rolled Prince Albert cigarette.

"Sheila, you need a scarf on, hon, the wind will blow out your style." Her mother's voice was loud. "What on earth do you have all over your mouth?"

"I don't want a scarf." Sheila sat her purse at her feet and slightly pressed her hands against the bubble of hair that ended in a flip.

Marilyn pushed back her shoulders, impatiently allowing air to escape through her mouth. "That's the style, Mother."

"Okay then, I guess we need to get there before the parade starts." Tiptoeing, her mother used one leg to pop herself up high enough to scoot onto the seat. As her mother swung her legs around and moved closer to her husband, Marilyn sat down next to her. She didn't need to stand on her toes. She was bigger than her mother.

*　*　*

The fifteen miles to Albertville had no stoplights. Her father drove slowly, commenting on everything he saw: the gardens, the pecan trees, and the increasing number of people growing bell peppers instead of cotton in the fields. After a few minutes, Marilyn stopped listening and tried to blow cigarette smoke against the blast of warm wind from the window. Closer to town, traffic picked up, and a long line proceeded to Main Street. As they neared the intersection, the town's one policeman motioned for the cars to turn right down a small road normally used for delivery to the back of the shops along Main Street.

"What's he making us turn for?" Her mother leaned forward. "We need to go straight and park on the other side. There ain't no good places on this side." She nudged her husband's arm. "He's just showing them people where to park. Go straight."

They continued straight, and the policeman continuously blew his whistle while motioning with both hands toward the side road to the right.

"We need to go straight." Her mother's head leaned in front of her husband to yell at the policeman as they slowly passed him and made their way to Main Street.

The whistle continued to blow, and her father looked in the rearview mirror. "I don't think I was suppose to go straight. He's still blowing the whistle. I'll have to turn around and go back." Slowing down to a crawl, her father looked from one side to the other and again up at his rearview mirror. "There are too many people in the way. I can't turn around."

Crowds of people were in the road, gathering on both sides of the street. Her father slowly maneuvered around the barricade at Main Street and stopped, tapping his horn at people before continuing and turning right.

"Honey, don't turn this way. Keep going straight!" Her mother's voice was unexpectedly loud and rushed, and she gestured with her hand in front of his face. "Go back. We can't park on Main. It's closed all the way."

"There was a barricade on the other side. I can't go back." He yelled, but his voice was nearly drowned out by the marching band that started up a song and was coming up close behind them. People moved in closer from the street edges, stretching to see the back of the truck.

Several boys darted from the crowd and ran up to the cab, slowing to walk along beside while looking over the girls in the back. "What you suppose to be? Who are you?"

One boy moved up even with the cab, catching Marilyn's eye, "What are y'all suppose to be?"

Taking a drag from her cigarette, Marilyn watched the tall, skinny kid with long hair continue to walk fast to keep up and then stop and throw up his arms as they passed. She flipped the lit cigarette out the window near him.

"They're getting too close, go down the center of the road. They think we're in the parade." Neither Marilyn nor her father answered her mother. "They've said no parking on Main Street the whole route. We'll have to go all the way to the end."

The truck moved to the center of the road, but Marilyn couldn't take her eyes off the row of store fronts, shifting, then bending forward as if they were trying to move in closer. Maybe they were looking to snatch the truck back to their side. Quickly she glanced back at her mother, who looked a little frightened too.

"Why are those people coming up so close?" Her mother's voice was a whisper and her breath blew against Marilyn's ear and she found it oddly comforting. The buildings straightened back up.

Older kids continued to come up close to the truck, their eyes wide and curious. Maybe they were looking for some type of sign on the truck door. A group of boys moved in close and stopped, moving at the last minute, but leaving only a narrow space for the truck to pass. Her father slowed down to a crawl and Marilyn moved her head further back from the window.

"Maybe they think we've got Miss Slick Chick." Marilyn quietly said the words and then laughed when she turned to look back behind her mother's head through the rear window to see the kids. Lenny lay flat in the truck bed. Both girls turned inward, burying their faces against their arms on the window. Ginny's eyes were closed and her lips were partially pressed against the glass. Her mother turned back to see and started laughing too.

"Turn around and wave girls. Turn around and wave at people." Sheila glared, and they both laughed harder.

"I'm glad the two of you think this is funny. I ought to just turn around and go home." The gruffness of her father's voice made her mother stop laughing, but Marilyn continued.

You couldn't turn around in this crowd even if you had to. You couldn't even turn around when there weren't any people there. Marilyn thought the words while glancing at the side of his face. She lay her head back and closed her eyes, suddenly tired.

Fewer people were at the end of the next block, and her father finally turned into a side alley and drove another block before stopping. "Get the kids out and watch this thing so we can go. I'm going up to the feed store."

Her father put his hat on as he got out of the truck, and her mother got out on his side. He took long strides and was quickly around the corner. "Come on. Hurry." Lenny opened the door and pulled on Marilyn's arm while she looked carefully at the buildings.

Her mother's voice was low at the back of the truck. "Goodness. That's why you need to keep a scarf with you." She moved up near Lenny and looked at her. "You coming?"

Marilyn looked at Lenny, "Go with your grandmother. Stay up in this area, and I'll come in a few minutes." Her mother took his hand, and one of Sheila's legs swung over the edge of the truck to the running board. Marilyn laughed out loud when she saw her windblown, ratted hair. Sheila quickly tried to smooth it down, and Ginny stepped down from the running board, both of them ignoring her and walking quickly up the block toward the crowd.

Marilyn got out, walking slowly while continuing to stare at the buildings until she reached Main Street and stopped near the storefront and leaned against a hand lettered specials sign to light a cigarette. The crowd was thick along the road, and young boys ran along the street in front, breathlessly proclaiming that the float with Miss Slick Chick was near. Marilyn leaned down to drop her cigarette and step carefully on the glowing tip before picking it back up and dropping it in her purse. Moving slowly through the crowd, she was surprised at how easy it was to step out in front of them and into the street.

The beat of the drums was loud as quiet was broken by the band starting a new song. Her heart began to pound with them, and she held a hand on her chest until the drums passed and the truck pulling the float slowly inched forward. It stopped near her, and Marilyn walked out into the road behind it, reaching out and touching a wad of pink ribbon and then looping her fingers through it while staring up at the pretty dark haired girl, who smiled, then waved at her. Startled, Marilyn stared at the girl's face, deciding she really wasn't all that pretty.

The float began to move forward, and Marilyn walked along, her hand still full of pink ribbon. With one hand continuously waving, the girl looked into the crowd on one side and then quickly back to Marilyn before turning to wave to the crowd on the other side. When the float moved ahead this time, Marilyn let the ribbon slip away from her hand. She walked a few more steps and then waved back to the girl; not smiling and fighting the urge to warn Miss Slick Chick that her parade was almost over.

Little girl dancers began whirling around her without music, and she quickly moved off the street and searched the crowd for Lenny and her mother or the girls. Other people began moving away too, not waiting for the group of old men on bikes who followed next. Walking back to the truck, she re-lit her cigarette and guessed Lenny would get his grandmother to buy the BBs.

The truck cab was hot as she sat inside. She was almost finished with the cigarette when she saw people begin to run down the alley. Her mother came around the corner, holding her purse over her head and clutching Lenny's hand. The girls were not with her.

Popping noises came in a wave as a shower of small white balls began falling onto the street as a crop dusting plane made a turn above them. Marilyn got out of the truck and ran back toward Main Street, dropping the cigarette butt, looking in the crowd for the girls. The ping-pong balls smacked into buildings and cars and bounced along the streets and into people who were racing around trying to grab them. People were stomping on the balls and taking out pieces of paper.

She saw Sheila grab one of the balls as it bounced up from the street. By the time Marilyn reached her, Sheila had taken out the paper.

"What is it?" Marilyn was slightly breathless watching her daughter's disappointed face.

Sheila flipped the piece of paper in front of her. "It's just a coupon for twenty percent off at Peppers and Company."

"Where's Ginny?" Marilyn followed Sheila's pointing finger while snapping, "Don't point!"

Ginny was squatting near the ground at the edge of the street, camera at her eye. Marilyn wasn't sure what she was looking at but her heart beat faster when she saw her father lean over Ginny, his finger pointing up, a scowl on his face. Ginny snapped the camera and stood, walking quickly while putting the camera in her bag. She glanced up at Marilyn, her face expressionless while she walked past, Father right behind.

He stopped in front of Marilyn, but leaned his head in near Sheila's face. "Everybody needs to get in the truck now." Sheila walked quickly ahead, and he turned to Marilyn, "We are going home now." She stared back into his eyes, wide and crazy. It was a temper tantrum; he was still angry. She wondered if it was because he made the wrong turn onto Main Street. He looked away, and she waited until he walked ahead of her before she moved. For a few seconds, she felt sorry for her mother.

*　*　*

The entire cab was full of the low, growling voice of her father on the way home. He was sure they knew about the ping-pong balls and not told him. He would never have allowed them to come if he had known about it. Her mother shouldn't have told him to pass the policeman; he was lucky he didn't get a ticket. The girls shouldn't have been alone on the street like that, with Ginny practically sitting on the street and Sheila with all that makeup. Marilyn closed out his voice, staring out the window at little houses lined up in rows.

When his voice became a shout, Marilyn realized he had worked himself up to one of his crazy fits. "It ain't right, and you know it ain't. You better watch her, Marilyn, 'cause I ain't going to have it."

Her mother opened a white paper sack and broke off a piece of coconut macaroon candy and held it near her husband's face. He ignored her, his breathing labored. After a few seconds, he let her put the candy in his mouth.

Marilyn didn't know what he was talking about, but she was sure her mother would remind her soon enough. They sat silent in the car, turning down the unpaved dirt road to the farm, clouds of dust flying alongside them, then drifting on past once they turned into the driveway.

CHAPTER 10

TATTOOED

GINNY, 1968

Lizzy winced as she took the straight pin and pushed it in and out of the inked flesh of her leg. With a steady grip on a kitchen-sized match, her fingers began rubbing the head into the design. After a few seconds she fanned her leg then started over with a new match.

Ginny watched her while trying again to think of a letter to tattoo on her own leg.

"Does it show when I'm standing?"

The edge of the puffy R showed even after Lizzy's hands smoothed down her short cheerleader skirt. Before Ginny could answer her, Lizzy was already in front of the full-length mirror, throwing her arms above her head and swirling around. The flash of contrasting gold shorts under the little, red skirt gave a glimpse of perfectly tanned legs with a large puffy R on the thigh. It was ugly.

How would she change the initial next week, when she got a new boyfriend? Lizzy stopped liking any of the boys at school, preferring the older, working boys who had money and cars. Most of them quit school and now came in big trucks to catch chickens in her daddy's chicken houses. Lizzy once explained that her daddy didn't raise chickens to lay eggs, preferring to raise pullets that were killed young. Crews of men came and quickly fanned through the chicken house, grabbing several chickens at once, holding them by their feet, swinging them upside down. Some of the boys always managed to linger at the house flirting with Lizzy long after the trucks left filled with crates of squatting chickens.

Once, Ginny asked her how she could let the boys touch her knowing what they had just done. Lizzy looked surprised. "That's their job,

Ginny." Moments later, her eyes narrowed, and her voice became cold. "My daddy's had chicken houses all my life. Why do you think you're so much better than everyone else?"

Ginny used the heel of her palm to rub inside her elbow where the skin was red and itchy. Mother said almost the same thing when she asked her to stop dropping ashes on the floor.

"Hurry, Ginny, it's almost time for practice." Lizzy's impatience made her perfect face a grimace. "Do you think maybe we should put peroxide on it to kill the germs?" Blond hair whipped forward as she flounced back in the lounge seat and examined her leg again.

"I don't know." Ginny looked at her own leg. "Maybe it would react with the match head if it got too hot."

"You mean like blow up or something?" Lizzy's face twisted into a sneer.

With a quick decision, Ginny scripted the letter G on her leg.

"So, who is G?" Lizzy looked curiously at her then nodded. "For Gary, right?"

Ginny nodded then thought about washing the G off and putting a T in its place. Tommy was whom she really liked, but he only liked Lizzy. But Lizzy would never like him because he was their age.

"I thought you didn't really like Gary."

"I don't."

"Then why are you putting his initial on your leg?"

"Because I'm beginning to like him."

"Oh." Lizzy looked uncertain, then went back to the mirror and began adding more lipstick to her red lips.

Gary was who she chose because G was her own initial, and when she stopped liking Gary, at least the tattoo could stand for her own name. Ginny decided not to explain.

"Come on, hurry up. Miss Smith will start searching the john for us soon."

Holding the pin straight, Ginny punched in and out of her skin. A slightly sick feeling stirred in her stomach, but she kept punching until she covered the entire initial. Next, she began burning the initial into her skin by pressing the match hard against the skin and rubbing. It didn't hurt, but the sick feeling stayed anyway. Sort of like the time when her aunt pierced her ears, and she could hear a slight snapping sound. The eye of the needle caused her aunt to tug at the earlobe; after it finally came through, Ginny had run to the bathroom and threw up.

"Ginny, why are you just sitting there?"

The loud impatient sound of her name made her flinch and drop the match. "Ok, I'll work on it tonight."

"You might not have time. Don't forget we're going to put peroxide on your hair. I think you will look great as a blond... shock everyone at school tomorrow."

Ginny wasn't sure she was the blond type, but Lizzy thought so. Just like she didn't think she was the cheerleader type, but Mother agreed to let her try out after Lizzy pleaded with her and then made all the boys promise to vote for her. The mirror was full-length, but Ginny's gaze carefully avoided looking at her legs that were too long and the baggy, poor boy sweater that hid the skintight undershirt she wore to flatten her breasts. Her dark hair was long, and people often said it was pretty so that's what she tried to keep focused on when she looked in mirrors.

"Do a spin, Ginny, so I can see the tattoo."

A slow turn made the skirt spin out.

"You can't even see the edge of the tattoo. Have you lost weight? Your skirt is a lot longer than mine."

"You know how my grandfather is."

"All I know, Ginny, is that you've got to let it show a little. How else will Gary know? You don't want for him to have to wait until the wedding night."

"I'm not marrying Gary." The words shot out quickly just seconds before the image flashed in her mind of her grandmother crying softly in the dark kitchen last Saturday after she heard that Sheila had gotten married.

"You might."

"No. I know I won't. He's too... dumb." Dumb wasn't what she meant, but she couldn't think of the right word. Instead, Grandmother's words came back, "That child doesn't know just how hard life is going to be now."

"Well then, I'll tell Gary. He will want to see it." Lizzy giggled, standing up.

"No, he won't." Ginny wondered why life was going to be hard for Sheila. Was it because of the boyfriend, Mike, now her husband? Maybe it was because of sex. Uncle Jack popped in her mind, and she pressed both hands down against her skirt.

"Yes he will." Lizzy moved in closer, latching onto Ginny's arm while the giggles increased. "He will ask you."

"No, he can't see it." Just shut up and let go of me. The words weren't out loud but she willed Lizzy to obey.

"You too scared to show him your thigh?"

A flash of Uncle Jack's nervous, pale hand touching her leg and then reaching up under her skirt made Ginny jerk away from Lizzy. "I don't want him to."

"You *are* afraid for him to see your thigh." Lizzy grabbed at Ginny's arm while laughing harder. "It's just your leg."

"Okay, I'll show it to him." The words weren't true. She pulled away from Lizzy's arm.

"It? Now what is it you going to show him?"

Just shut up. The words weren't out loud. She stuffed her hairbrush back inside her purse. Now that Sheila was gone, it would be harder to keep Uncle Jack away. Her fingers tightened on her purse. Whenever Sheila was with her, he didn't try to do anything.

Lizzy stood too close to her, "You know Gary will like that you tattooed his initial on your leg. Men like for their women to feel pain for them, that's why they want them to have their babies. They like to know a woman loves them enough to go through it. They don't even like babies much." Lizzy lowered her voice, "That's the closest a woman ever comes to death, just as the Bible warns. My momma and sisters have told me all about it."

"Oh, Lizzy." Ginny knew she was getting ready to describe the gory details of childbirth. "Lots of women have children. If it's so bad, why do they keep having them?"

She looked uncertain. "Probably because they can't help it; they get pregnant. Once you get married you have to give men sex whether you want to or not."

Ginny turned from the long, narrow dressing table. "Come on, Lizzy."

"Wait," Lizzy's voice was loud, and Ginny turned when she got to the door. "I started my period yesterday."

Ginny nodded.

"You're so lucky, Ginny. You don't have to worry about it yet. It's easier not having woman problems." Her hand smoothed her skirt in the back before walking across the room. "Have you asked your mother about going to a doctor to see what's wrong with you?"

Ginny shook her head, walking quickly ahead, wondering why Lizzy would think she could talk to her mother about anything. It was Sheila who gave her a little booklet about having periods and babies and told her to read it. Sheila also helped Ginny with her first bra. They got it from a box of old clothes given to them by relatives and used safety pins to make it fit. It struck her then that even though Lizzy came over to her house lots of times, she never seemed to notice her mother's crazy ways. Whenever she came over, Marilyn did act better, like she was flattered and interested whenever Lizzy talked to her.

The bell rang before they could get back to Miss Smith's class, and the hall filled quickly with students. Coach Nelson was in the hallway holding a basketball. He stopped to talk with Lizzy, and she turned back to hand her books to Ginny so she could show him the initial on her leg.

After she put both their books in her locker, Ginny walked back to the small crowd of boys surrounding Lizzy, all trying to see her tattoo. A slight fuzzy feeling was in her head, and Ginny leaned against the wall as she watched one of the bigger guys run his hand across Lizzy's backside, then laugh. The fuzzy feeling grew, and she looked away toward the other end of the hall. Blinking several times, she pretended to search her purse, ignoring Lizzy's laughter and then the commands that Ginny come and help her get away. When the commands got louder, Ginny pulled out the camera and quickly put it in front of her face. The image in the square seemed further away. After the first snap, Lizzy and all the boys gathered in a pose, and even though she knew it was too dark in the hallway, she snapped it again, thinking of the dark picture she would have to pay for anyway.

"Take another one." Lizzy raised her skirt higher. Coach Nelson returned from the office and barked orders for the hallway to clear and gave a halfhearted scolding to Lizzy before disappearing out the side door.

The fuzziness faded, but now she felt sleepy and not really there. Some of the boys quickly walked ahead with Lizzy, and she followed. Sometimes it seemed like Lizzy wanted someone dull like her as a friend so she would always be the center of things. The bell rang, and the boys raced ahead so they wouldn't be late for practice. Lizzy turned and waited for Ginny to catch up with her.

"I don't feel much like cheerleading practice. You know… because of my period."

Ginny nodded.

"I'm glad you're coming home with me tonight." Lizzy smiled into Ginny's face. "We are going to have such a good time. You are always so much fun."

Ginny smiled, feeling guilty at her earlier thoughts. They walked in sync around the corner of the building into the gym parking lot.

"Hey Lizzy." A chorus of whistles and screams showered them.

"Just keep walking, Ginny. They're all such idiots."

"Lizzy, Lizzy, you're making me dizzy."

Ignoring her own advice, Lizzy whirled around. "Will y'all just shut up?"

"You interested Lizzy?" A round of laughter and applause prompted Ginny to turn around just in time for a splat of water near their feet.

"Are those water balloons?" Ginny squinted up at the boys; some were sitting in cars and others were leaning outside. Most of them were smoking.

Lizzy looked surprised. "No, they're… you know." Ginny didn't know but was too embarrassed to ask questions. She nodded and kept her eyes away from the boys.

"Come on Lizzy, I got one for you." Davy yelled and stood up on the hood of a car.

"Keep it filled with water, Davy, that's as far as you'll ever get to using it." With that, Lizzy turned and pulled Ginny's arm to follow along with her. They heard more yells but continued to walk toward the gym. The quickening footsteps behind them made them walk faster; then Ginny heard the slap of Davy's hand smacking Lizzy's bottom.

Lizzy screamed and turned around, the top of her body tilted back, both hands in tight fists. Davy looked stunned, looking questioningly at his hand, stumbling back a little as Lizzy shoved him back and slapped him. He turned and ran back toward the other boys.

"I felt it! She must have done it last night 'cause she's got on a Kotex."

The girls looked at one another, and Lizzy burst out laughing, stopping to yell back at Davy, "How stupid can you get?" Some of the older boys started laughing, too, repeating what he said to others who didn't hear the first time. The second bell rang, and Lizzy and Ginny ran the rest of the way to the gym.

"I can't believe he thinks women have a period because they had sex." Lizzy laughed again while pulling open the door to the gym. Inside, it was so dark it took a few seconds for Ginny's eyes to adjust. Across the gym near the concession stand, Coach Nelson was unlocking the Coke machine while a couple of guys brought crates of bottled soda to fill it up.

Lizzy patted her arm, "Hold my purse for a minute. I'll be right back." Pushing her purse at Ginny, she ran across the center of the gym, stopping in front of Coach Nelson. She kept in step with him when he walked, patiently waiting when he stopped to yell out to the guys standing in three lines, some were throwing balls at the net while others dribbled over to the other line. He walked back to the Coke machine, giving directions to the guys carrying away crates before he pulled out a soda from the rack for Lizzy. He locked up the machine, throwing the massive key ring near his jacket on the bleachers just as Davy walked in the gym, his shirt partially unbuttoned and the sleeves rolled up. A large "Davy loves Lizzy" was inked on his left arm. His eyes found Lizzy, who whispered something to Coach Nelson and they both laughed. Davy blushed, and Ginny averted her eyes from his face and walked to the girl's locker room.

*   *   *

Lizzy insisted that Ginny should not rinse out the peroxide in her hair and let it stay in all night. They were both disappointed a few hours later that her hair was still dark brown. After rummaging through her mother's case of makeup samples, Lizzy found a tube of facial mask. They spread the pale, green liquid on their faces and tried not to laugh when it started to get hard like cement, making cracks whenever they did.

On their way to the kitchen, they paused to listen to Lizzy's strange older sister, whose bad singing could be heard through the closed bedroom door. Betsy dropped out of school years ago and thought of herself as a gospel singer, practicing for hours every day using a small microphone connected to the record player speaker in her room.

Lizzy stood in front of the door pretending to be singing along with Betsy, flapping out an arm and holding an imaginary microphone. For a second, Lizzy's cracked pale, green mask and jerky movements made Ginny slightly afraid and she nudged her forward. She was glad Betsy stayed in her room; she was loud and got too close to Ginny's face when she talked.

They passed her two brothers' rooms; both doors were shut. She knew from earlier visits that the bathroom was on the other side of the house, installed in a former bedroom years ago. The parents' bedroom was next to it, a large parlor with an outside door that opened into a small porch, now full of dead houseplants and two old overstuffed chairs that weren't supposed to be outside. Ginny had never seen inside it, but Lizzy spoke about it often, relaying the ongoing talks she had with her mother to let her have the room, giving her all kinds of reasons and making promises of what she would do if she could just move into the room.

The kitchen was dark, but a little light shone in from the living room. Ginny sat at the table, pushing her damp hair back from her face. Lizzy got them tall glasses of ice and poured in cups of sweet tea, dipping from a huge pot on the stove. Next, she brought saltine crackers and peanut butter to the table, prompting a smile from Ginny that she remembered peanut butter was her favorite food. The pinch near her mouth reminded her of the mask and she pressed her fingers in the spot. "Ouch."

"Here in the dark, you really make me a little scared with that mask on." Lizzy giggled, her fingers pressing against the cracked lines in her own face. Feeling relieved, Ginny laughed while digging a knife deep into the jar of peanut butter and spreading a thick layer on a cracker. She followed the bite by drinking almost half the glass of cold sweet tea.

The back door opened, and Lizzy's father came through the kitchen and to the back of the house. "Lizzy, fix me a glass of tea and bring it back. I'm going to lie down; you girls keep the noise down." His words ran together like it took too much effort to say them separately. He seemed to be the same age as her grandfather, except he was short, fat, and bald with overalls that were too short. He never cared much where the kids were and even now didn't seem to notice the masks on their faces. Lizzy's mother was short and fat, too, with very black hair that she wore in a tight bun. All the siblings looked a lot like the parents except for Lizzy and one of the married sisters.

When Lizzy got back from taking iced tea to her father, she reminded Ginny she had to call her boyfriend, Robert, who would be home from work now. "I always wait to make sure he's home 'cause I hate talking to his mother. Robert says she never likes his girlfriends." She walked into the hall way, then quickly turned back. "Hey, do you want to listen in? I could introduce the two of you."

Ginny immediately shook her head and pointed to the crackers still in front of her. "Go ahead, I'll just sit here and finish eating." She could tell from the frown that Lizzy was disappointed. Robert was older but didn't have a car and had to ask his mother if he could borrow hers. Even though he was old, he only worked part-time. Lizzy said he was going to start driving a truck cross country soon and that she planned to go with him.

The crackling amplified voice of Betsy started up again, and Ginny felt anxious, wondering if Betsy knew her father was home and if she should tell her. If it were at her house, both Grandfather and Mother would have already banged on the door and threatened something by now. She thought about how mad Betsy might get for being interrupted and decided not to say anything.

The front door opened and Lizzy's mother came in with Lizzy's youngest brother, Billy. They both glanced quickly at Ginny, still sitting in the darkness of the kitchen. Billy giggled, and her mother smiled. Billy ran to her, playfully poking one finger on Ginny's masked cheek. She laughed, pushing his hand away, glad that the mask and darkness hid her embarrassment that Billy seemed to really like her even though he was only ten years old and was probably the smallest kid in school.

Her mother, dressed in a long-sleeved black dress, flipped on the light as she walked into the kitchen carrying a paper sack and large Bible in one arm. "Hon, have you girls had that stuff on your faces ever since I left?"

Ginny nodded while moving her head to avoid Billy's hand as he tried to poke her again.

"I think it needs to be washed off now. Wearing it too long will make your skin dry." Glancing down at the peanut butter and crackers, she sat near Ginny at the table, dropping the sack and letting her Bible slide down from under her arm until it reached her hand and then set it on the table. The other arm swung slightly at her side. "Is peanut butter and crackers all you girls had for dinner?"

Billy's nose wrinkled, "Peanut butter." He turned to the stove and continue to mumble, "And crackers," while lifted lids to look inside several pots.

Ginny nodded and smiled, trying not to look at her bad arm before shoving half a cracker in her mouth. While sipping tea, she watched her mother use her good hand to lift her arm up onto the table. Lizzy said her mother had a heat stroke years ago while holding up and praying for a teenage boy outside after he collapsed in the cotton field.

"Billy, you need to get ready for school tomorrow." She watched when he tried one more time to poke her facemask, and then poked at his sister's when he passed her in the doorway.

"Robert says," Lizzy's voice was slightly irritated, "to tell you hello and that he will be plenty mad if you don't talk to him when he calls back later."

"Why don't you girls eat some vegetables? At least drink some milk." Her mother looked up to Lizzy, her eyes baggy with dark circles. Lizzy shook her head. When her mother shifted her eyes over to Ginny, she followed Lizzy's lead and shook her head too.

"Do you remember the Johnston baby at church?"

Lizzy nodded, scooping peanut butter from the jar with a finger and popping it in her mouth.

Her mother continued. "He's really sick again. The doctors say there ain't nothing more they can do."

Lizzy looked at Ginny. "He's only three and has been sick his entire life."

"We're going to lay hands on him later in the week. I want you to come and help out. We need to have a good group there. God can heal him. God can do anything."

"I will." The irritation came back into her voice. "I came when we prayed for him before." She quickly added, "As long as it's not the same night as the ball game."

Ginny wondered why they thought prayer would heal him now if it hadn't when they prayed for him before. As if hearing her thoughts, Lizzy's mother began talking about the messages that came to her in the church services this very night; she spoke the messages aloud to the congregation but didn't understand the language she was speaking until a translator stood up. He told them that he understood and that God said the child would be saved if they all believed enough.

"I need you to believe it with all your heart, Lizzy, and pray that way."

Ginny's leg began to twitch and she stood, walking toward the bathroom, ready to explain she had to go, but neither of them asked. Lizzy told her a long time ago that her mother spoke in tongues at church, and that it happened often. At first, Ginny felt sorry for Lizzy and wanted to tell her that her mother hears voices. But Lizzy sounded excited, "It's the Holy Spirit," she said, her voice going down to a whisper when she added that her mother also went to the church in Scottsboro at least once a month. Lizzy waited with wide eyes. When Ginny didn't say anything, she explained that her mother handled poisonous snakes and they didn't bite her, just like in the Bible. "It was a miracle considering her mother only had use of the one good arm."

After that, Ginny asked Grandmother about why people handle snakes, and she got upset, telling her to not to be friends with kids whose families went to those churches, especially the ones in Scottsboro, Alabama. She wanted to ask her about speaking in tongues, but before she could ask, Grandmother told her to never talk about this in front of her grandfather.

In the bathroom, there were dirty overalls and big underwear on the floor; razors, shaving cream, lotion, and tubes of pink and red lipstick on the sink. Boxes of makeup lined one wall. After a quick look in the mirror, Ginny chose an almost new green bar of soap to wash off the mask. She used her fingernails to scratch several really hard patches. There was no towel so she used her sweater to dry her face. The latch on the bathroom door wouldn't work, and now Ginny really had to pee. She paced, imagining herself pulling down her panties to pee just as Lizzy's father or brothers barged through the door. She wondered if she would be able to hear if

Lizzy's father came out of his bedroom next door, or if he would be able to hear her pee through the walls.

Finally, she pushed the overflowing hamper to block the door, pulled the crotch of her panties to one side so she wouldn't have to pull them down, and tried to pee quickly. Someone knocked on the door, and she quickly flushed the toilet before standing up so they would know she was inside. After a second knock, she quietly pulled the hamper away from the door and opened it.

"I have cookies. I'm going to the bedroom," Lizzy whispered, holding up in her face a pack of cigarettes as well as the cookies. Ginny whispered okay and then turned to the sink to wash her hands.

The bedroom door was locked when Ginny turned the handle, and she tapped quietly. The door opened, and Lizzy pulled her in, shutting the door quickly before taking a drag off the lit cigarette in her hand. She handed it to Ginny.

"Come over by the window and blow the smoke out. Luckily, neither Mom nor Dad can smell very well."

Ginny took a small drag and handed it back, noticing Lizzy's clean face was shiny like it was still wet. "When did you wash off the mask?"

"Mother took a wash cloth and insisted on taking it off while I was in the kitchen." Lizzy frowned, shaking her head slightly. "She says it will look bad tomorrow so she put some kind of gooey lotion on it."

"Has your mom gone to bed?" Ginny took a cookie from the bag and leaned against the windowsill, trying to only eat the parts with chocolate chips.

"No. She'll be up for hours, going through the orders for makeup, then the Bible study and prayer. She might go to bed earlier tonight since she went to church, but she usually doesn't."

Ginny wanted to ask Lizzy what it was like when her mother spoke in tongues, "Does your mom ever wear makeup?"

Lizzy shook her head, blowing smoke through pursed lips. "The church says women shouldn't wear it. I don't even wear it to church." She pushed the bag of cookies out of the way and sat on the edge of the bed. "Mother says makeup is important for me. I've got to make the best of what I have, but for her it doesn't matter."

That was the opposite of what Grandmother said, telling Ginny that Lizzy was too young to be so painted up. She was pleased that Ginny didn't ask to wear makeup. She especially disliked the red lipstick Lizzy wore, saying that red lips made men think of other parts of a woman's body.

Lizzy was quiet, one hand gripping her leg right above the knee, and the other holding a cigarette upright. She stood, picking up an ashtray before sitting back down. "Did you talk to Sheila this weekend?"

Ginny nodded, pulling up the cosmetic case that used to belong to her cousin and taking out a silky green gown. The gown was a Christmas gift from her aunt last year, and she wore it only when she was visiting somewhere.

"I bet she likes being married. I know I would. You do what you want instead of always having to ask."

"I guess so. She didn't really say." Ginny dropped the gown on the bed and thought of Grandmother's drawer full of new gowns and housecoats, Christmas and birthday gifts from past years that she had never worn.

"Did she tell you about it?" Lizzy eyes focused outside the window, and Ginny followed her gaze, seeing the street light in the distance and several cars parked on the grass in front of the house.

"About being married?" Ginny felt like she had missed something, that she should have asked Sheila about being married.

Lizzy nodded.

"No. She just stayed with Grandmother the whole time. Grandmother gave her a lot of food from the freezer, and Sheila was trying to write down how to cook things."

"Oh." Lizzy flopped back, lying flat. A breeze from the window rippled the open curtains, and a car drove slowly by the house outside. She turned on her side, "Robert hasn't called me. Maybe he fell asleep."

"He probably will soon. Let's turn off the lights so no one can see inside the room and we can get ready for bed." Ginny didn't want Lizzy to see the tight T-shirt she wore under her clothes.

"Okay, but we have to leave the window open while we smoke." Lizzy sat up, "Let me find a gown first." She rummaged through a drawer, stopping to pull out a blue stripped pajama top. "I don't know where the bottoms are."

A knock interrupted and Lizzy opened the door, pulling it wider for her mother before going back to the drawer, still holding up the top. "It's so big it's like a gown. It was Betsy's."

"Lizzy, I think you have something nicer to wear than that." Her mother's face was blotchy and red; her eyes puffy like she had been crying. Looking away quickly, Ginny grabbed another cookie from the bag even though she was beginning to feel slightly sick.

Lizzy continued to look through the drawer, "Ginny doesn't care what I wear to bed."

"Find something else, and stop smoking those cigarettes." Her mother set money on the top of the chest. "Men don't find smoking women attractive—at least not the right kind of men. That's your lunch money."

All of them jumped when Betsy flung open her bedroom door. "Momma? Momma?" At once, she was standing in the doorway of Lizzy's bedroom behind her mother, one hand reaching for her elbow, her voice louder, "Momma?"

"For God's sake, Betsy, say what you want. You don't have to keep repeating her name. You can see she's right here."

"You shut up." Betsy's thick finger pointed at Lizzy, while their mother slowly shook her head, her face disappointed and drooping more.

"What is it Betsy?" Her mother turned, her hand guiding Betsy away from the room.

"Momma, did you talk to Pastor after church tonight? Can I sing?"

Lizzy pushed the door closed behind them and grabbed the stripped pajama top, pushing the drawer partway shut with her hip. "You ready?" Before Ginny could answer, she flipped the light off.

Ginny threw off her blouse, the tight T-shirt, and the bra that was too small. The cool silky fabric of the gown draped loosely over her body. She loved the spaghetti straps, thinking it was a shame no one else saw how pretty it was.

"Do you know where the cigarettes are?" They both smoothed their hands over the bed, their eyes still adjusting to the pale light from the street.

"I bet we look strange." Lizzy giggled, then sparked the wheel of the lighter, holding the tiny light up over the bed, then the floor beside it. "There they are." She hesitated and continued to hold the light up, looking at Ginny.

"You look different. You look really good in that gown." Her head leaned to the side. "It makes your boobs look bigger."

Ginny turned away, facing the window while squatting down, and then resting her knees against the carpeted floor. With both hands on the windowsill, she looked up at the street light and it's reflection on the old cars parked haphazardly around it in the yard.

"Gary would love to see you in that."

Ginny didn't answer, hoping she would forget Gary. The lighter flickered again as Lizzy lit up a cigarette and slid down to sit on the floor; the familiar smoke circled them both. They were both quiet, staring out at the light because there was nothing else to see. It was the last light on the street right before the pavement gave way to a narrow dirt road just beyond the house.

"I feel like I can't stand it here anymore. She's always picking, telling me I can make things happen for God, do stuff to help the family. She says if I used what I was given…"

The cigarette butt glowed brighter. Ginny stayed quiet. Lizzy's mother was strange but always seemed kind.

"I'm not like her, praying and crying all night."

It was too dark to see Lizzy's face. Her voice was angry, but she sounded mostly sad.

"What does she want you to do?"

Lizzy shivered. "I'm too cold. Let's get in the bed."

Ginny pulled and pushed on the window and brought it down, hesitating, before leaving it open with a small crack. Lizzy pulled down the covers of the bed and got inside.

Once she got in on the other side, Ginny wanted to ask Lizzy what was wrong; to tell her about how hard it was with her own mother, even though she seemed different when Lizzy was around. Maybe Lizzy's mother was different when her friends were around too. Ginny lowered the covers, staring into the darkness at Lizzy's side of the bed, wondering if she was asleep already.

"You know how I used to babysit for my sister, Brenda?" Lizzy's voice was low and muffled, and Ginny strained to hear. "Brenda always put the kids in bed early, and they would be asleep when I came over about ten. She and her husband, Rodger, leave about ten thirty; they both work the eleven-to-seven shift."

The covers rustled and Lizzy spoke louder. "One night Rodger got sick at work and came home at two in the morning. He came in real quiet and tried to get in the bed with me."

Ginny slowly sat up pulling the sheet up high around her neck. "What did you do?"

Her face moved in close, her voice hissing out the words. "I had to fight him. You think I would let him touch me?"

Ginny pulled back, feeling Lizzy was angry at her.

"I fought him, screaming, kicking, and biting. The kids woke up and started crying, and I got away and ran across the street. I banged on the door, then Betsy's window. She let me in."

"Did he follow you?" Ginny covered her mouth with the sheet.

"No. But he came over the next day while I was at school and talked to Momma. Told her he was sorry, that he knows he did wrong. He just slipped up and that he and my sister have two little children to raise. So, she didn't tell my sister and told me not to either."

"Why did she do that?"

"He's so ugly, with his greasy hair and that big mole in the middle of his forehead." Lizzy's voice was cold, "I would kill him before I let him do anything to me."

"What did your mother say?"

"She prayed with him," Lizzy snorted. "Now he goes to church on Sunday with her when he's not at work. Later, she told me that he was truly sorry and she had forgiven him." Lizzy jumped from the bed and then turned back to lean toward Ginny with both hands on the bed. "Did you hear me? She forgave him, like he did it to her. Not that he would ever want to."

Ginny began to rock herself, while looking away from the shadowy Lizzy and trying not to think about what Grandmother would say if she told her about Uncle Jack.

"She says he can't help himself. That it's up to me to help bring him to God." Her voice was flat. "I stopped going to church most Sundays. He still stares when he's over here. He hasn't changed." She walked to the window and looked to the far left. "I can see the end of their trailer from here. I know he's off and at home tonight." Both hands covered the window in front of her eyes. "But guess what?"

Ginny didn't want to guess.

Lizzy turned suddenly and walked back to the bed. "He knows I'll fight, that I'll do anything to stop him. I told him I'd kill him if he ever tried to touch me again." She angrily jerked the covers up, "she can pray all she wants."

Ginny imagined Lizzy with a gun and shooting Rodger. He was home tonight just down the street where the dirt road starts and there are no lights. The big swing set in his yard somehow seemed wrong. She raised up to look at the window, wondering how hard it would be for him to push up the window a little higher, big enough to get in. She tried to imagine what Uncle Jack would do if she fought him, picturing the surprise on his face that would turn into horror when he saw she had a gun. Think of something else. Think of something else, she told herself over and over, blinking several times and refusing to witness his blood, even in a dream. She felt sick. Maybe she shouldn't have eaten so many cookies.

"Lizzy, I wish I was as strong."

Lizzy didn't answer. Ginny continued, "I have an uncle like that. I mean, he does things, but not as much now. But with Sheila gone…" Her voice broke off, and she felt her eyes tear up. She needed a drink of water. From the bed, her eyes could only see the street light against the dark sky. The air from the open window was cool, and she shivered. She pulled the covers up and covered her face.

CHAPTER 11

CATS

MARILYN, 1968

A fist was squeezing somewhere in her lower gut, then it let go. Shortly it grabbed her again, and she swore softly while going to the small closet in the girl's room and opening the door. Faint bad odors made her pull her head back quickly. She continued to sniff while prying apart the overstuffed hangers of clothes until she found an old shirt near the back to make into rags and quickly shut the door.

Her period felt more like she was giving birth. Lenny's tiny baby head popped into her mind. The last birth, the son CB always wanted, despite the daughters, the son he threatened to kill. Her left hand picked up the scissors from the dresser, punctured the old shirt, and then made several cuts. Both hands ripped the shirt into two big pieces. She continued ripping until the pieces got smaller and smaller, then picked up the scissors and carefully cut the buttons off the front strip and cuffs to save for a sewing project.

The odor in the closet was just as bad when she went back and she noticed for the first time the dirt on top of the small piece of linoleum in the floor. Ginny must have left the door open, and the damn cat dug up around the linoleum like it was a litter box. Shoving the door shut, she wondered if the scent would wash out of the clothes. Near the center of the room, she sniffed then again at the bed covers and the dolls on the shelf above the bed. The top drawer of the dresser used to be Sheila's, and she thought of her, living in Alabaster with her husband. She pulled the drawer open, took out two sweaters, and sniffed each one. The odor of cat urine was faint, but she could still smell it. Disgusted, she threw both sweaters on the floor and fanned the air with one hand, then went out on the back porch. Shivering in the cool air, she pulled apart several old boxes stored in the corner and took one back inside and set it on the floor.

Washing the clothes wouldn't help; they washed the clothes many times since the cat died, but the scent still lingered. Both hands pulled out clothes now. Two at a time, she pitched items into the box until the top drawer was empty.

The second drawer barely opened a crack when she pulled on it. After a few more tugs, she angrily slammed both hands against the chest until an old cracked Cinderella figurine fell to the floor, and this time lost her head. She sighed before searching the floor and picking up the head with the knot of upswept hair and put it on the dresser; it could be glued back later. But now she looked around for a tool to slide in the drawer and push down the clothes so she could pull it open. A butter knife came to mind, and she went to the wooden box of silverware stored in the big room cabinet. Next to the wooden box was an ice pick, and she took it instead.

She pushed it in the crack of the drawer and tried to press the fabric down. Instead the point punctured through clothes. The drawer only opened a little more before it stuck again. Angrily she stabbed at the crack in the drawer over and over, feeling it slide in quickly, snagging on threads and then stopping against something solid below the clothes. She wiggled it back and forth until whatever it was in the way began to give and she realized it must be papers. The sharp point pulled out a bit of black sweater; her fingers tugged but it wouldn't come through.

Leaning in closer, she saw red fabric at the other end of the drawer and carefully pulled at it with the ice pick. It was thin, and once she could hold it with her thumb and finger, it came out easily. The long scarf seemed to cling to her hand when she tried to snap it in the air. She sniffed and wrinkled her nose at the same time. Ginny must have worn it after putting VapoRub on her chest. It was musty but had no cat scent. Maybe she kept this drawer shut and the cat didn't get it in. She bunched the soft material with her fingers and squeezed it, hesitating for a moment when the softness seemed to be holding her hand. Quickly she slung her hand and let go, watching it land on the heap of clothes that now overflowed the box.

The drawer opened a little wider. The black material came out with a few more tugs. It was some kind of sweater. Without unfolding it, she threw it over to the box. Now she pulled out the thin box with no top holding magazine pages and photographs. She sorted out the magazine pages, looking at both sides of the top one. There was a mother-and-daughter Breck shampoo ad on one side, and part of an article on the other. Why did she save these? She stopped looking through them and dumped them into the box on the floor.

The photographs were mostly people she did not recognize. Some people were in stores, some from school. It didn't look like the people knew she was taking their picture. There were pictures of kids at school, Lenny, Sheila, cousins, and her grandmother, but no pictures of Marilyn. Of course, she would have noticed if she had taken pictures of her. At the end there were pictures of chickens, the cats and Lenny's dog. She began to sort them, pulling out the pictures of family, stopping to look at her mother making biscuits in the bread tray and another sitting in the shade under the cottonwood tree, her bonnet in one hand.

Marilyn stood and got her big box of family pictures and put them all inside before quickly flipping through the remaining photos; stopping to stare at a skinny, stringy-headed little girl leaning against a gravestone. The girl's skirt was too short and she was bare legged, but Marilyn recognized the scarf draped about her shoulders as if it were some kind of mink stole. While staring at the girl in picture, she lit a cigarette and sucked in the smoke, wondering what Ginny gave her for the shawl. The girl had a slight smile on her plain face but posed like she thought she was sexy with her skinny little arms and legs looking like sticks. Even her shoes were too big.

"Think you somebody." Marilyn said the words out loud and dropped her cigarette in a glass of water on the dresser before pitching the picture at the box. It landed near the fringe of the scarf. She squatted down and picked them both up, pushing the picture further into the overstuffed box while continuing to hold the scarf, reluctant to let go. Her knees began to ache. Finally, she dropped the scarf and quickly piled the rest of the pictures and old clothes on top before carrying all of it out the back door and past the outhouse to a small clearing where they burned trash. She set the box down and then lit the papers on fire before returning several times to take out the rest of the clothes and papers and throwing them in the blaze.

Marilyn didn't smell the clothes from the third drawer, but scooped them up and carried them out too. The clothes she threw on top made the flames of the fire die down. Some of the sweaters begin to melt over the pictures on the side and the smoke got heavier and darker before the whole thing belched tiny unburned pieces of pictures in the air. Marilyn wondered if one of the pieces was of the little girl and thought about catching a few of them to see. Instead, she watched little, red tongues of fire slip up through the clothes and grow bigger and hotter, then just as quickly they died down to embers that only glowed red with each breath of the wind.

She should have cleaned out this mess last year right after the cat died. Thinking about it made a quick shiver run through her body. Tiger jumped up near her, trying to rub until Marilyn pushed him away. He hunched up on the old kitchen table and stared at her. Later, he was stretched out in a lying position on the floor, continuing to stare but no longer at her. She left then, went out and got coffee at her mother's house. Later when she came back, the cat was still there, eyes looking straight ahead. Didn't move the whole time.

When Ginny got home from school, she tried to nurse him. "You didn't try and help him?" Her voice was angry, and Marilyn watched her force aspirin down his throat and try to move his stiff legs back and forth.

"That thing's dead. Exercise won't help." Marilyn repeated the words out loud now like she did then. "The cat is dead. Don't matter if the eyes are still open."

* * *

"Mother, where's my stuff?" Ginny came in the back door then quickly stepped down into the big room, her voice high pitched and alarmed.

The sun was low in the sky, but still bright with beams glaring through the window and the door. The school bus came by earlier, and Marilyn turned over and went back to sleep rather than get up and go to her mother's kitchen to get coffee and listen in at the kids while they got snacks and watched TV. She sat up in bed, hesitating before putting both feet on the floor. She stared at her daughter while reaching for a cigarette.

"Mother?" Ginny's forehead was frowning but the eyes were wide.

"I took that stinking mess out and burned it." Marilyn set the cigarette back down. "When you get home from school tomorrow you can clean out the mess in the bottom of the closet and hope we can wash out that stench from everybody's clothes in there."

"You burned my clothes, my pictures—all my stuff?" Ginny's arms flailed around as spoke, her voice shrill and louder. She stepped in, closer.

"I couldn't stand the stinking." Marilyn stood, her voice just as loud.

"What stinking?" Ginny was yelling.

"You'd better watch your mouth." Marilyn glared into Ginny's eyes. "If you had cleaned up that mess earlier, I wouldn't have had to do it."

"What mess are you talking about?" Ginny's eyes narrowed, but she lowered her voice.

"The mess that cat left when it died. I can smell it all over the house."

"The cat died almost two years ago." Ginny's face was flushed, her voice getting loud again. "This is crazy… you had no right." Ginny's finger jabbed in the air toward her, "You had no right to take my pictures—all my stuff. Nothing was stinking but…"

Marilyn thought about slapping her, but the expression in Ginny's eyes frightened her. Instead, she turned and walked to the sink and turned the faucet. Before she could dip her hands into the cold water, a quiver in her neck made her turn her head back. Ginny was still staring, her body trembling all over. Marilyn kept her eyes on Ginny, one hand patting the sink behind her for the towel.

Ginny's mouth barely moved, and her words were very low, "You really are crazy." For a moment they stared, and then Ginny turned and went back into her room. The back door slammed, and Marilyn struggled for air while holding one hand against her neck to stop the spasms. Voices repeated Ginny's words over and over, "You really are crazy, crazy.". She yelled back at Ginny and to the voices. "You're the one crazy. Go ahead. Wear clothes that stink. Go ahead if you want."

The towel was on the floor, and she stooped over to get it and then held it under the faucet until the cold water completely soaked it. She twisted it and held it to her face letting cold water drip down. The spasms continued, and she moved the towel to press against it on the back of her neck. Cold water soaked the collar of her blouse and ran down her back.

"Call me crazy… I'm not the one."

*   *   *

"Momma?" It was a whisper.

Her eyes opened, and she tried to see Lenny in his bed behind the couch.

"Momma, do you hear it?" Lenny whispered again. Before she could answer, Ginny sat up on the couch where she had been sleeping. It was Ginny who first saw an animal scratch off the linoleum and into the dirt when she opened the closet one night while getting her clothes ready for school.

A swishing sound came from the floor next to her bed, and she slowly inched herself back from the edge, straining her eyes to see in the dark.

"Momma, one's near the bottom of your bed!" Lenny's voice was muffled as he jerked covers over his head. Marilyn let out a scream; her hand grabbed the mop she propped nearby last night and scrambled to stand up in the center of her bed. For a few seconds, she hissed at the darkness while shaking the mop.

"Stop. You'll make them spray." Lenny was up on his knees in his twin bed. Ginny scrambled over the back of the couch into Lenny's bed, yelling for him to move over.

With a final shake of the mop, Marilyn hurled it toward the sound she heard earlier, and then dropped her body flat. The bed gave way from the headboard, leaving her head lower than her feet. The covers wouldn't budge as she tried to pull them up, so she stuck her head under the pillow. All she could hear was Ginny and Lenny giggling.

Moments later, the smell reached her. Not terribly strong; maybe they didn't spray and ran out. She cautiously rose up, her hand patting the nightstand until she found the lighter. Its faint light showed no signs of the polecats. Even so, the scent would be impossible to get out of the house. "I ought to just burn this damned place down."

Ginny climbed back over onto the couch but made no comment; she rarely did. She stayed with her grandmother every night until bedtime.

Marilyn thought about getting up and fixing the bed. Instead, she took the pillow and flipped around to have her head at the foot of the bed. After a few minutes of the smell, she sat up and scooted down until she reached her cigarettes and lighter on the table and dragged the ashtray stand closer. The glow from the cigarette reassured her with each drag that the polecats had not returned.

"Just burn the whole place down." There was no response from the bed or the couch. She crushed out the cigarette with each word, "Nothing… here… worth… saving."

Her hand wadded the edge of the pillow, and she shook it before flinging it across the room. Another cigarette was now tight between her fingers, and she waved the lighter flame back and forth making burn spots all along the cigarette before she lit the end. Once her lungs were full of smoke, she flicked ashes on the floor beside the bed, ignoring the ashtray, then flicked the cigarette harder, sending the glowing tip across the room.

"Burn everything, damn it."

"Mother." Ginny sounded irritated.

"What difference does it make if I dump ashes on the floor? Maybe it will smell better. Won't it smell better if it's burning up?" She looked over to catch Ginny's reaction. The blanket-draped figure was still, and she couldn't see her head or face.

Did she imagine her voice? Marilyn threw the dead cigarette toward the table and then sunk back into the bed, watching the glowing tip on the floor near the sink. She watched it until it darkened, disappointed in its death.

The scent was making her sick. How could they sleep? She got up and opened the front door, stopping to breathe in the cold air and look around the yard in the moonlight before picking up her pillow from the floor. The fire was out in the heater; it would get really cold before morning. Maybe it would air out in a few hours. She got under the covers and lay on her stomach with her face buried in the pillow.

She heard a car pass by outside. With her head at the foot of the bed, she couldn't see the door; it was open and unlocked. She flipped over on her back wondering why she worried that anyone would want to get in here.

Another car moved slowly down the road and pulled into the driveway and quickly backed out. For an instant, the headlights flashed light across the room and a face. Then the light was gone. Marilyn's body froze, her eyes continuing to stare at the spot where the face appeared, her heart beating faster. It wasn't human. It was an angel between her bed and Lenny's. Was it an angel here to take her? Or maybe it was here to take Lenny.

Nothing. No sounds. She inched both legs up toward her body, careful to not make a sound. Her fingers circled around the pole of the ashtray stand while she wondered if she would be able to lift it high enough to use as a weapon. No. Too heavy. Her hand went back to the top of the stand and found the lighter. Quietly, she sat up and put one foot on the floor, trying not to lose her balance from the incline of the bed. Biting her lip, she flicked the lighter. Nothing. No angel. Relief made her feel weak. The metal of the lighter was getting warm against her thumb and she stood up, instantly seeing the face again. It was an angel in the big picture on the wall, a big angel helping two kids cross a bridge in the storm.

She laughed as she flipped the lid back down on the lighter, her body shivering in the cold. Quickly, she got under the covers and pulled them up to her neck. Laughing again at how silly she was.

"Momma, what are you laughing at?" Lenny's bed creaked as he moved. "It's too cold in here."

"Then get up and close the door." Marilyn continued to laugh softly while hearing Ginny stand up. A few seconds later the front door slammed shut.

CHAPTER 12

THE ROOSTER'S CROW

GINNY, 1969

The new girl's name was Marsha Podder, and she had five younger sisters who all looked like her. On the third day of school, a car dropped them off in front, and Ginny's hand went to her camera when she watched the girls roll out of three doors, very similar but graduated in size. A skinny, pasty kid sitting on the front steps yelled out that the peas in a pod arrived.

By noon, older boys in the lunchroom were calling them the "pods," and Marsha was the big pod. Soon everyone was calling her Big Pod, but she didn't seem to mind. With light brown hair that came to her waist and very long legs, Marsha might have been very pretty if it weren't for the way the top of her mouth protruded out. Ginny kept expecting to see the rind of an orange slice tucked inside whenever she smiled.

Ginny smiled at Marsha several times, but Lizzy did not. After ignoring her for several more days, Lizzy walked up near her at the concession stand during recess and smiled. She bought a bag of peanuts and then casually suggested that Marsha sit with them at lunch. While walking away she whispered to Ginny, "We need to check out the Big Pod."

They had just set their trays on the table when Lizzy turned to Marsha as she sat in her chair.

"Who is that cute man that brings you to school every day?"

"Kevin. He's my boyfriend." Marsha sniffed while quickly stirring her fork through the noodle and ground beef dish on her plate.

"Really?" Lizzy leaned in.

"Yeah. I met him a couple of weeks ago while we were moving. He's a neighbor and helped us move some boxes. We've been together ever since." She tapped her fork on the edge of the tray, knocking drops of thin tomato sauce off before cutting into the edge of a canned half peach swimming in syrup.

"He seems older than high school. Does he have a job?" Lizzy's eyes lit up with interest.

Nodding, Marsha continued chewing before she paused to bite into a cookie. "He's eighteen, and such a good kisser. But he's real quiet." Looking at the boys at the next table, she frowned. "I don't like boys our age."

"I don't either." Lizzy rolled her eyes before taking her cookie off the tray and spreading a napkin over it. "I can't eat this."

Ginny started to suggest they try the hamburger and noodles; it was good. Instead, she took another bite and kept quiet.

"He brings us to school on his way to work. Since he's off today, he's coming by early and hanging out with Mr. Russ until time for us to leave."

A little wrinkle came onto Lizzy's forehead. "Mr. Russ? The janitor?"

Marsha glanced up at Lizzy, the last bite of peach on her fork. "Yeah, he knows him from somewhere.

Lizzy sat back in her chair, her eyes circling their sockets.

Quickly Ginny tried to think of something to say, hoping Marsha wouldn't notice Lizzy. "Only one more practice session and one more game."

"You going to try out for cheerleader next year in high school?" Marsha's hand brushed Lizzy's arm as she stood up. "You're so good."

"No. I'm not even sure I'll be here."

Marsha's eyes looked down her body. "Ginny, you're too… stiff and quiet to be a cheerleader."

Lizzy laughed while picking up her tray. Ginny shrugged her shoulders, knowing it was true but immediately deciding that Marsha was a Big Pod.

*　*　*

A few days later Big Pod stepped inside the heavy double doors of the school building with the two younger sisters hugged close, her coat draped over the top of them. The sisters took off once inside, and her coat slid to the floor. Her hair was now blond. She quickly glanced around the room before picking up the coat and then stopped to talk to a couple of older boys.

Lizzy watched and then quickly turned to her locker.

"Lizzy. Wait up."

Lizzy grimaced while closing her locker and turning toward her.

"Kevin is so sweet. He got paid yesterday and so he stopped at the store this morning. I brought you guys a Hershey bar." She held the two bars out to Lizzy and she took them, passing one on to Ginny.

"Did you bleach it yourself?" Lizzy's first words were loud, and she stared at Marsha's hair while biting off a corner of the chocolate.

"No! Of course not." Big Pod looked shocked, "I'm not crazy. Kevin took me to the beauty shop yesterday."

Lizzy's eyes narrowed but continued to stare at Marcia's hair until she turned abruptly and walked to homeroom. Later at recess, she quietly nudged Ginny and pointed to a side door, whispering as they went through it that she was not in the mood to listen to Big Pod's chatter.

It was muddy and wet outside, but the rain had stopped. The playground was empty except for one kid on the monkey bars. They made their way to the swings, wiping off the seats with their hands and sitting down, careful to avoid the little mud puddles at their feet.

"Big Pod keeps calling and asking to come over. She's been over twice this week."

A slight flutter started in Ginny's stomach, and she followed Lizzy's eyes and watched the little boy at the monkey bars, both hands holding tight while his body was hanging still below.

"She even wants us to go on a double date."

Lizzy tried to convince Ginny to go out with one of Robert's friends several times and she refused, too scared of her grandfather and too scared of the boy. She tried to make her voice steady, "Do you think Robert would like to double date with them?"

They both watched as the kid let go of the bar with one hand, his uneven body dangling off to the side, his hand unable to reach the next bar in front.

"Probably…"

Neither of them spoke, watching as the kid tried to go backwards and grab the back bar, dropping to the wet ground instead and lying still. After a few seconds he stood up, muddy and wet, and began walking slowly back to the building.

"He talked to her on the phone twice when she came over." Lizzy grimaced, "Momma really likes her." Raising a foot over the mud puddle, Lizzy allowed her bright white sneaker to tap just the top of the circle of water while they both watched the little waves push out over the banks. "But I don't care if he wants to or not," she shrugged then stood, careful to straddle her feet on either side of the mud.

Ginny sighed and stood up too. Lizzy and Robert were fighting a lot; he wanted sex, and she didn't. She wanted to go with him on one of his road trips in the truck, and he kept saying no. Finally, he told her that he couldn't take her because Lizzy's mother warned him that she would have him arrested if he took Lizzy anywhere. Since then, Lizzy wasn't speaking to her mother, insisting that Robert give her spending money because she didn't want to take anything from "that woman."

*   *   *

"Mother, Grandmother got you a new robe, since your old one is… wearing out." Her mother's breasts looked puckered and shriveled, as if someone had sucked out the insides and left small folds of skin held in place by the nipple. It reminded Ginny of her grandfather's mouth when he took out his false teeth. For a moment she couldn't look away, her body frozen, until the tightening of her stomach muscles made her eyes pierce her mother's for reassurance. Marilyn looked up, her dull eyes flickering over Ginny's face before returning back to the blue flame of the chunky lighter and cigarette.

The nails on Ginny's fingers were bitten into the quick except a small sliver on one thumb. She softly rubbed the edge of it with her forefinger, flinching when her mother suddenly dumped water from the metal basin into the sink. A washcloth slapped hard against the wall and fell back into the pile of dirty clothes on the floor.

"Mother, won't you at least try on the robe that Grandmother bought you?"

The silence was loud, pressing against the anger she felt rising in her throat. She kept Marilyn's figure slightly out of her direct vision, watching instead the stream of smoke that followed her as she walked from the sink to the bed. With her back to Ginny, Marilyn took her thin white and blue pinstriped housecoat from the chair and wrapped it tightly around her emaciated body. Several small slits of nude flesh showed through in the back where the material had simply given up.

It was useless to talk to her. Clenching teeth together, Ginny waited a little longer knowing that the new robe would be thrown in her room or burned after it draped the couch for a few days. Mother would continue to wear the old robe every day, refusing to get dressed when she went to Grandmother's house even if company was there. Both hands shook as she thought about yelling at her to put on some clothes, that no one wanted to see her like that. But she began chewing off the remaining thumb nail instead.

Why did she have to act so crazy? Or look so awful? Grandmother's quiet voice began speaking in her head, telling her that her mother couldn't help herself, she had bad nerves. Ginny violently shook her head no and flipped memories in her mind like a collection of photographs mounted as evidence that it wasn't nerves. She was mean, too. And the worst thing was that she didn't feel like Marilyn loved her and she couldn't remember a time when she ever did.

The old bed creaked as she flounced down, lying back against the pillows, her eyes tearing up and watching the door, wishing for the millionth time that her room had a door. She hated this horrible, old garage house. She hated living with Marilyn, especially now that she stopped eating, coming to every meal and only drinking cup after cup of black coffee while smoking and flipping ashes on the floor. Sometimes she lit up more than one cigarette, set them on the edge of Grandmother's dining room table, and let them burn up on their own. They always watched and tried to catch them before they burned the table. Grandmother warned Ginny to remind Marilyn to put out any cigarettes she left burning while at their house.

"You kids could burn up with the house one night." Her look was stern, but they both knew it wouldn't do any good to say anything. After that, Ginny tried to wait patiently every night until her mother went to sleep, pretending to get up for a glass of water while checking for cigarette butts still glowing in the dark on the furniture or on the floor.

Her fingers twisted around a small, fringed pillow that Sheila made last year in Home Economics class out of yarn and washcloths. While gripping the soft center of the pillow, she flopped on her stomach and stared at the vacant doorway. Why did she have to have *her* as a mother?

Ginny sat up, popping the pillow against the edge of the shelves on the wall behind the bed, then across the dusty face of her baby-sized doll sitting on the top shelf that always smiled through her own watery blue eyes. She hated her. She hated her own mother and wished she were dead. The next blow from the pillow toppled the doll from the shelf and knocked over a sack of Popsicle sticks saved from when she was younger, now sliding from a paper bag into the darkness between the bed and wall. She stopped and listened for her mother's footsteps, sure her thoughts were as noisy as baby doll's fall. There was only silence.

Dropping the pillow, she picked up baby doll and blew dust from her head. Guilty, Ginny held her tight in her arms while looking into the smiling plastic face, trying to remember the last name she had given her. Baby doll always smiles, even though Ginny had left her on the shelf for years.

She was still smiling when Ginny gently put her back on the shelf, somehow still feeling guilty that she didn't hold her longer. "She's only a doll," she whispered to herself and looked briefly between the bed and wall before standing up and leaving the Popsicle sticks in the dark.

As she walked across the yard to Grandmother's porch, she could smell frying sauerkraut and pork. The kitchen was hot when she opened the door. Dough was pressed out on a floured cloth and her grandmother's wrinkled hands were covered in flour.

"You're just in time. Do you want to set the table for me?"

"No." Ginny smiled when Grandmother looked up sharply from the dough, and then moved to take out a stack of plates from the cabinet.

"Did Marilyn try on the robe?"

Ginny was tempted to lie, to say she at least tried it on. "Well, she hadn't when I left. She was just getting up."

"She been in bed all day?"

"Just about."

Grandmother pursed her lips then went to the oven and set the pan of biscuits inside. Steam escaped from a pot of black-eyed peas when she lifted the lid. She poured them into a large earthen bowl that once belonged to Ginny's great-grandmother.

"Hanna plans to come this weekend and try to convince your mother to go stay with her in Florida for a while."

Relief washed over Ginny as she took forks from the drawer. Maybe Mother would go and stay with her sister, and Hanna would find a doctor that would make her well. With fingers tightly wound around forks and spoons, Ginny stood next to the table and tried to imagine Marilyn well, but no picture came to mind.

"You know your Aunt Hanna is always trying to help out." Years earlier, her mother and Lenny went to stay with Hanna. They showed back up two weeks later, returning on a bus after Marilyn insisted on returning early. There were packets and bottles of vitamins and herbs that Hanna had brought Marilyn, urging her to take them because she read they helped depression. The unopened packets were all stacked in the cupboard with the missing glass doors in their house, covered in dust.

Ginny quietly set the table. Hanna would not be able to get her mother to leave or to get well.

Grandmother set more bowls on the table, stopping to stand in the living room door. "Lenny, go tell your mother supper is ready."

He got up from the couch and continued to watch TV as he slowly walked to the kitchen. He took a hot biscuit from the platter, blowing it with short bursts of air until he got to the screen door and stopped to yell, "Supper's ready" before blowing on it again.

"I could have yelled. I told you to go tell her." Grandmother swatted a towel at him before turning back to the stove. Everyone got quiet when Grandfather came in from the shop and stood at the kitchen sink lathering up grease spattered hands with Lava soap.

They were all seated and had filled their plates with food by the time Marilyn came to dinner wearing her old robe, a cigarette already lit in her hand. The coffee was still perking. She turned her chair sideways away from the table and sat down.

Grandmother got up and went to the living room and back, setting an ashtray beside Marilyn's dinner plate, and then taking out mugs for both of them and setting them near the coffee pot. Marilyn's eyes didn't leave the ashtray while she flicked ashes in the floor. Once the pot stopped perking, she took a different mug from the cabinet, filled it with coffee, and left. They heard her laugh as she walked across the yard to her house.

* * *

The following Monday at the lockers, Lizzy grabbed Ginny's arm, pulling her close so she could whisper in her ear. "There's something bad wrong with Kevin!"

The immediate relief Ginny felt when Lizzy wanted to talk to her instead of Big Pod evaporated. "What's wrong with him?"

The whisper became louder and more breathy. "He can't talk, and he uses a little notebook to write down things and…." she stopped and leaned back to look Ginny in the eye before continuing. "When he laughs, he doesn't sound human." Lizzy shuddered.

Ginny repeated herself, "What's wrong with him?"

Lizzy shrugged, pulling a book from the locker and slamming it shut. "It's creepy the way he sounds. I don't know why Big Pod would date him."

Later that afternoon, Kevin was sitting with Big Pod in the bleachers. Big Pod waved and then motioned for them, while Lizzy turned her head back toward Ginny and made strange grunting sounds. "That's what he sounds like," she smirked, then continued, "Ask him a question like you don't know he can't talk."

"Are y'all going to play softball? I'm not." Everyone's eyes were on Big Pod's long legs as she slid one over the other, revealing a flash of pink before her knee rested against Kevin's. Ginny felt her face flush, and she quickly focused her eyes on a group of girls sitting on the top bleacher.

"Miss Winnie will probably come hunting us soon." Lizzy laughed while rolling her eyes, then stepped back. Her fingers began jabbing Ginny in the back, reminding her to ask Kevin a question.

Ginny shifted away from Lizzy and glanced at her before looking at Kevin, whose dark brown eyes were staring right at her. Feeling her face flush again, she turned quickly and began walking away, "We've got to go, we're already late." Once at the door she turned, expecting Lizzy to be close behind; instead, she had sat down next to Big Pod in the bleachers. "You're such a scaredy-cat," she told herself as she walked to the ball field alone.

Big Pod and Lizzy came to school the next morning wearing matching white go-go boots. The ring Robert had given Lizzy was missing from her finger and by lunch time everyone had heard. Several guys were sitting at their dining table when Ginny arrived late. She sat down at the far end, catching the end of Lizzy's story about hiding in the backseat of Kevin's car with Big Pod the day before, and skipping school. They had eaten burgers at the new Jack's before going to shop.

After several bites, Ginny stood and picked up her plate. She hesitated but no one seemed to notice so she walked away.

It had been raining all day so softball was canceled in the afternoon, and everyone was told to go to the gym. The smell of fresh popcorn from the concession stand greeted her when she went inside. The bleachers were crowded like it was a ball game, and Ginny's eyes searched slowly for Lizzy in the crowd. A hand touched her shoulder, and she turned to see Kevin, who seemed much taller standing next to her. He smiled, his eyes traveling from her eyes to glance down her body then back. With a nod, he smiled again, one hand sweeping outward toward the bleachers and the other holding a thick notebook.

She hesitated, and then walked ahead of him, climbing up three bleachers while resisting the urge to look back and see if he was behind her. He made sounds like Daffy Duck, and she couldn't understand what he was trying to say. She sat down quickly on the fourth bleacher near some elementary kids. Kevin made the sounds like a duck again, and she pretended not to hear, searching her purse for a reason to look away. He nudged her with his elbow, and she saw his notebook was open. When he flipped through the pages of Daffy Duck, it made it seem like the duck was walking, and he talked like Daffy Duck again. Ginny smiled. Several younger kids gathered around, begging for him to flip the pages again.

He opened the notebook further back, and an old gypsy woman with long grey hair and a peg leg began to dance across the page.

"I like this one the best." She whispered while patting the page, looking up to his face and then his eyes. He was smiling, and they stared for a moment before his eyes glanced away and then became focused behind her and she turned to see Big Pod and Lizzy pulling off letter jackets they were wearing and giving them back to two guys she didn't know. All of them had wet hair. One of the boys lit a cigarette for Big Pod, and she took it, her lips puckering out each time she sucked in the smoke.

Kevin stood, one hand patting Ginny's shoulder before he quickly went down the bleachers. Big Pod began talking when he stood in front of her, and the boy with the letter jacket walked away. Kevin lifted his hands up in a shrug over and over. Finally, he turned abruptly and went out the door. Big Pod followed.

*   *   *

"You ready for me to turn out the lights?" Ginny waited for Lenny to speak.

"Can't we keep them on?"

Ginny was silent for a moment. "Last night after you went to sleep I turned out all the lights, and the moon was so bright that you could see everything in here."

Lenny didn't answer, and she didn't tell him that she turned the lights back on later.

"Let me show you." Ginny turned off the lights, opened the wooden door and locked the screen.

"See?" The question was meant to convince herself as well as Lenny. Grandmother told her this morning to not leave the lights on at night anymore; they were too old to be afraid of the dark. The moon was very bright and after a few minutes to adjust, it was like daylight. They could see everything outside but no one out there could see inside. While wrapping the sheet around her and laying on the couch, she tried to think of something to talk about to make Lenny feel better.

"I wonder if Sheila's baby will be a boy or a girl? It will be born close to your birthday, maybe on the same day."

Lenny was still quiet.

"What do you hope it is?"

His voice was low, "A boy."

"After the baby comes, Sheila will stay here for a week, and then she says we can come and stay with her to help with the baby."

"I know, she told me already." He sighed. "What do you think Momma's doing?"

"Probably smoking." Ginny flippantly said the words, but immediately wondered if Lenny was upset that she had gone away. She felt guilty, but she wasn't sure if it was because Lenny missed her or because she didn't.

When she was sure Lenny was asleep, Ginny unlocked the door, slipping out to sit in the bright moonlight on the cinderblock porch. It was so bright that dark shadows appeared behind objects, like it did in sunlight. Everything had a shadow.

She quietly slipped back inside and took the camera from her purse. Pulling up the long shot lever, she pushed the shutter down and held it firmly in place while trying to hold very still. The manual said to hold it for five minutes to get a picture like their example of city lights at night, so she held the shutter down for what seemed like a long time and hoped it was five minutes. The moon filled the entire frame in her second shot, and she propped her arm against the house to help keep still. Moonlight washed through the chestnut trees, and she took two shots with different lengths of time, careful to watch for the sticky burrs on the ground.

Her last shots were of the swing set with the short shadows of the A frames on the ground behind it. She pushed both swings then stood in front and took the picture. Then with another push, she ran to the side, moving her body back and forth in movement with the one closest to her, holding the release button down, sure that the picture would show stringy ropes of light following the movements. While rolling the film, a strange sound snapped nearby and startled her. Had the slight squeaking sound of the swings woken someone up? Maybe it was her grandfather. She grabbed both chains to quiet them. Once they were still she went back inside the house and locked the screen door, listening for Lenny's breathing and carefully putting the camera back in her purse.

*   *   *

The bus was late the next morning, and the halls at school were almost empty except for the steady stream of mostly elementary kids from the bus. Lenny looked nice as he walked ahead of her going to his room, and Ginny felt a spark of pride as she left him and turned the corner to go to her locker. She ironed his shirt last night and set out his clothes, just like she did for herself.

The second bell rang while she turned the dial back and forth with her lock combination. A crumbled sheet fell out and slid to the floor while she stacked some books inside, keeping out English and Civics. After shutting the door and tugging on the lock, she reached down to pick up the paper and glanced at it while walking towards home room. Seeing a sketch of her face made her stop and smooth the crumpled edges. The long hair, eyes, and thin lips looked just like hers, but the breasts seemed too big with a hint of cleavage at the neck of the sweater. Her eyes glanced down at her chest where all but the top button of her blouse were fastened. The bottom of the sheet had a small drawing of the peg leg gypsy woman. There was nothing more on the paper.

Kevin must have slipped this in her locker. Why did he draw her? She stuffed it in her notebook and ran down the hall, feeling suddenly too warm. She stopped just outside the door of homeroom. Did this mean Kevin liked her?

Mr. Holcomb was near the end of roll call but glanced up and nodded as she came inside. Thankfully he didn't say her name or ask why she was late; hardly anyone noticed her. Across the room Lizzy was quietly talking to Floyd, the nice boy who sat in front of her whom everyone liked but no girls wanted to date. Ginny wondered what Lizzy would think of Kevin's drawing. Almost immediately she knew she would not show it to her.

*   *   *

Headlights shone directly in the house as a car pulled into the driveway. Ginny waited for it to turn around. The car continued forward, stopping near the porch. The door opened before the engine was turned off. Lenny pulled up to his knees from his bed behind the couch to peer into the darkness.

"It's Daddy. Ginny, it's Daddy!" Lenny climbed from the bed over the couch. He unlocked the screen door in time to hurl himself into his father as he came up the porch step.

"Lenny, are you glad to see me?" CB laughed, glancing up at Ginny when she walked to the door, "Marilyn?"

"It's me, Daddy." Ginny finished biting her fingernail then switched on a lamp.

"Hey, honey." His walk was slightly unsteady and he grabbed her in a bear hug. "You are getting prettier and prettier. Look just like your mother used to." He pulled his head back for a moment. "But don't you let any boys tell you that."

The smell of whiskey was strong. She wondered if her grandparents noticed the car and couldn't decide if she wanted them to or not.

"Where's Marilyn?"

Lenny answered first, "She's gone to Florida to stay with Aunt Hanna."

"What the hell is she doing there?" CB's forehead wrinkled with irritation as he sat on the couch and pulled a lock of Lenny's hair. "She is not going to take you kids down there, I can tell you that right now."

"They thought maybe a change would help her feel better." Ginny wondered why it mattered if they went to live in Florida, thinking she would like living close to the beach.

"Ain't nothing gonna make her any better." He flipped his hand like he was batting a bug away from his face. "Who thought it was okay to leave you kids alone here?"

"She isn't doing too good. She lost so much weight, and they thought…"

"Oh hell. I told you, ain't nothing going to help her." He reached in his jacket pocket and took out a small whiskey bottle that was almost empty. "She shouldn't have left you kids alone, not for any reason."

"Daddy, are you going to stay with us while Mother's gone?" Lenny sat down next to CB and patted his arm.

CB stared thoughtfully at his son, then nodded several times. "Well, I'll do even better. How about I stay the night, and both of you will go with me tomorrow?" He turned from Lenny to nod at Ginny before taking a drink, "Think Marilyn would like to come home and find you gone? She's done that to me more than a few times… didn't even bother to leave a damn note."

"Ginny, did you hear? We're going to go live with Daddy." Lenny looked to Ginny then back to his father. "Will it be okay with Grandmother?"

"Who cares if it's okay with Grandmother?" CB jerked his head to the side then stood up, glancing at Grandmother's house before running water over his hands and then patting his face. "Lenny, you go out to the car and bring my rifle inside. Be careful now, it's loaded."

Lenny nervously wiped both hands down his shirt before carefully opening the door.

CB pulled the straight chair from the kitchen table and placed it near Ginny, straddling backwards with both arms resting on the worn, ladder-back wood. "You've got to decide for both of you. I think you both should leave with me."

Ginny tried to swallow several times. Lenny came in the door, carefully holding the rifle up with both hands, "Dad, can I shoot it?"

"Hell, I guess so, that's what it's for." He smiled at his son before glancing at the empty whiskey bottle he left on the table.

"Daddy, it would wake up Grandmother and Grandfather." Ginny's words were rushed, and she wasn't sure he heard her. He took three small taped packages from his pocket and held them in his hands before looking to Lenny.

"Yeah, Ginny's right. I'll let you shoot it in the morning. Set it there on the table."

Lenny frowned at Ginny, before taking the rifle to the table. CB threw one of the packages to him as he turned. The package hit the floor.

"I thought you could catch better than that, boy." He laughed. "I didn't have time to buy presents while I was in Las Vegas, but I figured you'd like this just as well." He winked at Ginny while dropping a package into her hand. "We'll leave one for your sister. You put her name on it, 'cause your Momma won't get nothing when she decides to come back. Nothing."

After squatting to get the package, Lenny tore it open, spilling silver coins on the uneven floor. "It's silver dollars, Ginny. Open yours."

The silver coins clinked as she carefully opened the package and counted twenty. "Thank you, Daddy." She stood and hugged his neck, kissing him on the cheek.

He hugged her tight. "I've missed you, baby." She let go but he continued to hold on, one hand closing around a wad of hair that he pulled back. "I always miss you, Marilyn."

"Daddy, are you okay?" Ginny jerked back without waiting for an answer.

"Of course I am, baby." His bloodshot eyes looked sad. "I'm sorry, did I do something wrong?"

"No…" Her voice trailed away and she stood, not sure if he did something wrong or not. The dollars were still in her hand, and she took them to the table, stacking them next to Sheila's unopened package.

Lenny touched his father's watch, then the nametag stitched on his work jacket. CB tousled his hair. "You need to go to bed now. It's really late, and Ginny and I need to talk about things."

"Will you be here when I get up?" Lenny circled both hands around his arm.

"Of course. We'll shoot this rifle and go get something for breakfast."

Lenny nodded, walking slowly to the bed.

"You like pancakes?" Lenny nodded again, pulling the sheet up. CB stood and looked to Ginny, "I need to go back out to the car, baby. I'll be right back." He missed a step and stumbled off the porch but caught himself before he fell.

Ginny pictured them living with her father in a big house with a porch, as she often did when she was younger. Maybe he would quit drinking if they lived with him. She could help. She imagined them all sitting together in a swing on the porch, laughing.

The screen door creaked as CB came in holding a large bottle of whiskey. "I couldn't leave the good stuff out there."

She stood still watching him open the bottle and then sat in an old chair that used to have rockers but was now straight, close to her mother's bed and away from the couch. She didn't want him to sit next to her.

"Do you ever drink?"

She shook her head.

"Not even when you're out with boys?"

"I don't date."

"Your grandfather hasn't changed much has he? He was real hard on me when I tried to court your mother." His hands searched inside his coat pockets, and one made a fist around his keys and got hung in the pocket lining. He jerked his hand, but it stayed stuck. "But I found a way… told my friends I was going to get her." He tried to pull the coat off but the arm stuck with the pocket. He stopped struggling to look up and smile, "And I did find a way."

He slung both arms, then ripped the jacket until he could get it off his arm. He threw the torn jacket on the floor near the door. "Did Marilyn leave any matches? I lost my lighter."

Ginny pointed to the drawer. "Look in there." She pulled her legs and feet in the chair.

After rummaging through the drawer, he lit a cigarette, then took the bottle and sat down in the couch. "Tell me about your boyfriend."

"I don't have one."

He leaned forward. "Well, I'm not as old as your grandfather. I know how to take care of any boys that try anything." He leaned back and took the cap off the bottle. "In fact, it's probably good that I came tonight. You're at the age where you need to be with me." His hand tipped the bottle up then he laid his head back against the couch and slowly lowered the bottle where it rested beside him. He closed his eyes.

Ginny tried to decide whether she should slip out to tell her Grandmother he planned to take them. When she looked at Lenny asleep on his bed, she knew she couldn't leave him with CB, not even for a minute. He might take him while she was gone.

"What you thinking about? Women are always up to something when they quiet."

"Lenny's asleep, and I thought you were too."

"Naw, I'm just resting my eyes." He took another drink. "We'll leave early morning, before Grandmother even gets up." He nodded; both lips pressed together, his eyes suddenly wide.

"Maybe it's not a good time, Daddy."

"What's not a good time? Your momma left you. You're practically out of school for the summer. Your grandmother and grandfather won't come looking for you if that's what you're worried about." He sat up to the edge of the couch, his voice louder. "Hell, your momma won't come looking either 'cause she's not even here to notice."

The words were slurred, and the whites of his eyes were pink. He stared at her, but she didn't think he really saw her. He stood suddenly and put one hand on each of the arms of her chair. His face was inches from hers. "Do you think I don't have any control over you?" His bigness surrounded her. A lump would not go away in her throat. "If I tell you to get your things and leave, that's what you'll do."

She sat very still, the hope that he would pass out was gone. He stood up, kicking at something he saw on the floor. "You've been listening to your mother for way too long. She wasn't any picnic to live with. You remember?" He learned down close to her again. "Afraid of everybody and everything but couldn't listen to nothing. Sometimes all your mother could understand…" He stopped and abruptly walked to the sink.

A chill started at the back of Ginny's neck, and her hands began to tremble, then her legs. She held tight to the arms of the chair. Her stomach quivered. She did remember. Screaming. Glass breaking. The police.

He was standing still, his back to her.

"I… we can't go live with you, Daddy." He continued to stand at the sink in silence and she thought that maybe he didn't hear her. "Daddy? Did you hear me?"

He turned around slowly. "So… so you think you're better off by yourself than with your own daddy?"

"We're not alone. We have Grandmother… and them."

"Really, Ginny? Cause I don't see her or them here." He poked at things on the sink, knocking them down like he was searching, and then finally kicking the door shut.

She turned her body, putting her arm around the back of the chair, her fingers touched the sheet of her mother's bed, and she pulled it to herself. He threw the empty bottle against the wall. The sheet covered her shoulders and body and she tucked the edges under her legs and bare feet, resisting the urge to cover her head as well.

He picked up the rifle from the table. "Someone could have come in here tonight and killed you with one of these." He held it up to her. "I could kill you right now, Ginny, and Grandmother wouldn't be able to do anything about it."

He walked quickly and the gun barrel seemed perfectly still in front of her face. Then it all seemed far away like she was dreaming.

"What's it going to be Ginny?"

Slowly her eyes stopped circling the opening of the barrel and she looked at his face, his bloodshot blue eyes.

The rifle clicked, and her eyelids quickly closed and she heard him laugh. "It ain't loaded, baby. I'm not going to shoot you. You're whiter than that sheet."

Chills took over her body as if she had a fever. Her eyes refused to open, but tears leaked out anyway, and she felt them running down her face. His finger touched her face, dipping into the hollow below her right eye. She could not bear to see and forced her eyes tighter.

"I guess I should leave." His voice was a whisper. She felt him move away, and then he seemed very far away. The screen door opened and closed. When the car engine started, she pulled the sheet tight over her head and rocked, grateful for the bright, naked light bulb hanging above her head, even though she couldn't open her eyes to see it.

*   *   *

Ginny had been too sick to go to school for three days. Since the last day was only a half day, Grandfather and Grandmother dropped them at school and left to run errands in town. They planned to pick them back up on the way back home.

The locker had no new drawings from Kevin, and Ginny was unsure how she felt about it. She stacked up all the books and took them out of the locker and leaned against the door with her shoulder to close it. In homeroom, she stood in line to return the books, naming them off once it was her turn, and then getting in another line for her report card.

Before she saw her, she heard Lizzy's laugh. "Ginny. I heard you were sick." With all her hair swept up in a twist, Lizzy looked much older. Davy stood next to her, carrying her books to turn in.

Ginny nodded but didn't move from her place in line.

"Davy, go get in line, and I'll be right there." She looked at Ginny, "I'm just turning in these books, and then I'm leaving." When Davy walked away, she leaned forward, "Momma finally agreed to let me go with Robert on his trips during the Summer break. We're going to South Florida this afternoon." Her left hand waved in front of Ginny's face with Robert's old ring on her finger."

Ginny's face nodded and she was sure she was smiling, but she wanted Lizzy to go away.

"Well, I guess the next time I see you will be in the Fall. Isn't it strange that we will be leaving here for high school? Are you excited?"

Ginny nodded. Everything did feel strange, but she wasn't excited.

"Marsha's going to quit school. She wasn't going to pass anyway. She didn't even come in today."

"Did she and Kevin make up?" Ginny lowered her eyes to focus on the white eyelet edging on Lizzy's blouse.

"No. He won't even talk to her," she giggled and slapped her hand in the air, "Not that he ever did talk to anyone. She's dating Lem now."

Ginny couldn't help but smile, glad that Kevin was no longer with Big Pod. Lem was not anyone she could remember. Mr. Holcomb called out her name, and Lizzy waved and walked to the other line while Ginny took her report card.

After they got home and ate lunch, Ginny sat in the swing, her legs stiff and her feet still while watching Lenny line up all his toy cars and trucks in the sand. The morning after daddy left, she told him what their father was like when they all lived together and that she told him they couldn't go live with him. He nodded and then quickly asked if either Mother or Daddy were coming back. When Ginny nodded yes, she saw the relief in his eyes and felt the first of the churning in her stomach that made her throw up and unable to eat for two days.

Lenny's hand scraped a winding road through the sand, circling his manmade obstacle course of rocks, pinecones, and a plank, ending with a mountain of sand for his pretend people. He took a little red sports car for the first test drive. She left the swing and sat on the ground near him, reaching over and taking the big plastic convertible and driving it slowly along the road behind his new little, metal car. They continued until they had driven all the cars to the end of the road.

She stood and slowly walked inside, looking through the spiral bound notebooks for anything she intended to keep. Kevin's drawing was all she chose, and she smoothed out the wrinkles while memorizing the sketch before taking it to her box of pictures and papers hiding at Grandmother's house.

CHAPTER 13

GETTING DRESSED

MARILYN, 1972

The short dress stretched to hug her body, particularly her stomach and hips. Disgusted, she plopped down into the couch and heard the slight snapping sound of a ripped seam. The cold vinyl of the couch against the backs of her thighs annoyed her further.

"Must have gained weight." She talked more to herself than Lenny, who sat watching a football game on TV.

Scraps of dark, green polyester were heaped in a pile on the floor, and Marilyn pushed them aside to pick up the fat pattern envelope. Strands of hair fell in her face as leaned forward and tried to study the dresses on the cover. Maybe she should have used the pattern. She never used to. She just picked out a dress in a magazine and made it, adding special finishes like crocheted lace collars. People used to beg her to sew for them, but she never did. The envelope fell back to the floor as she tugged at the hem, forcing the material closer to her knees. It raced back up her thigh when she let go.

Nothing to do now. Her eyes glanced toward Lenny while reaching to find the remains of her cigarette on the edge of the sewing machine cabinet. She was hoping for a suggestion but with the flicker of her eyes, she was sure she saw CB sitting at the TV and looked back again. Fixing her eyes on her son, she wiped the cold ashes of her cigarette to the floor and relit the short stub.

Lenny coughed, then continued to force himself to cough.

She laughed at him, "Come get you a drag, baby, then you can really cough."

He ignored her. A door slammed from her mother's house, and Marilyn looked up as she heard footsteps race up the few porch steps and

Ginny came into the front door. Both of her hands held to an envelope, and her eyes shifted back and forth from Marilyn to Lenny, then back to Marilyn.

Her daughter's eyebrows bunched toward the center. "What happened?"

"To what?" Marilyn blew smoke up at her daughter.

"To your dress." Ginny's eyes looked up and down the dress, stopping at Marilyn's feet. "You didn't use the pattern… it's too tight… it looks…"

Her voice trailed off, and Marilyn twisted her cigarette several times in the ashtray and felt her face grow warm. "It's the style."

"I don't understand." Ginny's body shifted to one leg. "You used to sew such pretty things."

"Well, I used to be a pretty thing." Again heat rose in her face, and Marilyn brushed several small scraps from the couch to the floor. Just don't look if you don't like it. She waited for Ginny to comment again so she could say the sentence out loud. She was sick of the damn dress. With the cigarette pulled from the pack, Marilyn lit it, and then focused on the steady stream of smoke, glancing at Ginny, waiting for her to speak. She knew she was still standing here for some reason.

Her hands slightly trembled when Ginny took out the letter from the envelope and held it out to Marilyn.

"What is it?" Smoke escaped from her mouth when she spoke, and she quickly took another draw. The burning red glow of the tip got brighter as she sucked harder, racing the fire for the cigarette's last breath.

"It's my acceptance letter for college." Ginny continued to hold the letter out to her.

Something tightened in her chest, and Marilyn felt spasms rush up to her throat. She coughed, then coughed again, using three fingers to rub her chest. "I already told you when you started this mess that I wasn't going to pay for you to go off to no college."

Ginny's expression did not change. She opened the letter and began reading out loud, "We are happy to notify you of your acceptance, subject to medical clearance, as a student here at the University of Alabama."

"University of Alabama? Why didn't you apply to Auburn?" Lenny turned down the volume of the TV.

Without looking up, Ginny shook her head, a slight smile on her face. She folded the letter and put it back in the envelope.

The hem of the dress was high on her thigh again, and Marilyn pulled it down and tucked it tightly around her knees. The polyester fabric felt warm and comforting.

Ginny watched her pull the skirt down and now stared at the pile of scraps on the floor. "I'm going to get financial aid. The counselor at school helped me to fill out the papers. She told me I qualified for money for living expenses and tuition."

There were tiny flecks of yellow light in Ginny's eyes. Lots of people commented on them when she was little. Too odd, nothing like anything else she had ever seen, and Marilyn never really liked them, but she stared at them now, first the left eye then the right one.

"I am going to school this fall."

The same stuff again. Marilyn looked away. All this talk about graduation and school was tiring. She hunched forward in the seat, "Lenny, go ask your grandfather to go to the store." In an instant, the hem of her dress escaped and exposed both thighs. She stood and smoothed the dress down and walked to the sink, turning quickly to remark that the counselor could also pay for the dam school, since she was being so helpful. But Ginny had quietly left the room.

The shorts she wore earlier were on the bed, and Marilyn pulled them back on up under the dress. She took a deep breath before taking the dress off and dropping it on the floor.

Lenny turned to look at her and then frowned while looking away quickly. "You look like something bit you."

Without looking in the mirror her hand swiped at a bump on the side of her face, one that had been bleeding earlier. She feverishly snatched scraps of green polyester from the floor and dumped them in the trash. The back of Lenny's head bobbed, and he made sounds that reminded her of CB. She wasn't sure if he was mad or happy with the game he was watching. Either way it didn't really matter, he would get up and leave in the end.

The dress was still wadded up on the floor. She picked it up and flapped it in the air a few times before laying it out on the bed, lining it up carefully so that the shoulder seams touched the edge of the pillow. Her hands smoothed the bottom, and she thought about adding shoes and hose to look like someone real. A nervous glance at her son changed her mind, but she imagined someone there but no ideas came about what she could add that would look like arms. Gloves for hands would be easy. Maybe she could stitch the dress to a quilt top and add a hat for a head, maybe add another figure on the other side. Sitting on the edge of the bed, she ran her fingers across the fabric and tried to imagine the other figure but couldn't. Her fingers bunched the hem of the dress; it was lifeless and ugly.

She stood, rolled the dress up, and took it with the green scraps and pattern out the back door.

"Put a shirt on." Lenny yelled to her when the back door slammed. The white bra she wore had circular stitching around the pointed cups. What did it matter what she wore? No one saw her anyway. She didn't go anywhere. Then it came to her. She just wouldn't go to Ginny's high school graduation. There would be no need for a new dress. No need to listen to her talk about school. For a moment, she felt calm and slowly walked back inside the house still holding the green polyester and pattern.

*　　*　　*

Ginny and her mother had long finished the supper dishes and left Marilyn sitting alone at the kitchen table. Mother used to try and get her to join them in the living room for television after dinner, but she didn't want to be with them, instead she listened from the kitchen. The news blared from the TV. Things happened to people, but none of it seemed real.

The man on the TV said something about the University of Alabama, and she focused on the sounds of people yelling. He called it a riot and said students had burned down a building earlier in protest. Her leg nervously bounced up and down like she was playing horsey with a child, and she shuttered. Why would they be protesting? Why would Ginny want to go there? There was no place Marilyn really wanted to go. It had been a long time since she had been anywhere. She tried to remember the last time she actually left the farm. Must have been a few weeks ago when she went to the grocery store.

"Marilyn." Her body flinched when her mother spoke from close behind her. "I bought this dress for you yesterday in town. I thought you might like to wear it to Ginny's graduation."

Marilyn frowned at the sound of the voice but didn't turn around. Her mother draped a flowered dress over the chair next to her at the kitchen table. It was navy with big, pink cabbage roses. She hated it.

"I've already made a dress."

"Ginny said it was too small. I know you've gained weigh this year… so I got you a bigger size."

Her mother continued to stand beside her, patting the dress. Marilyn took the lit cigarette from the ashtray and stood, knocking the ladder-back wooden chair on the floor.

"Don't you like it?"

"It ain't my style." With cigarettes and lighter in her hand, she walked outside. No ugly big-flowered dress was going to change her mind. She wasn't going to her graduation.

* * *

It was late in the morning before Marilyn thought about getting out of bed and going for coffee at her mother's. The kids left the door slightly ajar when they left for school. Irritated, she slammed it shut and then waited with her hand on the knob for a few seconds, then opened it to leave.

Her mother's kitchen was silent as she stepped inside, but the coffee pot was still half full.

She poured herself a cup, added cream that was room temperature, and then pulled her chair out from the table. The flowered dress had been folded and was left on her seat.

"I don't want it!" She gestured toward the dress, her voice booming in the empty kitchen. Hot coffee sloshed over the back of her hand, and she dropped the cup, smashing it to pieces on the concrete floor and spattering hot coffee across the tops of her feet and canvas shoes. She turned and walked out, shoving the screen door back against the wringer washer on the porch. When the door bounced back, she shoved it again and again against the washer.

No one appeared, so she walked quickly back to her house. She sat in the cool dark room for a moment, and then took the green polyester dress and dropped it on top of the scraps in the trashcan and carried them out. Within minutes, a fire was blazing and the green dress was gone.

* * *

He was back behind her house in his shop. Most of the morning, she had felt the vibrations in the back wall they shared with scraping sounds. On and off, on and off. The voices warned her, they could feel it too. She didn't go back to his house to eat or get coffee since the warning.

The high-pitched sound began again, but louder; short bursts of screeching metal against metal. For years, she had warned him. Time and time again, she had told him that she couldn't stand being drilled, or sanded, or cut. But still he persisted.

Marilyn walked out the back door and slammed the door twice, warning him to stop. The late afternoon sun cast her shadow on the sheets of tin that separated her back porch from her father's shop. She was startled by her shadow on the wall. The dress looked like that of a child's, a short A shape. But the body was long, and the stomach stuck out like she was pregnant. Her eyes looked away, and she moved from the porch.

The blasts started again. Louder this time; she was outside and close. The voices were screaming, and she doubled over, squatting to the ground, her arms holding tight around her legs, rocking back and forth. He knew he could kill her this way. "Stop! Stop!"

The bursts of screeching metal stopped, and she stood, running around the tin wall and standing before the doors of her father's shop, an opening large enough to drive a car inside. Lightning bolts of light and sparks came from the darkness inside with more screeching. Her feet and legs could feel the rumbling of the sander wheel turning around and around making the trembling move all the way to the top of her head. He was in there, and she knew that soon the lightning bolts would be scraping and peeling the skin from her body.

"Stop it! Stop—you're killing me. Can't you see me bleeding?" The bright light from outside reflected off her father's glasses when his head moved in the darkness. He came forward, and she could barely make out his body but she saw he carried a pole in his hand and she braced herself, breathing hard and suddenly unable to scream for help.

He disappeared back into the dark. The rumbling stopped, then her father stepped out into the light toward her. "Marilyn? What's wrong with you?"

"Don't hit me. Don't you hit me. Can't you see I'm already bleeding?" She stepped in closer, holding out the palms of both hands, forcing him to see the blood. "Why do you do this to me?"

"Marilyn, stop this crazy talk."

"Crazy? You call me crazy?" She snatched both hands back while screaming louder.

"Marilyn!" He yelled while he moved toward her, throwing the pole to the ground.

Footsteps came up behind her, and she whirled around to see her mother. "Momma, he hurt me. Momma, he did this to me. I'm bleeding. See?"

"Marilyn, it's time to get on back to your house. Maybe you need to lie down for awhile." Both her mother's hands were up as if they were going to press against her.

Marilyn's body flinched and she stepped back. "Don't." She stared at her mother, then held both hands out again for her mother to see. "He did this. He did this to me."

"He has to sharpen the hoes, Marilyn. We have to have them tomorrow to work in the garden. You just calm down."

Her mother looked at her father and moved in closer to him, and they began to talk with low voices. She couldn't understand what they were saying. Mother wouldn't even look at the blood. Marilyn turned and ran around the tin wall and to the back of her house, slamming the door shut and bracing herself against it. It was difficult to breathe and the trembling of her body made it hard to stay braced against the door.

"What you going to do? What you going to do?" She repeated softly to herself, thinking of running out the front door, then wondering if that's where they were. Maybe they planned to come in the front door. She began sobbing. They would kill her this time.

The sounds of the school bus stopping out front made her freeze, listening for the children while still panting to breath. Children were laughing and yelling on the bus. She heard the door unfold open then shut, then the bus moved down the road. Relief flooded her body. They wouldn't dare do anything to her while the kids were here.

* * *

No one asked her again about the dress or Ginny's graduation. Lenny and Ginny dressed quickly and quietly, Ginny wearing a white dress while carrying the white graduation gown over her arm. Car doors slammed and the engine started up outside but she heard no voices. She resisted the urge to watch them leave and continued to sit on the couch.

Lenny said Grandmother decided not to go, either; said it wouldn't be right for the grandmother to go and not the mother. Grandfather would wait in the car for the ceremony to end and bring them home afterwards.

"Maybe you could go and wear the big-flowered dress you bought." Marilyn said the words to the wall while picturing her mother's plump body in it. She laughed. The smoke swirled around as she blew it out from her mouth, leaning forward to crush the cigarette in the ashtray, wondering how long it would be before they got back.

CHAPTER **14**

FLYING THE COOP

GINNY, 1972

The smoky, cool air felt good as Ginny climbed up the last step of the Trailways bus and inched her way back behind other passengers. At the first set of empty seats, she plopped down and lifted her big purse in the seat beside her, hoping that it would discourage anyone from sitting there. Her right hand automatically slid inside the bulky bag until her fingers felt the hard square camera.

She fought the urge to look out the window at Grandfather's car parked near the bus, knowing already what was there. Her mother and brother would be sitting in the backseat quietly staring at the bus, and her grandfather would be up front, a rolled Prince Albert between his middle finger and thumb. No one would talk about her leaving. Grandfather and Mother would smoke silently while memorizing the details of the passengers. Later Grandfather would describe the people during lunch with Grandmother, who was always hungry for the details of other people's lives.

A tall, thin man wearing jeans and cowboy boots hesitated beside her, and she quickly looked away from his intense stare. He sat across the aisle and she turned her attention on the dark brown pleats of her dress, smoothing down each fold until the hem covered her knees. The shiny, black straps of her sandals were dusty, and she licked a finger before lifting her foot and wiping a strap clean. The man in the aisle seat leaned toward her, and she turned to see him starting at her foot. He was so close she could hear him breathing. She partially stood and shoved her purse over and sat in the window seat, keeping her eyes out the window and away from the creepy man.

Grandfather's car was still parked nearby, and a small steady rope of smoke escaped from the back window until it rose above the car, then disappeared. The bus began to lumber from the station, and her heart beat faster when she thought about yelling for the driver to stop, about jumping off and getting back into the car. Instead, she swallowed again and again to keep down the fluttering in her stomach. There was no going back. Whatever happened, she wouldn't go back. But she wished she could have brought Lenny with her or at least hugged him again before leaving. She even wished she had found Grandmother and hugged her as well. They had all come out to see her leave, but tears had welled up quickly in Grandmother's eyes and she had twisted around and returned to her kitchen. Lenny crawled into the center of the back seat next to Mother. She hesitated, watching the door for Grandmother's return, and then crawled in beside Lenny, leaving Grandfather alone in the front. They rode silently to the bus station.

Shifting her eyes, she could see that the man in the aisle seat sat back, one leg crossed over the other, swinging like a woman. She thought of Sheila, fat and pregnant, waiting for her second baby to come. She brought Gilbert and spent a week with them before going over to stay with Mike's family for a few days. The fluttering rose again into her throat, and the bus turned onto Highway 431, passing the shirt factory where Lizzy and some of her other classmates had gotten jobs.

It made it easier for all of them when Sheila came with Gilbert. They lavished attention on him, especially Marilyn, who stood outside for hours early Saturday evening, snuggling close to Gilbert as she held him in her arms, giggling when he tried to reach out for the big moon she kept pointing out. Sheila brought stacks of pictures, giving Ginny and her mother little two-inch copies that replicated the bigger photos she kept for herself. The pictures were mostly of Gilbert taken over the past years. One photo was a close shot of Mother holding baby Gilbert back when she was terribly thin. Her frail arms wound around his chubby middle, holding him tight against her emaciated body. The slight smile on her face and half closed eyes were jarring to Ginny, and she put it behind the other pictures, not sure if it was her heart or her stomach that started thumping and made her feel sick.

Sheila helped Ginny sew two new blouses and pack boxes that they mailed to the university. She had seventy-five dollars in her purse, all she had left after buying some jeans and her bus ticket. Neighbors and family gave her money for high school graduation, and she cleaned house for an elderly woman down the road, saving everything for going away to college.

Leaning back, she closed her eyes from the sun brightly shining in the window and brought up her favorite image: the library steps at the university, a picture she frequently looked at from the catalog. She imagined herself walking up them with friends and commenting on the huge statues at the entrance and the paintings she was sure were on the inside walls. They wouldn't talk about diapers and trying to find a job.

The bus ride was slow and rumbling, stopping at so many little towns that she forgot the names. Three hours later there were more buildings, huge brick stores and factories with hundreds of railroad tracks. And then buildings taller than could be seen from the bus window. They were in Birmingham, and she instantly thought of her Daddy, the city he took them to live when she was in the first grade and the city where he still lived. "It's easier to get a brew there," he once said while winking at her, "not like these damn dry counties in North Alabama."

It was silly, but she scanned the faces of tall men as she stepped off the bus, looking for his familiar dark, wavy hair. While stepping up into the transfer bus, she imagined his surprise to see her; he didn't even know she was leaving for college. He had not visited them for almost a year, not since her mother told him that men from the FBI were looking for him. He apologized to Mother, looking both shocked and scared.

"Baby, I am so sorry they are bothering you. You sure, now? The FBI? I know the IRS is looking. Maybe it was them."

Her mother insisted it was the FBI while Ginny and Lenny rolled their eyes at each other. There were no FBI men, and it surprised her to see her father so scared over one of her mother's stories. She and Lenny continued to looked at each other, trying not to giggle when Daddy held his breath and listened intently two different times when cars passed by outside, peeking out from behind the curtains until the tail lights disappeared. Soon, he had quickly kissed them all good bye, and she had not been sorry to see him leave. Still, she wondered if he would be proud of her since he had never asked to see her report card or asked how she did in school.

The transfer bus was less crowded, and she didn't see the creepy man anymore. Soon they were rolling through more small towns, and then they drove through the campus, passing by Denny Chimes and the quad. Ginny squeezed her purse; it looked like she remembered when she had attended the orientation in the spring. They traveled further into the downtown streets of Tuscaloosa, and she grabbed the handle on the corner of the seat and stood. The handle was sticky, but she held on anyway, trying to balance as the bus turned through several small side streets. She was eager to get off quickly and find a hotel room before it got dark since tomorrow was the first day she could check into the dorm. Muggy air surrounded her as she stepped down the bus steps and stood at the side as a uniformed man flipped open the luggage compartment. He lifted a suitcase onto the cart. "You'll have to go into the terminal." He nodded past the bright yellow poles toward the door.

The cool air felt nice on her face when she entered, and she stood still for a moment. Another man with a dark tan helped pull the cart with suitcases though the door. He smiled moments later, looking through the suitcases, holding up blue ones until he could see they didn't match her luggage ticket. He explained to Ginny that her suitcase had probably not transferred in Birmingham from the first bus, and it would probably arrive on the next bus from Birmingham about an hour and a half later. The queasiness she felt earlier returned, and she glanced outside and wondered how much longer it would be daylight. What if it got dark, and she had no place to stay?

Telling herself not to worry, she went to the phone booth and looked up hotels. Dismay filled her as she realized she had no idea which ones were close by, and she didn't know how much it would cost to take a taxi. The man at the counter was pulling suitcases off the cart and tearing off ticket stubs before sliding them through the opening to waiting customers. The opening looked like a door for kids, and when he stepped up to slide the suitcases all she could see was his creased pants and shoes with a spit polished shine. She slipped back in line behind the last customer and asked his help.

"That's easy." He touched his hair with one hand while leaning on the counter. His dark oily hair sprung back into place after the touch, and his eyes slowly looked her over. "The Tide is about three blocks away. A nice little motor lodge, but reasonable. Call and see if they have a room."

After making the call and reserving a room, she realized she was starving and walked to the vending machines. She had been too nervous to eat her Grandmother's heavily buttered biscuits and strawberry jam at breakfast. Before she could find change for the crackers, the man behind the counter yelled back to her. "So the Tide was able to fix you up?"

She nodded and walked back toward the counter.

"You here to go to school?" His eyes crinkled when he smiled, and she felt relief at being able to talk to someone. She explained this was her second trip to Tuscaloosa, and she was here to start college next week. He said his name was Clyde and pointed to a piece of paper tacked to the wall that had his name and picture along with several other men who worked at the bus station. She asked Clyde if his children went to college here, and he laughed out loud.

"Honey, I'm only thirty. Do I look that old to you?"

The flush on her face made her warm, and she searched her mind for something else to say. A frowning woman walked up to the counter pulling along a crying boy. Ginny's hand slid inside her purse, and her fingers clutched the camera. She hesitated. The boy looked up at her through red, swollen eyes, one tiny arm surrounding the neck of a brown cloth doll half his size. He didn't return her smile, but lowered himself under the woman's hip and against her leg. He lost his balance when the woman suddenly turned around and reached down and grabbed his arm and continued toward the door pulling him along.

Ginny continued to stare after them, wanting to snap their picture but afraid the woman would get angry.

"That's some bag you got there. You carrying around a bottle of Jack Daniel's or something?" Clyde laughed, and Ginny turned back around to see his eyes rest on her chest before looking back up to her eyes. She turned quickly without answering and walked to the door.

"To the right for two blocks then turn left. Right?"

"Right." His voice was oddly soft, but she didn't look back. "Your bag should be here by the time you get back."

*   *   *

A young woman not much older than herself was at the desk of the motel, dressed in jeans and gauze top. She seemed nice but impatient to get back to her book. Ginny opened the door to her room and looked around before putting the key in the coin section of her wallet and taking out the camera to snap a picture of the hotel sign before heading back to the bus station. She felt relief. She had gotten a room and tomorrow she would be in the dorm. Everything would be okay.

Her eyes instantly recognized the old blue suitcase that had been handed down several times by aunts and cousins before Grandmother gave it to her for this trip. She smiled at Clyde. "It made it here."

"I told you it would. Hold on a second while I help this lady, and I'll get it for you." He turned to the elderly woman standing behind Ginny, who bought a ticket for a long trip, and it took a while for Clyde to write out all the different transfer tickets she would need at each place she would change buses.

Finally, he finished and smiled at her, his voice low. "Listen, I was thinking that instead of you lugging this big suitcase all the way to the hotel, I would bring it to you when I get off at seven."

The straps of her shoes were dusty again, and she busied herself wiping them off with a dry finger. Both of his hands were flat on the counter, and he stopped talking. She searched her mind for what to say.

"If you tell me what you drink, I'll pick us something up on my way."

"That's okay. I can take my suitcase myself."

"Oh come on now. It's pretty heavy, especially to carry that far. Besides, it's your first night in town. No sense in being alone."

It was hard for her to breathe. "Thank you anyway, but I need to get my suitcase now."

He pushed the suitcase partially through the opening in the counter, catching her hand as she reached for the handle and holding it tight. "Come on. I can still come over. I just thought I could make it easier and take the suitcase for you."

Without answering or looking at him, she slowly pulled her hand away from his and took the handle of the suitcase and pulled it through the opening and out of his grasp.

"Baby, if you don't give me your room number, I won't be able to find you… tell me what to bring to drink. You like rum and Coke?"

Her feet inched toward the door, and she finally looked up to him and smiled. "You have a nice evening."

There was not much time before Clyde would get off work. She ran toward the motel using both hands to hold the suitcase up. She ignored the stares from people walking by who could hear the loud panting and wheezing noise she made. Every car that passed made the queasy feeling come back. She was sure that Clyde would come, maybe even leave work early.

Coming up the sidewalk of the motel, she wondered if her room would be the only one without a car parked in front of it. He would be able to tell which room was hers, or even get it from the woman at the desk.

Once in the room, she locked the door and the deadbolt and sat on the bed. Seconds later, she got up and checked the door locks again before going to the bathroom for water. Car doors slammed shut outside before she could get the water, and she checked the locks again.

Close to seven o'clock she looked out the window and saw almost no cars in the parking lot. Did everyone leave? Maybe she should go talk to the girl that checked her in? Maybe she would know what to do about Clyde. She shook her head violently. No, that would mean she would have to go back outside, and besides it would be too embarrassing. Maybe Clyde would pretend he didn't say anything. The heavy drape resisted when she tried to put it back in place and make sure no cracks of the window was left uncovered. With several pushes, she moved the dresser so that it was blocking the door. Seconds later, tears rolled down her cheeks when she realized she had not gotten soda and cookies from the machines. There would be no dinner tonight.

She washed her face, shaking her head when she thought about the gown she had packed. Better to stay dressed in case she had to run for help. The suitcase was still near the door, and she decided to leave it there until she dressed in the morning, cringing at the thought of being naked in the shower if he tried to break in. She lay across the bed with her back near the headboard. The buckle on her shoe caught on threads from the bedspread when she pulled her knees near her chest. It was hard to hear unless she raised her head. She would need to sit up tonight, to listen for cars near her window. After turning off the sound of the TV, she flipped through the channels for some show she liked, avoiding police shows with bad people. Horses running through a small deserted town with big tumbleweeds made her pause then decide to watch. The pillows were small and flat, so she rolled the bed spread in a ball and leaned on it, exhausted.

Sometimes it made her feel better to think through what she would do if the worst happened, so she thought of it. If Clyde came to her door, she would have time to call someone before answering. The police? She couldn't do that; too embarrassing. He would just say she was lying. He would pretend he didn't say anything, and the police might tell her grandfather. If he thought a man came to her room, she wasn't sure what he would do, but she knew it would be her fault. Her hands shook with the thought. She should have asked a woman for help. Grandfather did not like it when she talked to strange men. It occurred to her she would just remain quiet and not answer the door. Maybe Clyde would think she wasn't in the room... that's it. She closed her eyes, exhausted.

*　*　*

The knocking was light, and she could hear loud breathing on the other side of the door. She reached out to make sure the door was locked, and then realized in horror that both of her hands had been cut off. She screamed while looking at the hideous scars at the end of her arms and the knocking became louder.

"Are you all right in there?" Ginny opened her eyes and quickly look up to the door after first glancing at her arms. It was a woman's voice and the knocking was loud. Ginny jumped up to go to the window to look out. The bright sunlight blinded her while the woman asked again if she was all right. All Ginny could see was a cart filled with folded towels.

"I'm o… kay." Her lips lightly brushed against the door while she spoke into the crack.

"Okay, miss. I will come back."

Her body surged with relief, and she pushed back the heavy curtain and smiled into the sun that covered her. The woman with the cart probably thought she was crazy, but she didn't care; it was no longer night.

By the time she called the taxi to come and get her, she had almost finished her third package of cookies. Clyde was probably back at work, but she decided to wait until she got to the dorm to take a shower or change clothes. She tried to smooth away some of the wrinkles in her dress but gave up and made up the bed instead. The elderly taxi man got out and helped her with her suitcase. She settled in the back seat, letting out a sigh as they pulled away from the motel.

CHAPTER 15

GO HOME

MARILYN 1972

A small envelope was partially tucked under her plate when she sat down to eat, and she reluctantly used her small finger to nudge it away. Marilyn was sure that she would not be interested in anything placed under her plate by her mother. Still, her eyes glanced at the return address: a small circle with a woman inside, holding some sort of twig and pointing down to a globe with her other hand. "UNIVERSITY OF ALABAMA" was printed beside the circle, and underneath Ginny had signed it and wrote *General Delivery*. It was not addressed to Marilyn, so she pushed it further away, then reached for the bowl of green beans and dipped a spoonful on her plate.

"Marilyn, that's a letter from Ginny." Her mother pointed a butter knife at the envelope. "She wrote to let us know she got to her schooling okay."

A strand of hair fell over her ear, and Marilyn twisted it back with one hand while taking a bite of cornbread, clenching it between her teeth.

"You going to read it?" Lenny picked up the letter.

Irritated, Marilyn pulled it from his hand and pushed it further from both of them toward her mother's side of the table. She picked up her glass of milk and took a sip, feeling the cornbread crumble in her mouth.

"Why don't you read it?" Lenny got closer to her face.

"It's not addressed to me." There was a piece of fatback in the beans on her plate, and she moved it to the side.

Everyone ate in silence until her father stood and poured himself a cup of coffee before going to the living room. Lenny stood, reached over the table, and took the letter from the envelope.

"Put it back." Marilyn said the words, then gritted her teeth. A surge of anger ran through her. She wanted to slap him but instead bit off another bite of cornbread.

"It says, 'Hello everybody,' so that means everyone."

"Well, I guess that's right, she did send it to everybody." Her mother smiled at Lenny, pleased with the answer.

Marilyn continued to chew the cornbread, letting it become mush in her mouth but did not swallow. She set her fork down and stood, taking her cup to the counter and pouring it full of coffee while Lenny continued to read the letter out loud.

"I walked down to the Union Station yesterday. I bought this stationary. There is a girl who graduated a year ahead of me in high school that lives in the dorm. She looked me up, and we went and got a hamburger for dinner." Marilyn stopped near the door to take a sip of coffee before walking outside and across the sandy yard. She walked up the steps and shut the door behind her, sipping coffee and feeling uneasy. The house was too hot, but she left the door closed and set the cup on the sink.

Little sparks shot out when she turned the switch of the fan on the table. She stepped back as the blades began to spin faster, and then looked slowly and carefully around the room thinking she had heard a hissing sound. There was nothing she could see but she couldn't be sure about where the sparks went. She shivered. Quietly picking up her cup, she opened the door but stood uncertain for a moment before stepping out on the cinder block porch then slowly sitting down, turning slightly so that she could watch the door.

There was a distant sound of a bird, or maybe some other creature and the constant hum of the fan from inside. She missed Gilbert. Sheila stopped by to eat lunch yesterday on her way back home after visiting her husband's family.

"Did Ginny get on the bus okay?" Sheila wanted to know about Ginny's trip to school, but Marilyn just shrugged and took Gilbert from her arms and took him outside to play in the sand. Nothing to tell. Ginny got in the car wearing no makeup and an ugly, brown dress with a striped tank top over it like a vest. If she had been nervous, she didn't show it and dressed like she didn't care how she looked. They drove to the bus station, and Lenny took Ginny's old suitcase out of the trunk while she and her father sat in the car. He rolled a Prince Albert cigarette, while she lit a Pall Mall; neither saying a word.

Lenny stood with Ginny at the bus door a few seconds and then got back into the car quickly and sat staring out the other side with his back to her. He did not turn to watch the bus pull away from the station. She wanted to tell him that Ginny would be back, just as she always came back. But something stopped her from saying it to him.

Thinking of it made Marilyn stiffen her back. She took a big gulp of coffee, feeling the hot liquid go down her throat. She had not told Ginny goodbye, thinking she would change her mind and not leave. Now, for the first time, she considered that Ginny might not come back.

Marilyn tried to get away. It was good with CB at the beginning. She had even tried to get away without him. She took Lenny to Florida to stay with her sisters. They had gone to the beach and spent most of their time with her youngest sister Hanna. After several weeks, she began to worry about whether CB might come to see her while she was gone and what he might think. That he might take the girls while she was gone. Even with her parents next door, she had been afraid CB would still try and take them like he threatened many times.

Hanna and her husband talked to her about getting a job and moving to Florida. They even pointed out small houses for rent near them. The voices reminded her no one would give her a job. Not even the chicken plant would hire her. But mostly she was afraid to be so far away from CB, afraid that without him there was nothing, no hope for anything.

The fear got bigger and bigger, swelling every time Hanna talked about her moving or getting a job. Voices whispered louder and louder, "Better go home. Go home. Get home." Marilyn shook her head constantly, trying to quiet the voices, but both Hanna and the voices kept talking, the voices so loud she couldn't hear anything else.

"Stop! We have to go back tomorrow. I can't stay here any longer." Hanna opened her mouth in response, but Marilyn yelled, "you talk too much!" She had grabbed her lit cigarette from the ashtray and escaped to the bathroom.

Hanna's husband took them early the next morning to the bus station headed for Boaz, the nearest station to home. The ride took all day, arriving at the bus station after it had closed for the evening. Lenny was asleep and she woke him, leading him to the side of the bus where they collected the suitcase and box tied with string. She ignored Lenny's whimpering and the voices, not really knowing what to do next since her parents had no telephone. CB had sisters in Boaz. Should she go to the phone booth and call or try to call the neighbor down the road from the farm? It was getting late to be calling the elderly neighbor.

A man got out of his car and walked toward her. She took Lenny's hand, the other on the suitcase. "Marilyn?"

His face was not familiar in the shadowy parking lot. She did not answer. Lenny held tightly to her hand and stared at the stranger.

"Marilyn? It's Jim. Nadine's husband. CB's cousin. Remember me?"

Vaguely she had remembered him. He ran around with CB and his friends before both of them got married. Jim walked in closer and then glanced around the parking lot.

"You waiting for someone?" Shaking her head no, she explained they just arrived, and she had not had time to contact family. After two offers, she agreed to let Jim take them home. He insisted they get supper first. Marilyn was grateful that Lenny was with her, knowing CB would not have liked it.

In the short drive to the diner, Jim asked her when she had last seen CB.

"It's been awhile." She stared directly ahead looking into the closed shops downtown.

"I can't believe you didn't have a way home. What were you going to do?"

She shrugged; glad the darkness hid the blush she felt on her face. In truth, she had not thought about it, she just wanted to quiet down the voices.

"Honey, you are too pretty to be alone at a bus station late at night. You need a good man to take care of you." He pulled his car into the parking lot. "I'm just glad I happened to be here tonight."

He did not say why he happened to be there, and Marilyn did not ask. He got out and came around the back of the car and opened the door. Lenny refused his hand and grabbed Marilyn's instead. She pulled her hand away and pushed him out. Sandwiches and fries were quickly brought to the table, and Jim mostly made small talk. He mentioned in an offhand way that it was too bad CB divorced her for that old woman. Marilyn did not look up and concentrated on trying to capture the last ketchup covered fry with her fork.

Later at her house, she had thanked him while getting out quickly and nudging Lenny toward the house. Jim insisted on carrying the suitcase and the box for her and set them on the bottom porch step. Lenny bolted and ran inside the door, closing it behind him. Jim stepped back and motioned with his head to the house next door.

"Your daddy live there?"

She nodded, and he followed her eyes to search the back door and windows of the house for signs of movement.

"He as bad as the stories CB used to tell?"

Both her hands grabbed the handle of the suitcase, knocking the box down. Jim picked up the box and took the handle from her.

"I'll carry these inside for you." He pushed past her through the door.

The light from the dangling center bulb was bright and swaying softly. Both girls froze and stood staring at them. Marilyn flipped her hand toward them, frowning. They both quickly disappeared along with Lenny into the other room. She thanked him once more for the ride.

"I see your girls have your looks." Jim smiled at her, and she stared into his brown eyes, annoyed. Neither one looked like her. She pulled on the doorknob, pushed the screen door open, and waited for him to step out. That was the last she saw of him.

A twitch made Marilyn's upper lip jump several times. She stood and walked back inside the house, letting the screen slam. She wondered if Jim told anyone about seeing her and why he said CB was with an older woman. Without turning on a light, she lay across the bed and was aware of how oddly quiet the voices were.

CHAPTER 16

FLYING THE COOP, PART 2

GINNY: 1972

It was almost three-fifteen when she finally found the white building and raced up the sidewalk and into the building, locating the office of Shelby Wright near the back. The vocational counselor assigned to her was a pretty, young blond woman with pink cheeks who smiled as she opened the door. "Ginny? Did you get lost? Many freshman do."

Ginny nodded, being too breathless to speak. It was a small, white room with kitchen cabinets and a sink that was now piled high with papers. A little, metal desk with chairs on either side filled the remaining tiny space. She sat down and tried to wedge her bag between the chair and wall. When it scraped she pulled it back up and quickly fingered the camera inside before trying to fit it underneath the chair, then snapping it back up as she imagined some unseen hand grabbing it from the door behind her even though it was closed.

"We could put your bag up on the counter if you like." The counselor's eyes were very intense, and Ginny nervously hung her head down so her long hair would cover part of her face.

"It's okay. I can just hold it, Miss Wright."

"No need for that… the floor is kinda dirty. Let's put it up on the counter."

Ginny quickly got up and placed the bag near the stack of papers in the sink. "I… it has a camera inside." The words darted out, and she was instantly sorry she said them.

"I prefer to be called Ms. Wright formally, but you can call me Shelby." She paused from the shuffling of files, "Have you been taking lots of pictures of the campus to send back home to your parents?"

Ginny shook her head. Why hadn't she made pictures to send home? Her fingers pinched the box pleat of her navy skirt. When she looked up, Shelby's brown eyes were staring.

"I… I don't take those kinds of pictures."

"Oh?" Her eyes warmed with interest. "So you are more of the artist-type?"

Ginny smiled, but didn't answer, hoping the questions would stop.

"I consider myself a bit of an artist as well… my undergraduate degree," the voice trailed off as she stopped to read something on the paper in front of her. "… but then I decided to come back to get a Master's degree in vocational counseling. I used to make collages."

Ginny wasn't sure if she knew exactly what collages were.

A long thin arm reached across the desk with several papers. "While we are talking about it…" her voice was almost conspiratorial, "look at the top sheet at the bottom. This is part of the results of those tests given to you when you were here for orientation."

Ginny took the papers and scanned quickly to the bottom of the page. Different careers were listed with numbers beside them.

"See, you scored high on aesthetics in the top part and as an artist at the bottom." Shelby's eyes sparkled, and she smiled. No one had ever gotten this excited before over any tests Ginny had taken. Shelby shook her blond locks impatiently and held both hands up for emphasis, "This confirms you are an artist!"

The stacks and stacks of pictures Ginny stored in boxes in the high shelf of the dorm fluttered through her mind, but she couldn't imagine anyone seeing them as art. "I don't think so."

Shelby sat back in her chair and lowered her voice. "All I'm saying is, you have the potential. Of course, it is all up to you." Her head turned sideways, "What were you planning on majoring in?"

"Nursing."

"Nursing?" She searched the sheet again. "That doesn't look promising… your math scores are kinda low for that. Teaching is high, but who really wants to be stuck in a box with children all day?"

Lenny popped into Ginny's mind, sitting at her grandmother's kitchen table working on math. She had tried to help Lenny with his homework, but yelled at him for not trying hard enough to get the right answers. "I don't want to teach." A dull ache started in her throat. She wondered what Lenny would be doing now.

"You okay?"

Ginny did not answer. Instead she read the scores on the print out sheet again.

"Has everything been okay since you got here? You seem a little anxious."

Ginny looked up at Shelby's head, nodding while waiting. "Yes."

"Are you having problems with depression?"

Marilyn's face came to her: dark circles and dull eyes, lying in bed for days without ever going to sleep and refusing to eat for days at a time. "No. No, I don't have a problem with depression."

Shelby's voice became softer. "We all get a little depressed at times, and there have been a lot of changes in your life recently, and... well, artist-types tend to have more than their share of melancholy."

Was melancholy worse than depression? It sounded worse.

"And as a woman artist, you will have to struggle even harder than men. Look at history. You will have to fight get the attention you deserve for your work." Shelby's eyes narrowed, one hand lightly tapping the desk. "There is therapy available through the Psych department that can help, and it's free."

"I'm not crazy." Ginny's eyes found her bag on the sink.

"No Ginny, not crazy." Shelby came to the edge of her seat. Her eyes were too bright, and Ginny looked behind her head at an old note taped to the cabinet warning staff to clean up behind themselves because their mother didn't work here. "Therapists can do very little for crazy people. It's too little too late. It's like a continuum. Therapy provides intervention for when you are having problems, before you get really bad. You know like doctors can't do much for dead people, but they can do a lot for people who are sick and might die if they didn't get help. Do you understand my analogy? Does it make sense?"

Ginny nodded, sure that Shelby would be crushed if she didn't understand.

"Good. You need to find ways to take care of yourself."

A smile and half nod got Shelby back to the papers and the test scores. Ginny knew she wasn't depressed like her mother. Was her mother less crazy in the beginning when she was younger? Maybe Marilyn didn't seem all that crazy back then. Maybe Ginny would be just as crazy in a few years.

"Ginny? You still with me? Let me finish going over these last percentiles with you, and I'll answer your questions. The one I particularly want you to see is the last one on page four. We compared you to former students that had your grades in high school and your ACT scores. They were successful in completing their degree eighty-three percent of the time."

Ginny nodded, wondering what happened to the ones who weren't successful. Did they go back home and work in the chicken factory? A slight chill started in her spine. Going back would be worse than if she had never left at all. She felt a flutter in her stomach. Did Marilyn's depression get worse when she went back? Ginny tried to remember the days before they moved back with her grandparents… it was like collecting pieces of scattered photographs.

"Ginny? Any questions?"

Ginny looked into Shelby's eyes for an instant. She wanted to ask if Marilyn was one of those people too crazy to be helped by counseling.

"What Ginny? You can talk to me about anything."

Ginny looked away and shook her head wondering if the throbbing pain in her neck and chest meant she was having a heart attack. Shelby reached across the desk, her hand patted Ginny's for a moment.

"Tell me what is upsetting you."

She searched her mind. She could not talk about Marilyn. She opened her mouth, and other words slipped out before she could think. "A man at the bus station. A man at the bus station tried…" A lump in her throat would not go down.

"What? Did he try to rape you?" Shelby's voice got lower.

Ginny shook her head, and two large fat tears escaped her eyes.

"He tried to follow you?"

Ginny nodded, then slumped forward and squeezed her eyes shut, hoping to stop the tears. "Kind of… he kept pushing me to give him my hotel room number and to let him come over. I was so scared he would, and I wouldn't be able to stop him."

"Did you tell him to get lost? Or threaten to call the police?"

"No. Oh no." Ginny hands shook, and her voice got squeaky. "I tried to tell him no, but I couldn't figure things out. I didn't do anything. I swear I didn't."

She looked up and saw the confusion on Shelby's face. "Why didn't you just no and leave?"

Why didn't she just say no? It never occurred to her.

"I did leave." But she was still afraid all night. Right now it seemed silly, but she couldn't say no. She could not explain this to Shelby and why no one at home could know what happened.

"Ginny, were you frightened because you don't like men… you know, bothering you?"

Ginny nodded, relieved.

"There are other women who feel the same way. Don't worry, it will be okay."

Were there other women who came from a family like hers? She twisted a strand of hair around and around her finger and thought about Lizzy, who now had a husband.

"Ginny, a group of women artists meet in town about once a month, usually on campus, but sometimes in people's homes or a bar. Most of them are older. Some are students. I think it would be good for you to come to one of their events so you can connect with other women artists. If you want to come, I'll introduce you around."

Shelby wrote down the directions to the next gathering and said their counseling session time was up. Haziness hung in her mind, but Ginny stood and stuffed test scores in the large envelope along with Shelby's notes. She was sure she had talked too much, for too long. While taking her bag from the counter, she wondered why papers were stacked in a sink. She resisted the urge to turn on the faucet and wash away the stack of scores and notes, knowing that later there would be written notes about her stacked in the sink as well.

*　*　*

At the last minute she wore the smock that Grandmother made for her. Pretty with tiny flowers and long enough to cover up the only jeans she owned. The legs were too skinny. Not like the elephant-leg jeans everyone else wore. She put the telephone number inside her bag and placed her hand around the camera for a second. She was nervous.

The party was at a place on the edge of campus. The walk would not be too bad, and it was still plenty light outside. She planned to arrive a few minutes after the time so she wouldn't get there before Shelby.

The bar was dark with lots of smoke just as she imagined while standing outside, hoping Shelby would see her through the glass and come out to meet her. When no one came out to meet her, she stood and watched different young women go in and casually followed one inside who had smiled at her. Candles stuck in wine bottles flickered on tables, and it took a for her eyes to adjust and to be able to see groups of women and a few men sitting in scattered groups, most holding plastic cups while talking and laughing. To her left was a long table with papers and cards. A tall, heavy woman stood from her seat behind it and smiled. Her jeans looked more like a skirt, and her halter top was made from bandanas.

"Ginny?"

Ginny nodded and tried to keep her eyes from looking at the woman's breasts spilling out from the sides and the front of her top.

"I'm Jan. Shelby may not make it tonight, but she told me to look out for you and to introduce you to some of the other women."

Jan handed her some papers and started walking before Ginny could answer or look at what she handed her. She followed close behind her, stuffing the papers in her purse. They stopped near a large group near the back where one woman was doing most of the talking.

"Everyone, this is Ginny. She's a photographer. She's a freshman…" Jan hesitated, "and Shelby said we need to make sure she feels welcome tonight." Jan flashed a smile in her direction and walked away.

There were no chairs left at the table, and Ginny wondered if she should go sit somewhere else or just stand there and wait. She took a deep breath and caught someone's left over cigarette smoke and felt comforted.

"What's in your pictures?"

The eyes never looked directly at her, but Ginny was sure it was the short, sandy-haired woman with the beer can tipped toward her face who asked the question. As the beer can lowered, Ginny saw the woman's eyes dart from the table to her and back several times.

"Mothers and children mostly." She answered slowly… just as she rehearsed, expecting that Shelby would ask but didn't expect to explain to anyone else.

The woman's nose crinkled and she leaned her chair back on two legs. "You have kids?"

Ginny shook her head and read the name embroidered on the woman's green shirt. "Gerrie."

"Why don't you pull up a chair Ginny?" The dark haired woman near Gerrie smiled while smoothing a long lock of hair behind her ear. "I'm Hazel."

A waitress came up and took her order for a Coke, and Ginny scanned nearby tables for a chair. Two older women nodded when she asked if it was okay to take one from their table. "Sure, honey." Kind eyes smiled up to her, and for a moment, she thought about sitting with them. A flutter of chairs scraped the floor as women moved over to make room for Ginny directly in front of Gerrie.

"Damn, I could use another cigarette. You got one?" Gerrie looked at Hazel, who shook her head. "Damn." She looked at Ginny again. "So, what's with the mothers?"

Ginny shrugged, not sure how to answer.

"Well, do you want to be a mother, or you just looking for one?" Gerrie turned and said something low to Hazel then laughed before turning and blinking her eyes several times at Ginny. Hazel looked at her too, waiting for an answer.

Ginny did a half nod. Didn't everyone want children eventually?

"You have a boyfriend? Or are you looking for a husband to have babies with?"

Ginny didn't know whether to say no or yes. "I want a husband and children one day. Just not now."

Gerrie's chair came forward with a thump and she stood and turned toward the front. "Jan! What the hell?"

"Gerrie, stop being so rude." Hazel's voice was loud then went back soft as she pulled on Gerrie's arm and whispered something to her.

"She likes weenies for God's sake. I don't have time for talking to no weenie girl."

Ginny head went back. Did she call her a weenie girl? No one had ever called her a weenie.

"Gerrie. Stop yelling. Maybe you should ease up on the beer." Hazel's voice was sharper than before, and Gerrie sat down and found Hazel's hand. Hazel pulled away and rolled her eyes at Ginny. "Ignore her. She's had way too much to drink."

Ginny's fingers found her camera and despite the fluttering in her chest, she wondered if she could snap a picture of Gerrie and Hazel before they noticed.

Hazel leaned forward. "Have you shown any of your work?"

Gerrie stood and steadied herself using the back of Hazel's chair, then walked toward Jan's table.

Ginny shook her head and let go of the camera. "Are you an artist?"

Hazel had already turned around to find Gerrie. "That's… what it's all about. Getting your work out there…"

Ginny was sure Hazel was still talking but she couldn't hear her. Jan was walking back toward them and sat down in Gerrie's chair and leaned in toward Ginny. "Gosh honey, sorry about that… Shelby thought that… well you know, that you liked women, and it might be nice for you to meet some… women."

Ginny studied Jan's face, noticing the sprinkle of freckles beneath the heavy makeup. She glanced back at Hazel. "I do like women."

A woman next to Hazel threw peanut shells up, and they fell to the table. "Good God."

Jan patted Ginny on the hand. "Come. Let me introduce you to some other women who are new tonight." She stood, and Ginny got her bag and Coke and followed behind her, feeling like something had gone terribly wrong at the table or maybe she was just wrong.

Jan stopped suddenly and turned to her and whispered. "Look honey, I like women too, but I prefer men. You know what I mean?" Ginny nodded, not wanting to appear dumb. She motioned to a table near the front with several young women. "Just don't take men seriously honey, and you will be okay. I like to think of men as life support for dicks, nothing more. You know what I mean? Just don't take them seriously, and they won't mess up your life or your art." Her voice got louder, and she pulled out a chair for Ginny. "Ginny is new tonight, too." With that announcement she walked away. Ginny sat in the chair, nodding at the girls who barely looked up then quickly looked back at the crowd. She did mess up. Jan had put her at the table for scared girls who sip quietly from their paper cups until they can escape and return.

What did it matter? A few days ago she didn't even think of herself as an artist. But it did matter. For these few days she had begun to feel like there was a reason for her need to take pictures.

She stood up and took her Coke and her bag and walked into the crowd and over to the wall to an empty table and sat down. Her hand instinctively slipped inside her purse and touched the camera before she leaned back in the chair.

CHAPTER 17

THE DEAD BOY

MARILYN, 1973

It was late Christmas Eve, and Marilyn was beginning to drift off to sleep when a car pulled up in the driveway. Sheila and her husband, Mike, were coming with Gilbert and Charleen and bags full of Santa presents for the kids to open in the morning. She quickly got up from bed and plugged up the colored lights on the small aluminum tree on the table before opening the door, just in time to take the sleeping Gilbert from his father.

"Put some coal on the fire." She whispered to Lenny.

Lenny stood as the door opened again, cold air blowing in along with Sheila holding the sleeping Charleen. He hurried to the potbellied stove and stoked up the fire, stepping aside to let Sheila pass by before adding coal.

Sheila leaned over Marilyn's bed to place Charleen in the center beside Gilbert. Marilyn quickly pulled the covers up around them as Mike came in with big plastic bags and a suitcase. He shivered, dropping the bags in the floor and getting close to the heater, "The wind is really blowing out there."

Earlier, Lenny had opened up the old couch, and Marilyn had made it up with sheets and several quilts and blankets. Sheila sat on it now, lying back with a sigh and closing her tired eyes. "So who all is here? There are cars in the driveway I don't recognize." Before Marilyn or Lenny could respond, she sat up, "Did Ginny get here?"

Marilyn felt a surge of anger at the mention of Ginny's name and saw Lenny glance at her before nodding to Sheila. "She got here the day before yesterday. Caught a ride with that girl from Sardis. She's staying at Grandmother's..." He nodded his head again toward the little bedroom before moving a straight chair closer to Mike, who had begun pulling out pieces of a little bike.

The bed in the girl's room had been good enough for Ginny to sleep on for years, but now that she was in college, it wasn't good enough. Marilyn opened her mouth to say so and then closed it, willing herself to stay calm while she sat down on the edge of her bed, lightly stroking Charleen's fat baby's cheek with the backs of her fingers.

Lenny continued, "All three of the Florida aunts are here and Robert. Everyone else is coming in tomorrow morning."

*　*　*

After two shifts of people eating Christmas dinner, the women sat down last. Her mother and the other women had cooked and cleaned since early morning and most of them looked exhausted. All the women but her. She held tight to Charleen, carrying her around to find little pretties on the tree and watching Gilbert play with the other children and sneaking peeks at gifts under the tree.

Marilyn hugged Charleen closer, feeding her little bites of mac and cheese from her plate. She waved Sheila away when she came to take her, only Charleen began to cry for her mother when she saw her, then reached out when Ginny showed her a plastic red cup. But Marilyn settled her back down and took the cup away, filling her mouth with more mac and cheese and giving her a spoon to hold. She only let her go when it was time for them to leave. As soon as she handed the baby to Sheila, she picked up Gilbert and kissed his cheek.

"Momma loves you."

Sheila laughed, "Yes, I do and so does his grandmother."

The comment stung. Shaking her head slightly, she reminded herself it was true. Gilbert was not her son.

*　*　*

It was Ginny's last night home, and Marilyn sat at the kitchen table drinking coffee, watching her mother and Ginny pour hot sorghum syrup over a large pan of popcorn. Lenny was shelling parched peanuts for the mixture, but managing to eat as many as he dropped in the pan.

"I think you all are just making a mess. You need Karo syrup to make popcorn balls. That stuff is too strong." Marilyn stood, leaving the cup on the corner of the table.

It was already dark when she walked outside to go to her house, and she wondered if Lenny was still planning on going to the party he had told her about yesterday. Just when she closed her door, one of Lenny's friends pulled up in the driveway in a car that sounded like it didn't have a muffler.

Lenny ran to the car with only a short-sleeved shirt on and spoke through the window to his friend. He rubbed his arms while talking, and Marilyn expected him to come home to change, but instead he ran back to his grandmother's. Marilyn turned away from the window but heard the car back out of the driveway and the muffler fade as it went back down the road.

* * *

"Oh goodness, just think what might have happened if Ginny had not been here?"

Her mother's voice was a little more than a whisper but Marilyn wanted to yell at her to hush, to let her think. She wanted to say that even if Ginny hadn't been here, it would have turned out okay but as she thought it, the voices wouldn't let her believe it.

As it was, Lenny decided not to go to a party because it was Ginny's last night at home. They had watched some old western movie and drank hot chocolate. (Marilyn noticed at breakfast the next morning that the popcorn and sorghum mess was still in the tub and no one ate it.) They took Ginny to the bus station in the afternoon and by that night, the news reported that eight students never made it home from the party, held in some warehouse near Carter, a town at the base of Sand Mountain.

Search teams had already spread out near the party site while students who attended the party were interviewed by police. Reporters said there were students reporting the use of mushrooms, drugs, and alcohol use outside the party, and about how five boys and three girls squeezed together to ride in the car that disappeared, that some were even in the trunk. Three of the guys were on the football team with Lenny last year; one was a friend he hung out with often.

Marilyn was shocked by the young girls leaving with the boys and wondered if they had just decided to ride to Birmingham or go somewhere else for fun instead of going home. She asked Lenny about the girls, but he didn't answer, keeping his eyes glued to his grandmother's large console TV until she left and went home.

Later, a friend came by and Lenny sat in his car in the driveway. Lenny got out and came inside and put clean underwear in the pocket of some clean jeans and folded a t-shirt and draped them across his arm.

"I'm going to go help with the search. I need to get out and do something. I'll be back tomorrow. Don't want him to have to drive back here again so late."

With that comment he left. It was only after the car was driving away did Marilyn realize he had not asked to go, just told her he was going. She held a fist in the center of her chest, sure that her mother's squash casserole was giving her indigestion.

Later during dinner her mother had barely sat down at the table when she looked at Marilyn, "Lenny had some clothes with him. Is he spending the night with that boy?"

Her mother continued without waiting for an answer. "Do you know the name of that boy? Lenny's friend? Or even where he lives?"

Marilyn shook her head. The pimple-faced, skinny boy came by often but always stayed in the car or on the porch waiting for Lenny.

"I'm not sure you should have let Lenny go out driving with a boy who probably uses drugs like his friends." Pursing her lips, her mother picked up a glass of buttermilk but then set it down without taking a sip. "I certainly hope Lenny's not involved in that stuff."

Burning leaped up in her stomach and continued to her throat. Voices were talking all day, telling her that she let Ginny go. That she let him go. That everyone was going. She gulped milk to cool the acid in her throat, and then held her lips firmly together. She got up and went back to her house without eating dinner.

*　*　*

Mid-day the next morning, her mother was talking and banging at her front door before Marilyn could get it open. "Marilyn, the newsman on the radio came on in the middle of gospel music hour to say the students had been found. Three are dead and the others are seriously hurt. Their car came clean off the winding mountain highway, clipping the tops of trees and falling into the canyon. The radio said it was near the scenic view picnic table area. The driver is one of the dead, and no one knows if he fell asleep or if he got distracted by friends in the car."

Marilyn bent forward, her empty stomach too full, the acid jumping up to her throat again and her mind racing, wondering where Lenny was and if he had heard the news. She held tight to the doorknob, then slowly stood up straight, swallowing over and over trying not to throw up.

"Oh Marilyn, if Lenny had been with them…" Her mother whispered, taking her glasses off and wiping the lens with her apron.

"He would never get in a car with kids using drugs." Marilyn's words were loud, but she knew since he didn't have a car, he would have had to ride back with whoever he came with, even if they were using drugs. He couldn't call home since they didn't have a telephone—not that he would ever call his grandfather. Time and time again she used to ride with CB when he was drinking, even putting the children in the car with him when he was so drunk he could barely walk.

"Maybe you're right, Marilyn."

Her mother's voice startled her and she looked at her sharply, wondering what she was right about.

"Those children were penned up with their dead friends for two days… they might not ever be right again."

"I need to call Lenny."

"You wouldn't know who to call, Marilyn." Her mother reached out and patted the air above her hand, "I'm sure Lenny is okay."

"No. There should be a phone." With that Marilyn stepped back and closed the door.

*   *   *

It was early morning and still dark outside. Lenny had not come home, leaving her to nap for short periods, worrying about where he might be. Surely he didn't come home because he just wanted to be with friends after hearing about the accident. The accident. The horrible accident. She thought again about what her mother had said about being penned up in the car with dead friends. She imagined herself at the party and then getting into the backseat of the car, sitting in her boyfriend's lap with his arm circling her back, fingers pressed into her breast underneath her arm. It felt good. He loved her, she could feel it, feel it in his arm holding her close and protecting her. She allowed her head to rest against his, her heart happy and full when someone began yelling and she realized the car was airborne, and then flipping, banging into trees with limbs that came crashing through the windows. Then they landed—a jumble of bodies, glass, and pieces of the car that came apart. Her breathing became shallow, and she screamed in the darkness, unsure if it was her boy or another, whose dead body pinned her against the broken window and door, now flat against the ground. Was her boy dead or did his dead body threaten to suffocate and kill her now? She heard others crying and screaming, and the smell of vomit and pee began to overwhelm her.

The front door jerked open and she jumped, relieved to see Lenny standing at the door and not some dead boy.

"Mother, were you screaming?"

Rushing toward him, she stopped suddenly, "Which boy was it that died? Tell me straight up, was it my boy?"

"Mother?" He stood still, looking at her, letting cold air come in around him. "You've never met the boys that died, Mother."

"Don't. Don't say that. I've met them all." She whirled around, allowing one arm to indicate all of them in the wreck, but there was no one there. "It was your dead boy." The voices wouldn't listen to Lenny.

"You need a cigarette, Mother? Where are they? Let's sit down."

She looked at him, a big boy, calm. CB never seemed calm. Lenny was a good boy, not like the dead boy. Not like CB. He deserved better… better than the dead boy. Better than this place. Her arm swept around and knocked things off the table, and she heard them hit the floor.

"Mother, calm down. Everything is okay." Lenny began walking towards her, shoving the door shut at the same time.

"You are going to go get your grandfather's truck." That was it, she told the voices, her breathing lighter. "It's yours now." She said it loud to drown out the voices that disagreed and kept saying that Lenny was riding with the dead boy.

"What?"

"I'm giving you your grandfather's truck. You don't have to ride with the dead boy." Both hands pressed against Lenny's chest, and he flinched. "I've earned it! I've worked in the fields all these years, and I am taking the truck and giving it to you."

"Mother, let's turn on the light. Where are your cigarettes?" Lenny moved to the center of the room, stepping on something that crunched. She heard the clicking of the metal chain, and then the glare from the bare bulb made her shield her eyes with one arm. He took a cigarette from the pack on the nightstand.

'He's riding with the dead boy.' The voice whispered, and Marilyn wondered if they saw Lenny in the truck would they stop saying it. "He always leaves the key in it. You can go wherever you want. Tonight. Now. You hear me?" She took the cigarette from Lenny's hands and watched him sit in the couch.

"Mother, Grandfather will have a fit if we get his truck."

"You think I care about what that old man thinks?" She dropped the burning cigarette into the ashtray and grabbed a sweater off the couch. "We are going to go get it now." She spat the words while picking up her purse from the dresser and walking to the door.

"Mother, I'm too young to get a driver's license. Grandfather will have me put in jail."

She slowly turned around, thinking about Lenny in jail. Lenny took the cigarette from the ashtray and held it out to her.

"How old was the dead boy?" Her two fingers circled the cigarette and brought it to her lips.

Lenny sighed, "One was sixteen, and one was seventeen."

Smoke filled her lungs. There were pieces of Gilbert's toy on the floor that she had knocked off and Lenny had stepped on. Picking up the pieces, she recognized half of a small clown face, empty on the inside, like half of a plastic egg. The other half had been crushed into pieces. After a moment she flicked ashes inside the half face and took another drag on the cigarette.

CHAPTER 18

GET THE PICTURE

GINNY, 1976

It was too hot, even in the air-conditioned classroom. For a moment the room was dark, then a flash as a slide dropped into the projector and revealed pale legs hanging from a bed with a pair of silky red panties draped around the ankles. A chorus of whistles came from the men in the room, and Ginny felt her cheeks burn with embarrassment.

"What color do you feel when you look at this picture?" The instructor, Lance as he asked them to call him, grinned at Kris, the tiny blond girl who shot the photo.

"Red!" A chorus of voices shouted out the color.

"Excellent, Kris. No doubt about it, everyone here is seeing red." Lance held up a thumb and continued to look at Kris with moony eyes, as all the girls called them. "Composition is great, particularly the viewpoint of the camera. You definitely have our interest, and we are all searching for clues as to what will happen next."

He jotted notes in his book near the slide projector table, and the slight quivering of Ginny's stomach got worse as she wondered if the next slide would be hers. It had taken an extra week for her to get up enough nerve to turn in a slide for this assignment. She actually liked the photography in advertising class. Each assignment was graded twice: once for the idea and set up and a second grade for the technical work of the finished photo due one week later. She exhaled slowly and tried to relax her shoulders. He had been lenient, telling them they could re-do it once. It was okay.

A new slide popped onto the wall showing a close up of a man mooning a crowd of people with his butt cheeks painted orange and blue. Lance laughed and then took notes while the chatter from the class got louder. "Tell me why Jim's picture doesn't work for this assignment."

The room got quiet, and the older female graduate student with long red hair spoke. "It's a documentary rather than a photo Jim set up and controlled."

Lance stopped at the woman's desk and stared at her. "And?"

"And… it has two colors not one?"

Lance looked back at Jim, "I'm assuming that you didn't get this guy to pose while you set up the lighting?"

Jim shook his head, still ginning.

Lance bent down toward his book. "Good photo but not for this assignment. You have one week to retake it, and I would advise that you do." He glanced up then looked around the room, "Remember, make your viewers see and feel a color."

A quick click and Ginny's slide was on the screen, red lighting jumping into the room before the eyes could focus on pieces of glass still in the air from a smashed picture frame on a wood floor. The eight-by-ten photograph was a black and white shot of her mother as a young woman in a pose that always made Ginny think she looked like Rita Hayworth.

Panic rose in her throat. It was all wrong. They could probably tell that the shards of glass in the air wasn't the really from the picture, and the red lighting was too harsh.

The class was quiet as Lance stared at the picture. "Whose picture is this?"

Ginny held her arm up until he began walking closer to her.

"Hmmmm. Class, what do you think?"

There wasn't enough air, and Ginny swallowed several times. She continued to look at her picture projected on the wall, avoiding any glances from moony eyes or anyone else.

Again, the older woman with the long, red hair spoke up. "The broken glass suggests something emotional is broken. But is it an accident or anger?"

Lance nodded his head, moved in closer to the redhead, placing one hand on her desk and squatting while keeping his eyes on the photo. "Is the red overall lighting saying anything to you?" After looking back to her for a few seconds, he stood, "Anyone?"

"It makes me see red, and I feel like I smashed the picture in anger." Kris looked over to Ginny, "How many times did you take the picture to get the glass pieces in the air in the right places like that?"

"Hold on. Let's stay with viewer thoughts. We can talk about techniques later." Lance walked to the wall and looked closer at the image. "Any more thoughts? What does the photograph tell us?"

The room was quiet.

"Come on people. What about the photograph?"

"It could have been an old man angry at his wife, and he smashed her picture… but it looks like an old picture."

Lanced ignored the comment, turned and walked back to the slide projector. "Do you all agree that you see and feel red, and it is anger?"

It was actually an accident. Ginny wanted to say the picture was knocked off the table when she threw jeans at the chair. Sharp tiny pieces of glass went all over the floor, and it came to her to use it to stage the photograph for the assignment.

Lance wrote a few notes in his notebook before looking up again at Ginny, not waiting for any more comments. "I assume you used red gels to cover the lights to get the red lighting?" She nodded. "Tell us about shooting the pieces of glass."

"The pieces of glass are actually thin pieces of ice."

He looked closer. "Did you try glass? Would glass have been more reflective of light?"

Ginny shrugged. She didn't have lots of glass to keep breaking over and over… but it didn't matter, Lance went back to writing without waiting for an answer. She wasn't sure if he liked it, but at least he didn't tell her to re-shoot it.

The next picture was a tiny, sleeping baby dressed completely in blue with what looked like pieces of dark blue metal in the background. She guessed blue for baby boy. Lance did not discuss it, but nodded at a guy near him. "Would a shot of the baby with a different expression help this photo?" He wrote notes in his book and looked back up, "Try that. Try taking pictures with other expressions." Two guys near her quietly got up and left through the open back door. Lance clicked on another slide. Class was running over time. She pulled her bag from under the desk and stood in the few seconds of darkness before the next slide. She heard other students following behind her.

"Cool photo." The words were a whisper behind her. Ginny caught the quick smile then the long, blond hair as Kris walked pass her and then turned as she got out the door to grab the hand of a long-haired hippie close behind her. He looked back at Ginny, nodding his head while allowing Kris to lead him by the hand, starring until Ginny looked away.

A feeling of satisfaction settled in but she cautioned herself not to think too much of it. Even though Kris was one of the best photography students there, Lance may not have liked it.

Squinting at the two figures walking ahead, she wondered if the hippie guy was taking the class? He didn't sit with her, and his photographs had never came up. Maybe he just stepped in the door when the photos were being shown while waiting for Kris. Ginny liked the way he stared at her. Immediately she felt guilty when she remembered he was holding hands with Kris.

The summer sun was too bright and hot. Why did she decide to go to summer school? Immediately her mind thought of summer with her mother and then guilt when she thought of Lenny alone with her. She swiped at the sweat on her face with her arm, thoughts of air conditioning and a cold Coke with a hotdog propelled her to walk faster up the grassy hill and still faster when she got to the sidewalk that led up to the small business district that catered to students.

A light turned red and she walked up behind three sweaty shirtless male students and two men in suits. The students were whispering about a crying woman, and Ginny moved slightly to the side into the grass to see her. At first, all she could see was long, fizzy hair, a white shirt, and jeans. The light changed, and the girl glanced back at them; she was maybe fifteen years old. Tears were streaming down her cheeks. She began to walk, pushing an empty baby stroller.

The camera came out while Ginny walked further to the right so that she could snap a profile from the side. She snapped a second shot before she thought about whether the girl might get upset with her for taking her picture. On the other side of the street, the young woman stopped for a few seconds staring at Ginny but did not stop crying or attempt to wipe away the tears. Ginny shot her picture again, then watched her turn and begin to walk up 12th Street.

Ginny hesitated then began to slowly follow her, wondering if the girl had broken up with a boyfriend. The girl began to walk faster, looking back occasionally.

Was she scaring her? Ginny slowed down, stopping at a tiny park with a picnic table. Bird droppings were on the bench, and Ginny tried to find a clean spot to sit. She opened her notebook while trying to catch glimpses of the girl's dark hair and white shirt. Once she couldn't see her anymore, Ginny quickly attached the telephoto lens to the camera and walked into the wooded area that separated the park from the back-yards of a row of houses. Looking through the lens, she searched between houses. She had disappeared. The lens continued to search for the girl in the doorways and windows of the small houses. Maybe she walked to the next block or was in one of the houses watching her. A slight shaking in her hands was making it difficult to hold the camera steady while she aimed it at the windows of houses and looked for any movement. There was no sound, not even much of a movement, but the lens caught something at the small window on the second floor of the house to the right. Was it an attic? She couldn't decide. The house had unfinished additions jutting out in the back and side.

After searching twice, she sighed and lowered the camera. Maybe it was the movement of the lace curtains or the shadows projected on the wall from the sun. Still, she was drawn to the window and walked further into the woods. She wondered if a second window would be on the side and moved to the left, trying to look without getting too close. There were no other windows, and she was now at the edge of the neighbor's yard.

Mosquito bites on her ankle prompted her to give up. She put the cap back on the lens and let the camera slide down to her side while holding the strap. One last look at the window made her feel naked, as if someone was watching. She backed up while pulling the camera up. At first the lacy shadow in the window reminded her of a little skull, then she sucked in her breath. It wasn't a shadow. Then there was nothing between the lace panels. The lens did not find the skull. Did she imagine it?

Several steps forward and she was out of the woods, cutting through a corner of a backyard, aware of some dog excitedly barking from inside the house. Once behind the house, she stopped and took shots of the window. Was it to prove to herself nothing was there? What was she doing running through these yards? This is crazy. She turned, thinking of whether to get to the road or go walk through the woods again.

Then she saw her. The young woman stood at the side of the house holding an emaciated baby in her arms. There were no sounds, and one thin arm reached up erratically, the skin tight around the bone. The child only wore a diaper, and the stomach was swollen.

For a few seconds, Ginny stared at the baby then looked to the young woman's face, her eyes unreadable, bottomless now that she wasn't crying. Ginny was unable to speak or look away from her or the child. Finally, her fingers pulled the camera up and snapped picture after picture, even a close up of the young woman's face, flinching when her eyes connected to Ginny briefly before becoming blank again. The young girl nor the child changed expressions.

"My God." The pounding of Ginny's heart grew stronger. This was why she was crying, pushing the stroller. This baby was dying. The camera dropped from her hand, the strap tightening where it was wrapped around her arm.

"I'm so sorry for your baby." She glanced around for signs of neighbors at home. Softly, the girl turned and walked around to the front of the house.

Ginny followed her, circling the corner, surprised by the fat, red flowers peeping from a little, white fence circling the porch. Taking up her camera, Ginny snapped a picture of the woman standing at the door, hesitating. Then she was gone. A heavy door slammed into place.

"Wait." Ginny felt wrong, unreasonable for expecting an explanation from the girl with the empty, dark eyes. A slight breeze made the sweat on her neck feel cold and the red flowers dance. One hand hurt where she had tightly wrapped the camera strap. Prickly heat began moving across her chest, and she turned around and around, lost as to what to do or where to go. There was no one. She stopped turning.

The baby was dying. The girl was upset watching the baby die.

Suddenly Ginny was running across the street, toward the next yard and past the empty park. She didn't want to see this, didn't want to see a baby die. Why did she follow this woman?

Near the intersection she saw students passing; none looked her way. She stopped to look back and catch her breath. While walking to the dorm, she held the camera away from her body. She imagined herself ripping out the film to expose it. She did not want to see this again.

CHAPTER 19

FLYING SOLO

Marilyn, 1976

The slightly sputtering sound of the old '62 Buick Special woke her up. It was hard to tell what time it was, but sunlight was scarce outside the window. The creak and slam of the car door prompted her to throw back the covers and sit up.

The dress she wore was wrinkled, but it reassured her that she was waking from a nap and that Lenny had not been out all night. It didn't particularly bother her for him to be out, especially since her father and mother would get all crazy about it. But she didn't like to think about what he could be doing all night. He was, after all, a boy.

Lenny came through the door as her eyes rested on a stick of ashes that used to be a cigarette. "Shit." She brushed the ashes from a burned out groove on the couch. A waste, a whole cigarette burned, and she only had a few left. How many days did she have before the check would come?

Her eyes quickly moved up and down Lenny's clothes for any sign of where he had been. He did not look at her. The flutter in her stomach reminded her again she had no cigarettes.

"What day of the month is it?" She looked up to Lenny seconds before he fell into his bed with the old rusting bed springs clattering in protest.

"The twenty-seventh, I think."

It was true, days before the check would come. "Where you been?"

"Ricky's." Lenny stayed out often since CB gave him the old car a few months back. Always saying he was at one of his friend's houses, mostly Ricky's. She wondered if it was so.

"What you going to bed for?" She didn't really expect an answer, but she wanted to hear him talk, hear his voice.

"Cat Fur." The muffled voice was barely audible.

"I didn't say 'fur.' I said 'for.' Sit up!" She felt her brows knit together as she took out another cigarette and lit it. Even though he was picking at her, she couldn't stand silence right now.

Lenny rolled over creating another chorus of squawking from the springs, but did not sit up. The smoke escaped through her nose while she tried to keep her mouth shut and wait for him to speak.

She flicked her finger against the cigarette, dropping ashes on the floor, while her eyes flashed back to Lenny's closed ones. Impatiently she tapped the cigarette again while continuing to stare at him, then sucked at the cigarette but the familiar draw of air did not come. The burning tip was missing. There was no sign of it on the floor, and she rubbed her hands over the bed and then down her dress, at once feeling it burn both the edge of her smallest finger and her leg.

"Shit. Damn." She stood and the tip fell to the floor, only a slight glow now.

"Watch the language." Lenny's voice was mimicking her, and it made her both angry and relieved.

A hole had burned into the dress and she poked a fingernail through it while walking to the sink, carefully setting the left over butt on the table. A wet washcloth was in the basin, and she pressed it against her finger then lifted her skirt to press the dripping cloth against the burn on her leg. She licked the paper edge of the cigarette, then rubbed leftover bits of tobacco from her tongue onto her lips, then softly spit them into the air.

Lenny raised his head for a moment, then dropped it back into the pillow. "What are you spitting at? The cat?"

A giggle escaped her throat despite her irritation. She spit again toward him then set the cigarette on the table to dry.

*　*　*

The door opened, and she blinked at the bright light surrounding Lenny's tall, thick body as he walked in and slowly sat on the couch. She stared at him, and then sat expectantly on the edge of her bed. Both hands smoothed down her dress, stopping inside her knees, which she pressed against them.

He had told her yesterday that he was leaving to spend the summer working for CB in Birmingham. She had managed to say nothing even though she wanted to scream no. When CB came and took Lenny to visit during Spring break she had worried that he wouldn't bring him back. But she told herself that Lenny was practically grown. She had to let him go to CB. Lenny drove back in his own little car.

Lenny reminded her several times that Birmingham was only a couple of hours away and that he needed to make some money for his senior year. But she knew he would not come back. He was like CB. He would leave her for good. She sat and watched him pack an old suitcase and a box, then put them in the car. During the night, she kept recounting what he put in the box. Why had he taken an old worn out billfold from Ginny? In her dreams, she had chased Lenny and tried to take something he held in his hands high above his head. Then CB sneaked inside the house and whispered to Lenny what to pack. It was still dark when she opened her eyes and got out of bed, pacing the floor and thinking about the box. Tiptoeing into the early morning light, she went to look, to see what he had taken. After circling the car several times with the key in her fingers, she felt tears on her face and had quickly came back inside and to her bed.

"I'll be back to visit in a couple of weeks." The voice was soft and unlike Lenny. She followed his eyes as he looked around the room and wondered why he would come back, but was grateful that he said he would. Questions burned in her throat. Was CB living with a woman? Did he live in a house? But she sucked in her lips and bit them together. Pain in her chest made it difficult to breathe. She just lit the last cigarette when he stood to leave.

With a throat full of smoke, she followed him out and stood on the cement block porch and watched as he rummaged in a black case for a music tape to play. When her mother came out too and stood watching him from her porch, Marilyn gritted her teeth and stepped back inside, not wanting to hear her talk or even let her think she was going to be heard. The car started up and quickly backed out of the driveway. At first it was quiet, then she heard a bird chirp outside her door.

*　*　*

The ticking of the clock was loud, and she was sure she heard something at the door more than once. It was nothing. She refused to give in to being afraid and continued to lie in the bed. If someone came in the front, then she would just run out the back door.

A thud against the door made her sit up. Then it sounded like someone was trying to cut the screen in the door. Had she locked it? Quietly pulling the sheet around her, she stood and softly walked to the back door and hesitated. Silence. Maybe she scared away whoever it was. Was she dreaming?

The ripping sound began again, faster and louder. Dropping the sheet, she reached for Lenny's BB gun and raced to the front door, smacking the gun against things to make noise, to scare off whoever was there. One hand jerked open the door and slammed it back against the dresser. Darkness. The screen door uncut. Finally, her eyes adjusted to the slight movement of the hairy stomach of Ginny's cat, Cinnamon, that was near the top of the screen door and whose claws popped the screen with each movement. A pitiful cry filled the air. A pounding heart kept Marilyn still for a moment. She didn't much care for this or any cat and thought about shooting it off the door with the BB gun. Cinnamon cried again and Marilyn stepped back, watching her inch down the door backwards to be even with Marilyn's face. Throwing the gun backwards into a chair, Marilyn opened the screen door then shook it back and forth until Cinnamon dropped to the ground and raced inside.

"Go kill some rats." The cat's tail began to flap back and forth in jerky movements. Marilyn scooted across the floor and jumped into bed afraid now that the thing would try and bite her feet. The cat roamed the room, jumping into Lenny's bed then back down, finally walking the back of the couch, stopping to sniff a spot of a cigarette burn.

"Lenny ain't here to feed you… you better start looking for a rat." Cinnamon responded with a short cry while squatting on the edge of couch arm. Her tail began to impatiently thump the green vinyl seat behind her. Marilyn stuck her foot out from under the sheet and wiggled her toes, then screamed when Cinnamon's body mildly rocked back and forth before pouncing quickly from the couch to her foot then back to the floor and under the bed. Moments later, Cinnamon jumped on the foot of the bed and settled into a tight crouch. Then the buzzing sound started and the skin on Marilyn's neck prickled. She pushed the cat into the floor with a covered foot.

"Turn off that damn noise and find you an empty bed to sleep in."

* * *

It was barely light outside. Marilyn wasn't sure what woke her up but she could hear the bumping sounds from next door of her mother's bread tray when she kneaded lard and buttermilk into flour for biscuits. She allowed one leg from the sheet to test the morning air and brought it back into the warm spot, while looking over to the empty bed behind the couch.

Lenny is gone. The thought came like she had read the sentence into her mind. Seconds later a rush of pain like she had just plugged into an electrical current. No point in getting up. She flipped over facing the wall, pulling the sheet higher to her head and as her eyes closed she flinched suddenly when almond-shaped yellow eyes blinked at her from CB's side of the bed. Cinnamon was between the pillow and headboard. Marilyn stared back, one hand softly raking her hair closer to her head while willing the cat to move. Her hand softly gripped the other pillow and pushed it at the cat.

"Git. Git down."

Cinnamon did not move but flattened her ears and backed her head into her neck. Her checks pouched out, and Marilyn wondered if she had something in her mouth. She pushed the pillow at Cinnamon again and watched the head retreat further back into the neck. This time the tail unwrapped from her body and began to thump the bed in even strokes.

"Sit there then. Damn cat." Marilyn looked away then turned back over. "Stop staring."

Lenny's empty bed. A clatter of empty pans out at her mother's. She wondered if Lenny was up eating breakfast, if CB had a mistress who made biscuits. CB used to always eat a full breakfast he cooked himself. "That was because you didn't like my cooking." She said the words out loud while sitting up in the bed. "Well do it yourself then!"

She imagined him standing near the sink, shoulders slightly slumped and his blue eyes cloudy with the bottle in hand that always kept him company. Her mother and father both blamed CB's drinking for their split-up. This morning she didn't believe it was the drinking. A jagged breath made her tremble for a second. Did he ever really love her? She frowned at his imaginary spot. He never knew her; he always talked and she was always quiet. For a while it had been enough to just be beautiful. He bragged about that all the time to anyone who would listen. Then only nasty comments came out of his mouth.

The white slip came over her head easily, and she threw it at his spot. He was younger, the man standing at the sink. She couldn't even remember the details of how he looked now. Why was he here now? Why was he looking at her now? She sat back down and pulled the sheet over her naked body. She couldn't look away. She saw it in his eyes. He did not want her. She was no longer beautiful.

"Leave me alone." She screamed the words at him and threw a pillow, then searched the bedside table for something to throw—anything.

Nothing. There was nothing. She had nothing, and he had everything. She sat back, willing her breath to calm down.

She needed a cigarette. Her father would give her a few of his cigarettes. Some coffee and cigarettes and then she would feel better.

She felt the movement beside her and turned her head to watch the cat walk in close beside her. Turning, she lunged her body and grabbed the cat with both hands feeling claws from the cat's back legs scraping her arm as she threw her to the floor.

"I said to git down."

CHAPTER 20

THE EYES

GINNY, 1976

Ginny sucked in her breath briefly to lift her suitcase and slide it through the opening at the bottom of the counter at the bus station. Money for the bus ticket was folded in her pocket, along with quarters for the vending machines. After counting out the exact change and getting her ticket, she went to the vending machines and eyed the packages of candy and crackers, then made a quick search among the photographs of employees. Once reassured that Clyde's photo was not among them, she walked away. It had been gone for several years, but she still checked every time she rode the bus.

The small terminal was nearly empty, and she hesitated before sitting in one of the scooped out plastic chairs, feeling dread for the trip home to take Marilyn to the doctor. Should she get a Coke? Without caffeine she might actually sleep through the endless small towns on her way home, towns she memorized the first year of taking the bus back and forth, but were of no interest anymore.

At least this bus trip was only one way. Even though CB had discouraged her, Ginny decided to ignore his advice and drive Lenny's old car back to campus since he now had a newer one. Years ago, she had dubbed the old murky brown car with the bigger back wheels as the Roach because it resembled a giant roach bug. Now she liked the knowing smiles and nods some people gave her when she mentioned the name, even though she knew they thought she was referring to pot. She wasn't sure what the big deal was with pot. She occasionally took a toke at parties, but never felt anything resembling a high, only burning in her throat and lungs.

Lenny was agreeable to her taking the roach. He even left the old eight-track tape player in it, now that he had money to buy a new cassette player and better speakers for the car her father used as incentive for getting him to come and work with him. Despite telephone calls, an occasional check for spending money and a couple of visits to have lunch with her, Ginny was still nervous around her father and always felt she was betraying her mother. Her stomach fluttered in fear when Lenny called to tell her he was going to live with CB and Marcelle, the woman who acted like his wife. Lenny was only a baby when CB lived with them and didn't even know how violent he could be. It didn't matter that CB and Marcelle swore that CB didn't drink anymore.

Ginny's last visit with CB was different. Instead of him coming to Tuscaloosa to meet her, she agreed to take the bus to Birmingham for an overnight visit with him. CB was on edge, easily offended. He made a blanket apology for her childhood while criticizing and blaming her mother in the same sentence. Then he quickly turned to the freezer and began eating ice cream right out of the carton, something he repeated whenever he became upset. He suggested that she join him, to just choose a flavor she liked from the cartons in the freezer. Ginny saw they were all opened and partially eaten and declined, flinching when she turned to find Marcelle frowning at her from across the kitchen.

It was still dark outside, and the bus station began to fill with passengers carrying suitcases and big shopping bags. She was careful not to look in the eyes of any of the men. Shelby coached her on how to act to keep men from approaching, and she had reminded Ginny again when she dropped her off at the bus station. "Don't look open. You never look into their eyes and for God's sake don't act like you are lost or need help. If you do talk to a man, pay attention to the eyes. They should look kind and relaxed. Avoid the ones that stare or have too much eye movement. It means they are excited, because they are crazy, want sex or your money."

A stack of newspapers on the seat next to her caught her eye, and she searched through the pages to find her horoscope. Reading it gave her hope. "Today, important information will be made available to you." She thought of Marilyn's doctor's appointment and wondered if that would be the important information, but no, the appointment wasn't until tomorrow. She sighed and dropped the paper back in the chair and looked at the clock. Why did she get here so early?

She thought of the psychiatrist referred by the Welfare department after Ginny asked the social worker for help getting a disability check for Marilyn. Once Lenny left, no more checks came. The social worker said they had to prove Marilyn was too mentally disabled to hold down a job and referred them to a psychiatrist. She was stern and asked Marilyn all kinds of questions, looking at Ginny for confirmation after each answer. Marilyn denied that she had ever tried to commit suicide or that she heard voices, glaring at Ginny when she told the truth. After a few questions, she continued to stare just at Ginny, waiting for each question to be asked twice before responding, usually with a no or a shrug. Finally the meeting ended, and the psychiatrist insisted that Marilyn must get a full physical and come back again before she would recommend anything.

Last year, Ginny volunteered at Bryce State Mental Hospital while taking Abnormal Psychology, hoping to learn more about what would help Marilyn. Two visits to the hospital and she couldn't go back. Dreams filled her nights after the visits, including the last one where hundreds of Marilyn's were following her, each carrying or pulling a metal twin bed like the ones that patients slept on. They stacked them all up, pushing them closer and closer, imprisoning her in a corner. She knew they were going to crush her, and she should escape, but she had been more afraid of slipping through the openings in the metal frames and having all the Marilyns physically hold on to her.

A group of passengers began to line up near a bus outside, and she rolled up the paper to read on the bus later, slipping it in the canvas bag, alongside the stack of photographs she brought to review for class. She stood up, stuffing her hand in her jeans pocket and pulling out quarters while walking over to the vending machines and began feeding coins to the first one for a pack of crackers, then a Coke.

A uniformed man with kind, crinkled eyes punched her ticket at the bus door, and she smiled at him before moving quickly up the steps. The front seats were already filled with people, most of them old. No college students would be going home now, not at the beginning of finals. The first empty set of seats was third from the back. She sat down then frowned at the line of people coming behind her. The bus would be packed. She should just as well slide over to the window.

A man with a short afro wearing a brown plaid leisure suit carefully sat on the edge of the seat next to her, placing a cane between the seats and using it to brace himself while he slid back. His right hand held the cane while his left hand set his leather briefcase on the floor, before shuffling it between his feet. He took a pressed handkerchief from his pocket and snapped it open, holding it against his face and then up over his forehead and back against an uneven hairline that disappeared when the hair popped back in place. The right hand still curled loosely to the cane, creating an inside circle of lighter skin that made Ginny want to take a picture of it.

She looked up to his face, expecting to look in his eyes, but they were closed. The eyebrows were a bit bushy, and there were small pouches of puffy skin under his eyes like he had not slept in a long time. He frowned as the bus pulled out of the station and then jerked as they rolled over a curb. The hand grew tighter around the cane, and Ginny glanced back to his face wondering if he was hurting.

"Young lady. It is not polite to stare." Although his eyes were still closed, Ginny sat back in her seat too embarrassed to answer. Even so, her eyes kept sliding over to watch his hand, wondering if he would get upset if she asked to take a picture of it. He would get angry; she was sure about that. Turning away, her eyes scanned the blur of trees outside the window while she tried to think through how long it would take to get Marilyn to go the doctor. On the way home from the psychiatrist, Marilyn asserted that she was not going back to the psychiatrist and she would not go to a doctor either. The third time she said it, Ginny blurted out, "If you don't go, they will not send you a welfare check, and you won't have money for cigarettes."

Marilyn's eyes narrowed and she stared at Ginny for a long time. Ginny thought she might slap her. Instead she puckered out her lips and sucked on an unlit cigarette. Moments later she rolled down the window and pitched the cigarette, then sucked on another one, continuing until they arrived home. Most of the cigarettes were gone when Ginny got out of the car. She hurried away in case Marilyn decided to throw more out the window. She did not want to be around in case her grandfather saw Marilyn throwing away the cigarettes he bought her.

The bus slowed down and turned into the small bus station. Ginny watched a mother and several small children get in the back of a truck. There were two men in the cab, and she wondered why one of them didn't ride in the back and let the tired looking woman sit inside. Looking away, Ginny glanced back at the man's face beside her. His eyes were still closed, but the hand on the cane was relaxed.

She took the paper from her bag and looked again at the horoscopes. Her birth was only a few days before the horoscope changed signs, so she usually read two of them and chose the one she liked best. The second one predicted a troubling time, but she already knew that. It was always troubling to go home. She continued to read the comics for a moment until the bus lurched forward then she stopped, feeling the familiar queasiness of motion sickness starting in her stomach. Bunching up the paper, she reached in her bag for the Coke, which usually helped. The man stirred besides her, using the cane to shift his body toward the aisle.

It was only a short time before they stopped again. The bus driver told them they would have twenty minutes in Birmingham, and Ginny asked the man if he would let her out to go to the bathroom in the station. He sighed, but moved his legs and cane aside quickly, allowing her to get by.

"Young lady?" His deep voice startled her, and she turned back. "Would you mind if I read your paper?"

She shook her head and took it from her bag and held it out to him. His eyelids stayed low and she could not see into his eyes. Now she knew what Shelby meant: he knew the secret of how to keep people from talking to him.

After she got back on the bus, the man's head stayed inside the fold of the paper, even when he moved his legs for her to get in to her seat. The trip was feeling longer than it ever had, and some of the queasiness stayed with her. After tilting up her head for the last of the Coke, she took out the stack of photographs in her bag. She needed to turn in several photographs on Monday or take more pictures in a hurry. The first picture was for her photojournalism class: a picture of the first black homecoming queen at the University of Alabama. She snapped several pictures from the stands with a telephoto lens as Governor George Wallace tried to place a crown on her head from his wheel chair in the middle of Denny stadium. Other newspaper photographers snapped pictures when he kissed her cheek, so this was not that great.

There were several shots of two artist friends painting each other's nude body. The unplanned stripping and painting at one of the artists' parties had been so unnerving that Ginny started snapping pictures to keep from being embarrassed. The best picture was cropped to a close up of one woman's painted face looking like a moon with stars in an inky background staring intently at a streak of purple she was painting on another woman's soft belly. The full shot showed the women painting in a smoky haze with a few close onlookers and other women sitting at tables with lit candles stuck in dark bottles along with a few beer cans and wine glasses. This one was better for the documentary assignment, but the nudeness still made her nervous. If the shot had been for Lance's class, she knew he would like it.

At the thought of Lance, she pulled out the mounted photo of the broken glass picture of her mother from the bag and quickly placed it over the nude women while glancing up to the newspaper when it began moving. The man was only turning pages and kept his head buried inside.

The actual photograph of her mother's broken framed picture was now covered with tiny cracks, like a glass with tiny cracks all in it had been placed on top. John, the instructor for the lab, told her he had never seen anything like it, perhaps the film had gotten too hot and that made tiny cracks in the emulsion that showed in the printing. He assured her that the photo looked better, like she had done it on purpose, but agreed that since it was unintentional, Lance might lower the technical grade. "You didn't do it on purpose did you?" He had looked at her then with a twinkle in his eye. She did not answer, confused, since she already told him she hadn't. She put the picture to the back of the stack, still not sure what to do.

The pictures of the girl with the skeleton baby were next. She forced herself to pull all of them out. The queasiness in her stomach increased when she saw the tiny baby arm caught in an erratic movement in the air. Her finger rubbed the tiny hand until her heart seemed to stop for a second before the next beat. She closed her eyes and swallowed several times knowing she would never be able to lose this image. For the first time in a long time, she wanted to curl up and rock herself—an old childhood habit. She told herself that a photographer has to see, even when things are hard to look at. Words from a professor in an earlier class but somehow it did not comfort her.

Forcing her eyes to open, she looked again, this time to the mother's face. The skin on her face was puffy from crying, but there was no spark of light, no hint at feeling in the eyes. There was nothing. The eyes were dark and flat.

A sharp sucking of air from the man startled her, and she quickly turned to look at him.

"Is that the Davies girl? And her baby?" His voice was deep and loud, and his eyes were wide open. He leaned in toward the picture. "Where did you get that, young lady?"

"I don't know her name. You know her?" She whispered, aware that other people were turning in their seats to look back at them because his voice was so loud.

His eyes narrowed and the frown in his forehead deepened as he looked at her in disbelief.

"I followed her one day and took her picture." Ginny was still whispering but turned back to the picture. "Who is she?"

He snatched the paper together, turning pages before pushing it in front of her face. At first, she looked at a well-dressed woman sitting rigidly straight at a wood table. Then she saw the teenage girl at her side with four fingers of each hand pressed tightly against the edge of the table, making her elbows jut out on either side. She was the same girl as the one in her picture. Moving her eyes up, Ginny read the headline, "Mother Will Not Be Charged In Deliberate Starvation of Her Daughter."

Her stomach sucked in but no air came in or out of her lungs. Ginny held a finger on the headline to hold her eyes in place to read it again, but a switch had been cut off to her body, and she began to slowly crumble forward into the newspaper, her head swiping against the back of the headrest in front of her and then the seat. The girl's photographs slid a few at a time from her lap to the bus floor, disappearing under the seat in front of her then all the other photographs followed.

CHAPTER 21

THE BABY

MARILYN 1976

It was hot and the little oscillating fan seemed to do nothing more than warm the air it pulled in over its hot motor. Marilyn held the hem of her housedress and grasped the switch to turn it off so it would cool. She couldn't remember exactly when she turned it on, but it had been running night and day ever since the heat had gotten so bad it made her face turn red and skin prickle.

It was barely daylight this morning when she got up to do laundry before it got so hot. She wanted to make sure her good dress was clean in case she decided to go to the doctor with Ginny. Her mother insisted it was too early to pull out the old wringer washer and washtubs on her porch, but Marilyn paid her no mind since there wasn't anyone asleep that it would bother.

Ginny would be here soon; her grandfather left to go pick her up at the bus station. Even though he asked Marilyn if she wanted to go, she did not answer, letting him stand on the porch watching her dunk clothes over and over in the cold water. He shifted his weight once, then suddenly turned and walked back into his house.

Ginny's letter said her bus would come in around two. Marilyn read the letter at the kitchen counter while her mother and father were at the grocery store. Right now she wished it was Sheila coming to take her to the doctor. She sorely missed Gilbert and Charleen since they all moved to Mobile for Mike's job. Her wet thumb softly stroked her own finger remembering Charleen's perfect tiny fingers circling around hers.

A washcloth she used earlier was hanging to dry at the sink, and she soaked it with cool water from the tap and pressed it against her face, then the back of her neck. Feeling better, she rinsed it with water again, not minding that this time the water dripped on to her dress.

The old truck pulled into the driveway and stopped with the motor still running. It continued on past her house to the garage when Marilyn looked out the window and watched Ginny carrying a suitcase and some sort of cloth bag to her grandmother's house. Marilyn felt the quick familiar irritation noticing Ginny's quick steps and that she didn't even glance in the direction of her own home.

*   *   *

Supper was called, but Marilyn was in no hurry to get to the table. It had gotten cooler in the afternoon, even when she had stood in the sun gathering in the dry clothes. She ran her fingers through her hair and glanced in the mirror. The curls around her face lay flat, probably because of her sweating so much in the morning. She tried sweeping them to one side, and then got a white headband and firmly pulled all the hair back, making her look almost like she did when she was a school girl, only back then she had always used cloth headbands with bows.

There was noise from the shop behind the back wall of the house, and Marilyn sighed before lighting a cigarette and sucking in the smoke. Her father must have already eaten and left the table, hoping to make a lot of racket in his shop while she was away eating dinner. Walking out the door, she took another draw on the cigarette before slamming the door to let him know she was still at home.

Although the kitchen was silent, no one seemed to notice when she came inside through the screen door and sat down. Looking at the table loaded with food, Marilyn saw that her mother had fixed lots of Ginny's favorites, but that Ginny was stirring the food on her plate with her fork rather than eating.

"I just hope he's a good man and won't steer you wrong." Her mother was looking at Ginny when she spoke but her eyes wandered over to Marilyn, where they rested on her headband.

Could Ginny have a boyfriend? Her mind could not accept an image of Ginny with a boyfriend. "What man?" Marilyn asked while taking a piece of cornbread that was already cold. She picked up the bowl of black-eyed peas then set them back down, feeling the headband slipping up the back of her neck. She tugged it back down with fingers from both hands while looking at Ginny, who was stirring her mashed potatoes.

"I followed a girl home and took her picture and she brought a sick baby out and I took pictures of both of them and I met a man on the bus today who says that the baby died and they have charged the girl's mother with the baby's death but my picture shows that the girl had access to the baby and so she may be charged as well—assuming they get a copy of the picture."

Ginny's flat voice was irritating. The corn, peas, and okra were all stirred together with the mashed potatoes on her plate and now she was crumbling cornbread on top. Why Ginny took pictures of strangers had always seemed more than crazy.

"Why would you take their picture? Getting caught up in a big mess. That's what you're doing."

"Ginny made a mess with a dead baby." One of the voices hissed, and another one kept asking where were the pictures of the dead baby. Marilyn ignored both of them. "Why were you following someone?"

"I told you. To take her picture." Ginny looked up at her grandmother, a slight frown on her face. "I don't have a choice as to whether or not to trust him. He's willing to help, and I can't afford to hire a lawyer to tell me what to do."

Fluttering started in Marilyn's stomach. The voices were loud, "Where's the pictures? Look at the dead baby."

Ginny continued talking about lawyers until her grandmother interrupted, "Don't tell your grandfather anything about all this…"

"Mess." Marilyn finished the sentence while dipping heaping spoons of peas and potatoes onto her plate. The voices began mimicking Ginny, "Can't afford a lawyer. Tell me what to do."

Lawyers would cost a lot of money. She knew that from when she and CB had first talked about getting a divorce. "Don't be asking me to pay for no lawyer." She frowned at Ginny, who made a loud sigh, "You taking everything I got for your college already. Left me with nothing."

Ginny turned to her then, both eyes staying at the top of her head. "I didn't take anything from you, Mother." Ginny's cold voice startled her, and the voices got silent.

"Ginny." Marilyn's mother interrupted.

"You used to get checks because you had dependent children at home." Ginny hesitated, her voice lower, "But now no children are living with you. That's why I'm here to take you to the doctor, so you can get a check again."

Anger surged through Marilyn's body, and she leaned forward, the prickly heat coming back into her face. "You watch yourself talking back to me. I'll mash your mouth!"

Ginny started stirring the mess in her plate again. The headband begin contracting slowly, sliding up from Marilyn's neck and away from her face until it slipped off and limply held to the hair in the back of her head. She snatched it off and threw it to the counter and thought about leaving. Instead she grabbed the watered down ice tea and took several long sips while eyeing the plate of food she had taken.

Ginny got up and dumped the food from her plate into a bowl of scraps for the dog, circled around her grandmother's chair at the table and walked out the screen door. While still chewing on her last bite of food, Marilyn stood, taking her cup to the pot of coffee. Her mother began clearing the table, and Marilyn picked up her cigarettes and walked outside.

The cat had arched her back to rub under Ginny's hand while she sat still in the swing. Marilyn watched them until she reached her house, stopping briefly to yell back at Ginny, "You ain't getting the cat back, he's mine."

*　　*　　*

The bucket tinged as it bumped against the doorframe, then her mother knocked. "Marilyn, you need to get up and get breakfast. You and Ginny need to leave for Gadsden soon."

Marilyn had been up for a long time and had gotten dressed in the dark, first using the chilly cold water from the faucet to wash her face. The pins were all out from the curls she had set and she ran her fingers through them, gently shaping them away from her face. In the mirror, she saw tiny red blotches on her face and resisted the urge to take tweezers and pull away the little scabs, instead taking the washcloth to wipe clean her black flats and slip them on her feet.

A strong breeze blew at her hair when she came outside, and she searched the sky for signs of clouds, but saw nothing and held a hand over her hair as a shield while walking quickly into her mother's kitchen. She set her coffee near her plate and took two buttered biscuits and spread them heavily with pear preserves.

Ginny came into the kitchen with an empty cup and walked to the counter. Her long hair was pulled into a ponytail on top of her head. Her shirt was made out of thin, flimsy white material that looked like the stuff used by doctors to bandage up cuts.

"Where did you get that thing?" Marilyn bit into the biscuit, instantly tasting the sweet tangy pear.

"What?" Ginny was still acting absentminded.

"Your shirt." Marilyn took another bite and continued to look at it while chewing.

"I bought it." Ginny poured herself another cup of coffee and added cream. "I'd like to leave in about twenty minutes. I'm hoping they will get to you faster if we are early. I'm going to Cullman to see the attorney after we get back and from there I'll go back to Tuscaloosa."

"You better check to see if there's any gas in the car." Marilyn wasn't going to talk about the dead baby mess. Ginny should just give the girl the pictures she took and leave her alone.

"We will fill up when we get on the road."

"Did you even check to see if it's running?" Marilyn took another bite.

"No, Mother, I didn't." Ginny's voice was mildly irritated. "I'll go get the keys and check now."

Marilyn took the last bite and chewed it slowly, watching Ginny set her cup down and walk out the screen door. By the time she drank the last of her coffee, the car started up outside, sounding as it did when Lenny was here. The voices whispered Lenny was with CB, and she quickly tried to block the sound and to not let herself wonder what he was doing. Instead, she moved out the door to go brush her teeth and get her purse before her mind changed about going to the doctor.

*   *   *

She was surprised that Gadsden had not changed much over the years. It was still a lot like it was when she and CB lived here. They passed a sign giving directions for Noccalula Falls, and she remembered helping Sheila collect pennies that the school turned in to use for the bronze statue of the Cherokee Princess who jumped from the falls because her father wouldn't let her marry the man of another tribe. Marilyn snorted while lighting a cigarette.

Ginny turned down the tape player, "You say something?"

Marilyn shook her head. The princess was silly. She should've just married someone that could take care of her. The voices began jabbering about the princess then one louder than the rest accused her, "You tried to jump. You tried to jump off the bridge'. The bridge flashed before her, the tall metal arms; the dark forest on the other side. "You should have jumped." The other voices began to join in. Strands of purple-black, then yellow, began swirling in her head, becoming big like clouds and filling her with dread, with anxiety. It was quick when it began sliding around. Now she knew the dark feeling never left; it only made itself smaller.

"I think this is it." Ginny turned the car into a new shopping center where one whole side of the building was a medical office. Relieved, Marilyn opened the door before Ginny turned off the engine. Ginny caught up with her at the door and continued up to the receptionist. Marilyn frowned at her, "I don't need you to come in with me."

Ginny looked unsure, and Marilyn turned to the receptionist who pointed to a sign in sheet. Marilyn signed her name.

"Mother." Ginny was holding out an envelope, and Marilyn took it. "This is the psychiatrist's letter to the doctor with instructions for what the doctor needs to send. Give it to the nurse. Mother, you have to do this right, or we won't get a check for you."

The voices repeatedly asked Marilyn what was in the envelope. The nurse came out quickly, and Marilyn gave her the letter from the psychiatrist and then followed her to the exam room. The nurse stopped to read the letter. Both of them stood at the closed door of the exam room until she finished, then she opened the door.

Marilyn tried to ignore the voices, that were now alarmed and repeatedly telling her to get out, to leave and to take back the letter. The nurse asked Marilyn to sit down and began asking questions while holding a pen mid-air. "Did you have any of the following childhood illnesses?"

As the nurse named them, Marilyn shook her head or nodded, but couldn't remember the exact birth dates of her three children. After naming a few known diseases in the family, one of the voices commanded her to be quiet, to stop answering the questions.

The nurse spoke louder, "I really need for you to answer the rest of these questions the best you can." Marilyn looked up at her, and she continued. "How long have you been depressed?"

Their eyes met, and then Marilyn looked her over, noticing for the first time how small she was and that her forehead had a red rash with caked up makeup on it. It was too dark for her pale skin. The nurse stepped back a baby step and looked back to her paper, the hand with the pen reached up and two fingers brushed the rash slightly before marking something on the paper.

"Do you know when you last had a menstrual cycle?" Marilyn shrugged her shoulders, wondering if she knew her uniform collar was twisted up on one side. The voices were louder, telling her to leave… repeating it over and over, making it hard to hear the nurse or think. How much longer, how much longer?

The nurse abruptly turned, picked up a gown, and told her to take off her clothes and put it on. She showed her the little green and red buttons near the door and told her to press the green one when she was ready for the doctor. Grabbing the file, she left and closed the door.

Marilyn continued to sit in the chair, imaging herself naked and needing to get out, running out the door and people staring at her, chasing her. For a second, her heart skipped a beat and then began racing faster and faster. She looked down at her chest, expecting to see the heart pushing out, bulging against the skin, beating harder and harder, so rapid she felt breathless. Ginny would just have to take her home.

Marilyn threw the gown to the floor and jerked open the door, startled at the young man with a white coat who was blocking the door and reading papers in a file.

"Good morning, you must be my new patient." He held out his hand, "I'm Doctor Gregory."

She didn't answer but stood frozen, waiting for him to get out of the way.

"Is there something wrong?" His large hand reached up and patted her upper arm, then rested there.

The voices became more alarmed and kept murmuring about the man in the white coat holding on to her.

The doctor patted her arm again and then dropped his arm to his side. "Let me come inside and close the door where we can have some privacy to talk."

Slowly she stepped back, confused by the voices but allowing Dr. Gregory to come in, his hand raising up to pat her shoulder and resting there for a few seconds before motioning to the examining table.

"Have a seat and let me take your blood pressure, get a little blood and see if we can make you feel a little bit better. Is that all right?" He smiled and took her hand as she stepped up to sit on the exam table. "Tell me about anything that hurts, okay?"

* * *

Ginny turned a chair backwards from the reception area and sat facing the glass window, watching children playing outside. Marilyn gave papers to the receptionist and tried to keep from dropping the four sample boxes of vitamins the doctor had given her, with instructions to take one every day, no exceptions. While at the desk, she squeezed two of them inside her purse, along with the receipt. With an eye watching Ginny, Marilyn rushed toward the door, needing to get to the car for a cigarette.

As if she felt Marilyn's eyes on her, Ginny turned and then stood up quickly while capping her camera lens. Marilyn searched outside the window while Ginny met her at the door.

"What mess you taking a picture of now?"

Ginny took out her keys without comment. "Did you give the doctor the instructions from the psychiatrist?"

Marilyn ignored her question and walked ahead to the car, quickly rolling down the window and lighting a cigarette. The outside heat made her face prickly hot again. She tried to keep her mind blank and not think about what the doctor had said.

"What are those?" Ginny glanced at the boxes in Marilyn's lap while starting the car and backing out.

"Vitamins. I got to take them every day and come back…" Marilyn stopped herself, aware she had said too much. Ginny was not going to bring her to the next appointment.

"Okay." Ginny glanced at Marilyn before pulling out into the road. "Did he say why?"

"He took some tests and wants to go over them."

"Did they give you an appointment?"

"No. He will send me a letter."

"A letter?"

The car turned left at the light, and Marilyn quickly read the street sign. "This is the wrong way. You turned too soon."

"You sure?" Ginny's eyes were doubtful.

"I lived in Gadsden." Go ahead and drive all day in the wrong direction if you want. She said the words in her head while noticing the little frame house on the side of the road; boarded up but with bright blue flower boxes that were empty.

The car slowed and Ginny turned around in the driveway of another abandoned house. She pushed the tape in the eight-track player, and Marilyn's hand cupped her belly, anxiety trickling the back of her head remembering Dr. Gregory's words: "You're likely pregnant.". He gave her a pregnancy test but wouldn't have the results for days, and then he would have to mail them to her. But he had felt sure enough to give her prenatal vitamins. Her head began to nod. A baby.

She glanced to Ginny, whose eyes were darting back and forth from the road to the boxes of vitamins in Marilyn's lap. Dark blue labels across the boxes had PRENATAL in bold white letters. Marilyn set the two boxes and her purse on the floorboard. She wasn't about to tell her about the baby. She wasn't going to tell anyone.

Seconds later Ginny turned up the music, her lips mouthing the words of the song without sound. Neither of them spoke again as they left Gadsden and rode the forty minutes it took to get back home.

CHAPTER 22

SPECK

GINNY 1976

The attorney's full name was printed on the card he gave Ginny when she got off the bus. James "Speck" McMillan, with an office in downtown Tuscaloosa, was on his way to visit his mother in Cullman, a town about sixty miles from her grandparents. It seemed odd now that an attorney would be riding a bus, but she was too upset to even think about it.

Two thoughts popped into her head when Speck, as he told her to call him, said he was en route to Cullman. The first was of the Ku Klux Klan and their rumored training camp there. The second thought was of the Ave Maria Grotto, a miniature of the city of Jerusalem that was built by a monk at the Abbey in Cullman before she was even born.

When in high school, boys from her class once bragged they found the location of the KKK camp and were going to a meeting. Later in the week, they told of how they hid from a distance to watch but were disappointed that there was just a bunch of old men standing around smoking and talking in voices too low to hear. They didn't even light up a giant cross like the meetings they had seen on television. That was years ago, but close enough that she wondered why Speck's family would live there, close to such people.

As a kid she visited the Ave Maria Grotto with the other kids, her Uncle Jack, and Aunt Kate, even though Grandmother did not really approve of anything Catholic. Grandmother whispered her concerns to Uncle Jack, but it was Aunt Kate that assured her it would be about history and learning about Jerusalem, the Holy City. Grandmother gave in, seeing as how she didn't think they would ever get to visit Jerusalem, but she had stuck her head inside the back seat car window to tell them they needn't tell their grandfather they went to a Catholic abbey and not to listen to the teachings of the monks. That was the first time Ginny realized that adults had not figured out who was the real God and that she might be praying to the wrong one.

They drove to the little Jerusalem, and she had stuck close to Aunt Kate, avoiding Uncle Jack and his hands even when he challenged the kids to race him. They marveled over the marble buildings the size of dollhouses, but she was disappointed to find the buildings weren't open in the back, like a secret life was going on inside them. For a while, she kept checking every angle of the buildings, even though Aunt Katie kept reminding her not to touch.

Ginny slowed the car, searching the cluster of road signs for one that indicated Highway 278. Turning left, she took a sip of Coke and sped up, grateful that her grandmother found an old map so she could check the highway numbers and make the shortest route all the way back to Tuscaloosa. She would be early to meet Speck and wondered if she should stop at a gas station and call him before continuing on to his mother's house. Thinking the call might still be long distance, she continued driving and took a tea cake from the bag of goodies grandmother packed for her.

One of Marilyn's cigarettes was on the passenger floorboard, and she set the cookie down to reach for it while quickly popping her head back and forth to watch the road. Holding the cigarette between her fingers, she thought about lighting it up like she did in Junior High, but instead let it slide down to the base of her fingers. She squeezed it, holding her fingers together as long as she could, then let go. She liked the feeling of the spongy cylinder and continued to squeeze it while clinching her teeth at the same time.

She remembered how Marilyn moved quickly to get out of the car when they got back from the doctor, carrying the prenatal vitamins inside her house and slamming the door. Ginny sat in the car staring at the closed door, wondering why the doctor gave them to her. Maybe the doctor's office only had this type of vitamin for patient samples. Maybe she had a vitamin deficiency, and he wanted to make sure she had some vitamins since she was poor. A fear curled up tight in her stomach and then got tighter when she thought of her mother being pregnant.

No, her father stopped visiting her mother after Lenny left. Or so they thought. The tight knot expanded when she tried to close off a flash of anger at her father. If Marilyn was pregnant, her grandparents would be shocked, and Grandfather would go into a crazy rage. The theme from *SWAT* came on the radio, and she quickly turned down the sound, frowning. No one suspected all these years that CB still had sex with Marilyn when he visited; she never told Grandmother and never brought it up with Sheila or Lenny.

What if she was having sex with someone else? The image of her mother having sex made Ginny fling her hand to let go of the cigarette still between her fingers. She pushed a tape into the player and turned up the volume, tapping the selection button until Linda Ronstadt was singing "You're No Good." The cookie was still on the seat, and she took a big bite, willing herself to think of the words to the song while chewing, but an image of Marilyn's nude body came to her mind anyway, quickly changing to a nude, pregnant body.

*   *   *

After turning the car around, she slowly drove on the dirt road, looking carefully at each house she passed since none of the mailboxes had names or numbers. Dust blew in the windows, and she could feel it with her tongue when she licked her lips.

The small shotgun house with brown shingles had to be the right one. She turned into the sandy drive way and drove until it ended near the house, underneath a water oak tree. The house had a large old porch with a bench swing hanging by only one chain; the other end resting on the ground. Two straight back chairs had worn out cane bottom seats, but a mixture of bright flowers bloomed in two giant clay pots.

No barking dogs ran up to greet her, but she hesitated a moment longer, then opened the door and stood outside the car. The screen door popped open, and Speck came out in dress pants and a tank-style undershirt, his head snapping back a little and his eyes blinking in the bright sun, looking at the Roach beside her.

"Damn. 1963." He didn't smile but nodded at her and then went back inside.

She stood there, uncertain what to do, shifting her weight from one leg to the other. Slowly, she walked to the steps of the porch and sat. A fat, wiggly hound dog ran from across the road toward her, an older puppy. She stood and opened the car door for a tea cake and held it out for him. He took the cookie but did not eat it, instead stood holding it in his mouth, waiting, his tail whipping back and forth. She reached back inside and took out her camera and snapped his picture.

"Eat it." She whispered. But they both quickly looked back at the house when they heard Speck's voice sounding angry from somewhere inside, and the puppy immediately trotted back and crossed the road, stopping to eat the cookie and look at her before running back toward a house far off in the distance.

"You still here?" Speck's voice was louder than it needed to be, and his eyes squinted at her when he came out onto the porch, "Why do you have your camera out?" His voice became edgy.

"I took a picture of the puppy." She smiled at Speck then turned to get the camera case from the seat and close the car door.

"Don't encourage that dog! Comes behind the house and tears into the garbage and drags it all over the place." His arms flipped upward in the air, and he quickly reached back to hold to the wall to steady himself. He was frowning, his eyes narrowing to search the weeds across the road. "I keep some little rocks in a bucket to throw at him when he comes up in the yard."

"Maybe he's hungry." Ginny spoke softly, but felt little sparks of anger at Speck for throwing rocks.

"His owner should feed him. Besides, he's fat. He's not hungry. He can go hunt something if he's hungry."

"Maybe his owner doesn't feed him, and he's fat because he eats a lot of garbage." Her voice got louder, and the sparks had given way to a flame, "He's only a puppy, not old enough to hunt. You need to stop throwing rocks at him."

Speck looked at her, startled. He slowly nodded his head. "Okay." His voice was gruff, and he turned back to go inside but hesitated. "Come inside and have some tea with my mother while I take care of some things."

She walked up the steps, shifting the camera case and camera to her left hand in case she needed to shake hands with Speck's mother. There wasn't a bucket of rocks on the porch, and she wondered if Speck was just teasing her. Still, the puppy seemed to be afraid of him.

Inside the door, the room was darker and cooler with the faint smell of Vicks VapoRub and sweet flowers. Emotions overwhelmed Ginny. She felt both happy and sad, and she stood still for a moment, not sure why she was so emotional. Once her eyes adjusted to the darker room, she saw Speck's mother in a four poster bed under the window on the right side of the room. Several plush, old-fashioned chairs circled around the three windows that opened to the porch, all separated by small narrow tables. A metal tray with bottles of medicine and equipment was beside her bed along with a wheel chair. Some sort of old chaise lounge was against the wall on the left with a wadded up white sheet and pillow. There were large, potted plants in two corners and flowers on several tables.

"Mother, this is Ginny. Ginny, this is my mother, Mrs. McMillan." Speck's mother quickly glanced at her son before smiling at Ginny. She did not speak. She was a tiny, frail woman with almond shaped eyes, and coarse straight hair that stood out around her small face. Her skin was a much lighter complexion than Speck's, and her tiny body was lost in a huge, dark blue robe. He motioned toward a chair and Ginny sat down, feeling like she could easily cry. She stared at the squares of light falling across the bed through the window, highlighting patches of faded material from a threadbare quilt.

Slowly and silently, Ginny took the cap off her camera lens and dropped it into the camera case. She was going to take this woman's picture. Would it be enough to brace her arm against the chair to keep the camera still since it was dark in the room? Her hand reached back inside the case for the small tripod that she could brace against her chest. She didn't want to take any chances.

Speck returned to the room and quickly set two glasses of iced tea on the small table beside her. The table was made from a beautiful, dark wood with carved feet, but the top was covered in water circles and now there would be two more.

Ginny quickly twisted the tripod to the camera as he walked away and braced it against her chest as Speck gathered his mother up carefully into his arms. Ginny snapped the picture just as he impulsively kissed her cheek. His head quickly turned to her at the sound of the shutter, his body becoming still, eyes glaring. While winding the film she attempted an apologetic smile, waiting while he put his mother into the wheel chair. She pointed the camera up again, hesitating when he growled at her this time, putting his hand up, the open palm in front of his mother. Then her hand reached out and clasped his, and the frown softened then disappeared when he saw her smile for the camera. Ginny shot the picture, winding the film quick enough to shoot another after his hand dropped, his eyes continuing to watch his mother smile.

Ginny lowered the camera in her lap when he pushed the wheel chair past her to the other side of the table, facing the window. They smiled at each other, and Ginny took a sip of tea. Mrs. McMillan's eyes quickly found the flowers in the big clay pots outside on the porch, and she took a deep breath. Ginny pulled the camera up and took a close up of her profile. She turned to face Ginny, her eyes quizzical and bright, full of light.

Embarrassed, Ginny whispered to her, "I'm sorry. I'm being rude. But could I take one more? Just one more picture?" She held up a finger for emphasis.

Mrs. McMillan smiled, her eyes softer. Ginny got up and pulled yellow flowers from the rubber band that held the store-bought arrangement together in a pot near the bed; then felt compelled to pull a few more from the plastic arrangement on the table in the corner. Her thumb pressed in the center of the plastic rose, and lingered there for a moment, thinking how simple the man-made pieces were put together and how easy it would be to take them apart and then put them back together again, unlike the fragile real flowers. She quickly made a bouquet and put them into Mrs. McMillan's hands, positioned against the dark blue robe below her face. The light from the window was perfect, and she pushed the button and quickly prepared the camera for another image of Mrs. McMillan nuzzling flowers under her nose against her lips, not seeming to favor the real flowers over the plastic ones. She had closed her eyes. There was no sound, but Ginny felt Speck's presence in the room. She turned to him, but his eyes were on his mother.

"It's time to get back in bed to rest. Miss Anna will be here in a few minutes." Speck's voice was soft and when Ginny turned back, Mrs. McMillan's head had drooped to the side and only one flower remained: a plastic yellow rose pressed against the table by her hand and without thinking she backed up and catching the image as Speck stepped up behind the chair and placed his hands on the handles in back. He acted as if she were not there, backing the chair slowly away from the table and taking care that his mother did not slide down any further. Ginny picked up the flowers from the floor while he positioned the chair near the bed and then turned to her.

"Could you wait outside please?" Speck's voice was soft. A dull ache started in Ginny's chest, and she put the bunch of real and plastic flowers into his out-stretched hand, turning quickly to say goodbye to Mrs. McMillan, but she seemed to already be asleep. Ginny impulsively picked up the plastic, yellow rose left on the edge of the table.

"I need to catch a ride back with you to Tuscaloosa. We can talk about your pictures on the way." He tapped her shoulder lightly, his hand still holding the flowers, and then he turned back toward his mother without waiting for an answer. Ginny watched him set the flowers on the table and lift his mother from the wheelchair, a slight fluttering in her stomach. The trip would be almost three hours. She didn't really know him. How did she know he was even an attorney? Just because he had a card? He glanced up to her, but went back to putting pillows around his mother, his voice low, telling her he would turn on her music.

Outside, the sun was bright, and the warm air cleared away the scent of Vicks. Quietly, she closed the screen door behind her and walked over to the clay pot of flowers.

She had to talk to him about the pictures. She didn't know what else to do. Find another attorney? Walk in the police station and tell them she had pictures of the girl and try to explain why? The flutters in her stomach turned to churning. If he didn't sound right—like an attorney— she'd have to think about someone else. Maybe Shelby knew someone. Her mind thought of the crowds of friends Shelby invited to parties. Most of them were women artists she collected in order to feel like she was an artist herself, rather than a graduate student in counseling. An attorney was not likely as it would serve no purpose to her. Ginny stuck the plastic flower into the center of the pot with the real ones and walked down the steps.

She hoped the pictures would turn out well because she knew she would most likely never see this woman again, like… Like what? It felt like she had done this before, been in this same place. An image of Lucile popped into her head then, and the sadness she felt earlier came back over her while images flooded her mind of Lucile posing with her mother's scarf on her tombstone, the one picture of her Ginny had taken, studying it every day for months after Lucile left. Even now she sometimes wondered what happened to Lucile and if she still had the picture Ginny took of her and her mother walking in the rain. Her chest ached more, and she opened the car door, busying herself moving things from the front seat to make room for Speck. Finally, she picked up the cigarette from the floorboard and threw it in the back seat with a warning to herself to not to think about Marilyn. Not now. She quietly sat behind the steering wheel and leaned her head against it.

Speck came out shortly with his briefcase, cane, duffle bag, and pil- low. He had on jeans and a Jimi Hendrix T-shirt, making him seem a lot younger. He stumbled when stepping down the steps, and Ginny won- dered if he needed to use his cane. He threw things in the back seat and got in, shifting his body several times while she backed out of the drive way.

The sun was getting low by the time they pulled onto Interstate 65. Speck had not spoken since he came out of the house, he didn't act like he even knew she was there. Minutes later, he had a flask in hand and took a long drink from it. Dread filled her body, and she avoided looking in his direction when he took another drink. She wondered how long he had been drinking and thought of how unsteady he had been on the porch. He shifted in the seat again, then leaned back against the door, raising up once to stuff his pillow behind his head.

She would not to try and talk to him. He would probably keep drinking until he became belligerent and unable to be logical, getting nasty if crossed. Her face felt feverish. Just get home she told herself. Speck is not saying anything, maybe he'll fall asleep. It is going to be okay. He isn't her father; he is an attorney. People drink all the time without becoming mean. Hadn't she been to lots of parties where people were drinking until they were drunk? Why was she getting so nervous now?

He began snoring, and she sighed with relief.

A sign announcing the exit for Jasper in two miles startled her. When she planned the trip this morning, she thought she would go the shortest distance, get off the interstate and go through the scenic back roads through the small town of Jasper and then through Bankhead Forest, including the Sipsey Wilderness Reserve. The artist group once drove up from Tuscaloosa, stopping at a camp site a few miles into the twenty-five thousand acres of trees and winding roads. It was such a peaceful, beautiful place. In a split second, she decided to continue with her plans and turned off Interstate 65 toward the small town of Jasper.

*　*　*

It took over an hour to reach downtown Jasper, and the sunlight was gone. After they passed through the small city, the road narrowed down to such a little street that Ginny was sure she missed a turn. She pulled into the first driveway on the right. It was a used car sales business. The car hesitated, then lurched forward, and she realized the driveway had a small chain across it to keep people out and she had run through it. There wasn't enough light to see Speck's face, but she could hear muffled, grunting sounds and wondered if she should check to see if his face was buried in the pillow. Maybe he couldn't breathe. Instead she took a slow breath, then jumped when she heard a siren nearby and wondered if there was an alarm attached to the chain she broke and hurried to get back on the road in the direction they had come.

After driving back for miles, she realized there was no missed turn, so she turned back around until they passed the used car sales lot and then narrowed onto a small two-lane road with no streetlights. The forest was completely dark on both sides of the road. She sped up to make up for lost time but slowed back down to stay inside the sharp curve. Her foot kept tapping the floor for the high beam light, but one headlight was off, throwing light into the tops of trees instead of the road. Curve after curve, she tapped the light high then back to low trying to see.

Her father had warned her that this car was not safe for distances. He had bought it from a man who used it to go fishing on weekends. If she broke down, what would she do? There were no phones here, and she didn't have much money. Maybe Speck was good at working on cars? She glanced in his direction and saw his body slid further down and his knee was near her in the center of the seat. Maybe he passed out. When she was younger, her father had been drinking and getting belligerent, and she had prayed for God to make him pass out before he got violent; she believed it was God's way of saving them. But when Marilyn left to visit her sister and he came to see them, God didn't answer her. Her stomach fluttered remembering the small round circle of the riffle pointed in her face and the suggestions that he could kill her if he chose. Speeding the car up, she wondering if God would help her tonight if Speck got drunk enough to be crazy or if the car broke down.

The next curve was sharp, and the car veered over into the oncoming lane, then the outer rim of the curve. She sucked in her breath sharply and stomped on the brakes with both feet. The car screeched to a stop, still on the edge of the road but there were no longer any headlights and she wasn't sure how close they were to the edge. Even though it was totally dark, relief slowly coated the inside of her body. They were still on the road.

"What's going on?" Speck's body was moving.

Sitting still in the darkness, Ginny noticed the moon. It was almost full. She continued to stare at it, ignoring everything else. It would be okay. They didn't go off the road and die. Even if they have broken down and have to wait until morning to get help, it would be okay. Even if Speck got crazy, she had gotten through worst; he could never be as bad as her father.

"Where the hell are we?" Speck's voice changed to alarm, and he was sitting up straight.

She took her left foot off the brake, and they rolled forward before she realized her right foot was not on the brake but holding down the button controlling the light beam. As she raised her right foot to press the brake, the car headlights came back on. Sucking in air first, she changed gears and slowly backed up, then turned the car quickly into the right lane.

"Bankhead Forest."

"Bankhead? What the hell are we doing in Bankhead forest? Are you trying to get me killed? This ain't no place for a black man riding in a car with a white girl in the middle of the night."

Ginny could hear the sound of sloshing liquid and knew he had taken a swig from the flask. The KKK camp was miles away, at least a two hour drive. She glanced in his direction but couldn't see his face. "It's only about nine o'clock."

"Some of the people living here have never been outside these woods or seen the real light of day for that matter."

"I'm sorry. I wasn't thinking about that. It looked like it was a closer route on the map."

"Closer? All these winding roads?"

She tried to answer, then coughed several times.

"You should have asked me." He bumped the flask against his chest then held it straight up to his mouth, then quickly back down. "I could have told you."

"You were drunk and asleep. How could I ask you?" She kept her eyes on the road and carefully turned the curves.

"I was not drunk. Are you one of those teetotalers who think that anyone having a drink is drunk?" He waited for a few seconds before continuing, "I was up all night doing things for my mother, excuse me for falling asleep."

Some of his words were slurred. If she stayed quiet and didn't argue, maybe he would fall back asleep.

He leaned his head against the window and stared into the woods. "You see the movie *Deliverance*? Enough to make any man paranoid to go into these backwoods."

"No."

"No?"

"No, I didn't see the movie."

"Don't bother." He reached into the back seat and found his duffle bag and brought it to the front, squashing it onto the floorboards at his feet. She heard him unzip the bag.

"Oh, and I want all my mother's pictures you took."

Without looking, she knew he was searching for another bottle of booze.

"I'll give you copies. But do you think you could you stop drinking now?" The sharpness in her voice surprised her, and she held her breath for a moment.

"Look here little girl, I ain't done nothing to you. So whoever it was that hurt you, you go tell them about it. I ain't done nothing. Just trying to soothe my nerves. I got my own problems, you see?" He stopped and took a drink from the full bottle he pulled from the bag.

She sighed loudly.

"I don't want no copies. I want the negatives and pictures. All of them. Anything you took. You like taking pictures of other people's problems I see, the girl and her baby and now my mother. Does it make you feel like you ain't got any or do you just forget them when you're clicking the camera?"

She flinched, then quickly tried to forget the girl with the baby and focused instead on the image of his mother, the tiny woman in the blue robe. Speck continued to make clicking sounds like he was shooting a picture.

"Your mother is a problem for you?"

"No. She is not a problem for me."

"You said I was taking pictures of other people's problems." She glanced in his direction but unable to see his face. "I liked her eyes. She seemed… peaceful and caring, and couldn't stop looking at the flowers. When you held her, the two of you seemed so close."

"I don't want to hear what you think about me and my mother. I just want the pictures and the negatives. Consider it payment for my services when I make sure you are protected when we turn in pictures of the Davies girl." The bottle sloshed again. "Your picture will likely put her away for a long time."

The base of her head was aching and pain came from nowhere and quickly circled her head. She remembered once again the girl's eyes. She didn't need the photograph to remember their vacant look while she held the dying child in her arms.

"Speck?" Ginny whispered. "Did you see her eyes?" She began quickly swallowing over and over even though her mouth had become too dry.

"Did I? No. Never seen her. Just the pictures in the paper."

"They weren't right, Speck. It's like she wasn't in there."

"She let her baby die, Ginny. Her own helpless baby. She knew it was wrong or she wouldn't have helped hide it. Just because she's crazy doesn't mean she isn't responsible."

"Maybe she was too scared. She seemed scared. She…" Ginny hesitated, swallowing again, her mouth so dry she could barely speak, "Maybe she was trying to help… when she showed the baby to me." Her body cringed and nausea overcame her. She quickly pulled over onto the shoulder of the road and jerked open the door, but not before she began vomiting.

"Oh God."

She couldn't tell from the comment if Speck was disgusted, but she kept her head down and used one hand to hold back her hair. A car slowly passed them, and she saw from the headlights that vomit was dripping from the door and she began again. Speck was sloshing the bottle then moments later he nudged her arm.

"Here's an undershirt from my bag doused with some cognac. Wipe off and throw it out. If I start smelling puke, we will both be puking the rest of the way."

She wiped her mouth and then the side of the door before dropping the shirt on the ground.

He poured more from the bottle into her Coke can and held it out to her. "Take a sip."

Instead of taking the can, she put her hands on the steering wheel.

"Take a sip or you'll be tasting puke all the way to Tuscaloosa and start heaving again."

Keeping her foot on the brake, she took the can and took a mouth full of the vile liquid and sloshed it around in her mouth before letting it burn down her throat. She handed the can back, tapping it against his arm and then she drove back onto the road.

The darkness around them seemed thicker, and she clicked on the high beams, trying to calm her need to see more of what was to come. They rounded another curve. They had to be getting closer, she just needed to stay calm and watch the road. After two more curves, the road straightened, and she could see lights in the distance. They were finally out of the forest.

CHAPTER 23

THE BURNING RAYS OF THE SUN

MARILYN, 1976

"Freedom is the most precious thing we have."

Marilyn did not look up to her mother and continued to break off pieces of biscuit to drop into the bowl of sliced sweetened strawberries in front of her. She was sick of hearing about the Bicentennial, especially from her mother.

Her father didn't comment, and Marilyn watched the red juice soak into the pieces of biscuit. Her mother continued to talk about freedom, and Marilyn's eyes were caught by the movement in the window. Ginny's cat, Cinnamon, was on the outside windowsill looking in at them, her tail politely wrapped close to her body. A smile came to Marilyn's lips, remembering the dozen or so thick, long nails her mother had pounded into the wooden sill yesterday, leaving them only halfway driven into the wood, hoping they would poke the cat if it tried to sit there again.

Cinnamon's mouth was moving, but they could not hear a sound. Her mother was softly arguing that a picnic at the lake for the Fourth of July Bicentennial would be just the thing since many of the grandchildren would be coming, and they could swim to get away from the heat.

"I don't want to sit in those old folding chairs all day." Her father's voice was irritated; his head wobbled back and forth with the words and then became still, his eyes staring at Cinnamon in the window, hunched over the nails; mouth still moving. "That nasty thing is sitting over the food again."

Her mother looked back over her shoulder through the window and shrugged. "Well, I don't know what to do about it. Maybe he thinks Ginny is in here."

"I could shoot it." His jaw clenched, and he pushed his food away. "Can't even eat with it sitting there."

"I could shoot it." The voice repeated her father' words, then said it again, "I could shoot it." Marilyn frowned and swallowed a mouthful of cold strawberries and sweet juice, her lips shaking slightly.

"Dead cat. Dead cat." Then a difference voice, softer, "Don't kill it."

A bit of strawberry juice made its way out and rolled quickly down her chin. She rubbed it off before reaching for a biscuit from the platter and then stuffing it with a piece of fried pork before standing and walking out the door. Marilyn squashed the pork biscuit between two large nails on the windowsill, watching the cat begin to eat before coming back inside and sitting down. Both her mother and father glanced at her several times, their eyes moving from their plates to her face, then back again. No one spoke, and Marilyn took another bite of strawberries.

Her mother stood and turned toward the counter. "I'm going to turn on the radio. It's too early for the community show, but the news will be on." The announcer's voice started low then filled the room. Marilyn imagined his tongue being stretched as her mother turned the knob around.

"This comes after Governor Wallace left the presidential race last month after carrying only three southern states: Mississippi, South Carolina, and Alabama. This was his fourth bid for president."

"Thank goodness. Maybe now he will stop running." Her mother had never liked George Wallace, once turning her back to him when he rode past them in the Christmas parade sitting in the back of a Cadillac.

"Well, he carried Alabama." Her father's voice had a trace of humor. He always enjoyed arguing politics with her mother. "Well, he done lost his fire anyway. Looks to be in bad health and having to be in that wheel chair all the time. I would think you would have some sympathy."

"I'm sorry that man shot him, but I still don't like him. Acting like a banty rooster. I saw the kind of man he was back when he first ran. Now he tries to say he is different." She nodded her head. "Remember when Marvin Gates came by here and tried to talk him up."

Her father frowned, "When?"

"Right after Marilyn first moved here. He stopped out by the side of the road and walked through the cotton field to where we were. Said if we would come and vote for him, he would personally pay the poll tax for us. And Marilyn, too."

Marilyn saw her mother glancing sideways to her. She used a piece of biscuit to soak up the last traces of strawberry juice from her bowl before popping it into her mouth. They didn't know that Marvin stopped by the house after leaving the field, knocking on her door and then acting surprised when he saw her. She was holding Lenny, trying to quiet him by patting his back while he was propped up on her shoulder.

She looked a mess and tried to get rid of him, nodding while he talked about voting and poll taxes but keeping her eyes on Lenny. He insisted that he would personally drive her to the poll to cast her ballot for George Wallace.

She finally stopped nodding and looked up to stare into his eyes. Years before she married CB, she heard the rumors that Marvin was crazy about her. Her mother had heard them too and tried to talk her into dating him, telling her that even though Marvin was not a good looking man, he had substance. He started taking over his daddy's business and was already a deacon at the church. But CB was the only man she wanted. Even that day, he acted bashful and looked away but continued to talk.

"George Wallace is opposed to drinking and would eliminate liquor agents and would not allow drinking at the governor's mansion." She was unsure what liquor agents were, but before she could ask, he patted her hand.

"I've heard about CB's drinking, Marilyn. I'm sorry. A beautiful woman like yourself shouldn't be in this situation."

"Marilyn, are you finished eating?" Her mother was clearing the table. Her father walked past her with a cup of coffee, staring straight ahead and, she turned to look up to the window. The cat was gone.

*   *   *

After getting her father to agree to the picnic, the kitchen table was covered with coupons Thursday afternoon in preparation for the trip to the grocery store on Friday. Her mother clipped them for several months, determined to buy real picnic food: hamburgers and hotdogs with store bought buns, pork and beans, potato chips, and Coke. She bought a few things each Saturday during June while listening to her husband complain that they were too poor to be buying all that for the Fourth of July.

Marilyn originally decided not to go to the picnic until Sheila wrote that she would be coming with the kids and that they would pick up Lenny in Birmingham on the way. Ginny told them she would not be coming back home for the Fourth of July when she came home to take Marilyn to the doctor.

Marilyn took a sip of hot coffee and sat back in the chair to light a cigarette, staring at coupons arranged in piles across the table.

"Isn't it too hot for coffee?" Her mother pulled at the neckline of her housedress and faced the small fan when it oscillated so that it was directly blowing on her. The air blew high enough to not hit the stacks of coupons even though a few of them danced across the table anyway as it turned slowly a half circle.

Marilyn ignored the remark, too tired to talk to her. Maybe the coffee would give her energy. She thought again of Sheila's letter with several comments about Lenny and wondered if Sheila recently visited Lenny at CB's house. She thought of CB holding little Gilbert and Charleen, acting like a proud grandfather and then she sucked in her breath. What if he had a woman there, acting like the grandmother?

* * *

Five of Marilyn's siblings came to the picnic, along with their spouses, but three did not make it—and they lived further away than Ginny. It seemed to take hours to line everybody up in various family units to take pictures under the pine trees with the lake in the background. Marilyn stood between Sheila and Lenny for their picture and held Charleen while Gilbert rested in his father's arms. She resisted looking at her brother taking the picture, preferring to watch the pine needles waving at her far above his head. Wafts of smoke billowed upward too, coming from the free standing grills that were now burning the charcoal her father fought so hard not to buy. She smiled remembering the little tiff her parents had in the grocery store after which she went off to the candy aisle to buy Tootsie Roll Pops for the children.

The sun flickering through the trees was hot, and she was extremely tired. Once the picture was done, she quickly turned to thrust Charleen in Lenny's arms. "Take her down to the water's edge to watch the other kids." She moved toward a picnic table far from those near other family and sat on the cement slab, closing her eyes for a moment, wishing her cigarettes were nearby.

"Mother, you all right?" Sheila's voice was near, and Marilyn opened her eyes to watch her slip her legs underneath the table. Gilbert sat close to his mother, his back to Marilyn. She watched other kids running from the lake in their swim suits to get the burgers and hotdogs stacked up on plates on the other table.

"I guess. I just feel tired." Sheila frowned. Marilyn knew she was remembering last night when she asked her to go to the store to buy pads for her. Marilyn didn't tell her she was losing the baby, that she had begun to bleed the day before.

"Maybe you need something to eat." Sheila rose up from the bench. "I don't remember you having breakfast this morning, except for coffee. Let me fix you a plate."

Marilyn shook her head slightly at Sheila's back, watching her hold Gilbert's hand while making her way to the food table. No use telling her about losing the baby since she didn't know about it in the first place.

*   *   *

Her brother-in-law, Jack, asked her again if she would come with them for a boat ride, and she looked down at the half-eaten burger on her plate. How would she explain that she was too tired to get in the boat? It would take too much effort to explain, so she stood and followed him and Sheila, holding Gilbert's hand while listening to several young nieces giggle while following along behind them.

Jack lifted a life vest from the pile on the shore near the boat, the red color faded to a pale orange. Her nose wrinkled when he lifted it over Sheila's head while apologizing that it was damp and a bit musty. He lifted another to put over her head, but she moved her head back, letting go of Gilbert's hand to wave it away. She helped put a smaller one on Gilbert, then took his hand and led him to the boat, frowning when the water from the shore licked her feet through her canvas shoes then hungrily swallowed both feet as she stepped in closer to the boat.

She motioned for Gilbert to sit near Sheila, and then sat down next to him. With the sound of the motor starting up, he immediately stood, turning back toward shore to smile and wave. The smile on his lips opened to let out an excited cry when the boat lurched forward. He sat down and raised himself back up to look on either side of the boat, his eyes growing large while watching the continuous waves coming up beside them as they sliced through the water. Thankfully the motor was too loud to allow small talk, and Marilyn took a deep breath and then coughed to exhale the lingering gas fumes.

As they picked up speed, the air felt good on her face, even though the sun was too bright and harsh and she wished she had brought sunglasses. When they turned the curve, two boats passed them on the left, the families waving as if they knew them. Lots of other families were sitting around picnic tables on the shore, miles of them. Some of them smiling and waving as the boat passed, but she couldn't bring herself to smile or wave back, not even to the children. Gilbert waved for a while then stopped with his arm still in the air, looking up to her, uncertain as to whether he should continue.

She smiled at his too-pink face, patting his arm and pushing it down. When she looked up, she noticed the blue line crossing the lake in the distance. Jack saw it too and yelled to the kids they would be going under a bridge soon. Gilbert patted her arm and then jabbed his finger in the air to show her, and she nodded, shielding her eyes with her hand and shivering slightly despite the relentless heat of the sun. Soon the blue line looked like a train of metal boxes, not moving and arching slightly over the water.

The bridge trembled then and the arch slowly sunk, flattening down and straining metal cables. Marilyn crouched forward, her face close to her knees, glancing sideways at Sheila, who was pointing at something on the far shore to Gilbert. She glanced up again and watched the thick metal arms holding the metal cage stretching, making bigger holes. No one else seemed to notice that the bridge was falling. She hugged her legs, seeing that her canvas shoes were ruined from the lake water and she should have taken them off. Her head was quiet, and she worried that the voices had left her. Where could they have gone?

She pressed one hand against the bottom of the boat then rose up so she could look again. Several cars were stopped along the bridge. Were they moving and then stopped when the bridge dipped? She slid her bottom off the seat, squatting, one hand accidentally brushing her niece sitting in front of her, who turned; her eyes startled to find Marilyn so close. Marilyn ignored her, her eyes searching for people inside the cars. No one else around her seemed alarmed that the bridge was moving even though they were staring right at it. How could they not see it or at least hear the sounds of twisting and straining metal? She shook her head and told herself the bridge must not be moving.

Voices shouted out then, loud and sharp despite the boat's loud motor. Her back stiffened, and she glanced around her before looking up at the cage with the rest of them. Had the voices left her for the bridge? It was directly in front of her.

The kids began yelling and pointing with wide smiles. A woman began screaming and at once it felt familiar, like remembering something the voices had said. Marilyn arched her back to look for the woman until the boat slid underneath the bridge, the sun blocked and the cool shade a relief to her face. Muffled sounds came from people above them and she shivered, the damp, moldy air filling her lungs and leaving the taste of fish in her mouth. She leaned forward, anticipating the light on the other side, needing the sun to burn away the darkness even though she could feel its earlier burn on her face.

The light struck the front of the boat first, then sharp sounds came from above, an outcry from a man and exactly when the sun struck her face, she could see a woman jumping from the bridge, right above them, falling slowly, then faster. No time to warn the others. She grabbed at little Gilbert's hand just before the woman fell directly onto her and they both plunged into the lake.

Her tongue pushed out words, but cool water took them, filling her mouth and swallowing her body. It was too cold now; her body becoming numb, sinking and drifting away from the sun, away from the boat. She was helpless to stop. Then suddenly it was completely dark, and there were no more sounds from above the lake.

CHAPTER 24

KISSES

GINNY, 1976

Her earth shoes did not make a sound as Ginny hurried down the hospital hallway and looked for Marilyn's room. Lenny talked to her early this morning after trying to reach her all night. He kept repeating over and over that Marilyn had a stroke, that she just fell into the lake from Uncle Jack's boat; but all Ginny could say in response was, "What?" He finally asked Ginny how much she had to drink at the party. Now, she guessed it was a lot, her aching head flashed with memories of glasses of sweet, cheap wine that kept getting replaced while she danced in a circle of friends who encouraged her to enjoy the music and just forget all her troubles. It seemed simple enough. Forget the pictures of the starving baby. But there was also a flash of her bursting into tears and talking about the dead baby to a total stranger who sat beside her at the bar and then the sensation of panic when she remembered Speck telling her not to talk about the baby to anyone. Later she tried to find the stranger, mistakenly telling different women at the party to keep quiet about the baby.

The door to her mother's room was closed, and she quietly slipped inside. Her mother's face looked red and blistered with several bruises around her mouth; both eyes were closed even though Lenny told Ginny her eyes opened and followed him for a while after they brought her into the room. The closed eyelids looked thin and pale in their sockets.

The doctor admonished Lenny several times that the family should not talk freely around Marilyn, that she might hear them even if she didn't show signs of being conscious. Ginny frowned and wondered if she should say something encouraging just in case. Instead she sat down, rubbing her throbbing forehead, wishing Lenny and Sheila were here now so they could think of something encouraging. They waited until she arrived at the hospital before leaving. Lenny needed to be dropped off in Birmingham to get his car and some clothes before coming back, and Sheila's husband had to return to work. There hadn't been much time together, just an update and a hug.

Ginny blinked back tears, quickly standing and studying her mother's face again for signs she might have awakened. Her fingers tore open a pack of artificial sweetener and dumped it into the glass of iced tea from Marilyn's food tray. She quickly swirled her finger in it to mix it up, then used the same finger to lift the metal lid off the plate. The heavy smell of tomato sauce and bell peppers made her stomach lurch, and she quickly let the metal cover drop, returning to the chair beside the bed, her body exhausted but her mind racing around like the little silver balls spring-loaded from a pinball machine. They were smacking into one thought then another. She took a sip of tea, and then drank it quickly to ease her dry throat.

Sheila said that Uncle Jack immediately killed the motor to his boat and jumped into the lake to save Marilyn when she fell. By the time he swam around then pulled her head to the surface, other boats came in from the shore after hearing them scream for help. Eventually someone called an ambulance.

Ginny tried to imagine being paralyzed and drifting around the bottom of the lake. Her mouth opened wide, gasping for air as if it were true. Then she imagined Uncle Jack's hands grabbing her to him and pulling her head up. Violently, she pushed the thought away and quickly stood up, keeping her eyes half closed against the glare of the sun reflecting off parked cars from the window. Turning back toward her mother, she took a deep breath, allowing her hand to briefly touch the top of Marilyn's cool one before instantly pulling it away and then returning it to hover just above it.

Just a day earlier, she called Lenny to tell him to go through Marilyn's mail while he was there for the Fourth of July and see if the doctor sent a report about her pregnancy test. Since Marilyn kept every letter ever sent to her in dusty stacks on the table behind the small television set, it had been easy for him to find. The doctor's report said she was not pregnant. It was at least one problem solved.

The door silently swung open, and Uncle Jack came into the room, one arm hugging a brown grocery bag. He nodded, and she quickly looked away to her mother's face.

"Any change?"

Ginny shook her head while glancing sideways to Uncle Jack, focusing her eyes on his short bristly grey hair before noticing his eyes were intently watching Marilyn. He set the sack on the floor next to the nightstand then walked quickly to the padded chair near the other patient bed and began pulling it toward Marilyn. It had been a while since Ginny had been alone with Uncle Jack; she avoided him for years and always avoided looking into his eyes. She searched her mother's face and wondered if she ever understood what happened.

Ginny shoved the food table from over Marilyn's bed and turned away to sit down, her body facing away from Uncle Jack, who sat on the edge of the chair in order to be high enough to watch Marilyn.

"I know everyone left. They all had to get back home… to go to work. I've got to leave soon myself to get the boat and get home."

His voice sounded strange, a little like he had a cold and couldn't breathe through his nose. She stood, checking his face to see if he had been crying.

He continued in the same nasal tone, "I want you to know that I will be back to help out… however you kids need me."

Lenny told her that Uncle Jack followed the ambulance and stayed at the hospital through the night. Most of the family left to go home from the lake, not stopping at the hospital at all. Maybe none of them had anything to say to Marilyn, that talking to her at family gatherings was enough. Or maybe they thought Marilyn was going to die and didn't want to be here if she did. Panic rushed through her veins. Her mother was going to die. Tears came to her eyes, and she blinked over and over, turning her back and studying the cars outside the window before sitting back down.

Would it be better if Marilyn died? Her life seemed so hard. In the past they wondered what they would do to care for her when her grandparents were no longer able. The panic started again… she felt the need to run from the room. She twisted both feet up inside the rungs of the chair and pressed them still. She could not leave her… could not run away from her.

"I'm sorry I didn't insist your mother wear a life jacket." Uncle Jack's words were not loud, but they startled her. When she twisted to see his face, a cramp started in her foot and moved up into her leg. She tried to straighten her foot, removing it from the rungs of the chair and pressing down against the floor, but the cramp continued slightly higher sucking up the side of her leg. She cried out softly, removing the shoe, then rubbing the spot, making it worse.

"Cramp." She offered the quick explanation and looked up, seeing that Uncle Jack's eyes were still on Marilyn and he didn't seem to be aware of her. Never before had she experienced a cramp like this and wondered if it was something else, like a blood clot. She stood, and the cramp stopped moving up. Almost paralyzed with pain, she stood very still. She tried to relax by breathing through her mouth, hoping it would soon end.

"I'm so sorry." His words rushed out, and when Ginny glanced at him, his face was low. Was he talking to Marilyn? Stripes ran across his face from sunlight filtering through the blinds in the darkened room. Why was he sorry? Did he feel guilty that he did not make Marilyn put on a life jacket? The rush of anger Ginny felt surprised her, and she tried to close it off, already nauseated from the cramp. She bent down to massage the leg not wanting to have to think about him and his feelings. But still, at that moment she also felt sorry for him.

"You pulled her out of the lake. If she makes it, it will be because of you." Despite her pity, irritation was in her voice.

"I'm sorry for everything." His voice was so low she could barely hear him, but she understood he was no longer talking about Marilyn.

First her face, then the rest of her body turned clammy and yet strangely cold as if she had frozen her body from the inside. She dropped to the edge of the chair, accepting the shooting pain, allowing it to continue its course and move up the muscle. Both of her hands held tight, her thumbs digging in and pressing the most painful spot; she was panting, trying not to throw up and no longer caring if Uncle Jack heard her.

There was a burst of air when the door opened then closed, and she knew he left the room. She was gritting her teeth when the pain slowly began to ease up, leaving the muscle trembling, then the pain stopped altogether. With a sigh of relief, she reached for her shoe and slipped it back on her foot.

Did her mother hear Uncle Jack apologize? Did she ever suspect what he did to her when she was little? She walked slowly around the bed, stopping to stand on her tiptoes to stretch her foot then she began to walk again. Maybe she imagined he apologized. Why would he say he was sorry now? She looked at her mother's face. Was it because he thought Marilyn drowned and was scared of dying?

She sat in Uncle Jack's chair. Her eyes rested on the sack Uncle Jack left near the table. A big plastic bottle of soda, various bags of chips, and a small bag of chocolate Hersheys Kisses were inside.

*   *   *

Nurses and attendants frequently came into the room all night, ending all possibility of tortured sleep in the hospital chair. She finally sat up fully, quickly checking Marilyn's face before reaching for her paper cup to take a sip of melted ice and watered down Coke. The back of her fingertips brushed against the plastic bag of chocolate kisses she left on the table. After swallowing the Coke, she carefully set the cup closer to the edge of the table.

The telephone began ringing, first with her grandmother, followed by Sheila. Both asked if there were any changes, and Sheila told her that Lenny would be driving back to the hospital today. When she picked up the phone again, she didn't immediately recognize the voice.

"Hello, young lady. How is your mother?" While the gruffness was gone, she recognized Speck with his second sentence.

"There is no change."

She heard the deep sigh on the other end of the phone. "Are you okay?"

"I'm okay."

"I had to come back to Cullman but will be leaving soon to go home. Abrial called this morning to give me your message."

The image of Speck's slightly arrogant law student assistant came to mind. After a few seconds Speck continued, "As we expected, the Davies girl was charged with murder yesterday."

The clamminess began to come back to her body. "Okay."

"Ginny, since the newspapers ran stories about the new evidence and pictures of the Davies girl, there are people who have become interested in why you took her picture. Why you didn't call the police. There have been letters to the editors of the paper, and a few people have been waiting outside your classrooms, asking about you. We think it is probably reporters trying to get an interview and get copies of the pictures. But it is only a matter of time before they show up at your home, if they haven't already. I've asked the University to take precautions to keep any information on you private, including your grandparents' address. Is your grandparents' last name different from yours?"

Fear felt like a wad of cotton in her throat, and she couldn't answer. She tried to clear her throat, but no sound came out. She sipped more of the watered down Coke.

"Ginny?"

"Different than mine."

"Good."

"You said you thought it was probably reporters. Who else would be waiting for me?"

Speck cleared his throat before speaking, "The trial against the grand-mother will be over soon, but more people are upset about the baby's death since they charged the Davies girl. The letters are angry, saying the baby would have been saved if you had called the police. They have increased security at the courthouse for the mother and daughter, and the prosecuting attorney is concerned that you take precautions too." Ginny's hands began to shake, and she set the paper cup down.

"This kind of thing brings out crazy people, Ginny. I just think that you need to hide out, at least until the trials end and the publicity blows over. Maybe take this next semester off."

"Hide? Where will I go?"

"I know this is fast, but call your landlord and let them know you're moving. I will get my assistants over to pack up your things today."

Her lungs strained for breaths while Speck continued, her mind having trouble following his words, thinking instead of moving back home, returning to everything.

"Call your professors about turning in assignments without attending these last few classes. It is so close to the end of the semester. Maybe they will allow you to do that without penalties. If nothing else, you could take incompletes and finish them later."

Speck had gotten her though the police talks and the meeting with the district attorney. She trusted him to help her, but she couldn't go back home. She promised herself she would never come go back there.

"I know you're overwhelmed." He hesitated, "Why don't I talk to some folks at the University? Is it okay for me to talk to the dean?"

She nodded, her mind already walking into her mother's house, seeing her mother in a hospital bed, smoking. There were flashes from cameras stuck in the door by reporters.

"Ginny, you still with me?"

She shook her head, "Yes. I'm here."

"Do I have permission to talk with the dean on your behalf?"

"Yes."

"Let me know how things are in the morning. We can put some stuff in storage. But no pictures. Okay? Keep all pictures. You don't want some snooping reporter to find them."

The door popped opened wide, and a patient on a gurney was brought to the edge of the other bed while a nurse pulled the curtain separating the beds. Ginny turned toward the window.

"Ginny, I'm trying to think of anything that might happen, so that we can be prepared. I've got to go. I'll call you first thing tomorrow morning. Okay?"

"Okay." She almost had the phone on the receiver before she jerked it back against her ear, her hand still shaking. "Speck? Thank you."

He mumbled something, or maybe it was a grunting sound. Then he hung up.

*   *   *

She could smell the dinner that had been delivered, and when she quickly checked on Marilyn, a nurse was standing near her, fingers on her hand. Ginny had fallen asleep in the chair. She straightened and scooted to the edge before standing, rubbing her neck and wondering how long she was out. It seemed impossible that she would nod out with the television so loud for the patient next to them, but it was already dark outside.

Marilyn's face looked ruddy and damp against the pillow. The skin on her forehead and nose was beginning to peel from the sunburn, and Ginny felt compelled to pull the little bits of skin away, but was afraid that Marilyn's eyes would suddenly open like Lenny said they had the first night. Her stomach fluttered, and she moved back, unable to find a place to put her thoughts so that she wasn't filled with fear. What scared her the most, that Marilyn might die or that she would live? Would she have brain damage if she survived? And what about school? Would she ever be able to go back if she left? What did these strangers want from her in Tuscaloosa? Despite the noise from the television, it suddenly seemed quiet. But there was no space in her head for all the noise, either.

She took the cover from the plate of food. The piece of baked chicken was already cool, but she pulled a piece from it and tried to chew the rubbery white strip. The tea with melted ice was unsweetened, but she didn't take time to add sweetener before taking large gulps while replacing the cover on the plate, pausing a few seconds to stare at the square piece of cake with pink icing.

"Nothing pink." She spoke to no one but imagined Marilyn's eyes opening now, knowing how much she hated people to stare at her. Ginny turned her eyes away, first looking at her feet, then twisting her body slowly around as far as she could without moving them, searching the room for a place to stop. Her head snapped back to the chocolate kisses on the table.

All those years he hurt her… why? Why did he do that to her? She walked back to the chair and table. What did an apology matter now? Was it because he thought her mother was dying? Or did he see his own death? Her hands tore open the bag of kisses, and they scattered across the table. She picked up all the pieces and carefully put them back into the torn bag.

After she got to high school, her father apologized whenever he visited them. Never specific about what he was sorry for, but he was always drinking and often he'd cry. But nothing ever changed. After she realized he only apologized to make himself feel better, she stopped whispering okay or nodding like she understood. She even moved away when he tried to hug her. Finally, he didn't hug her anymore, and he stopped apologizing. Did Uncle Jack apologize so he wouldn't feel bad about what he did? Is that why he said he would help with Marilyn?

She took a piece of candy. The foil wrapper came off quickly, and she opened five more of the kisses before popping them all in her mouth, closing her eyes, and thinking of nothing but of the melting sweet drops coating her tongue. Before they were gone, she quickly unwrapped more, letting them sit on her tongue until they melted.

Get out! It was as if she had screamed the words; her heart pounding and body moving to a crouching position. She wadded up the bag with the candy and stuffed it in her purse, walking quickly to the door, her eyes watching her feet, unwilling to look back at Marilyn.

She left the hospital vowing not to think about Marilyn, her father, or Uncle Jack. She couldn't stay another minute. Sleep. Maybe if she went to Grandmother's and got some sleep in a bed rather than a chair she would feel better. Maybe she should plan to go back to Tuscaloosa tomorrow and get her things while Lenny stayed here.

By the time she had turned onto Highway 168, her mother crept back into her mind, riding along with her and expanding until she was the same as the night air. What should she do? Stay by her mother's bedside and pray for her recovery? What had the stroke done to her mental condition?

She pulled the car into the driveway at her grandparents' farm, driving up close to the front of her mother's house. Her house. What if Marilyn didn't make it? Some part of her felt relief, then she felt horror at the relief she felt. Quickly she got out of the car, then paused, staring at the cinderblock porch and remembering all the times when she walked up these steps, hating the house and hating Marilyn. A dark fuzziness seemed to cover her, weighting both shoulders down and filling her brain. The walk to the back door of her grandmother's house was slow and drained all the remaining energy in her body.

Grandmother was standing near the TV in the living room, and she punched the off button before coming toward her, pausing in the door-frame. "Is Marilyn any better?" Ginny continued to take baby steps when her grandmother briefly put her hand on her shoulder. "Do you want some dinner? I can heat something up for you."

Ginny shook her head, once for both questions, while stuffing keys into her purse, her feet continuing to shuffle forward to the bedroom. Grand-mother asked no more questions. She probably felt Marilyn in the air too.

The bedroom was dark and much too warm, but Ginny closed the door behind her and sat on the edge of the bed, her hand pulling out the bag of chocolate Kisses and the other pulling off her shoes. Without turning on the light, she pressed her back against the headboard, gently knocking her head against the wall several times.

I will not get stuck back here. The words repeated over in her mind while her fingers began peeling, then tearing away foil from kisses. Mari-lyn was still in the air; she was here in the room. Ginny whispered the words aloud to her, "No matter what it takes, I will not get stuck here. I will not live here again. You hear me?"

She popped unwrapped kisses in her mouth while tears began rolling down her face. She softly rocked herself, refusing to wipe the tears away, but when they came close to her mouth her tongue licked them in with the chocolate.

CHAPTER 25

THE MESSENGER

GINNY, 1976

Speck's assistant, Abrial, sounded irritable this morning, telling Ginny they packed and removed all her things from her room before going into the office "to work our regular jobs." Ginny thanked her twice, telling her how much she appreciated her help.

"That's why I'm in law school. To assist people with legal problems."

Ginny knew from her tone the comment was meant to be sarcastic. Remembering it now made her fingers grip the steering wheel tight and wonder again why Speck would have such a difficult assistant.

The car was speeding down the interstate; she was in a hurry to go somewhere, anywhere to get away from the hospital. A park. With lots of trees and hiking on a trail. She imagined it and briefly thought of stopping en route to Tuscaloosa. She would pass several parks. She could shoot some pictures, but with no people around. That's what she wanted right now. No people. Sighing, she tried to remember the last shots she took. At the party before she got so drunk? There were people dressed up in various Fourth of July outfits that night, including a shirtless man walking on stilts, leaning over to get in the door, blue stars covering his nipples. Thinking of the party made her want to call Shelby. When she told Speck this morning that she planned to spend the night with Shelby while in Tuscaloosa, he insisted she stay with people he knew. He reminded her that reporters were waiting outside her classroom and angry letters continued to be sent to the paper, upset that Ginny took the baby's picture instead of calling the police. "We need to be cautious."

A tightening of her chest now reminded her of the fear that held to her body when Speck told her about the letters. Shelby was unsympathetic and offended when Ginny called her back to say she would be staying with Speck's friends instead of her, snapping that her network of people would have been able to keep Ginny hidden away, no matter what Speck thought. Later in the conversation, Shelby apologized for her outburst, but asked if Speck was expecting Ginny to stay at his place, maybe this was what he had in mind all along. Ginny simply hung up, certain Speck would never plan such a thing. With the phone still in her hand, doubt began to creep in, and she wondered why she trusted him so much.

Lenny looked tired this morning, driving in from Birmingham and getting to the hospital before her. The table was stacked with sodas, sandwiches and packages of cookies as well as a half-eaten biscuit oozing red jelly that dripped onto the wax paper wrap. He seemed to be spooked when Ginny told him that Marilyn had not opened her eyes since he left.

"Are you going to be okay?" She asked more than once. Each time he waved her away, cutting his eyes sharply back to Marilyn as if he thought he might catch her eyes open. Now she felt bad about leaving him there alone.

* * *

William and Becky Winters lived in a house that resembled a giant barn set back into acres of wooded land contained within a spiked black metal fence and no visible neighbors. The gate was open, and she drove inside the fence slowly, braking to study the abstract metal art piece that rested just inside that resembled a giant lion with a fan-like head that twirled with the breeze. She backed up and pulled the front of the car closer to the edge of the drive and to the lion, glancing up to the house to see if someone was watching. The upper sidewall of the barn-like house had rows of glass brick running the entire length of the house, but no other windows faced the gate. Grabbing her camera, she got out of the car and walked up the drive and then framed them with little background; the roach with its higher back end and lower front, seemingly bowing down to the slight whirling of the lion's head. She took several shots, calculating the shot so that the motion of the fan would blur in the shot. Smiling, she walked back. Lenny would be amused.

Getting back in the car, she took a deep breath and began moving slowly down the drive, wondering if anyone knew she was here. Speck told her this morning that Bill was an editor of a magazine in Birmingham and his wife Becky was an artist. Bill was a reporter in the early Sixties, writing stories about civil rights in Birmingham, and according to Speck,

216

he had paid a high price for it. She guessed the lion was Becky's work, and somehow, it made her feel better about coming to their place.

The gate began closing, and Ginny softly braked and began chewing a nail while watching through her rear view mirror. She could no longer get out. Slowly she continued up the drive, parking near the front entrance. Immediately, the heat cloaked her body while she reluctantly rolled up the windows and picked up her portfolio and purse. The heavy front door opened to the house and a short, plump woman came out, her white hair cut short on the sides but much longer in the back. She had a wide smile on her face and waved. As soon as Ginny stepped out of the car, the woman was beside her with hand outstretched.

"You must be Ginny. Welcome to our home."

Ginny shook her hand and smiled, relieved that she instantly liked the woman.

"Most people call me Beck," she stopped to shrug, "except for Speck. He says he doesn't like his friends' names to rhyme with his own." She rolled her eyes, one hand resting for a few seconds on Ginny's elbow.

"I have warm chocolate chip muffins and iced tea, or milk if you prefer. Let's get out of this heat." She led the way to the door, and then turned back to her. "Let me get your suitcase for you while we are out here."

Despite Ginny's protest, Beck got the small suitcase from the trunk. "I called Speck as soon as I saw you were here, so he will be on his way soon. Bill will be in later. He was trying to get away early, but we will see if he manages that."

The front door opened into a large foyer with a large mirror on one wall and an old life-size fortune-teller booth across from it on the right. A mannequin stared up at them, her hand full of tarot cards, seemingly watching as they set her things down in the corner and continued to the right through a heavy swinging door. They were immediately in a compact kitchen with steps on the left that went down into a long room with a wall of windows to the right that started waist-high and ended at the ceiling. An old, wooden bar ran the length of the windows with metal stools underneath. Several large, leather chairs circled around a coffee table on the left.

"What a great room." Ginny was immediately drawn to the windows and stepped down and stood next to the bar to peer out into the surprisingly dense forest outside.

"Thank you. I loved tree houses as a child, and this is the compromise Bill and I worked out when I wanted us to build a tree house. We have a house in the trees instead." She threw up her hands, "Have a seat wherever you like."

Beck busied herself putting ice in glasses, and Ginny sat on a stool, first noticing the movement of two birds in the trees and then a squirrel below them on the ground. She made out a large lantern hanging from a black metal loop, then realized it was the paw of a giant bear outlined in metal.

Beck stepped down from the kitchen behind the bar and set down two glasses and small plates in front of Ginny, then quickly stepped back up. Although heavily laminated, Ginny's fingers followed several large cuts in the old wood bar.

"The bar used to be in an old hotel in Atlanta before they tore it down." She came back on the outside of the bar this time and held out a plate of muffins to Ginny before setting the plate down between them, along with a small, thick pitcher. "This is warm chocolate-orange sauce for the muffin, if you like."

Beck sat on the stool next to her, "Sometimes I feel like a waitress running back behind the bar to serve guests that are sitting in a straight line instead of a circle around a table."

She poured glaze on her muffin and took a bite. "Mmmm… This is so good."

Ginny followed her lead but started with a smaller bite with only a bit of sauce. The tang and slight bite of orange liqueur in the warm dark chocolate was so good that she closed her eyes for a second and then poured more on her muffin. Beck nudged her with her arm, motioning toward the top of the windows where a bird was fluttering all along the top, apparently trying to find a way to get inside. It finally fluttered down to the bottom, bumping into the glass several times before moving back up from where it started.

After taking a sip of tea, Beck paused to look at her. "How is your mom? I meant to ask earlier. All of this must be so hard for you… and your family."

It was like tight strings in Ginny's stomach had been pulled, and she bent forward slightly to ease the pain, setting the muffin on her plate while trying to swallow the small bite. She picked up the glass of tea, unable to drink, but desperate to delay giving an answer, fearing that Marilyn might come here and fill this house with her presence once Ginny spoke of her.

Her hand got cold holding the glass, and it seemed as if a long time had passed. She set it down, her eyes quickly searching the top of the windows for the bird trying to get in, but it was gone.

"My mother is still in a coma. My brother is with her now." Would that be enough, she wondered? Should she say more? Beck was silent. Ginny glanced at her, saw her eyes were concerned, still looking at her. "My father does not visit her, not for a long time now."

"I'm so sorry." Beck's voice was soft. "You are so young to have to handle this and the death of the baby." Her hand reached out, grasping the top of Ginny's, the edge of her fingers bumping the small pitcher of chocolate orange sauce that fell over, creating a partial circle that began to spread out.

"The pitcher." Ginny used her other hand to quickly set the pitcher upright, but it was mostly empty.

"Honey, don't worry about that. I'll get it." She squeezed Ginny's hand for emphasis; her voice very soft.

Ginny face was getting warm, and an uncomfortable shyness bubbled her apart from Beck. Her eyes focused on the chocolate sauce circle.

"Tell me about your mom." Beck let go of Ginny's hand, but Ginny didn't look up. The chocolate circle was now contained within its own thickened border that had cooled faster than the insides. A deep longing welled up inside her and she wanted to puncture the edge of the chocolate border with her finger to allow the insides a way out. Instead, she looked up at Beck, her sentences pouring out.

"My mother was… is not normal." Beck nodded and looked away before quickly looking back, "She hears voices. She's depressed all the time. She's difficult. She doesn't…"

A loud buzzing startled them both.

"That's probably Speck and Abrial at the gate." Her voice was low, but Beck remained still. "Your mom doesn't what?"

Ginny grabbed several napkins and pressed them onto the circle of sauce, leaving the paper stuck there. Why was she telling Beck this? She felt confused and uncertain; her hand picked up the glass of tea and held it in front of her mouth before continuing, "She doesn't act like a real mother."

Beck nodded, waiting until there was another buzz before she got up and walked toward the swinging door. Sipping the sweet tea, Ginny stared at the trees before her, still uncomfortable, wondering what Beck thought of her talking about her mother like that. Her hand pressed the napkins down to soak up the sauce before she wiped them in a circular motion and dropped them into her plate. Speck's voice was loud in the foyer, and she quickly poured a few drops of tea on the spot before wiping it again with a clean napkin so that the circle would be completely gone before he could see it.

Abrial had helped Speck bring in two boxes with the photography things and left them in the foyer. Ginny thanked them both again, pointedly thanking Abrial for remembering to bring them in from the heat. Abrial shrugged, frowning at the chocolate-soiled napkins on Ginny's plate after Beck told her there was no more chocolate sauce for her muffin. She quickly left without telling anyone goodbye.

Speck sat down at the bar after Beck excused herself to begin preparing for dinner; his eyes narrowing when they looked into the forest, but Ginny was sure he was not seeing the trees. Tiny fingers of fear squeezed her stomach, and she rushed words from her mouth without concern for being within earshot of Beck, "What are they going to ask when I testify?"

He turned from the window, his words quick as if he had anticipated the question. "It will be similar to the questions they already asked you when we first took them the pictures. I will go over what I think they will ask. You are just going to tell the truth, but you are only going to answer the question they ask—the specific question, nothing more. No additional explanations or saying what you think."

She took a deep breath, looking down at her hands, remembering the tiny hand of the baby, the tiny arm reaching out and captured forever in her head and in the picture. Was the girl trying to get Ginny to help the baby? It did not occur to her that the baby could be saved. Why didn't she think to call the police or insist that the girl tell her what was wrong with the baby? Now what was going to happen to the girl? As quickly as she thought it, she tried to stop, but blurted it out instead, "What's going to happen to her? The mother?"

Speck frowned, his eyes intense, studying her. "Ginny, you have no responsibility for what happened to the baby or what happens to this girl." He paused, "Don't try to help her in your testimony. Comments you make could make it worse for her. Just answer the specific questions with the truth and nothing more. Everything is out of your hands, understand?"

* * *

Bill was a tall man with a stocky build. He limped and used a cane, his leg difficult to bend when coming down the step. His white dress shirt was rumpled but still tucked in his trousers and the sleeves were rolled up. He smiled when introduced to Ginny, but his eyes were sharp and unblinking. Her body stiffened from his look, fearing he was making some type of opinion of her guilt and going to ask about the Davies girl. He did not.

They had a late dinner, and Ginny was happy to quietly sit at the end of the bar, listening to the conversation as it switched among Speck, Bill and Beck, often erupting in laughter. Beck served cold sweet potato soup, salad with nuts and dried cherries, and some sort of cold fish that looked raw but tasted like pickles. Even the crackers on the side were brown and grainy, not like regular saltines. Ginny tasted a little of each but found she could not eat much.

Bill laughed easily with Speck, most loudly when he implied he lost money at their last poker game to Abrial. Speck turned to Ginny and explained proudly that Abrial paid most of her tuition in law school by playing poker with a local group of men who drank more than they played.

"Some of us don't drink that much. We're just lousy players." Bill retorted, smiling at Beck as she stood and motioned toward the chairs.

"Let's move over to the circle and get more comfortable." She picked up two serving bowls, "First, I'll make us some coffee." Speck stood, stacking up bowls and small plates before following her to the kitchen.

Before Ginny could decide if she should help carry dishes to the kitchen, Bill smiled at her, a hand waving toward the big chairs, "Shall we move to the circle?"

She nodded and stood.

"Maybe you could show me some of your work?" He held to the counter for a few seconds while moving his body slowly forward and then shifting his weight to his cane.

Nervousness came over her, worse than it did in class, but she nodded. "I'll get my portfolio." She walked up the step past the kitchen, hearing Speck tell Beck her coffee was too weak.

"It's a whole scoop per cup."

In the foyer, Ginny opened one of the boxes brought in by Abrial, filled with papers, books and pictures from her desk in her room. The other box held plastic sheets of negatives, about a hundred small boxes of slides, and a stack of photographs she developed in the dark room the day before the Fourth of July party. She would need to go through these for class shots to turn in. She was at once grateful the professor was willing to grade her final assignment without her going to the last week of classes. She grabbed the portfolio sitting near her purse and the stack of photographs and went back, setting the portfolio on the coffee table in front of Bill. She sat on the edge of another chair, ready to flip through the stack but instead watched Bill.

He turned pages quickly, slowing down to look carefully at a few shots, before flipping quickly through the rest.

He nodded at the stack in her hands while sliding the portfolio to the center of the table.

She hesitated, "These I developed right before my mother… I haven't really looked through them since they were developed. Abrial packed them this morning."

Some of the assignments were dumb, and she thought of quickly fanning through the pictures to take them out, instead she gave the stack to him. Maybe he expected her to show him shots of the Davies girl. Even though Speck had said he wouldn't, he also said that they talked about whether Bill might do a story about her or her work later to help direct some of the speculation about her. She declined, feeling scared and uncomfortable and Speck did not mention it again.

Bill set the stack down on the table in front of his seat. He flipped the first one over face down.

"I turned in all the pictures I had of the Davies girl… if that is what interests you."

He looked up into her eyes briefly, making a slight nod before he looked back down.

The smell of coffee brought Marilyn to mind and guilt that she had not called Lenny to check on her or him. It was probably too late or maybe not… she tried to pull her thoughts back, wanting to be without Marilyn in her head a little longer tonight.

"Is this a picture of Grace LeRaunt?" Bill was looking at the photo up close to his face.

"Grace LeRaunt?" She questioned, not recognizing the name.

Bill's eyes bunched up more while he studied around the edges of the photo. Still holding it, he looked at the next picture in the stack, and they both saw the photograph of Speck carrying his mother.

"And Speck with Mrs. LeRaunt." There was surprise in Bill's voice.

Speck's mother. Of course. The pictures had been part of the last rolls she developed. Dread stiffened her body when she glanced toward the kitchen and saw from his expression that Speck had heard and was walking toward them, an empty cup rattling in the saucer he carried.

"You're showing those pictures? I told you I wanted the pictures and the negatives." Speck's voice was stern, his jaws tight and barely moving.

They both looked at her, Bill's eyebrow raised slightly and Speck's cup still rattling. Bill spoke first, his voice low, directed at Speck. "She's not showing the pictures to the public, Speck. She has only shown them to me—unless Abrial saw them when she packed Ginny's things."

Beck came up behind Speck holding a tray with coffee, cream, and sugar.

"These pictures are private." Speck looked from Bill to Ginny, "You didn't have permission to take them in the first place."

Anger and a rush of adrenalin pushed Ginny to speak. "Actually, I did ask your mother if I could take… some of them."

"Grace LeRaunt is your mother?" Bill's voice was very low. "People have speculated all kinds of things, since she disappeared shortly after her husband's death."

Speck ignored him and glared at Ginny, setting the coffee cup on the table. His eyes went to the picture Bill still held in his hand, it was of his mother holding flowers to her chest. He inhaled quickly, his face softening before it quickly tensed again. His eyes danced all around the photograph, and Ginny looked with him at his mother's almond eyes almost closed, a serene expression on her face that belied the tightly wound fingers squeezing and crushing the flower stems at her chest. Ginny remembered this photograph had been taken while Speck was out of her room.

Beck poured coffee in Speck's cup, her eyes intense and looking at Bill. She frowned, and he cleared his throat.

"Ginny, would you and Beck give Speck and me a few minutes?"

"Let me show you the guest room, Ginny. We can get some coffee later."

Ginny followed her, hesitating briefly at the door while she fought the urge to go back and grab the pictures from the table. When she looked back, Speck's eyes were still accusatory. Would he get angry enough to take the prints? She reminded herself that the negatives were still in the box in the foyer. Surely he wouldn't take the negatives and burn them. A quick sharp pain in her chest made her stop walking, and then it was gone, but not before a vague image came to mind of her mother burning Lucille's picture years ago.

The guest room was down a long hallway with rows of glass brick near the ceiling but no windows. Beck opened a door and turned on a lamp between twin metal beds. The walls were painted a dark blue and held different sized black-and-white photographs in ivory frames. A table and chair set in front of large windows that looked into the forest, almost dark now, with a faint light from a different lantern.

Beck closed the blinds. "The bathroom is next door, and there is one more guestroom after that. I thought you might like this one because of the old black and white prints."

Ginny continued staring at the closed blinds, her skin at once prickly. She forced herself to glance at photograph near her; a woman in ragged dress holding a child at her side. It was a picture she recognized but could not think of the photographer. She turned back toward the door. All she could think about were the photos she left on the table and the box of negatives in the foyer, both near an angry Speck.

"Speck seems really angry with me."

"I suppose he is." Beck busied herself pulling down the spread and removing the sham covered pillow. She sat on a bench at the end of one bed. "You will find that your art will do that sometimes."

"Art?"

"Art often shines a light on things people don't want to see. Instead of dealing with what they don't want to see, people frequently get mad at the messenger. The artist."

Were her photographs art? Is that why people seem to react so negatively, even Marilyn?

"Regardless of how angry Speck is, he will do his best to protect you from people who want someone to hold accountable for what happened to that baby. Nobody is even thinking about who is accountable for what happened to this girl for all these years."

Everything seemed to be getting fuzzy. Ginny was feeling dizzy, as if she had dropped down into a strange river in a boat that kept moving through dangerous rapids and she was helpless to stop. She moved to the table and chair and turned the chair outward as she sat down. Beck's smile had become more of a straight line, tight against her teeth.

"Speck has his blind spots. Your pictures probably make him see things he does not want to see either."

What was she not telling her about Speck? Maybe she should have asked more questions when Speck said he would help her. She whispered to Beck, "What am I suppose to do now?"

"You keep moving forward. Most of what you are going through right now will work itself out shortly." Beck's face relaxed, "In terms of Speck, give him a little time. He has problems of his own. All of us do."

"Why doesn't Speck drive?" Ginny wanted some answers now, but already knowing it was related to his drinking, just like her father, who could no longer drive.

"His license was suspended after an accident. I'm not comfortable in giving details." Beck pushed up a sleeve before continuing, "He and Abrial live together, but she prefers not to socialize with him in public—just so you understand that. She grew up in France, but her mother is an

American. She can sometimes be difficult but does appear to care deeply about Speck."

Beck stood and straightened pictures that were already straight then turned quickly. "Now that I know about Speck's mother, his attraction to Abrial makes sense."

"Becky, I'm leaving." Speck's voice came from the hallway, "Abrial is here."

Beck frowned and then quickly walked from the room and down the hall with Ginny close behind her. "Speck, don't leave now. Ask Abrial to come in and have coffee."

Ginny tried to imagine Speck and Abrial living together as a couple, but couldn't. Her head hurt, and she wished she might just get her photos and go to bed.

"I need to go." Speck answered quickly. He was already at the door and continued talking without turning back. Ginny saw he did not have the photos in either hand.

"Ginny, remember there's a student from the dean's office bringing over paperwork for you to sign in the morning." He opened the door and walked outside. "Thanks for dinner, Becky. It was great as usual." The door quickly closed behind him.

*   *   *

The sky had been overcast all day, making the drive from Tuscaloosa to the hospital much cooler. It was almost four p.m. when Ginny pushed open the door to Marilyn's room at the hospital and quickly walked past the other patient and the center curtain.

"How is she?" Her eyes met Lenny's then switched to check Marilyn's face, quickly moving down to her sheet-covered body when she noticed a slight movement, perhaps a shudder. Ginny's heart beat faster and she walked closer. Marilyn had no expression, although her face was more flushed than usual and her once beautiful hair was tangled and bunched back with a plain rubber band. Another shudder moved the sheet again.

"They say it's her body reacting to the ice packs they have all around her." Lenny stood and was on Marilyn's other side. "She has a high fever."

His eyes looked glazed, perhaps from fatigue or maybe it was sadness. Ginny looked away quickly, allowing her hand to smooth the blanket at Marilyn's feet. For a moment she had hoped things were going back to normal; normal was what she needed. Something to be normal. She wanted to scream at Marilyn to wake up and act normal.

"You're back early."

She chewed at her bottom lip, "Speck canceled our meeting this morning. I stayed long enough to sign some papers from the University." She pulled the blanket up to cover more of Marilyn's body after watching her shiver again.

He shook his head. "The blanket won't help the fever to go down. Why did he cancel?"

"His assistant said he had an emergency during the night and had to leave town." She stopped herself from saying that Abrial had gotten angry when she'd asked why he was canceling and if he was still angry over his mother's pictures.

"You're not the only person dealing with a sick mother, Ginny, and he also has other clients."

The pictures were still on the table after Speck left, and she packed them back in the box. She also checked the box again after Bill left for work. A pang of guilt edged in her head now. She should trust them. All of them were trying to help her, and she was so suspicious and was worried more about the pictures than their feelings. Beck insisted on making breakfast and told her to call if she needed anything, or even just to talk. "After the trial next week, we'll figure out something relaxing to do."

Ginny opened the drawer on the bedside table and took out a hairbrush before gently taking the rubber band from Marilyn's hair. "Did you spend the night here?"

Lenny nodded.

The biggest tangle was in the back of Marilyn's head, and Ginny brushed the bottom of it while pressing against the scalp to ease the strain. With each pull of the small brush she hesitated, glancing at Marilyn and imagining her awake, angry that she was being touched. The last snarl resulted in a small knot of hair in the brush, and Ginny set it on the bed and used her fingers to try and detangle the other side.

"Let's go get dinner somewhere. I need to get out." Lenny slid several neat stacks of coins off the windowsill into his hand and then into his pocket.

Ginny hesitated, should they both leave with her fever so high?

As if he read her mind, he answered, his voice flat. "The doctor said this morning that she could be like this for a long time. After they get her fever down, they will help us move her into a nursing home."

He walked around and took the brush, staring at the knot of hair before pulling it out and holding it up to Ginny, his eyebrows raised.

"I know. I'm trying to do it with my fingers."

He dropped the knot in the trash and set the brush back on the bed before running his fingers through his own hair. "They will call Grandmother if anything changes. We just need to check in with her several times."

$$* \quad * \quad *$$

Maybe it would have been better if she slept on the couch. At least there wouldn't be a dip in the center. There were no extra sheets that Ginny could find, so she lay on the top of the spread on her mother's bed, flipping over again while pulling at her shorts that were twisting. She willed herself to go to sleep while facing the front door, left open to let in air and aided by an oscillating fan going back and forth. It lulled her into thinking a cool breeze might comfort her, but it didn't and the sound of the whirling blades irritated her each time it turned.

Marilyn was all she could think about here. She supposed this was why they were spending the night, a chance to pretend things were normal. She swallowed. Maybe Marilyn would be okay. Maybe things would go back to the way they were. But somehow she knew they would not for Marilyn. Her presence was softer, less intense even in her own room, her own house.

"Are you asleep?" She smiled at Lenny's whisper, loud enough to wake her up even if she had been sleeping.

"No."

The metal bedsprings of his old bed creaked loudly, and she knew he was getting up. There was no moonlight with the cloud cover, and the air was muggy and thick. With the click of the chain, the single dangling light bulb was bright in the room.

"Could you please find a lamp instead of that damn glaring bulb?" She held a hand over her eyes while sitting up and putting her feet on the floor.

Lenny sighed but disappeared into the smaller back room and brought out a lamp, setting it on the dresser before plugging it in and pulling the chain of the overhead light bulb. His T-shirt was wet with perspiration.

"God it's hot in here. Whose bright idea was it to spend the night here anyway?" She smiled at her brother while pulling her T-shirt sleeve up to blot sweat underneath her hair.

"At least you were getting some air from the fan. The back of the couch blocks my bed."

She grabbed the strands of her hair up and tied them in a knot on top of her head while walking to the sink and patting cool water on her neck and face. She soaked a washcloth with water and threw it to Lenny, who caught it with one hand.

He sat on the couch. "Why did we move in here?"

Sometimes she envied him being too young to remember the earlier years. Images came at her from when they moved in, when he was only a baby and her grandparents were in the final stages of building a house to replace the one that had burned. She sat in the straight back chair near the table. "Daddy was drinking a lot and hitting Mother a lot. Mother's mind got worse. She thought people were trying to poison her and you."

"She wasn't worried about you or Sheila getting poisoned?"

Ginny's body flinched and she stopped talking. Why did Marilyn leave them out? Did she no longer care what happened to them? Did Lenny understand something she didn't? She glanced at Lenny leaning back in the couch, the washcloth spread over his face.

She pushed the question aside and continued talking, her words rushed. "She had tried to commit suicide several times." Lenny sat up quickly and stretched to reach his soda cup on the nightstand.

"The neighbors in the apartment building convinced Mother to let them bring us here while Daddy was at work. They told them," she nodded her head toward their grandparents' house, "that Daddy had gotten so violent that they believed he would eventually kill us all."

Lenny took the plastic top off his soda cup and shook ice into his mouth, crunching the pieces with his teeth.

"We were only supposed to be here awhile, but we ended up staying here. For years. And years."

The skin around Lenny's eyes crinkled, and his shoulders moved slightly up and then down; his fingers rubbed across the series of burned out grooves from cigarettes on the arm of the couch. Ginny quietly stood and reached out with cupped palms and Lenny shook ice into them. She sat back down, biting into several pieces while allowing the rest to melt in her hand. She transferred the ice to the other hand and patted her face. The melted ice felt good on her face, and she could finally feel a breeze from the fan as it turned.

A bracelet with red glass sets was on the table, and she picked it up, letting her fingers rub over them before taking it to her mother's dresser and dropping it inside the clear plastic jewelry box. She hesitated before replacing the lid, taking out an emerald earring with tiny rhinestones and clipped it on her ear, wincing with the pinch of pain. She fished out the other one and a matching necklace, feeling like she did as a child, playing with her mother's jewelry and trying to imagine a time when Marilyn would have worn these things. There had also been party dresses, long ago altered into something else or thrown out, but she could only remember them bulging out from the back of the closet of this house; never a time when Marilyn had dressed up in one of them. Her thumb and finger pressed open the spring-loaded clasp of the necklace and put it around her neck, letting the clasp close on the loop.

Lenny sat forward in the couch and stretched to reach her portfolio in the chair. He glanced up at her, "Those don't look good."

"What? Not right with my sweaty T-shirt?" She smiled but left them on and sat down beside him.

"Too old-fashioned." He flipped through the pages of photographs, stopping to look at pictures of Gilbert she shot for a class assignment.

"He looks a lot like you when you were a baby."

He held the picture closer. "His hair is getting dark."

"Just like yours did."

"Wasn't Sheila's hair blond as a baby too?"

"No, she was bald. No hair at all." Ginny stood up and went to the closet in the small room and pulled out the large red box from the shelf where her mother kept pictures. She sat back down on the couch and opened it, rummaging her fingers through pictures, pulling up first one then another, pointing out to Lenny that his hair had been so blond it looked white in the black and white baby pictures. There were two baby books in the bottom of the box, and she opened the first, showing Lenny the bald-headed Sheila with the toothless grin attached to the first page.

"I've seen that before."

"Bald-headed until she was almost two. That's what Grandmother says."

"Ginny? Lenny?"

They both jumped, looking up at the door where Grandmother was standing on the porch, the light reflecting off her glasses and her old white housecoat buttoned up wrong; her open palm patting against the screen.

"The hospital called. You need to get back. The nurse doesn't think Marilyn will last the night."

CHAPTER 26

THE END

GINNY, 1976

Her feet hurt, and now a headache surrounded her eyes. She nodded again to Mrs. Jackson, a neighbor who had come by Grandmother's house earlier this morning to drop off a banana pudding and was now repeating herself from that conversation, expressing shock that Marilyn was dead. She had not made it to the hospital to see her before she died. Would they be able to forgive her? Ginny could not recall Mrs. Jackson ever visiting Marilyn when she was alive, but she nodded until the woman finally turned to the young teenager standing behind her in the line and introduced him as her son before she moved on and started at the beginning of her speech with Lenny.

Ginny shook the son's hand, who simply said, "Sorry." From his expression Ginny wasn't sure if he was referring to Marilyn's death or his mother's speech. They stood uncomfortably face-to-face until his mother completed her comments to Lenny.

Breathing in slowly, Ginny took a step forward and looked down the long receiving line--most people here barely knew her mother. If they did, it was when she was a girl. Most of them came because of her grandmother or one of her mother's siblings. There were no friends of hers, either, no Shelby or any of the others in the artist's group or anyone from high school—not that she had expected anyone. She winced, shifting her weight to one leg, temped to kick off the shoes. Why did she buy high heels to wear to the funeral?

"How are you, hon?" The kind, round face smiled as the shorter woman reached both arms out to her.

"I'm doing okay." Ginny uncomfortably leaned down and accepted the hug. The last two days had been filled with hugs from strangers.

She patted Ginny's back. "I know you don't remember me, but I'm Patsy, your father's oldest sister. I'm so sorry about your mother."

Ginny drew a blank, but noticed Patsy looked a little like her grandmother did years ago.

"Have you heard from your father?"

Ginny shook her head, "Lenny talked to him the night before Mother died. I believe he is out of town."

"Really?" She frowned. "Divorce makes things hard. I hated we never got to see you kids much after that."

Divorce? She guessed her father had told his family he was divorced. Which probably meant that he also told them he was married to the woman he was living with now. Her stomach drew up tight.

"Honey, don't try to pretend everything is okay and be so brave," Patsy squeezed Ginny's arm while slowly moving forward, her head turning back, "take it from an old woman who has been to many funerals."

She *was* okay. She just had to make it through this day, and then there would be the trial in two days. When she and Lenny got back to the hospital and accepted Marilyn was going to die, they positioned chairs on either side of her bed and sat for hours. Without any noticeable sign that she was aware of them, Marilyn stopped breathing shortly before sunrise and before Sheila could get back to the hospital from Mobile.

When they first arrived at the hospital, she held tightly to Marilyn's hand, not wanting her to feel alone, but Marilyn's hand never cupped around her own. Finally, it had felt so pointless, just as it did whenever she tried to be close to Marilyn as a child. Marilyn never wanted Ginny to hug or touch her, telling Ginny she was too old to be "wanting all that attention." After a few hours that night, she let go of Marilyn's hand, feeling oddly hollow like a chocolate Easter bunny shell with nothing inside.

The funeral felt like a play; they were all instructed on their parts, and she moved quickly to say and do what she was told, feeling more and more empty.

"Honey, I'm so sorry you're going through this," a woman with thin, wispy brown hair moved in close, the smell of cigarette smoke becoming stronger as she did. "Just remember that God don't send you nothing you can't handle." She continued to nod, a knowing smile on her face, a thin finger quickly pointing up close to Ginny's face. "You just remember. Nothing you can't handle."

She was sure the woman was implying something about Marilyn with her comment, and the knot in Ginny's stomach formed into a fist, rushing upward and making her body shake. She clasped both hands together, fighting the impulse to shove the woman back, but her voice blurted out, thick and low, "Then why are there so many people who crack up or commit suicide after God sends them stuff?

The woman's head jerked back, her brows bunching together over startled, wide-open eyes. "Girl, don't ever, ever question God."

Feeling Sheila's hand on her trembling arm, Ginny willed herself to keep quiet, beating down the adrenalin that made her want to scream at the woman who started again with her finger pointing, "Suicide is a sin. Those people burn in hell!"

People where staring, and Ginny allowed herself to be pulled closer to Sheila.

"Who is she?" Sheila whispered, but not waiting for an answer and immediately speaking louder, "Lavonne, you remember Ginny."

The tall, pretty woman was near her mother's age and wore bright red lipstick. Ginny forced a smile, immediately remembering her from years ago at another funeral or gathering.

"Goodness. Some people really shouldn't try to comfort people." Lavonne smiled. "I have pictures of your mother from back in Junior High. I'll have to look through them and let you girls get some copies. We went everywhere together back then."

"Mother has… had a bunch of pictures too. We should get together and look through all of them." Sheila continued, and Lavonne shared a story about her and Marilyn cutting each other's hair in Junior High School. Ginny kept losing threads of the story so she smiled whenever Sheila did; her hands still tightly clasped together.

Lavonne moved forward then, stretching to hold her hand out to Lenny. "I'd know you anywhere. You look a lot like your daddy."

A man had taken Sheila's hand, and then Ginny's, squeezing tight, his solemn expression unchanged as he walked past. Sheila murmured, "Don't even know who he is."

Lavonne quietly walked from Lenny to the exit; not stopping by Marilyn's coffin. Ginny wondered why she came. The funeral seemed silly, people pretending Marilyn had been a close part of their life. Stepping behind Sheila, she faced the wall, her face close enough to see brush strokes in a painting with dark murky brown shadows surrounding fruit in a bowl.

Her fingers grasped underneath her black shirtdress for the chain around her neck and slid down to the emerald stone, her hand forming a fist around it. An impulse urged her to jerk the chain and break it away from her neck, but she froze, breathing in and out, her hand staying tight.

Grandmother leaned over from the other side of Sheila, pressing her finger and thumb into the flesh of Ginny's arm as if to pinch; her voice a loud whisper. "What's wrong?"

"Nothing." Ginny quickly returned her grandmother's gaze until her eyes dropped to the fist she had made underneath her dress. Another finger nudged her in the back, and Sheila whispered, "It's the funeral home guy."

Ginny let go of the stone and turned, glancing at Lenny first, but he was already watching the young man, smiling in an odd, apologetic way at Grandmother. His hair was combed back, puffy on top, like the men from gospel singing groups in the Fifties. Yesterday he had pressed her to pick out at two songs for the funeral service, even though she told him that as far as they knew, Marilyn had no favorite hymns. After more insistence, she chose the only song she recognized on the list, "The Old Rugged Cross". After reading to the end and going back up, she chose "This World Is Not My Home". Even though she had never heard of it, the title seemed to fit.

"We need to start the service now." His whisper was loud, then he turned and announced to the crowd that only immediate family should remain for a final viewing and that visitors intending on staying for the funeral should exit through the doors on the right and take a seat in the chapel. As people moved out, he turned and took their grandmother's arm, ushering her toward Marilyn's coffin, her grandfather following behind.

Ginny averted her eyes from her grandmother's tears instead they followed the curve of the heavily padded, silky cream-colored lining inside the coffin. Marilyn's sisters and brothers chipped in to pay for the sleek shiny brown coffin that would be Marilyn's forever home. The funeral director had already known before Marilyn's three children arrived in his office that they had no money. He checked the standard boxes all the way to the end of the contract before handing Sheila his Cross pen for their signatures. Later he chased after them into the parking lot, breathlessly asking if one of them still had his pen. Lenny had mindlessly stuck the pen in his pocket, and he took it out, apologizing. The funeral director did not answer, quickly taking the pen from his hand and turning back to go inside.

Each of the siblings and their families lined up in front of the coffin. One by one, they walked forward and then were directed to go through a back door that would take them to the family section of the chapel, a platform with a podium, separated by drapes from the general public who were seated below the staging area.

People did not linger long at Marilyn's casket for the last viewing, except for Uncle Jack, who stood uneasily at the head of the casket as others walked past him. Ginny looked away, breathing in deeply as her eyes tried to count the number of roses in the casket cover. The florist assured them she would make sure it was beautiful even though it was the cheapest price. It was beautiful, even though it had lots of baby's breath.

"Baby's breath." She murmured it out loud, making her own breath shallow. Why did they call it that? Baby's breath at a funeral. Baby breathing. Baby not breathing. The Davies baby stopped breathing. How long had she struggled to breathe? Quickly Ginny sucked in air, closing her eyes and picturing the Davies baby in a casket, the tiny arm still up, erratically searching. Tears streamed from her closed eyes, and she bent over, sliding a foot out of one shoe, then the other, demanding her mind to stop thinking of the baby. Start counting the roses again. You just have to get through this day. Would it be easier after Marilyn was buried?

They chose a spot of land for her grave near her great-grandparents' plot as her grandmother wished. For years her grandfather's family had been buried at the same small church where her great-great-grandfather had donated the land for the building and the graveyard. The church property was attached to her grandfather's inherited land, and even though no one in the family participated in the church for years, the family continued to bury their dead there.

The room was now almost empty. Sheila and Mike walked up to the coffin, Charleen and Gilbert in their arms. Gilbert stared at Marilyn and then quickly looked back to Sheila, eyes wide in his confused face. He quickly hid in his father's neck, refusing to look up again after Sheila told him to tell Marilyn goodbye. Instead Charleen waved goodbye at Gilbert, closing and opening her hand completely, while looking back at the tears on her mother's face.

Lenny wiped tears from his eyes several times before offering his arm to Ginny. She picked up her heels with one hand and took his arm, noticing the silence when the background music stopped. She saw Marilyn's body last night and avoided it when she arrived early this morning. The thick crown of Rita Hayworth curls normally circling her head was gone; her hair was pulled back, flat and straight. She wore heavy make-up and a dark green silky dress with a mandarin collar and empire waist her older sister bought for her. Marilyn was still not herself.

"The Old Rugged Cross" began to play over the stereo system— loud, as if to simulate a live performance. Ginny dropped her shoes and reached for the emerald rhinestone necklace, circling the chain around her neck until she found the clasp.

"Lift her head a little."

"What?" Lenny whispered, giving her a wide-eyed look while watching her take the chain from her own neck. He carefully put his hands around the sides of Marilyn's head and lifted.

Ginny cringed when her fingers touched Marilyn's neck, hard and unyielding. She quickly pulled the chain around but sighed when the emerald stone slid to the side instead of lying flat on Marilyn's chest.

"You really think she would have worn that here?" A touch of humor was in Lenny's whisper.

"No, but it matches her dress, and she wouldn't have worn that either." Ginny nudged him with her shoulder and instantly felt sharp physical pain in her chest. The numbness she felt earlier had lifted. Quickly her fingers loosened a few tendrils of Marilyn's hair, pulling them from the clasp that held them tight, but they remained straight and stiff, falling back into the same place.

"Ready?"

Lenny glanced at her, and they stepped back. The funeral director and an assistant silently closed the coffin.

The music was louder in the next room where they were directed through a short narrow aisle to the front row. The folding front chairs were up too far to be protected from view by the drapery and as they sat down, "The Old Rugged Cross" ended and in the silence she glanced out to her left at the small crowd slightly below them, feeling again as if she were in a play. She flinched as a voice sang out loudly over the speaker without accompaniment.

"This world is not my home, no, not my home."

A giggle escaped as Ginny looked toward the speaker on the wall, expecting others to be startled as well but no one seemed to notice. The piano accompaniment began, striking and irregular, then matching the woman's next line.

More giggles bubbled up, and she leaned forward, arms wrapping tight around her own body attempting to hold it still. The song continued and more giggles erupted and then she was laughing with her whole body, hysterical, never-ending laughter, and she buried her face in her hands, bowing her head low and leaning into Lenny. Her body shook from the laughter and refused to stop, the muscles hurting and wheezing erupting from her lungs. She rocked herself slightly and tried to think of something to make it stop. But the song continued on and on, and she imagined

Marilyn laughing too, the way she always did that made them think she was crazy. Maybe Ginny was crazy now.

There were sounds of movement and chairs scraping the floor as others stood and came in closer, touching her, different hands squeezing her arms and patting her back and head. A cousin leaned in from behind her, whispering words that left her breath in Ginny's right ear. Then the song ended and in the crush of silence she began to cry, continuing to hold herself crunched together, her head buried inside the crook of her brother's arm.

*   *   *

It was after three o'clock before people begin leaving her grandmother's house, having come over after the funeral to eat. Neighbors brought in food, and it covered the counter tops and the large chest-type freezer. Her grandmother sent whole pies and pieces of chicken home with each of Marilyn's siblings as they left.

They changed into jeans before getting into Sheila's van to go down the road to the graveyard. They stood at the canopy of flowers covering Marilyn's grave and continuing on the ground around it and other graves.

Sheila set Charleen down and allowed her to pick flowers from the arrangements at the edge. "Mother hated the hospital. Maybe now she feels like she's home."

Ginny nodded, trying to reassure her that Marilyn would be at peace here. The bright sun was hurting her head, and it was still hot. She guiltily remembered her assertion only a few nights ago that she wouldn't come back home to stay, no matter what happened to Marilyn.

Charleen dropped her flowers and tried to lift up the flowerpot. Sheila took the pot from her and picked her up, ignoring her screech of displeasure. "Momma got so many flowers."

Ginny picked up the flowers with the crushed stems and waved them in front of Charleen's face. Baby fingers with tiny nails snatched flowers from her before struggling to get from her mother's arms and back on the ground. Were there flowers at the Davies baby's funeral? Had the mother attended the funeral? How could she have stood it?

Ginny began to feel dizzy and turned quickly away. "I'm going back to the van." She managed to smile as she passed Gilbert running through the headstones with his father close behind him. She opened the van doors and sat inside. She didn't even know the baby's name. Taking several deep breaths, she wiped the sweat from her face on her T-shirt and picked up her camera. She twisted on the telephoto lens and removed the lens cover. Lenny was holding Charleen, her hands full of new flowers. She took several shots and then refocused to shoot the grave and flowers. Did Marilyn ever get flowers when she was alive?

* * *

After Lenny and Sheila left for home, Ginny took a bowl of banana pudding at her grandmother's insistence, stirring it over and over while seated with her in the living room watching the news on TV. Her grandfather's truck returned from a run to the store for tobacco, and grandmother hurried back to the kitchen to put two buttered biscuits on his plate.

She returned to her seat in front of the TV, and they sat silently until the news was off and her grandfather sat down. Ginny and her Grandmother cleared the table of food and began to wash the stacks of dishes, and she was grateful that earlier someone washed many of the dishes from the first round of guests. Neither of them talked, Ginny patting her shoulder and softly whispering good night when she left to go back to the bedroom.

She stretched across the bed and closed her eyes, her body too exhausted to move. She was grateful that Lenny brought her suitcase in from Marilyn's house. She could not visit or sleep with Marilyn tonight.

* * *

It had to be early morning, but it was still dark. Her feet were cold and hanging off the bed and the muscles in her calves were sore. She also had to pee. Rising up, she saw she was still lying across the bed on top of the covers and in her jeans. Slowly she sat up and then stood, turning down the sheet and spread. The fan in the bedroom was loud and drowned out her noise while she walked quietly in the dark to the bathroom and pulled down her jeans and panties and sat on the commode.

She stood, flushing the toilet while glancing out the small open bathroom window, eyes drawn immediately to the light in the distance. It was the single, pale street light near the edge of the graveyard—desolate and full of shadows—just as she had seen it a million times growing up. When passing it at night as kids, they had often dared each other to take a flower from a grave.

Now she searched to see through the bushes and trees, their leaves full and green and alive, her mother's body dead in the grave on the other side. Was Marilyn scared out there all alone? She began to weep remembering how she let go of Marilyn's hand at the hospital. An image of Marilyn came back to her now, eyes stern and cold when her own tiny hand reached out to her in fear. It was a quick flash and Ginny could not remember more.

It was like the baby's hand, the tiny arm searching for help. They baby that was also alone in a grave somewhere. Ginny didn't even know where the baby was or where to go to comfort her. Had there been a time when she felt love or comfort? Was her whole life spent dying? Why didn't she insist that the girl tell her what was wrong with the baby? Or called the police?

A small scream escaped from her mouth, and she could no longer stand. She sunk to the commode while slapping both hands over her open mouth and leaned against the wall. Her nose was running while she rocked back and forth. Tearing off tissue from the roll, she wiped her nose and stood, taking the small hand towel and quickly walking to her bed and getting underneath the covers, rocking until the darkness began to fade outside.

She heard her grandparents move about and in the bathroom. When she heard her grandmother making breakfast she got up and got dressed, exhausted and numb. In the bathroom, she splashed cold water on her face and brushed her teeth, avoiding even a glance at the window.

At her grandmother's kitchen table, she took a cup of strong coffee and stared outside at the bright sunlight. The smell of bacon was real. She promised herself that things were going to get back to normal. But she knew they would never be the same without her mother.

She quickly hugged her grandmother and put her bag in the Roach and drove out, speeding up when the church and graveyard became visible, and then screeching to a stop. In the sunlight the shadows from the night had burned away, but the car jerked forward as if her foot had decided to move on without her conscious thought. She felt relief that she was staying with Beck tonight before testifying at the trial tomorrow afternoon.

*   *   *

The drive to Beck and Bill's home seemed short, perhaps because she was racing against the gathering dark clouds. Today when she turned into their driveway, the gate remained closed and she pressed the call button and waited before pressing it again. Seconds later it slowly began to move and she drove inside, noting that the lion fan head was turning fast and the backdrop of trees were swaying wildly behind the house as the storm got closer. Once parked, she got out, her hair blowing back as she faced the wind and looked to the sky. She was both excited and afraid of the murderous black clouds.

Picking up the fat envelope of photographs on the seat and her purse, she walked quickly to the front door and saw it was open. Once inside, she shut the door and shook her head to get her hair back in place while setting her things on the table. The fortune-teller's eyes were watching, and she stood in front of the booth, wondering if fortunes here still available for a nickel as it advertised. The card of death was in the mannequin's hand, a giant figure dressed in black with small naked people holding up offerings of coins and flowers. Ginny shivered, grateful to hear footsteps hurriedly approaching from the hallway.

"Ginny!" Beck smiled as she came through the left side hallway wearing a long sleeved coverall. Her hair was flat against her head and her face flushed. "Good to see you got here okay, and before the storm."

A pop of thunder accentuated her sentence, and they both smiled again. "Let's get something cold to drink."

Beck led the way through the swinging door to the kitchen and began naming choices of drinks. A torrent of rain began pelting the windows, and the trees bent so far over Ginny expected some to snap. Beck stopped talking, and Ginny realized when she glanced back that she was waiting for an answer, standing in front of the refrigerator, a Coke in one hand.

"I'll have the same."

"I tried to finish a piece I was welding but had to stop to bring in some things before the rain started." A white, hot flash of light made Ginny shut her eyes tight, cringing when thunder rocked the house. "Wow," Beck continued, and Ginny opened her eyes. "At least this will cool things off."

They sat in the large chairs, Ginny choosing the one facing away from the windows, feeling nervous and jumpy with the flashes of lightning and thunder.

"How are you doing?" Beck looked concerned.

Ginny nodded, "Okay."

"I know funerals are difficult."

It was an image of the Davies baby, lifeless and still, that popped in her head, and she blurted out the question she needed to know. "Did the Davies baby have a funeral?"

Beck blinked before nodding then quickly took a sip of the Coke. "A group at the Circle of Light Church raised money for a casket and planned the ceremony. Belinda, the mother, attended but the grandmother had already been arrested."

Belinda. That was the young woman's name. Drinking quickly from the Coke, she was satisfied with the burn of fizz in her throat and continued to drink. She readied herself to ask about Belinda, jumping when a loud clap of thunder was followed by odd, loud pop. The room was suddenly dark and quiet except for the sound of rain and wind against the windows.

"I don't like how that sounded." Beck scooted to the edge of her seat. "I'm going to look around and make sure nothing was hit by lightning." She stood up and looked out the windows before turning back to Ginny. "I'm going to check out back. Doctor Bell called you here this morning. She said something about trying to catch you at your grandmother's yesterday. Her number is on the pad."

Another clap of thunder kept Ginny seated, her eyes closed and her hand tight against the soda can. The lights flickered and then came back on along with the hum of the refrigerator.

Beck came back through the swinging door. "Well, I can't see anything wrong in the front or back. I'm going to check outside after the storm passes."

Adrenalin surged in Ginny's body, and she squirmed to the edge of the seat, ready to ask Beck more questions, but stopped herself. Even though they had agreed yesterday that Beck would drop off her class assignment to Lance at his apartment, Ginny would do it herself. Maybe she could find the church.

The rain was soft when Ginny picked up the packet of pictures and walked outside with Beck, telling her she was taking her assignment to Lance. Beck turned toward her, their umbrellas touching.

"Ginny, I think it's better if I take it for you. The trial is tomorrow and you don't need to take a chance and run into anyone. It is very possible someone has gotten a picture of you."

"I just want to go do it, to keep busy." Ginny's eyes did not meet Beck's, and she sighed.

Ginny took the sigh as an agreement and got back inside the Roach, waving at Beck as she continued to the gate. It did not open immediately and Ginny got out to push the button to remind Beck to release the gate, hoping she was back inside by now. When she pushed the button again, the gate began to slowly open.

Moments later, she was on University Boulevard, and the sun was shining hot. She passed the turn off to Lance's apartment. She was making her way west of the campus to find the Circle of Light Church and the baby's grave. Shaking off feelings of guilt for not telling Beck, she tried to remember the location of the church from her freshman year when she visited several churches near campus. After two more turns, she saw a cluster of old gravestones standing tall behind a chain link fence and she slowly continued up the block to the church building. She passed the church and noticed cars in the parking lot and a few parked along the street next to the fence. The gate was open and several people were inside, so she stopped to read the small sign that said the gate would be locked at dusk. Three older men in dress shirts came from inside the fence and glanced at her before crossing the street and getting into their cars.

She took the wallet and hairbrush out of her bag, leaving them on the floorboard covered with papers along with the class assignment envelope. Attaching the telephoto lens to her camera, she positioned it in her bag and then got out and leaned against the car for a moment, hoping to locate the grave before going inside the fence.

There was a young woman smoking at the far corner, walking slowly along the path next to the fence. Ginny put the camera to her face and circled around the graves and saw the back of a young man standing near a grave covered with flowers and no headstone. There were no other freshly dug graves. The large number of flowers on the grave comforted her. Surely the baby felt the presence of people near her, even in death. Her hand lowered the camera back into her bag, and she moved forward through the gate, walking straight across the graveyard in order to miss the woman walking toward her from the left. She would wait until the man left before getting a shot of the grave.

The man circled around the grave, his hands and arms gesturing wildly. Was he angry? She put the camera up to her face to see him more clearly. He was facing her now, sobbing, his mouth open, the shrieks loud. Her finger wavered before snapping a picture, her stomach quivering, and tears blurring her own eyes before she determinedly snapped several more. He leaned over, screaming sounds that were unearthly, a tiny rope of saliva escaping from his lips.

"Who are you?"

The angry female voice was behind her. Ginny didn't answer, her fingers frozen. She blinked away tears and looked away from the camera.

"You a reporter?"

Ginny turned to the woman, whose long hair was greasy, a lit cigarette still in her hand.

Ginny didn't answer but shook her head.

"This woman's been taking your picture." She yelled out, her eyes looking to the left, but behind Ginny, "Says she ain't no reporter."

They continued to stare at each other, the woman's cigarette smoke around them. The young man rushed up to them and then he stood beside the woman, breathless. "Why you taking pictures?"

For a moment she stared intently into his eyes. Who was he?

Both arms pulled back slightly from his chest. "Who sent you?"

Even while angry, Ginny could see the pain in his eyes although now they had gotten narrow, and his chest rose and fell in deep heavy breaths. Glancing toward the gate, she began to back up slowly, realizing that the only way out was behind these two people.

"You're that girl who took pictures of Belinda and the baby. Took her picture and didn't do a damn thing to help her." His face was puffy, but she couldn't stop looking at his mouth visibly twitching.

"Answer me! Are you that woman?" He was screaming now, "Why didn't you help her? Why? She might be alive now." He suddenly moved forward, both hands shoving against her shoulders. She stumbled backwards but managed to stay on her feet, her fingers tightly holding the camera. Quickly, she moved to the side, scrambling to circle a large head stone, hoping the spirit of the dead body underneath would forgive her when she trampled through several pots of plastic flowers.

He turned as she moved, slapping his body up against the headstone, flinging both hands toward her. "Answer me!"

Glancing quickly at the church, she hoped someone would hear and come out. The young woman saw her and looked up toward the building too. She threw down her cigarette and grabbed his arm, "Gary!"

He looked at the woman, grabbing her hand, his face contorted in pain. She frowned and stepped back, pulling her hand away and he bent over, putting his hands on his knees, his breathing loud.

Ginny stomach tightened, tears in her own eyes. "I didn't know."

His face turned back toward Ginny, his voice cold, "You're lying." The woman stepped closer to him. "I saw the pictures. Anyone would have known that she was dying."

Ginny's pictures had not been published. If he had seen them, he had to have seen them while being questioned by the police, which meant he was close to Belinda. She was surprised by the anger that surged in her voice. "Why didn't you call the police? Why didn't the family or the neighbors call the police?"

"I didn't know." His voice was quieter, and the eyes were pleading. He was now looking at the young woman. "I didn't know she was pregnant. I swear. I didn't know about the baby until they told me she was dead." He was sobbing again, and the young woman moved in trying to hold him as he fell to his knees. "She never told me."

"I know. It's okay." The woman tried to comfort him. They held tight to each other and for a moment seemed to forget about her.

Ginny's fingers loosened on the camera, and she wanted to touch the man's shoulder. But she stopped herself, remembering she needed to get away. Thorns from a small rose bush tore at her jeans when she tried to step back out of the squared off gravesite. Her ankle was bleeding.

The woman frowned up at her, and Ginny began to run, continuing until she got to the gate. When she turned, they were huddled on the ground. Lifting the camera, she saw there was no lens cap. One hand searched her pocket while she watched them through the telephoto lens, her shaking finger lingering over the shutter button for several moments before finally pressing the button.

While walking across the road to the car, she patted the other pocket for the lens cap, but knew it dropped off somewhere in the graveyard. Once seated in the car, she quickly turned the camera toward her face, checking for scratches. Looking back toward the gate, she set the camera against the passenger's seat with the lens up.

* * *

With her eyes open, she felt as if she were melting into the pitch-black darkness of the guest room. Some part of her was glad, aching to be to be part of something besides herself. The fuzziness she felt for days lifted away at the bathroom window this morning, revealing raw fear that ate at her, made her want to rush to do something—anything—to make it go away.

Last night the fear got so loud, she couldn't understand her own words when she spoke, much less those of Beck. When Speck came over he asked her to please focus when he explained how the court would proceed.

Was this how madness took over? Was she becoming like Marilyn?

Throwing back the bed sheet and spread, she quickly sat up and stood, straightening her T-shirt and jeans before pulling the cords to open the window blinds. Her clothes had been a layer of protection that she was unwilling to remove earlier, now she wanted to take them off to blend into the darkness outside. She shook her head. The thought remained, and she forced herself to put her shoes on by the slight light of the lantern outside, slowly, meticulously tightening and tying the laces as if this could keep her together.

Straightening her back, she breathed in slowly and looked out at the trees, following the slight movements of the leaves. Then there was a tiny, red glow, moving down, then back up, and then a brighter glowing speck of fire.

Was it a cigarette? She moved closer, her forehead touching the window. The red glow was there, and then it was falling quickly to the ground, disappearing completely.

Stepping back from the window where it was darker, she kept her eyes on the same spot, looking for movement. Was it Marilyn? Would she come back to her in this way? Each beat of her heart was now pulsing in her right eye. Years ago, Lucille described how her dead mother came to her at night. Ginny strained to see through the forest, remembering Lucille and her mother walking in the rain, almost blending into the gray sky. An unbearable sadness rushed tears to her eyes. She shook her head again. She and Marilyn were different. Why would Marilyn bother to come to her?

The cigarette belonged to the living, and they were outside her window. She stepped further back where it was darker and wiped her eyes. Was it Gary and his friend? Had they somehow followed her this afternoon, slipped inside the gate, and were now waiting for her? Shivering, she turned and opened the door, quietly creeping down the hallway.

Bill was not home. Beck was in a room jutting off the other side of the foyer, and Ginny doubted she could hear her but she stopped and listened before cautiously moving forward again.

In the den, she looked through the large windows, straining to see through the trees illuminated by the dim yellow light. There was nothing. Did she imagine it? No. She was sure she saw a burning cigarette, and whoever it was probably saw her open the blinds. She slipped quietly through the kitchen. The peephole in the front door would allow her to see if the gate is closed.

The mannequin looked up at her through half closed eyes when Ginny carefully pushed open the swinging door. The light from inside the booth was bright, and she blinked before walking to the door. Closing one eye, she looked through the peephole at the closed gate and before she could take a breath, her eye caught a movement beside her and she jerked her head to the left, catching the movement of the mannequin's hand as she laid out three new cards.

The fortune-teller was wearing an old ratty white blouse, and there was a small crack over her left eyebrow. The first card in her hand was the

Ten of Swords with three wild- haired discombobulated heads with hands resting on nine swords stuck in the ground and a woman pointing at them while holding her large sword upward. The human man is curled up in a ball at her feet. The second card was difficult to see, but the third card was the Fool and a young man is unaware he is about to step off a cliff.

This is crazy. Why is she looking at cards when there is someone outside the house? Did she imagine the cigarette? Should she wake Beck? And tell her what? That she went to the graveyard?

She turned away from the fortune-teller and quietly slipped back through the swinging door and sat in the big chair facing the window. Shivering, she curled her feet up in the chair and laid her head on the fat, padded chair arm, keeping her eyes on the part of the woods illuminated by the lantern held by the bear.

CHAPTER **27**

WHAT HAS BEEN BURIED

GINNY, 1976

There were two men checking the grounds of the Winter home. Ginny was supposed to be taking a shower, but felt uncomfortable taking her off her clothes until the men reported back to Beck that no one was still inside the gate.

Beck woke her early this morning. Ginny was still in the chair and quickly told her about the cigarette and then about the visit to the graveyard, and was relieved when Beck accepted the information calmly and called her security company to come and check out the grounds. She also called Speck and Ginny could tell from the one sided conversation that he was angry that Ginny went to the graveyard, insisting on coming back over this morning even though he talked to her last night.

The dress she wore to the funeral was on a hanger but draped over a chair. Beck suggested she wear flats instead of heels, reminding her that if they were followed, they might have to run quickly. Speck enlisted a law student to come to court with him and Abrial, hoping reporters would think the student was Ginny and follow them instead of Beck and Ginny, who would slip in afterwards. The tricky part would be getting her out of the building afterwards because everyone will know what she looks like after she testifies.

Think of something else… think of something else. Ginny looked around the room and then sat at the table and began reading through the list of things she had to do. She searched for something she could do now. Just focus on the list and stop thinking. Beck's note about Dr. Bell's call was with the list, and she read through the number before cautiously picking up the phone, listening to make sure it was clear before dialing Dr. Bell's number.

"Good morning Ginny. I hope you are doing okay. I know it's very stressful right now. I'm calling you about an internship, and I have to get back to the committee today."

Ginny waited silently for her to continue.

"There is a team of graduate students and professors working on an archeological dig in Costa Rica. One of the students who had been photographing the stages of progress of the dig had to return due to a family problem. The director of the project is willing to hire you for the position if you are interested."

"In Costa Rica?" She thought vaguely about Central America and tried to place Costa Rica on a map. People would speak Spanish. She would have to fly there by herself—her first flight. Butterflies came into her stomach, and she pulled her legs up into the chair. She struggled with what to say next.

"Thank you for your help, Dr. Bell."

"Think about it, Ginny. It is part time so the pay is not a lot, but room and board are provided, as well as tuition if you want to take a class. The assignment would be for the fall term. They expect to return before Thanksgiving. You will need to get some shots and a passport."

It was happening too fast, and it was difficult to think. Could she do this? She needed to think, yet didn't want to say anything to offend Dr. Bell. A strange sound came from her throat.

Dr. Bell continued after a few seconds. "I was thinking you could take an independent study class on some area of photography and shoot it while you are there. It is a beautiful country with so many distinct landscapes. The volcanoes, the flowers, and wildlife. Not to mention the people. A different culture."

"Okay, I'll think about it and call you back. Maybe tomorrow?"

"They really wanted to know something today, but because of your circumstances I'll let them know it will be tomorrow. Give it serious thought Ginny. It is a great opportunity and it sounds like it will work out great given your situation."

She breathed out slowly while hanging up the phone, then jerked the phone back wondering if she had even said goodbye. The line was dead. It would be interesting to travel, to have her first real photography job. She closed her eyes and imagined traveling to the site and then holding a large view camera over an unearthed grave, a skeleton still partially buried with ancient jewelry close around the neck. She stared at the skeleton through the camera, and then glanced up at a shadowy man on the other side of the grave, his thumb and middle finger holding a lit cigarette, silently waiting for her to push the shutter button. Waiting—but for what? Was he offended? Had this been his ancestor's grave? With her heart racing, she watched herself look back through the camera, now seeing the glimmer of green jade from the necklace that had fallen through the rib bones of the skeleton. She pushed the shutter and looked back at the man and watched his lit cigarette drop to the ground. She threw the camera with its skeleton image into the gravesite and ran. But where would she run to in Costa Rica? Both her eyes popped open. She was sweating. What was wrong with her?

Outside the window one of the blue shirted security men moved by slowly, bent at the waist with his hands carefully holding back bushes while he studied the ground intently. She stood and then moved away from the window, lying down on the unmade twin bed in the darkened room, one hand pulling the bedspread up to meet her chin. When she realized she was rocking, she willed herself to stop, to lie quiet and still.

*　*　*

Speck was showing only slight irritation, asking her why she went to the baby's grave. She tried to think of a satisfying answer, but her mind had refused to settle after Beck told her that the security men had found two cigarette butts near her window and footprints in the ground made soft by the earlier rain. The prints circled around the house, and another cigarette butt was found near Beck's bedroom window. They could not tell if the prints were male or female, but it appeared to only be one person.

"I don't know." She knew this wasn't exactly the truth, but the truth seemed as shapeless as water, needing too much thought to find some type of container that she could hold out for him to examine.

He continued to hold a steady gaze so she preferred staring at his hand and the index finger that repeatedly patted against the bar in Beck's dining room.

She tried again. "After my mother's funeral, I kept feeling like she would be scared to be alone in the graveyard. Then I thought of the baby, alone in a grave. I wondered if there was a funeral and if anyone came and put flowers on it… I just needed to see the grave… and to take a picture so I could look back at it again later."

He nodded. "Why did you take a picture of the boyfriend?"

"So, he was the boyfriend?" The sobbing young man came to mind. "He said he didn't even know about the baby." Apparently Belinda didn't tell him or couldn't tell him. Breathing in, she wondered if the fullness in her stomach was air or something else. She suddenly needed for Speck to understand and looked into his eyes and tried again to explain.

"He was crying. He loved the baby even though he had never even seen her."

Speck's eyes dropped to his hand pressed hard and flat against the bar. "Not necessarily, Ginny. He probably feels guilty that he got this girl pregnant and left her to handle her monster mother and his baby by herself and something horrible happened. There are many people in this situation that share guilt for what happened to this baby."

Beck came in from the foyer. "Speck, Abrial says you guys are already late picking up the student. Ginny needs to finish getting dressed."

Speck glanced at Beck and then quickly stood. "Don't mention the visit to the graveyard or the boyfriend when you testify. Do not take off and do anything else."

She nodded, but stared down at her shoes.

"There are people who are looking for someone to blame to get themselves off the hook. We are trying to protect you. Do you understand what I'm saying?" He waited several seconds before continuing, "Hopefully the boyfriend hasn't told anyone." He got up abruptly, and she watched his feet in loafer-type shoes. "This will be over soon, Ginny. Just hold on. Stay as calm as you can. Don't do anything else without telling us. And remember, only answer the questions you are asked while on the stand."

She glanced up to see him pull his hand back that was about to touch her shoulder.

*　*　*

The walk up to the court house steps was easy despite the crowd that had gathered, many of them women, whispering to one another while studying the people who went up the steps and inside. Several people walking past called out a friendly greeting to Beck.

"You know everybody." Ginny whispered to Beck just before an elderly man stopped them on the steps and tightly grasped Beck's hand while speaking of his grandson, who had gotten a scholarship to attend a University in Boston. Ginny stepped back while they talked, her eyes scanning the crowd until her head jerked back to a homemade sign that was shoved high above the heads, a poster nailed to a crossed piece of wood with "Baby Killer" scrawled with red ink and an enlarged grainy black and white copy of one of Ginny's pictures of the mother and baby. The figure holding the sign was far behind the crowd, in the parking lot of the next building with a group of about fifteen people.

"That's my picture. No, you can't use my picture like that." Anger made Ginny's face flush, and she stepped down steps and into the crowd. Beck immediately grasped her arm.

"They got my picture. Look—there in the back."

"Lower your voice." Beck warned her before scanning the crowd, stopping for a few seconds to look at the sign, her hand pulling Ginny toward her.

"How did they get it?" Ginny's body stiffened, and she resisted Beck's efforts to pull her back up the steps.

"Mr. Naylor, I'm sorry, we've got to go." Without waiting for a response, both of Beck's hands here pulling and Ginny allowed herself to be guided up the steps and through the door. There were fewer people inside, and two more people greeted Beck, but Ginny did not hear her respond. They continued to walk quickly through the hallway and then slowly through glass doors and into a large room. In the far corner were two more doors that led to a small room with four pew-like benches and a wooden desk at the front. Beck closed the door behind them and they sat, staying close together.

Were other people holding signs made of her picture? Her hands shook with the image of someone nailing the picture to the wooden cross bar. Do they have copies of all the others? Of course they would. Why would someone only give them one of the pictures? She looked quickly to Beck to comment but stopped herself. Beck was sitting still, her face red and her forehead covered with little beads of perspiration.

"Are you okay?" She whispered and glanced around the tiny room feeling like they were in some sort of small church. Beck had been quiet this morning on the way to the courthouse. Maybe she was upset with her for going to the graveyard. Was she sorry she had agreed to help Ginny?

Beck didn't answer but stood and reached over into the next bench for a small newspaper left in the seat and used it to fan herself as she sat back down.

"I'm sorry I went to the graveyard, Beck. I didn't mean to upset you."

Beck stopped waving the newspaper for a moment, "I know you didn't."

Ginny searched for something else to say. "You know a lot of people here."

"A few years ago, I was here often. The same people still work here." Her breathing was shallow, and she sounded anxious.

"Are you nervous about the trial?"

Beck shook her head and touched Ginny's arm. "I was here when they prosecuted two men who were responsible for blowing up a church where a man was killed and my Bill was injured. It took years for them to come to trial. I was here every day of both trials. Mr. Naylor was too. He is the father of the young man who died."

Ginny sat very still, wanting to ask Beck questions but wasn't sure she wanted answers. Guilt rippled through her for all the problems she was causing Beck and Bill. Speck told her this morning that Beck worried that the cigarette-smoking intruder was more likely someone related to Bill's past rather than the young couple following Ginny from the graveyard. Or it might be a prowler who just happened to come through the gate the night after a lightning bolt had struck it. The security company confirmed that while the gate still opened and closed, it no longer locked.

"I'm sorry. I caused so many problems."

Beck's hand patted Ginny's, "Don't worry about that. Right now, let's just breathe and take it one step at a time. We just need to do the next step. This trial is the next step, and it will be over soon."

Ginny leaned back. Lenny and Sheila would be waiting for her call after court, and she thought of driving down to stay at Sheila's for a while... she couldn't bear to go back to Marilyn's and see her mother's grave every night. Now there was Costa Rica, and she realized with a sudden fierceness that she wanted to be far away from here, to not think of Marilyn, the baby, or of people smoking outside her window. She *would* go to Costa Rica.

Filling her lungs, she counted to ten before exhaling in several short bursts to propel her mind forward, like a boat. Yes, she liked thinking of being on a boat and gliding through this and then leaving it all behind. But her mind resisted her attempt at calm. Like a jolt of electricity, dismay filled her when she thought of Marilyn falling from the boat.

The door opened and the assistant district attorney came in with Speck behind her. "Good morning." Beck stood, and Ginny followed her lead. Both their eyes were on Speck.

The Assistant DA set her briefcase in a chair, "Ginny, I just need to remind you of a few details for your testimony and to answer any questions you have. First, I want to make sure that you remember the exact date of when you took the pictures of Belinda Davies."

Ginny nodded, her eyes darting back and forth from the Assistant DA to Speck while he walked to the side of the room where Beck met him. They were whispering while Speck continued to watch the Assistant DA. A frown was immediate just before his eyes met hers, and she looked away quickly back to the assistant district attorney's eyes, at once startled by their impersonal coolness. As she continued to talk, Ginny chewed the small sliver of nail left on her thumb and felt the panic growing inside the pit of her stomach.

* * *

Later in the courtroom, Ginny could hear the quiet rustle of people turning to watch her make her way up to the witness stand. They called her name, and she nervously got up from the bench outside the courtroom when directed by the officer and walked inside, now standing still while glancing around the room. Her brain felt confused for a moment, weak and scattered. She quickly looked at her feet, worried that she might faint.

The sounds from the room became muffled as if she were under water. She watched herself walk forward, feeling as though she were watching herself on television. Glancing up on her left, the faces of strangers strained to see closer. A few were glaring. On her right, she immediately saw Abrial, who flashed her a tight-lipped smile and turned to whisper something to the other law student beside her. Ginny allowed her eyes to linger momentarily on those of the boyfriend, Gary, feeling their penetrating hardness as if he could break inside her head. Her eyes swept over the rest of the crowd while walking forward faster.

With one hand up, she stated her name as Ginny Jackson and was sworn in while she searched for Speck, who was sitting in the front row behind the district attorney's table. His nod comforted her, and she cautiously looked to the right at the Davies' girl, who sat slumped at the table, her face puffy, her eyes down. There were women on either side of her, and Ginny recognized the defense attorney who asked her questions weeks earlier.

Somewhere someone was talking, but she couldn't pull her eyes away from the Davies girl, Belinda. It was the district attorney's voice, and as it got louder, Belinda seem to shrink and pull her arms closer together in front of her thin body. Ginny worried that she might slide out of the chair and disappear underneath the table. She's melting. Maybe she feels hollow inside too, like the hollow chocolate bunny that Ginny felt like at her mother's funeral. At once she wondered if being pregnant made Belinda not feel so hollow?

"Miss Jackson? Could you please answer the question?"

The district attorney was now in front of her, and the sounds of the court room were no longer muffled; there was a piercing silence while everyone waited, staring at her. For the first time she understood that this must be what Marilyn felt like when she worried that people were staring at her, waiting for her to do something crazy..

Ginny cleared her throat, "I'm sorry. Could you repeat the question?"

The DA was a nice looking man, often smiling at her in the past with kind eyes when he asked questions. Now his head was turned a bit toward the judge and his eyes narrowed, darting back and forth from her to papers in his hand.

"Could you tell us what happened the day you saw Belinda Davies for the first time?" His body blocked her view of Speck, and he walked in toward her. Her heart began to race, and she looked at Belinda, whose face had gotten closer to the table.

Ginny opened her mouth and began speaking, careful to keep her eyes at the D.A.'s neck tie with dark and light blue stripes, telling how she left her photography class and saw Belinda crying while pushing an empty stroller through the red light.

"I took her picture. She looked at me but kept walking and crying. I followed her. Then I slowed down. I thought I might have frightened her. There were a few neighbors that passed in cars but it seemed very still and quiet. I wasn't sure which house she went to, but I kept looking for her through my telephoto lens. I thought I saw her and went to the yard of that house. Eventually she came out holding the baby, and I took several pictures before she disappeared back inside."

The district attorney turned suddenly and picked up a stack of photographs from the table, and fanned them apart before holding one up to her. "Is this the picture you took of Belinda Davies pushing the stroller?"

She nodded, struck by how much better Belinda looked in the pictures compared to now.

"I need for you to verbally answer the question."

"Yes, I took the picture of Belinda Davies pushing the stroller."

He said something about an exhibit and handed them to another man before turning back to her with the second picture of Belinda holding the baby while standing beside her mother's house. Ginny swallowed several times. It was the same picture that the woman had blown up as a poster in the crowd outside. She quickly shifted her eyes to the fat flowers growing at Belinda's feet near the house.

"Yes, I took the picture."

The DA continued through two more pictures, and Ginny stated each time that she took the pictures that day.

"Did you see anyone else at the Davies home that day, besides the mother and baby?"

"No."

"So the grandmother, Miss Davies' mother, was not there?

"I did not see her, but I did not go inside the house."

"Did Miss Davies ask you for help?"

Ginny readied herself to say *no* but hesitated, her eyes searching for Speck, still blocked from her view by the DA.

"Miss Jackson, did Miss Davies ask you for help?"

Ginny sucked in air and spoke before she let it out, her voice weak. "She did not ask me for help. She did not speak at all. But maybe that's why she brought the baby out to me."

This wasn't what she was supposed to say. Glancing sideways at Belinda, she saw the tiniest quick movement of her head. Did she look up?

"Miss Jackson, please do not speculate, just answer the questions that you factually know." The district attorney stepped toward her. "You stated that Belinda Davies did not ask for help when she brought the baby out. Did *you* ask her if she needed help?"

Ginny didn't expect this question. Speck was sliding forward in his seat, and she blinked several times before quickly looking down at her hands, the nails chewed deep, her fingertips raw and red.

"No. I did not ask her if she needed help."

"Did you ask her what was wrong with the baby?"

Why didn't she push Belinda to talk or call the police? People would now blame her for not saving the baby, but she knew she already blamed herself. She blinked, a few tears leaked and clung to her eyelashes.

"No, I did not ask what was wrong. The baby looked like she was dying, but I thought she was sick. It never occurred to me that she was being starved to death. There were neighbors all around the house. Surely someone would have noticed."

The defense attorney had jumped to her feet and people were talking while the gavel was banging. The judge demanded order and once it was quiet, admonished Ginny to only answer the questions she was asked. The district attorney said that was all of his questions and walked back to his table. Speck's hand was flat and slowly going downward as if pressing down and gave her a slight smile. Her breath was ragged and wheezy.

The defense attorney did not sit back down, but picked up a photograph before turning and walking to stand in front of Ginny. Her auburn hair was pulled back into a tight bun, and she wore a navy suit. Ginny glanced at Belinda, her eyes still studying the tabletop in front of her.

Did she understand what was happening? Ginny clenched her jaw, understanding that this would never be over for Belinda regardless of what happens in the court room today. Then immediately she realized that Belinda and her baby would be forever in her own head.

"Miss Jackson, why did you decide to take this picture of Belinda Davies?"

There was no way to explain her need to take the type of pictures she took; this she already knew. They had not prepared for this question. Why *did* she take the picture? "I guess it was because she was so inconsolable, and it looked odd that she was pushing an empty stroller."

"Yes, the photograph clearly shows that she is… inconsolable. Did an empty stroller signify something to you? Is that why you followed her?"

An objection rang out from the district attorney, and short arguments started between him and the defense attorney before the judge told her to answer the question.

Ginny thought back to when she followed her, feeling her sadness and, yes, fear. "She acted scared and was crying. I didn't know why she had the stroller, but knew something was wrong. Her eyes were odd, almost like she wasn't really present… no hope, almost dead-like."

"Dead-like?"

Ginny looked down, aching to cover her own eyes; tired of explaining. She looked back to the defense attorney, "Like people's eyes get when they've seen too many bad things. They can't bear to see any more, and they can't bear to remember what they've already seen."

"Why did that compel you to follow her? That her eyes looked this way?"

Ginny glanced at Belinda, head still down and suddenly she remembered an old family picture shot in front of Grandmother's Christmas tree. Marilyn was holding baby Lenny in her left arm and Sheila was beside her on the right with Ginny in front. It was Christmas; they were smiling with shiny eyes and baby Lenny was holding a toy but also reaching for Ginny's hair. Marilyn was completely alone in her head, the misery in her eyes solid, captured by the camera even though she was staring off to the left, completely captured in there with all her pain. Startled, she closed her eyes, and realized that this was the reason she had not taken pictures of Marilyn all these years. It wasn't fear of her, but it was that she could not bear to see her so disconnected; trapped alone inside her head with so much pain.

The defense attorney repeated the question, her voice softer. The answer was there in her head, but Ginny was reluctant to say it.

The judge told Ginny to answer the question.

"I was afraid she might hurt herself."

"What do you mean by hurt herself?"

"I was afraid that she might try to kill herself."

Again there were objections and people talking. But it didn't feel as loud. She shook her head, feeling like water was filling her ears, making it hard to hear.

"Have you ever known anyone that killed themselves or tried to commit suicide?"

Ginny's stomach lurched and fear passed through body as a quick memory flashed of her mother angrily lashing at Ginny with a belt for talking too much, for telling a neighbor that Marilyn had tried to kill herself.

"Yes." Ginny's voice was a whisper. The room was quiet. "My mother tried to commit suicide several times."

"Ginny, we need for you to speak a little louder."

Ginny looked at the defense attorney's shoes. They were chunky tall heels, beige with black stitching around the open toes, yet it was quiet when she walked.

"So, your mother was mentally ill?"

"Yes." Ginny's voice still whispering.

"Did Belinda remind you of your mother?"

There was an objection about leading. Ginny glanced at Belinda, but she was not looking up. Terrible longing and sadness filled her. Was it for Marilyn? This girl? The baby? Tears rolled down her cheeks, and she silently wiped them away with her fingers. She missed the opportunity to save the baby and was now unable to save Belinda.

"Miss Jackson, did Belinda remind you of your mother?"

"Yes."

* * *

Speck slipped out and was waiting outside the courtroom door. He took Ginny's arm and ushered her back through a small group of people standing in the hallway and around the corner to the small room they had been in earlier. They slid into the back pew, and he began talking but all sounds were still muffled.

Did she say her mother was mentally ill? Did she say that Belinda was like her mother and that Ginny was worried she might kill herself? Yet on that terrible day, why didn't it occur to her that Belinda might be letting her baby starve to death? Crying about the coming death while doing nothing to stop it. Why would a grandmother starve her own grandchild?

Closing her eyes, she tried to shut off the questions, squash them down along with the terrible anxiety rising in her. She put her head on her crossed arms propped against the back of the pew in front of her. Don't think about the baby. Don't think.

"Ginny! Ginny, listen," She heard Speck and felt his fingers pressed hard into the flesh right above her elbow. Her head jerked up, the light of the room making her blink.

His eyes were intense, but she welcomed him in her head, welcomed the jab into her arm. She needed someone to stop the thoughts to bury the bad feelings and forget what was happening. Bury the feelings? Like the baby? She looked away, her body shaking.

"It's over. You hear me? It's done. There is nothing you can do." His fingers pressed harder. She focused on the pain from his fingers and not jerking her arm away, staring at his fingers and allowing the pain to pull her thoughts toward it. She stopped shaking.

His voice lowered, and he relaxed his grip. "This tragedy started long before you took a picture. A lot of people failed to help this baby. Nobody stopped Belinda's mother from locking her up when she was pregnant. People just dismissed her as crazy so no one even gave a damn when she disappeared."

"I made it worse… I could have saved the baby." Her breath was shallow and short. She put her head down again, swallowing over and over.

Speck's hand rubbed her arm. "We don't know if the baby would have lived even if you had called the police. At least you didn't ignore Belinda like most people did." His hand lightly smoothed her hair on the back of her head for a moment. "Hopefully she will get help now. Just about anywhere she goes has to be better than living in hell with her mother."

Ginny resisted the urge to rock herself. Speck's hand smoothing her hair was comforting, and she wished he hadn't stopped.

The door opened to the room, and he quickly stood. She looked up at the older man with a shiny, bald head, watching the two speak softly so that she could not hear. She allowed her body to rock slightly while she watched them, thinking of Lenny and Sheila, eager to go to them and get away from here.

Speck turned and walked her way while the man went out the door. "Beck is feeling unsafe. Because someone leaked your photos, we think you may be unsafe in Tuscaloosa. She is packing your things and will meet us in Birmingham tonight. One of the security team is going to drive you and I there now to meet her. She will make arrangements to have someone drive your car there tomorrow once she gets your keys."

"Birmingham?" An image of her father came to mind but she quickly pushed it away.

"Bill arranged for a place there for a week. You will be safe. This is just a precaution for a few days."

She understood now how sadness and anxiety could completely fill you up, leaving no room for anything else. Even though Speck and the Winters were doing this to help her, for the first time since she left for college, she just wanted to go home. She wanted to be with Sheila and Lenny. She nodded to Speck, and they walked out the door and followed the man waiting in the hallway.

There were no people outside the side door, and the car was right at the curb with a driver. The bald guy gave him some instructions, and then they drove away. Speck leaned back, his eyes closed, so she did the same. The driver stopped shortly for burgers and colas, holding them over the back seat, before driving smoothly back onto the road. They quietly ate while the driver turned on the radio to classical music.

Without turning to her, Speck broke the silence. "I told Bill I would do an interview for his magazine, talk about my mother." He dropped the last bite of burger in his mouth before wading up the wrapper and drinking a sip of Coke. "We want to use your pictures, to print with the interview."

"No." The word popped out, and she shook her head for emphasis, chewing hard on the bite she had in her mouth.

"It's okay Ginny. I talked to mother, and she has agreed that I should do the interview, to give the story about her life—our life. This isn't going to be like the pictures of the baby."

She pressed her lips tightly together but her brain kept repeating, "NO, NO, NO".. The pictures may have been of Speck and his mother, but they were hers. She did not want to share them, not with Speck, and certainly not print them in a magazine.

"Regardless of whether we use your photographs, we are doing the story. They will just send someone else to take pictures and I don't want it to feel stiff, although she might prefer to be more dressed up." He smiled slightly at that and turned toward the window, staring at old military barracks that the University rented as housing for married students, looking as if he was searching for someone.

When he started speaking again, she glanced at him still staring out the window. "My mother met my father when she was fifteen and he was eighteen. She was visiting Cullman one summer with her grandmother. She got pregnant, and her parents decided that her grandmother would hide her away in a rental house until I was born and then they left me with my grandmother and father."

Ginny could not eat any more but put the last of the burger in her mouth anyway. Her cheeks puffed out with the big bite, and she immediately regretted it.

Speck seemed not to notice her, continuing to speak, but now with an edge in his voice. "After having me, my mother returned first to New York and then to France, where she grew up and became somewhat famous as an opera singer." The fingers on his hand fluttered when he said somewhat famous. "Later, she moved to New York and married a civil rights activist and minister. She was beautiful and charming. There were pictures all over the place of her marching at rallies and then later at events when her husband campaigned to became a senator. I knew who she was before I found out she was my mother. I met her for the first time at age fourteen, right after my father's funeral. Right at the gravesite."

Ginny tried to swallow, thinking Speck expected some comment from her. He had a frown across his face, not acting like he was happy that he had a beautiful, famous mother. Maybe it was because of his father's death. She tried nodding slowly as she had seen Shelby do when someone was upset and talking.

"She kept me a secret from her husband, insisting that it was our secret, arranging to visit me at my grandmother's, bringing me clothes not suited for Cullman. She once said she had an agreement with her husband that she would never have children, that she just couldn't be a mother."

Napkins were in the bag between them, and she took several, turning toward her window and spiting the burger out, scrunching the napkin up and putting it in the sack.

"I stopped seeing my mother for years, although she would think of me occasionally and buy something to send to me. She helped me financially with law school. But even that was a secret. When her husband died years ago, nothing changed. I know that some of the time she tried, but I always needed more from her than she could give."

Speck turned to face her. "Your pictures showed me that. She is just unable to love me like a mother should. Not once has she looked at me the way she does in the photographs you took. It's all for the camera."

He turned back to the window, and she at once thought of the picture of his mother squeezing the flowers until the real stems were crushed. At the end she had only hung on to the plastic flower.

Ginny touched his arm, sad for him. But she knew he would not like her sympathy. He had been wrong when he said the photographs were not going to be like those of the baby. It's just that he is the baby, still not claimed by his mother and her photographs had caused him pain.

"I have taken care of my mother for over a year now. She is very ill. But now I want her to publicly acknowledge me as her son. No more secrets."

How could she say no to giving Speck the pictures?

CHAPTER 28

THE EXCAVATION

GINNY 1976

Although she insisted to Beck she was ready to go back home and pack for Costa Rica, now she wasn't so sure. After lunch with her grandparents, she had brought her box of pictures stored at her grandmother's, several smaller boxes, and an empty suitcase so she could pack what she needed and sort some things to leave behind.

The darkened room and the scent of stale smoke—everything seemed the same, yet somehow Ginny felt like an intruder. A carton with several packs of cigarettes was on the table, and Ginny tore one open and shook out a cigarette. She held it to her nose inhaling the scent before picking up the small gold lighter with a broken chain. How many of these things did Marilyn have? There was a box of dead lighters under the kitchen sink that she had refused to throw away, but there must be five or six lying around the room.

It had been six days since the trial. The first night she called family and then stayed in front of the TV, unable to sleep. She resisted Beck's suggestions they walk in the park for some interesting images and by the third day, Bill insisted she come to the magazine office with him and use their dark room to develop the photographs she shot. He introduced her to a few people, including the staff photographer, who asked if she would like to go on a shoot with him. She quickly declined, not wanting to answer questions about Belinda to the young man whose quiet glances seemed to be sizing her up. Once she started printing pictures she felt better and returned the next day. On the fifth day, Beck insisted they go shopping to buy a few things for her trip. Last night, Speck and Abrial came up and they all went to dinner. She took pictures of Beck and Bill and of Speck with Abrial. They even had a group shot taken by a stranger. Now all she needed was a few family pictures to take with her.

The box of her mother's pictures was still on the couch; left when she and Lenny quickly went to the hospital early that morning. She took out a handful, stacking them until they fit neatly in her hand. With her other thumb, she repeatedly slid pictures from the stack as she looked through them.

It was strange looking at the old pictures she had seen over and over in her childhood, knowing there would be no more of Marilyn. She set two pictures aside and took more from the box. With the next stack, a cut out circle in a black and white photo made her stop and bring the it closer to see Daddy towering over little girl Ginny and a headless Marilyn near a big rock. There were more cutouts. Marilyn cut herself out of pictures not long after the first long separation from her father. When Ginny was younger she tried to figure out why Marilyn did it. Did she not like how she looked or was she just trying to separate herself from them? It would have made more sense to cut out her father since he was the one that was gone. She took out one more picture and dropped the others back in the box.

There were three pictures she kept out, lined up even with the edge of the table, side-by-side and not touching. A younger Marilyn was one of them and she picked it up, feeling a surge of anxiety, immediately wondering if she should take Marilyn on this trip. A trip where Ginny would be photographing unearthed skeletons, the dirt swept away from their buried bones and things they would need in the afterlife.

The image of her mother's grave under the streetlight twisted back to her mind. She stood, wondering what things Marilyn would have wanted buried with her in that dark graveyard. The little gold lighter came to mind—light so she could see. Ginny shivered, grateful that this house was back and to the left of Grandmother's with no windows on the side to allow even a glimpse of the light at the cemetery. She would be spending the night at her grandparents' house, and this time she would avoid looking out the window.

Earlier she organized her pictures into separate stacks and took care to put all the negatives and pictures of Speck and his mother into a separate envelope as well as her final class assignment photos to take back to Birmingham in the morning. She put them in a box and carried them through the screen door and down the steps to the car, shifting the box to her hip while opening the trunk. The sun would set soon and she looked up into its fierce glare, feeling the heat on her face and then her body flinching when she saw the sun was almost directly behind the graveyard. One hand pushed down the trunk lid, and she quickly walked back to the porch.

Did Marilyn dread the nighttime at the graveyard? Images of her mother smoking in the dark slid past and all the nights she checked to see if the glow of a lit cigarette was left somewhere in the room. Ginny pushed the thought away and ran up the steps. The house seemed hotter, and Ginny turned on the old fan and draped a sheet over the couch to keep the vinyl from sticking to her legs when she sat down. She pulled at her shorts, thinking of the list sent to her yesterday, along with a letter and booklet, specifying that trousers or jeans would be preferred for students on the project site and that girls should wear bras while in Costa Rica. She smiled, thinking that some of the artists in her group didn't even own bras. But, in just nine days she would be on a plane and headed for Costa Rica for four months.

She set her mother's box of photos on the dresser. Of the two remaining stacks of her own photos, the smaller one would go with her on this trip. A close-up of Belinda was on top, blown up so that only her face filled the frame, the only shot where Belinda looked straight at the camera. Ginny quickly developed it in the darkroom at Bill's workplace, along with pictures of Speck's mother. She wasn't sure why this photo would go with her.

Belinda stared up at her now, eyes dull and flat, half covered with eyelids and thick lashes. She was pretty. Gary would have thought her pretty. Maybe she didn't act odd back then, and talked to him. Did her silence start after her mother locked her up when she got pregnant? Did she deliver the baby all alone? Speck said no one asked about her. They dismissed her because she was mentally ill, so she must have been that way all along. Ginny slowly sat on the couch. The image of the baby came back, the tiny little arm. Tears came to her eyes, and she swallowed several times. How could she not feed her baby? How could she not help her? Did she love her? Ginny wished she could understand Belinda. Maybe she didn't understand what was happening to the baby until close to the end.

Stop! She admonished herself while continuing to stare at her picture. "Not now." She said the words out loud but still could not cover Belinda's face. Maybe she would find out more when she returned.

She picked up the other stack of pictures. These were for storage. Bill promised Ginny that she would be in Costa Rica by the time the article came out about Speck with his mother's photographs. He promised to save copies for her. Bill said it would help her reputation as a photographer to publish them. Her work was being discussed, especially since her pictures of Belinda had been picked up and published by newspapers outside the state. Bill even asked if she wanted copies of these newspapers with Belinda's pictures for later, and she had shook her head, wondering, but not asking how he knew about this.

The photographs not going went into an old box that had once held new canning jars, now filled with her photographs she had hidden at Grandmother's after Marilyn burned her clothes and pictures she had hidden in a drawer. She had kept a few and put them in her photo box, but Ginny had taken them out later. These photos were some of the worst she had taken, but they were the most precious.

Taking a washcloth from the stack on the sink, she put it under the faucet to get it damp and then wiped layers of dust off the top of the box. She threw away the washcloth, sure it was too dirty to ever be clean again, and taped the top closed before sitting it back down on the sheet draped couch.

The two baby books were on the far end of the table, and she reached for them, dropping Lenny's book inside her mother's box of pictures but continued to hold her own. Maybe she should take it now, keep it with her pictures. Marilyn wasn't here anymore to care. Quickly she glanced around, before leaning back and opening her blue baby book, knowing already that her parents had hoped for a son when Ginny was born. Marilyn had crocheted a pale blue cap and sweater for her, so pale it was almost white. When Santa Claus brought her a baby doll, Marilyn gave her the cap and sweater for the doll.

Only the first part of the book was filled in—short, choppy sentences describing the first visitors, the trip home and her grandparents waiting to see her. There were five congratulations cards toward the back, sent after Ginny's birth. She remembered this from looking at the book many times when she was younger. She leafed through it again, looking at the picture of herself in Marilyn's arms wearing the blue sweater and cap, then one with Daddy tightly wrapped in a pink blanket and another with Sheila sitting on porch steps while stiffly holding her in the same blanket. The yellow, cracked tape let go of the greeting cards and she pushed them deeper in the spine of the book to keep them from falling out.

With her thumbnail, she zipped through the remaining pages as if shuffling a deck of cards; one by one the pages of printed lines flipped by, all blank. Near the end, she almost missed a few scribbled sentences and shifted the book to her other hand so she could turn the pages back to find it.

"Baby's First Birthday!" the heading announced, and then Marilyn's tight, scrunched, right-leaning words. Ginny pictured her mother's left hand curled around a pen with her whole arm curved over the top of the book and moving to make the letters rather than her fingers.

"Ginny is one today. She smiles all the time. We love her so much. Sometimes Sheila gets jealous of her little sister, but mostly she picks her up and carries her around. I made a new dress for her with a cancan slip and took her picture. CB let her eat a piece of birthday cake all by herself."

*   *   *

The room was dark except for the faint moonlight coming through the window and door. It reminded her of many summers ago when Marilyn had gone to Florida, and she slept in this room with Lenny, convincing him that the outside moonlight was enough for them to see without keeping a light on all night. Now she was sure that if she pulled the chain of the dangling bulb above her, the light would permanently burn images into the pain already in her head. She could not bear to see anymore. Soon enough the morning light would get here, for now all she could do was sit in the dark, her head back against the vinyl couch and her eyes unable to close.

She had tried but failed to move several times, to push herself to the edge of the seat and go to her grandmother. Grandmother did not come to her. Everything about her was paralyzed but for burning in her throat.

Trying again, her body moves this time, slowly forward until she stops to glance around, at once grateful for the darkness and the inability to see clearly anything of Marilyn. Seeing her things or her picture would make it worse. Old thoughts from the past were circling around and around in her head, once familiar but now murky and blurred. Once she gave them words, they would be wiped clear and sharp.

The three family pictures she took out earlier were still on the table underneath where she set the baby book. Her index finger jabbed at the book as if it were hot until it fell. The first picture was the little family portrait taken when Lenny was still a baby in diapers. It was too dark to see the image, even when she picked it up and held it close to her eyes. The details came to her mind and she projected it on the wall in front of her, just above the dresser. Words circled around and began to come quietly from her mouth to the woman in the image in her hand that she could not see.

"You loved me. You did love me. When did you stop?" There was no answer from the paper Marilyn in her hand. But she had felt it at a very young age, the loss of love. Was it her mental illness as her grandmother suggested? Or worse was it Ginny? There had to be some signs. Of course. There would be signs in her pictures, just as there had been signs in all the pictures she took of strangers, especially the mothers with their children. If she could figure out when she stopped loving her, then maybe she would know why.

She stood up slowly. How could she find the signs? Compare them? She needed to see them together… see the pictures together and compare them. She took down the small paint-by-number painting of the *Last Supper* from the wall over the dresser. There were signs of his betrayal in the picture… just as she would find.

Fingers searched around the table and then took the roll of tape and snapped a piece over tiny plastic teeth and taped the small picture to the unpainted wall. Quickly she taped the other two pictures on either side, pushing the dresser to roll further down the wall until she heard the crack of the straight chair falling, and it stuck in place. Using her hip, she pushed harder against the dresser but it did not move. She quickly walked around and grabbed the chair, throwing it out the screen door into the front yard and then pulled the dresser until it was pinning the front door open back against the wall. She stood staring at the three dark spots where the photos were taped. It would take more for her to see signs. Much more.

Busting open the box of old photographs, she pulled some from the top, glancing at them but unable to make them out. It was okay, she had long ago memorized all of them; this would be Speck's mother with her hand covering his; this one the scared kid at the Tuscaloosa bus station, crying while leaning in against his mother's leg and holding to her dress; her cousin's friend holding the edge of her mother's robe while watching the mother hold tight to the hymnal.

Ginny took out more, taping them to the wall, circling around and around the three family pictures; no longer looking at the images but slapping them against the wall and taping them in place until the circle expanded out to the edge of the dresser again. She pulled the dresser outward so she could get behind it; her eyes glancing over the big family Bible, the darkness hiding the cracked picture of Jesus she knew was embedded on the cover. Marilyn had long ago ripped out the family tree, with the proof of her marriage written on it. Ginny picked it up and after a second glance, took the jewelry box as well and threw them both out the door.

When she returned, the squat, uneven circle of pictures drew her back to the center. She stood up close, staring, wanting the signs, the details, and the eyes. It was too dark; but she still feared the light.

"They are dead-like." The words she spoke in the trial came back to her, and she sat back on the couch, rocking. If they are dead-like, it is already too late.

"Just enough light, just a little light," she pleaded softly. The index finger and thumb showing her that a little light was about an inch. Both hands began patting her thighs before she stood, moving to the sink, running her fingers along the smooth cool metal of the table until she found the lighter. Pushing her thumb against the tiny wheel and then instantly, there was a burst of light. Her eyes burned, and she averted them but also kept them down, not looking around the room—Marilyn's room. Looking back to the uneven circle of eyes on the wall, she felt them, all the eyes looking into the room at Marilyn's things. And at her. Are they seeing me?

Marilyn was the center, and the eyes looked from the direction of the graveyard. She sucked in a deep breath. Had she made eyes for Marilyn to see inside the house? The lid clicked as she quickly flipped it over the flame, her hand swallowing the lighter with its light. The darkness returned. No dead eyes anymore.

A deep, deep pain was in her chest. Marilyn was dead. Sinking back down in the couch, she felt the heat from the metal lighter in her hand and squeezed tighter. The only answers would come from the pictures— the captured life. Did she want to know? She walked back to the wall and the family portrait in the center and pressed her thumb against the lighter wheel again, both dread and longing making her feel faint.

There was Marilyn wearing shorts, tightly holding a shirtless Lenny, still only a baby. Sheila stood next to her with Ginny on her other side. One of Ginny's hands was holding to Sheila's and the other to a tall thin doll that belonged to one of her cousins. She brought the lighter in closer. Although she couldn't see Marilyn's eyes, she knew they were looking away from the camera. There was no smile on her thin face.

Disappointment bubbled up and then anger at Marilyn. Ginny remembered that day; she didn't have to see Marilyn's eyes close up. She smacked her free hand against the wall; just as quickly a shriek escaped from her mouth as she began to cry. Marilyn had already stopped loving her; she had known it even back then. Ginny's body pressed in flat against the wall, and she closed both eyes. Maybe she stopped loving her when Lenny was born. Maybe one baby was all she had room for. Daddy left her, she was depressed, her head filled with voices. There was no room for Ginny. No room for anything else.

She felt the warmth of fire near her hand and let go of the lighter, turning her head up to see fire jumping from a picture to the old linen wall calendar. She froze watching tongues of fire leap higher from the calendar and hungrily lick the ceiling. For a moment she was glad. Burn it all. Hadn't Marilyn herself tried to burn it all down?

The blaze grew bigger, and she stepped back, bumping Marilyn's picture box to the floor, photos scattering across her feet. She couldn't see the images but knew they were all there: pictures of Sheila's sixth birthday, Lenny crying while sitting in a stroller, a very skinny Marilyn dressed up and posing with her father. Instantly she was horrified. If the pictures burned, Marilyn would be gone forever, their childhoods erased except what they could remember. Sheila and Lenny would be crushed.

Despite the blaze she bent down, her hands shoving pictures from the floor into the lid and then back into the box. One arm swept all that was left on the table and she ran out, pitching them to the ground before grabbing the outside water hose at the corner of the house and turning it on. She pulled it up the concrete porch and into the house, coughing violently and stepping back, and then bending down to avoid the worse of the smoke.

She began spraying at the burning eyes. The fire had eaten through the wall and was now in the ceiling. Jerking the hose up, she sprayed at the ceiling and moved toward the bedroom door to look into the other room when she saw her grandfather rushing onto the porch. He turned on the outside lights.

"Ginny!" It was her grandmother's voice.

There was no time to explain. A fit of coughing made her hesitate, then tug harder on the hose and it slid in effortlessly. Her grandfather pulled the hose further inside the door from outside. Her grandmother had grabbed her other photo box and the portable TV and rushed out. Despite her protests, Grandfather took the hose from her hands, and she tried to figure out what else to grab. Mostly she wanted to save baby doll, but he was blocking the door with his body and the hose was spraying in the direction of the shelves where baby doll was sitting—right behind the circle of eyes.

He turned and came toward her, respraying the wall. He urged her toward the door, but she wrapped her arms across her chest and held to her arms, backing up against the sink, wheezing, sobbing and afraid. Grandfather's hand pulled on her arm.

"Come on, get outside. Out of the smoke."

Grandmother was yelling, too. Something about getting outside but Ginny couldn't hear her. She ran out, sobbing, sitting on the porch and pulling her knees close to her face, her head bowing down. Grandmother came to her and held out the Bible. When Ginny did not take it, she carefully set it next to her.

This body no longer felt like hers. Nothing was in the right place in her head. Wind had blown through, shifting so much that at this moment she didn't know what she really felt or what to think. But there was a hole without Marilyn. It had been empty for a long, long time.

"A lot of these pictures are wet. I don't know if we can save them." Grandmother had pictures in each hand, picked up from the sand.

They would need to separate them before they dried stuck together. Wiping her face on her dirty T-shirt, she stood, surprised by traces of early morning light. She ran back inside and winced at the smoky walls but turned to grab the small bucket underneath the sink and towels from the shelf.

Grandmother had picked up pieces of jewelry and more pictures, setting them on the porch near the Bible.

"Why in the world did you try to save this old thing?" Grandfather lifted up the old straight back chair she had thrown out. She did not answer but bent over and gathered up more of the wet pictures.

EPILOGUE

With a hand holding to the shoulder strap of the new canvas bag, Ginny slowly walked up to the counter while checking the ticket stub to make sure she was at the right gate. Nervously, she waited for the woman at the counter to look up.

Another passenger brushed up close beside her, "Excuse me."

She glanced at him, and then looked again. He was Kris's boyfriend, from photography class. His long hippy hair was cut short now, and he had a very dark tan. She wasn't sure if she liked the hair cut so short.

The woman at the counter nodded at Ginny's ticket. "We will begin boarding in thirty minutes." Kris's boyfriend turned his head toward Ginny, his eyes quizzically staring into hers for a moment, before briefly dropping down to scan her body before returning. With a slight smile, he nodded in recognition and turned his attention back to the woman behind the counter. "I'm flying standby."

Ginny hurriedly walked away, wondering if he was going to Costa Rica. Her fingers stuffed the ticket stub into one of four pockets on the front of her bag, a gift Beck gave her yesterday. It was big enough to hold her camera along with a small purse that was stuffed with her passport, part of her traveler's checks and cash. Bill paid her for the pictures of Speck and his mother, giving her the check before they were published so she could take the money with her to Costa Rica.

"Whoa, don't walk so fast." The voice was close behind her, momentarily making butterflies in her stomach. A finger pushed into the soft flesh of her upper arm, then again like he was ringing a doorbell.

She turned slowly, feeling her face flush, grateful when he quickly smiled before squatting down to rummage through his duffle bag that looked as if everything had been dumped inside it. "Hold on. I've got to find my passport." He pulled out a small brown envelope then continued to rummage.

"So you're going to Costa Rica?"

He looked up at her with a smirk, "I have to. That's where this flight is going." He zipped up the bag and stood, "I've been working on a project there. Started last semester then took off a semester to work on my thesis. Dr. Michaels called to give me the go ahead to take this flight. So, I threw my stuff together this morning and here I am." He held out his arms slightly and smiled. "He also said someone else working on the project was leaving from Birmingham. A student photographer. I'm guessing that's you."

"You only found out this morning you were going to Costa Rica?"

"Back to Costa Rica. Actually he told me yesterday, but there was a going away party last night, and I was pretty wasted until early this morning."

"You have a hangover?" She thought wistfully of the parties of her artist group. She had not said goodbye to any of them.

"Never do." He smiled. "The trick to never stop drinking."

She looked closer at him. Was he still drunk?

"I'm kidding. Don't look at me like that. My name is Ben Scatterfield. But everyone calls me Scatter, and my parents call me Ben."

"Scatter?"

"Don't ask. Nickname the guys gave me."

"I'm Ginny Jackson."

"Yeah, I know. Kris talked about you a lot, particularly during the trial. She showed me your pictures in the paper. She didn't know you were doing this gig. Actually, she called and asked about the internship herself."

Ginny smiled, unsure what to say. Mostly she didn't want to talk about Belinda or the trial. "Sorry. I guess you're disappointed that Kris isn't going to be there with you."

"Not really."

Something about his earnest look made him look like a kid. She returned his gaze for a moment and then looked away, smoothing her hair with one hand.

"Kris and I are friends right now. Too much distance, school and all that. You know."

She didn't know what he meant but nodded anyway. Did that mean they were not dating right now but would again when he got back?

"And now I have the opportunity to get to know you." He leaned in closer. "I always noticed you in the photography class, but you never even looked at me. Except that last time you looked back. I thought I had missed my chance since you never came back to class. And here you are. Ever been to Costa Rica?"

She shook her head.

"It's great. I'll show you around. Lots of outdoor cafes. It's just beautiful." He stopped for a moment. "You have beautiful eyes."

"Ginny."

She turned. Speck and Abrial were standing behind her. Smiling, she felt both happy to see them and worried that Scatter would go talk to another girl.

"You're here. I didn't think you could make it."

Speck smiled, his eyes shifting back and forth between Ginny and Scatter.

"Sorry. Speck and Abrial, this is Scatter, or Ben. He's working on the Costa Rica project too."

Scatter reached forward with outstretched hand. Abrial nodded, and Speck extended his hand to Scatter and put two small books in hers. One book was a Spanish-English dictionary and the other was titled, *The Costa Rican Life*. Scatter moved in close, "Yep, that's the standard book for students in Costa Rica, written about twenty years ago." He smiled at Ginny then at Speck, "Some things are still the same."

"Beck didn't stay with you?" Speck glanced around the room but immediately his eyes were studying Scatter.

"She is on her way home to Tuscaloosa. She had a meeting, so she dropped me off."

Abrial smiled. "I'm glad we came then. We should have planned all along to bring you to the airport." Her smile deepened. "Are we interrupting anything between you two?"

Ginny shook her head.

Scatter's hand waved slightly, "Just telling her about San Jose. She's going to love it."

"Are you a student too?" Speck asked the question politely and then continued with several questions about the dig and where the site was located.

The boarding call began and Scatter grabbed his bag from the floor. "I'm flying standby, so got to go check on things. Nice to meet both of you."

"Have a good trip, Ben." Speck watched Scatter walk away and Abrial pressed an envelope in Ginny's hand. "Don't open this until you are on the plane."

"Thank you." She slipped the card in her bag and then turned to Speck. "Thank you for all your help, Speck. I don't know what I would have done without you."

He put a hand on Ginny's shoulder. "Send a post card every now and then and let me know how you're doing. Call if you need anything. It's okay to call collect."

She nodded. "I will."

He smiled, his hand patting her shoulder before dropping down. Ginny turned to walk toward the door and suddenly he was beside her again. "Ginny, be careful and watch out with him." His head nodded in the direction of Scatter, who was walking out the door talking with an older couple in front of him.

She searched his eyes for a moment. What did he mean by that? He turned back to Abrial and she continued forward and held out her ticket to the attendant. She looked back at them and smiled before walking through the door. Did Speck think Scatter was a bad guy?

Scatter was waiting for her right outside the plane. "This flight has a bunch of empty rows, so the stewardess said we can change seats so we can sit together."

Ginny flashed a smile but felt her heart fluttered when she stepped inside the plane and noticed how thin the walls were. People fly all the time; there is nothing to worry about. The stewardess beckoned Scatter further back on the plane and Ginny followed.

"Do you want the window seat?"

Blinking her eyes was all she could do. Maybe it would be better to not look out the window.

"Is this your first time flying?"

She nodded.

"You must sit in the window seat. You got to see yourself flying out of the country."

She sat down and fastened the seatbelt. Scatter pulled out a magazine from his bag and put it in the pouch on back of the seat. The safety procedures card was there, and she pulled it out, her eyes falling on a note that the bottoms seats could be used as flotation devices. For the first time, she wondered if the plane looped around in such a way that they would travel over water.

She took her camera out of the bag and remembered Abrial's envelope and tore it open.

"I won big at poker Monday night. I decided to share a little with you. Buy something nice for yourself while in Costa Rica." Ginny counted the bills and smiled. A hundred and forty-three dollars. Wow. Why would Abrial do that for her? She wished she could go back and thank her.

The stewardess began explaining emergency procedures, and Ginny picked up the folded card again to follow along.

"Don't worry about all that. I'll save you if there is an emergency." He leaned in towards her. "If we crash there will be no time for all that stuff anyway."

Her hand pushed him back, and he chuckled out loud after she frowned at him. "Hush Ben." She found her place on the card and continued to follow along.

"Ben? Now you're sounding like my mother. Are you always so serious?" He took out his card, nodding seriously while pointing out the words on the card and nudging her.

"I'm a little scared of flying."

"Okay, tell you what. You and I will talk and have a few drinks, get to know one another, and you will forget you are flying until we land in San Jose. Well, unless we crash."

His eyes were sparkling with merriment. She smiled but shook her head. "I want to remember all of it. Nothing buried, nothing lost." She startled herself with the comment, but quickly removed the lens cap from her camera and shot a full frame close up of Scatter.

"My eyes, my eyes," he joked.

When the plane lurched and lifted up, she adjusted the camera settings and straightened her arms, holding the camera up over her head and shooting an interior view of the plane. Quickly, she focused outside the window and shot the edge of the wing and the ground below, feeling momentarily uneasy with the unsteady movements of the plane.

"Relax. Everything's fine." Scatter whispered softly, his hand resting on hers. "It will smooth out once we've climbed to the right altitude and very quickly we will be in San Jose."

She took a deep breath and smiled, allowing his hand to stay on hers, sure that for the moment, everything was fine.

ACKNOWLEDGEMENTS

On the occasion of this new edition of *The Memory of Flight*, I am grateful for the assistance and services of the Authors Guild and the Independent Publishers Group that helped make it possible. I have much gratitude to Little Feather Books, the original publisher in 2014, as well as to the Georgia Writers Association for honoring *The Memory of Flight* with the 2015 Author of the Year Award for First Novel.

As noted in the original edition, there are many friends and family who have offered encouragement and support for which I am grateful. In particular, I thank my brother, Joe, for going above and beyond and listening for hours when I needed to talk about "the book." Finally, I thank three people whose attention and encouragement at different times many years ago helped light a path for me: Maxine Bittinger, Hellen Marshall, and Dr. Robert Sigler. Much good in my life would not have come to pass without you.

ABOUT THE AUTHOR

Debra Bowling grew up in North Alabama and graduated from The University of Alabama. She currently lives in Atlanta, Georgia. The Memory of Flight is her first novel. Check out her website at www.DebraBowling.com.

www.ingramcontent.com/pod-product-compliance
Lightning Source LLC
Chambersburg PA
CBHW071427200726
48294CB00002B/542